Desert Fables: Bedtime Stories for the Child Within

Ann McDermott

First Printing: August 2013

Copyright © 2013 Desert Fables:
Bedtime Stories for the Child Within

Ann McDermott
Desert Drifter Publications
261 Maya Dr.
Litchfield Park, Arizona 85340

E-mail the author at annfmcdermott@gmail.com
Write "Desert Fables" in the subject line

Printed in U.S.A.
ISBN: 978-0615957739

Prologue

At the point of encountering your own being, you either have to remain silent or start singing. If you're going to talk about "being" in any meaningful way, you may have to use special language, perhaps mythic language. Myth, in this context, is not falsehood. It's the language of the heart and mind together, and it surpasses our ordinary way of expressing ourselves. Nature often speaks to us in mythic language. We tend to paper over nature with scientific language and think we've fully described it, but to look at nature only in that way is to muzzle it.

...from an indigenous perspective, [nature] is always speaking to us and yearning to be heard. The typical modern reaction to nature is instead to manipulate it or cover it over with our own artifacts. We're constantly muting the living presence of nature in our lives.

But if you really give your full attention to nature, it does speak to you. If you've ever been out in the woods and suddenly experienced a shock of grief or awe or a sense of belonging to something greater, that's because nature has spoken to you. That's why there's a timeless, universal tradition of experiencing God in nature. It's one way of recognizing that we're part of something greater than ourselves.

Jacob Needleman

For Pete's sake, don't read this book like a novel. It's not. Treat it like a book of bedtime stories. Take one or two a night before bedtime. No more.

Adults need bedtime stories too. The child within needs the pleasure, and the adult needs reminding.

Who am I?

The child knows. The adult must remember.

Remember.

Unfold Your Own Myth

Who gets up early to discover the moment light begins?
Who finds us here circling, bewildered, like atoms?
Who comes to a spring thirsty and sees the moon reflected in it?
Who, like Jacob blind with grief and age, smells the shirt of his lost son and can see again?
Who lets a bucket down and brings up a flowing prophet?
Or like Moses goes for fire and finds what burns inside the sunrise?

Jesus slips into a house to escape enemies, and opens a door to the other world.
Soloman cuts open a fish, and there's a gold ring.
Omar storms in to kill the prophet and leaves with blessings.
Chase a deer and end up everywhere!
An oyster opens his mouth to swallow one drop.
Now there's a pearl.
A vagrant wanders empty ruins.
Suddenly he's wealthy.

But don't be satisfied with stories, how things have gone with others.
Unfold your own myth, without complicated explanation,
So everyone will understand the passage,

WE HAVE OPENED YOU.

Start walking toward [your spiritual inspiration].
Your legs will get heavy, and tired.
Then comes a moment of feeling the wings you've grown,
Lifting.

Jalal ad-Din Muhammad Rumi (1207-1273)
translated by Coleman Barks

TABLE OF CONTENTS

Remembering

It is said that there was once a time before time.

It was a Presence. Or maybe just a potential for what might be.

Nothing was there. Everything was there.

But no one observed it. To be seen, it had to change. So it became two.

Day and Night came forth. Together, they saw and understood the creative Presence. Then, they too created.

They made the elements: Earth, Wind, Fire, Water and Connection. Day and Night began to coax these forces into play. Different combinations created different beings. Connection was that element that held everything together. All of the diversity of creation was alive and each individual knew its Connection to everything else. Through Connection, each one also knew the original Source.

Because of Connection, each creature could also create. They interacted with Day and Night, the elements, and one another. Creations unfolded with astounding speed. There was no telling what would happen or who would be created next.

The process continues to this day. All of it Connected.

Everyone occasionally forgets that.

But all are destined to remember again, eventually.

Soul's Equinox

It is said that there is a time in the desert when everything is crystalline clear. Often it happens after Wind has blown Air clean of dust. Then Sun sets and rises with a thinner, more desperate set of colors, for it is Earth's contribution of dust that makes a cloud-free sunset glorious.

But sometimes it just happens.

Edges stand out more blatantly. Nothing blends.

The essence of everything is somehow visible in ways it normally isn't. Trees, grass, hills, saguaros, they are all different from their every day selves. They stand apart from their surroundings, unusually distinct entities, and they radiate with beingness. Coyote spooks walking by a palo verde tree he has seen every day of his life because he senses its presence in a powerful, new way. It is itself, but more.

Time slows then, occasionally even standing still. There is nothing but the present and everything is starkly "there" to everything else, glowing with every inner aspect of its essence. The light is more revealing, almost painful to the eyes. Colors are more vibrant and everything vibrates with clarity.

This is the time of Soul's equinox, when all of creation is perfectly balanced. Energy is renewed. All things are awake and waiting.

Yes, that's it. Everything has paused and is waiting, shining in full manifestation of everything it is.

And what is that? It is perfection.

On any given day, if you should suddenly notice that Air is unusually transparent and everything trembles

with magnified life, be sure to pause. Soak up the moment.
It will pass.

     But in such moments,

          it is well known,

               anything can happen.

Sun's Awakening

It is said that there was once a time when Sun wandered overhead unregulated. Consequently, some days were very long, others much shorter. Sometimes he barely cleared the horizon in the east, then hung there all day without purpose, and set again at night, without bothering to cross the sky to the west first.

It's true that Day and Night, the two primary creators, were only just starting out in the business, so they too were uncertain of how to set boundaries and just what would happen if they did this rather than that. It had seemed a grand idea to have an Earth and a Sun, Wind and Water, but now what? They were stymied.

This is the point where that other Element, Connection, came on the scene. I wish I had a more impressive name for it, but we take what we are given, after all. Connection was that awareness of one another that allowed the other Elements to know each other, and more importantly, to know their interrelationship. Neither Day nor Night could really take credit for Connection. It just sort of happened.

Through Connection, Sun woke up. He saw that he charred Earth if he stayed too long in one spot in the sky, and that ice formed if he remained away too long. He became aware that if he watched the other Elements, he could see how his actions affected them and he knew he was part of a larger wholeness he'd never imagined.

Of course, Sun wasn't the only one to wake up. They all did. Day and Night began to see patterns, to which the Elements began to conform. They became self-regulating because they saw the patterns too and the vast potentials they held. This gave them all a sense of meaning and purpose. Sun was no longer bored. Life on Earth quickened exponentially.

For a time, according to pattern, Day would grow in power, then Night would have her increase. But what sign would mark the turning? When would Day and Sun begin to diminish their hours? All eyes turned to Saguaro. Why? Because Saguaro was and is a huge hub of Connection throughout the Sonoran Desert.

Saguaro had been storing Sun's increasing fire in his fruit.

"When you see my seed pods burst open, revealing your flames in the red of my fruit, you'll know it's time to stand down," directed Saguaro.

Sun nodded.

"Then I will rise with Wind to bring monsoons," said Water. "To entice Night to begin her return."

"Agreed," said Day and Night, and all the Elements.

As it is with Sun, it is with us. Our pattern, purpose and meaning will be found when and where we most feel Connection.

Bowlesia incana: The Mediator

It is said that there was once a time when Day and Night, the two primary creators of all and everything, were so busy with their own projects that it was long hours since they'd last spoken together.

Day was working with Sun and Rain, experimenting with them to create a larger, brighter Rainbow.

Night was in counsel with Moon. Those two were practicing casting moonglow against Cloud, tinting him pinkish-orange where he surrounded Moon, and measuring how far Moon could spread the gilded light, depending on whether or not she was full. Wind kept busy with both projects, as he was in charge of rearranging Cloud as the tests were running. So wrapped up were Day and Night in their investigations, they stood in one spot so long that a plant began to grow between them, completely unnoticed.

Bowlesia incana emerged from the lack of communion between Day and Night, to fill the spaces between them, so naturally, it was a plant with trailing tendencies. It crept around and over stones, preferring the shade under taller shrubs, yet weaving itself through them in its efforts to reach the sunshine with at least a few of its broader-than-long, lobed leaves.

For all its capacity to connect one thing to another, it was surprisingly inconspicuous. This was due, in part, no doubt, to its tiny, five-petaled white flowers, hidden at the base of each leaf. Such tiny flowers called the attention of only the smallest insects to pollinate them, so no one noticed Bowlesia incana spread and vine its way to Day on one side, and Night on the other. They didn't notice it either, until it touched their ankles. And even then, only when they moved slightly to speak with the elements.

Day shifted his weight and called to Wind to open a bit of Cloud at a slightly different spot, so Sun's ray could be ever so minutely adjusted to heighten the colors of Rainbow. In so doing, he discovered his foot had been covered by a strange green plant that crept over the hills, to where Night worked with her crew.

"What the heck?" asked Day to himself, attempting to disengage his leg from the vine.

"What?" said Night, turning toward her partner and scanning the hillsides to where he was shaking his leg from the clinging Bowlesia incana.

"You heard that?" asked Day. "I wasn't even talking to you and you heard that from your great distance?"

"I did," answered Night, bending over to examine her own leg. "I seem to have the same stuff growing on me."

"What is it?" asked Day.

"No clue," said Night. "It must be new, but I didn't make it."

"I didn't either," declared Day.

"And yet, here it is," said Night.

"Such odd leaves," she muttered to herself. "Some have five lobes, some six--here's one with nine, even."

"I see what you mean," answered Day.

"You heard that?" marveled Night. "I was talking to myself. I can't believe you heard that."

"Loud and clear," assured Day.

"Do you suppose it's this plant?" asked Day. "I think it might actually be connecting us across these hills. Maybe that's why we can hear each other even though we're so far apart."

"Well, I can certainly hear you experimenting with Rainbow. Mind if I use some of your lighting variations with Moon and Cloud?"

"Not at all. This is hardly a competition," Day answered.

"Of course not," Night agreed. "We could never come up with such assorted colors as you and Sun can."

"I like it," said Wind.

"Like what?" asked Day and Night.

"I like that you're both connected by that plant--and, through you, I am too."

"It does help us communicate," admitted Night.

"That could help speed up the work," added Day, ever the practical and results-oriented one.

"Just be sure you focus on Rainbow and not Moon's halo," teased Night.

"I would never take over your project," said Day.

So Bowlesia incana connected Day and Night and, through them, all the Elements, helping everyone to hear one another just that much better than before.

Inconspicuous, yet invaluable.

The Origins of Sound

It is said that there was once a time when there was no noise anywhere throughout the whole of creation. Day and Night, the two primary creators, did not need sound waves to "hear" their creatures, since they were connected to everything and heard it by means other than ears. Through them, creation heard itself, but only through Day and Night. When Day and Night became aware their offspring did not have the ability to hear one another directly, they wondered why they had not thought to incorporate that from the start. But since they had not, they next wondered what would be the best remedy for the soundless situation.

The elementals were gathered: Earth, Wind, Fire and Water. After consultation, Wind was picked to be in charge of sound-making because he could flow most readily through all living things. He could even flow through the spaces in non-living things, giving them voice when needed, something beyond the capacity of the other elementals. Even stones could sing when Wind entered the open spaces between them.

For those who wanted and needed them, ears were fashioned. For those who wanted to speak, some manner of funneling Wind through vibrators was developed so sound waves could be formed. Designs were considered and rejected, installed and removed, reworked again and again until they were comfortable and convenient to the beings who would use them. The work went on for quite some time, and during the whole of it there was only silence. It seemed all had unanimously agreed to hold off making any noise until everyone was ready. Until all could hear and speak, no one would.

Producing and hearing sound would allow creation to bypass the creators in communicating with one another, but no one quite knew how to do it, even once they all had the equipment to do so. Everyone was too self-conscious to begin.

As Night fell, Day's creatures went to their sleeping places in silence. Night's creatures moved through their activities without a sound. Quiet reigned supreme. Creation remained reticent and mute.

Then, as Night leaked away over the western horizon and Day rimmed the east with pink, Curved-billed Thrasher stirred from his rest and without thinking, called his greeting to Day.

"Whit-it-rit," he sang, shattering silence forever.

All the rest of creation joined in, and continues always.

The Marriage of Air and Water

It is said that there was once a time when Air sighed with jealousy. Three of the other elements, Water, Earth and Connection, had recently designed the amphibians.

"How perfect is that?" marveled Air. "These creatures truly are the marriage of Water and Earth. They are born and spend their youth in Water, then mature to walk on land. Yet, they retain their association with Water even then. They are Connection made manifest. They're beautiful."

Sun overheard. He stopped showing off with Rainbow long enough to say, "You have an odd notion of beauty. Still, I know what you mean. I can't say they impress me as lovely, but the new creatures are perfect. They unite Earth and Water as only Connection can do."

"I want to make someone with Connection and Water," announced Air.

"How could you not?" asked Sun. "Don't they all breathe?"

"Oh, sure. But you know what I mean. I want that perfect marriage with Water too."

"There are none so blind..." quoth Sun.

"Shut up!" said Air.

So Wandering Glider was created. Water was world to eggs and larvae, but only for six weeks, an unusually short time for a dragonfly. As an adult, the Glider was all about Air, but this too was for a short time, about as long as it lived under Water. Its short life cycle allowed it to use ephemeral Waters for egg-laying. Wandering Glider was quite the opportunist. And the visible balance of Water and Air.

11

In addition, the newest dragonfly could store fat. None of the elements expected that, but this let the creature fly long distances without eating, and fly it did. Give it a moist wind and it crossed oceans to become almost world-wide in range. Strong enough to fly in thunderstorms, it was even tough enough to fly over the Himalayas. The dry winds off the Sahara prevented it from colonizing Europe. Cold kept it from Earth's poles. The rest of the planet was home.

But not in any stationary sense. Always migrating, always seeking change, nearly always airborne--this was Wandering Glider.

"It's perfect!" declared Air.

Water was pleased too.

"Oh look," smirked Sun. "It has my eyes."

Indeed, the creature had huge eyes, the color of gold.

"Shut up!" said Air.

Connection chuckled.

Of Graybirds and Power

It is said that there was once a time when two Graybird grasshoppers sat near one another in the same basil bush on a hot, summer's afternoon. The aroma of crushed basil filled the air as the two insects chewed their lunch.

One grasshopper was an adult. He was three inches long, grayish-brown in color, with short antennae. A cream-colored-central stripe ran from the top of his head to where his wings sprouted from his thorax, and faint barring marked his well-muscled femur. Yes, femur. He only had one, having lost a leg to a bird days before. He would not live to see another season.

The other was an inch smaller in length, bright green in color and had no wings. He was a Graybird nymph, an immature, with several more molts to go before reaching adulthood. He would accomplish this by winter, and if it were a mild one, he'd survive until spring, the season of his birth this year--after a good, drenching visit by Rain. The moisture had helped him break out of his egg by softening Earth, in which he was buried, so he could force his tiny, but fully-formed grasshopper body upward to light.

Now, he ate and grew. Mostly, he ate.

The old one eyed the spring-green youth. He adjusted his position on the basil branch he grasped, wobbling clumsily due to his handicap. The neophyte watched back, pitying his elder's difficulties. How will this crippled one escape next time, he wondered?

"I am not out of danger yet," he said, as if he'd heard the juvenile's thought. "But there are some perils that are behind me. Yours are still before you, and I'm considering whether I should warn you of one of them."

"If it's something I can avoid, I would appreciate the warning," Young Grasshopper said. "If it cannot be avoided--well, I would still appreciate the warning."

The oldster chuckled, pleased by the youth's answer. "I can't promise you can escape it, but perhaps you could, if you recognize the signs. Yes, perhaps escape is possible if you know what to look for and have someplace to slip away to. Still, it is an experience you might want. Like all things, I suppose, there is the good and bad of it."

"What are you talking about?" asked the nymph. "Tell me so I can choose for myself."

Old Grasshopper stared intently at his companion, amazed by his clarity and confidence. Perhaps this one can choose, he thought. Perhaps he will find a way.

"There is an enormous strength within," he began. "It is huge and powerful, but also destructive. As we sit now, with enough to eat and no overcrowding, we are one thing. We act as we are acting now. We recognize and expect this of ourselves."

"I do think of myself in particular ways," said the green adolescent. "Do you mean there are times I might not recognize myself?"

"I mean there are things about yourself you do not know. They are hidden until we grasshoppers are gathered together in regions where our numbers are too great for the food available. When we starve and scramble over one another for food, a great change comes over us. When our hind legs are bumped and brushed by others of our kind-- several contacts per minute, over a period of four hours--a rush of serotonin is released in our bodies. This chemical makes us strangers to ourselves. Our color changes; we eat more, and we breed more easily. No matter how many of us there are, we fly as one. We ravage the countryside in

14

our hunger, destroying everything within reach. We can fly three hundred miles at a stretch, as a cloud that hides Sun from those below. It is rumored that one such flight, across a great ocean, is how we got to this fair land. Our people originated on another continent."

"Three hundred miles!" marveled the youth. "Having no wings at all, I can't imagine it!"

"Alone we are grasshoppers; together we are locusts," continued the senior. "The power of locusts is beyond imagination. It must be experienced to be believed."

"And you have? You know this wonderful side of yourself?" asked immature Graybird?

"I have. I have felt the power. I have felt it flow through me, change me, into something unthinkingly destructive, yet stronger than anything I'd ever known. We flew miles and miles, eating fields and forests in our path, leaving Earth uninhabitable for ourselves and most other life."

"How did it end? How is it you are here now to tell the tale?" asked the nymph distrustfully.

"As we migrated, our numbers became fewer and fewer. Some creatures crushed us defending their homes. Some ate us. Some of us tired and fell from the sky, weak and wingworn. After our reign of terror, I crawled under the root of a tree and in my muddleheadedness and exhaustion, could not find my way out. In my dark hole, I returned to myself. I became a grasshopper once again. I was one of the few who survived to do that. Most died as locusts, unable to break the chains of their communal mindlessness. I persisted, with the memories of both the glory and the insanity. I don't know why. Perhaps so I can tell you."

"The energy to cross oceans and whole continents," gasped the amazed youth.

"And at the same time, destroy entire ecosystems," responded the ancient insect.

"Can I have the power without wrecking havoc?" asked the younger.

"Such does not seem to be our nature," assured the elder.

"When Graybirds gather in numbers, beware. Then it is time for you to choose. Will you mingle and be swept away by mass-mind? Or will you remain an individual and think for yourself? Now you know the possibilities. Now you can choose. I did not know, so I had no choice. But you do. You are aware."

How Owl Proved His Wisdom

It is said that there was once a time before anyone thought of Owl as wise. Able to fly quieter than any other bird? Yes. Able to hear the smallest movement in the darkest night? Yes. The most dangerous hunter after sundown? Yes. But wise? Not especially. Then this story made the rounds amongst the desert folk.

A boy lived in the camp of humans who farmed the flood plain of the nearby river. His special talent was making nets. His quick fingers spun snares of fine hairs with large, medium or tiny mesh, depending on the need. His skill benefited all his people because the nets he crafted were used for hunting small game, scooping fish from the river, harvesting mesquite bean pods, and many other tasks.

When the pods were dried properly on the mesquite trees' limbs, the nets were spread on the ground below. The women and children then grasped branches, careful to avoid the thorns, and shook the pods from the tree. They fell into the net, along with leaves, but when the nets were lifted up, the small leaflets fell through the holes, but the long, twisted pods caught in the webbing. Later they would be ground into flour and eaten.

In preparation for a harvest, the boy had taken a newly prepared net and hung it on a tree limb to spend the night. In the early morning he would come back to spread the net on the ground before the women arrived for their duties.

In the dawn's first light, he returned to the stand of mesquite to go to work. As he approached the tree where his net hung, he felt the eyes of another watching him. Still

17

fifty feet away from his net, he saw the snared creature he'd sensed. A Great Horned Owl stared from his perch in the mesquite, one foot tangled in the net, unable to fly away and quivering in fright.

The boy's breath caught in his throat. His people believed Owl to be a messenger of Death. Would this one tell him of his own or someone he knew? It remained silently staring, though deeply alarmed, not uttering the name of the condemned. If he released Death's cohort and Owl remained silent, would he and his people be spared? How could he loose the huge bird without getting bitten or clawed by sharp talons? He too trembled in fear.

The boy considered abandoning the net, but it was needed for the day's work. He took one step closer. Owl raised his wings threateningly.

"I wish you no harm," the boy said soothingly. "I hope you also wish me none. Perhaps you just meant to pass in the night and carried no message for me or my people. If you will allow me the privilege of setting you free, you can get on with your task and I with mine."

He approached slowly, one step at a time, bowing with each pace and holding his arms out at his sides in an attempt to imitate Owl's stance. By this behavior he meant to convey his good will and respect as an equal--and perhaps conceal his own fear. He did not stare directly at Owl's face and kept talking gently to the fierce bird, telling of his plans for the harvest and how it would help feed his people. He knew Owl would understand about hunger and their need for food.

When he stood by Owl's tree, he reached very slooowwwly and with many consoling words, to the bird's tangled foot. Owl leaned away, and spread his wings farther, but said nothing and did not attack. His eyes burned the boy, but the human refused to see anything but the claw in his hands.

18

Deftly he untangled his net from the talons and toes. When Owl felt the last bindings stripped away, he launched quickly and departed with no thanks but his silence and the good will shown in not harming the human child. Now the boy looked, but Owl was gone. He bowed one last time to the direction Owl fled and gave thanks Death left no warning. Sighing with relief, he began picking his net out of the tree to spread on the ground.

"How did Owl know the boy wouldn't kill him?" squealed Antelope Squirrel when Dragonfly finished recounting what he'd witnessed that morning.

"I have no idea," answered Dragonfly as he finished cleaning his wings.

"Perhaps he decided he had no choice but to risk it," speculated Verdin, pausing in his own search for small insects in Palo Verde tree leaves long enough to ponder the question.

"Or perhaps he took the measure of the boy's heart as he was approaching," suggested Curve-billed Thrasher. "All humans aren't unkind."

"Plus he had little choice," repeated Verdin. "Not if he wanted to live."

"Still, it was very brave not to struggle," said Dragonfly, preparing to depart.

"And wise to trust, in this instance," added Antelope Squirrel in amazement.
"How did he do it?"

Thus began Owl's reputation for wisdom, one that continues growing with each telling of this tale.

19

Cottontail the Courageous

It is said that there was once a time when Coyote headed for the shade of an ironwood tree after a hot summer morning of catching ground squirrels for breakfast. As he neared the great tree, however, a rumbling warned him another had beaten him there beneath its cooling branches. When he spotted the immaculate, tawniness of a full-bellied female cougar, he started to shy away, then realized the grumbling sound was not about him, and not a growl. The huge cat watched a scene unfolding in the creosote bushes a hundred feet away. Coyote, always curious, sat and watched too.

"Look at that!" said Cougar. "Who would ever have thought? Normally, she's first to run in the other direction. Have you ever seen such a thing?"

"You talking to me?" asked Coyote.

"You see anyone else around?" asked Cougar.

"Not at the moment," allowed Coyote, realizing the huge beast must have heard him walk up, though she did not divert her attention from the drama she viewed.

"Rabbit," Cougar snorted. "Rabbit, the little one with the big reputation for cowardice. The one who breeds so we predators can eat."

"Kinda small for you, isn't she?" commented Coyote, wishing he wasn't too full of ground squirrel to care about catching a rabbit.

"True, deer are more my style. Still, I do savor rabbit in a pinch."

"Who doesn't?" asked Coyote.

"Exactly," laughed Cougar. "But I think Roadrunner must be changing his mind right about now."

"Probably," giggled Coyote.

The two hunters watched as Cottontail Rabbit chased Roadrunner around and through the creosote patch. She would not let up. Roadrunner tried to convince her he was leaving, only to circle back, but she would have none of his trickery. Roadrunner was becoming more and more exasperated.

"She dogs him even better than I could," said Coyote, grinning.

"She's at least as lionhearted as I," acknowledged Cougar with a smile.

At this point, a pair of nesting curved-billed thrashers joined in the routing of Roadrunner until the 24 inch long cuckoo decided he had had enough. He shot off through the bursage to find his next meal elsewhere.

Coyote watched Cottontail Rabbit break off her chase and disappear into the desert.

"Must have young nearby," he observed.

"Easy pickings for that roadrunner," agreed Cougar.

"I saw him shake and beat a sparrow to death with that bill once," said Coyote. "Very impressive."

"I've seen him kill a rattlesnake," said Cougar. "Now THAT was impressive!"

"No kidding!" said Coyote. "Baby bunnies wouldn't stand a chance."

"Not a chance," agreed Cougar.

"Maybe I'll just go have a look for them myself," said Coyote.

"Not today," announced Cougar, licking her paw and eyeing Coyote.

"What's it to you?" asked Coyote.

"Let's just call it a little bonding between mothers," answered Cougar.

Coyote trotted away, wisely deciding that messing with mothers was not a good plan--at least not for the moment, and that another shady spot would undoubtedly be much more to his liking.

Sewing Together Earth and Sky

It is said that there was once a time when Day sought to honor the moment of birth he shared with Night. He had been a little unavailable, of late, passing eons of time decorating the heavens with supernovas and stars. Although Night had not protested, Day thought a nice present might please her and appease her, if she should be miffed and not immediately overjoyed at his homecoming to Earth. He found many changes, upon his return. Night had been busy with her crew of assisting Elements. There were many faces he did not recall, new plants and animals he'd never seen.

"What shall I give her?" Day asked. "Have you any ingenious ideas?"

"Well," Wind replied, giving it some thought, "I happen to know she's currently crazy for insects. All kinds. Of course my favorites are ones that can fly, and a great many of them do."

Wind spent time with both Day and Night, dividing himself between them, so he was aware of the projects they each had going. He had no problem with swirling up either cosmic dust or Earth dust and was vital to the plans of both primary creators.

"Insects," mulled Day. "Six legs--head, thorax, abdomen--isn't that the basic plan?"

"As a start," answered Wind, shaking his head. "You really have been away for a while, haven't you?"

"Yeah, but that's exactly what I don't want her to think about, so help me out here, will you?"

"Sure, Boss," agreed Wind. "Whatever you say."

"So you suggest something that can fly?" prompted Day.

"I do," said Wind. "Dragonflies are on her agenda today. They're cool. You'll like them."

"But will she like one of mine? That's the point."

"I guarantee it, but you'll want to surprise her with something a little unique, won't you? How about a variation on the general theme that's all your own?"

"Such as...?"

"Something smaller, more delicate, that shows her how you feel."

"That's the ticket," Day said excitedly. "Exactly what I'm looking for."

Wind began with a reconstruction of the dragonfly mold he'd seen earlier. He tweaked it here and there, creating a long, thin, abdomen, but keeping the double-winged format. The wings were held perpendicular to the body when at rest and were clear, but marked with veins throughout, making the wings appear paneled. In the leading edge of each wing, out toward the tip, he darkened a tiny panel with black, Night's favorite color.

"Trust me," said Wind. "She'll love the wing-mark."

About two-and-three-quarters inch long from stubby antennae to tip of abdomen, the creature, still the color of dirt except for the wings and wing-mark, began to buzz its wings.

"Wow," said Day. "Already?"

"Yeah," answered Wind. "They're designed for flight. In fact, they can't walk. They rest by perching, but their legs are all up front on their body, so they can't walk. They use their legs for snatching insects right out of the air, and holding them while they devour their prey in mid-air. I'm not surprised it's trying to fly already. I'll get started on his mate while you figure out how to color them."

Day started with the very large eyes. He made them the same blue as Sky during Sun's reign. The thorax he left brown. The long abdomen was his special delight. He created a beautiful mosaic pattern of browns, blacks and blues.

"Very impressive!" admired Wind. "The colors almost look braided together."

"A melding of Night's Earth and my Sky," explained Day.

"Good thinking!" raved Wind. "A sewing together of Earth and Sky. She'll have to love that. Here's his mate. What are you going to do with her?"

"Same pattern, I think," said Day, searching his pallet for just the right color combination. "But how about green rather than blue."

"Nice," agreed Wind. "But you know what would be even more appealing to Night?"

"What?"

"If you let the female choose for herself. Let her decide how much green or blue she'll have in her abdominal mosaic."

Day whistled. "You are absolutely right. Night will go for that."

The two creatures sat side by side, their eight wings eagerly buzzing against Wind's restraining hand.

"Stand back," came an announcement from above. With that, a bolt of lightning split the air, unleashed by Sky out of his clear blue. "I couldn't let you two have all the glory. I want to impress Night too."

Now each insect sported two blue stripes on top, and two diagonal stripes on the left and right side of its thorax. They were profoundly gorgeous. Off they raced to become the predators of the air they were meant to be.

"Oh how beautiful," Night exclaimed later, watching Day's gift sport amongst her new dragonflies. "I love them.

Such a fabulous blending of Earth and Sky, of both our realms. And I adore the wing-mark. What are they?"

"They forever sew together Earth and Sky," quoted Wind importantly.

"They're Darners," declared Day, smitten with inspiration. "Blue-eyed Darners."

"Darners, huh? Wonderful. Let's make some more."

Bumblebee Song

It is said that there was once a time before Bumblebee Song. In those days the competition for pollen at the blossoms of desert plants was won largely by the smaller and faster insects. With over two hundred different kinds of native bees, the largest renown for pollination efforts was theirs. But many insects got "honorable mention," including ants, who by their shear numbers and tendency to swarm were bound to accomplish fertilization more often than not in the flowers they scurried through. Those insects that were slower and more cumbersome still collected pollen, but frequently the task of impregnating the blossom had already been accomplished.

Bumblebees and Carpenter Bees belonged in the "cumbersome" category, and you may be sure they knew it. Not only were they bungling giants, they were also solitary. They did not form societies or live communally as the ants did.

Ants were a force to reckon with wherever they were, at home or abroad, for there were hordes of them, each of whom had her sister's back. Mess with one, you messed with all.

Many bees were solitary too, but they were also quick on the wing. Fleetness of flight plus their wide variety of shape and form put them way ahead of their competitors.

Bumblebees perceived themselves as nothing less than handicapped in the race to help procreate their food plants. Though solitary, they were large in body and voice. When they had a gripe, it could not go unnoticed. No less a force than Wind heard their whining and determined he should petition Day and Night, the two primary creators, for some way to level out the pollination path to the flowers, so that all might share in the privilege of plant production.

"Does it really matter?" asked Day, not sure he should interrupt his nap for this interview. He was currently primarily concerned with hastening along the burgeoning life processes in the far north where he'd been working nearly twenty-four hours a day to pull off the birthing of everything from tiny krill to vast stretches of tundra growth in a few short months. Naps were almost non-existent and he was ill-tempered without them.

Night, who was equally as busy at the South Pole overseeing the deep-freezing of all life there, had been working closely with Wind to create the blizzards that cleansed Antarctica during her winter season. She was more willing to hear what Wind, her right-hand man, had to say.

"It seems minor to us, rushed as we are for time, but Bumblebee is unable to rush, which is precisely his complaint. He has not the wherewithal to accomplish what he most dearly desires: to take part in creating the seed of the plants he loves, without which he cannot continue."

"But so what?" carped Day. "It's not as if others aren't filling that gap more than adequately. Why do we need one more?"

"If you could hear how he moans and groans, you'd understand," declared Wind. "It's quite amazing how loud his complaints have become when he lumbers to a flower only to find seed manufacture already underway. He feels quite useless. Yes, that's it; he feels his life's without merit. He is fed by the pollen, but gives nothing in return. He feels non-essential to the plant so vital to him. I swear, this depression makes him fly all the slower, and I, for one, would hardly have thought that possible."

"That is something you'll never feel," Night asserted gently, "because nothing is vitalized without you. But put yourself in Bumblebee's place. Would you find purposelessness becoming? Is it garb you'd gladly wear?"

Day yawned and shrugged. "I suppose not," he admitted. "Although it might be quite agreeable for an hour or two so I could rest. Well--what's the remedy? You two got something in mind?"

"Not really," admitted Night sheepishly.

"Not right off the top of my head," Wind sighed.

"Then bring Bumblebee here, quickly," snapped Day. "I'd like to think I could still get some shuteye today after our meeting."

"Take your nap," Wind advised. "I'll bring him, but not quickly. That's the issue, remember? We'll be here as soon as we can, for while he's brawny of wing, he's about as streamlined as a box of rocks. We'll be back tomorrow," he promised.

Day snored within moments. Night sipped an iced tea and rested too.

In two days time--the trip took longer than Wind thought, even with his assistance--Bumblebee arrived. He hovered a full minute, then tumbled gracelessly at his creator's feet, awakening Day, who was once again catching a quick nap.

"Oh, it's you," Day grunted, stretching. "I thought Night'd set the alarm clock to awaken me for the second round of Mosquito hatchings."

"No," Night countered. "The whining of Mosquito is infinitely more irritating than any alarm clock. I knew it wouldn't be necessary."

"We finally made it," announced Wind. "We're here to discuss plants for Bumblebee."

"He expects his own plants?" asked Day.

28

"I don't ask for many," Bumblebee spoke up for himself.

"But you do expect some," Day continued. "I thought we were going to discuss this and come up with a plan together."

"Well," Wind began. "We did hash it about a little as we traveled and we thought perhaps a number of plants that could only be pollinated by Bumblebee would be the way to go."

"His own private plants?" asked Day, a tad incredulously.

"I'd share," answered Bumblebee defensively. "I'd share with other pokey pollinators--like Carpenter Bee," he offered.

"That would be fair," Wind said hastily.

"We've done something like that before," Night remembered. "Made such close ties between specific plants and animals. What he's asking is really not that unreasonable. We'd have to come up with a plant only Bumblebee could collect pollen from. That shouldn't be too difficult."

"Well, what sets Bumblebee apart?" Day asked, warming to the challenge. "He's slow, we've established that, but we can hardly develop plants that are any slower than what we've already got. And we can't slow down the rest of the insect world to give him a better chance at snagging a flower before anyone else."

"No," Night agreed. "Still, it's plants that give us our best options. Bumblebee is also a little clumsy. Remember your crash landing when you arrived?" she said to the bulky bee with a smile meant to tease and not humiliate.

"We should call you 'Tumblebee' instead of 'Bumblebee,'" joked Wind.

"How does that help anything?" Day wondered

"I'm just tossing around ideas here," Night responded. "Maybe we'll use them, maybe we won't. Let's hear some from you."

"He's chunkier than most everything else that visits flowers," Day stated. "He's just plain heavier. Can we work off of that?"

"Maybe," said Night. "Because that means he's usually pulling the blossom over while he's on it."

"Hanging upside down," added Bumblebee, the voice of experience.

"How about a flower that spilled pollen down onto him," asked Wind. "It would only dump out when it was upside down."

"That's a thought, but you might spill the goods in that case," said Day reflectively. "Many's the time you blow plants hard enough to bend flowers toward Earth. That'd be nothing but a waste of good pollen."

"Give Bumblebee a key," Wind responded. "Some way only he can unlock the flower, not me and not any other major pollen distributor."

"What kind of key?" asked Bumblebee, trying to imagine flying with additional weight. "I'm already husky, as you've pointed out. Now I should carry some sort of key too?"

"You just need a means of identifying yourself to the flower," said Wind. "Then it would open and dump its pollen on you as you pull it upside down. Not all means of identifying yourself are carried," he added. "Wolves listen to calls sung out from a distance and know each family member's songs from another's. Can you sing?" he asked Bumblebee as an afterthought.

"Never tried," Bumblebee bumbled in his surprise. "Never thought to try."

Desert Senna was just beginning to bloom. Intrigued by the conversation it overheard, she considered her qualifications. Being a perennial, she had main branches that already could bear the weight of Bumblebee. But her clusters of yellow, five-petaled flowers were easily bent earthward too. Not by bees, but she was sure Bumblebee could do it. She offered herself for modification so the big black and yellow insect could have a chance at fertilizing blossoms.

"That way you don't have to start from scratch," she said to Day and Night. "And I've always thought we went well together, my flowers and your stripes," she nodded to Bumblebee.

"You're willing to go back to the drawing board?" Bumblebee asked. "That's very kind of you."

"Not really," laughed Senna. "I'm thinking of myself too. Your voice has always been a pleasure to me. I hear you coming from far away and look forward to your visits." Her gray-green leaflets jingled as Wind looked her over.

"You'd be depending on him to form seed," Wind reminded her. His numbers aren't as great as the other bees. There might be some risk involved."

"I'll trust in his strength," she replied.

"It could work," Bumblebee declared.

"I admit I had something in mind with larger flowers," began Day, but maybe we could come up with a plan."

The rest of the day was spent trying on differing styles of flower construction and having Bumblebee give each a test run. He blundered in for a landing pretty consistently--as if he were blind and landing by smell and touch, but that was normal for him. Nothing worked in the way of anther design to deliver pollen to him exclusively until Day thought to seal away each anther's pollen instead of leaving it on display to any and all comers. The new anther just had a tiny pore in the end of it, large enough for pollen to pass, but not insects, no matter how small. Needless to say, it was off limits to Bumblebee too. He hung and tipped the flowers with his bulk, but no pollen was dislodged, though he jiggled and bobbled with all his might.

Everyone was disappointed, and everyone was oh so tired of trying. Wind and Night pleaded off, saying they had a blizzard to attend down south. Day threw in the towel too, having run out of all ideas to help. He shrugged and headed toward the Arctic. Poor Bumblebee still hung upside down on sore Senna's golden flowers, not willing to surrender, but not sure what to try next.

"Well, it seemed like a good idea," Senna sighed. "I'm so sorry it didn't work out."

"We gave it our best," groaned Bumblebee. "My wings are so tired I'm not sure I can leave. Do you mind if I just stay a while?"

"Suit yourself," Senna responded. "Perhaps we can try again ourselves tomorrow."

Bumblebee was humbled by her devotion. She'd said she liked his voice better than anyone else's, hadn't she? Too tired to fly, he could still buzz, he decided, and did so. It was a different tone than when in flight, but a buzz is a buzz, he reasoned.

And that's when it rained pollen. His voice vibrated Senna's anthers at just the right frequency to rattle the pollen lose. It cascaded out the little hole in the anther's end to dump all over his body, where fine hairs caught and held the golden stuff of both their lives.

Senna laughed with delight. Bumblebee floundered to another flower and sang again, resulting in another downpour of pollen.

"You've found the key!" exclaimed Senna.

"Your patience and selflessness have taught me to sing," replied Bumblebee gratefully.

"Welcome to my world," Senna sassed playfully.

"Look out seeds, here I come," shouted Bumblebee, as he lifted off for another flower and another song.

Jumpstarting the Creative Process

It is said that there was once a time when Day and Night sat together, hard at work hammering out the fine details of Creation.

"Geez. Another bean pod? Aren't there enough pods bursting and beaning all over? Can't we do another fruit-like thing. Berries maybe? Burrs?

"Burrs? Oh yeah. That's original. Your desert landscaping is already full of burrs."

"OK. Berries then."

"We just did Heliotrope. You want berries again already?"

"But Heliotrope is an annual, and short. This is perennial and larger, a bush, even. That's not being repetitious."

"I suppose it has to reproduce somehow."

"It's tough, this creation-thing. It's hard to come up with new angles all the time."

"I'll say. I'm exhausted. Maybe it's time for a nap."

"Hey, didn't we just make one plant?"

"Yeah."

"So how come there's three now?"

"Three?"

"See for yourself."

"Son of a gun! You're right. You're usually not, but when you're right, you're right."

"Yeah, yeah. I'm right as often as you. It's hard to foresee every possible outcome of every act of creation. Besides, we're in this together."

"True. We are. And it is impossible to know everything beforehand. Obviously. Because how did the other two bushes get here?"

"Beats me."

"Well, help me look. There has to be an explanation somewhere. Hey, what's this? A root came from the original bush and sprouted a new plant at the soil's surface. Have we done that before?"

"Yeah, but not so often as the burr-thing. Didn't we call it a rhizome? When the root-like thing sprouts a new plant?"

"Rhizome!? You must have come up with that name."

"Yeah, I did, as a matter of fact."

"So why did you use that with this bush without discussing it with me?"

"I didn't do it. I thought you did it."

"Well, I didn't, but it's done now. I don't feel like un-doing it, do you?"

"No, I suppose not. But then, why the flowers? We just spent all this time designing the flowers--the deep dark purple of your influence below, the white-ish upper lip and tube showing my touch. All that debating and we're not going to have flowers?"

"We can still have flowers."

"Well, are they going to produce seed?"

"Sure, why not?"

"Because now we have to decide what that's going to be like. I still lean toward berries."

"Berries schmerries. I'm sick of berries."

"What then?"

"I don't know. Do I have to think of everything?"

"Like I said. It's hard to come up with anything novel after a while."

"Like I said. Maybe a nap would help."

"Come on. It's only mid-morning. If we can't do better than this, we're never going to finish."

"Sometimes it seems that way."

"Deep sigh," said the silver-green leafed bush.

"What was that?"

"What was what?"

"Hey look! What's that?"

"Wow! The seed maybe?"

"Ya think?"

"Got any better ideas?"

"You do that? It's fabulously original."

"I thought you did it."

"No. I like it though. How about you?"

"Seed pods that look like paper lanterns? Who would argue with that kind of creativity?"

"You, if I had thought of it."

"Yeah, but you didn't."

"True, I did not."

"So it's a 'keeper'?"

"Agreed."

"About time," said the bush.

"What?" said Day.

"What's next?" said Night.

And that's how Bladdersage created it's own methods of reproduction and came by another of its names--Paperbagplant.

Despite Day and Night.

Black-throated Sparrow Confronts Chaos

It is said that there was once a time when Chaos reigned. Nothing happened on a regular schedule. Sun rose whenever. Moon was always full. There were no seasons, for when Sun didn't show, it was cold. When he did appear, he was often so close to Earth that he scorched her. Water washed over the land and only the highest mountains were not subject to periodic floods. Wind blew constantly.

In spite of the difficulties, there was life. It was precarious, but there was life. In those days, Coyote called almost incessantly. He could be heard wailing all Day and all Night, irregular as Day and Night were. Sometimes he was broadcasting news. Mostly he was complaining about how hard his life was. Such constant practice vocalizing rendered him a wonderful vocabulary. The stories he told as he called to the elements and anyone else who would listen! He developed a reputation: if you wanted everyone to know something, tell Coyote.

Coyote wasn't, of course, the only one who had it hard. Everyone did. No one knows who first thought there might be a way to organize Chaos, but everyone knew who to ask to spread the word. Coyote called from one edge of the world to the other, and soon all the plants and animals knew there was to be a meeting. They began to gather at Earth's middle, where they agreed they would guarantee one another's safety. Even Coyote agreed not to eat Rabbit while on the meeting grounds. If there was a slight glint in his eye as he promised, a glance at stern Cougar convinced him to obey.

It was the birds who seemed to have thought the most about their dilemma. They led the discussion and made the most suggestions. They suspected that order might be brought out of Chaos if importuned diligently.

Sun would respond, perhaps, if regularly petitioned to rise--then thanked for his appearance. He should also be reminded to leave, in case he forgot and hung around too long.

Moon might be convinced to vary her light--leaving room for more dark of Night, when creatures could sleep most deeply and stars were better seen. Stars too were erratically bunched. They could be organized and made meaningful. But if there was to be variable light, Moon would need to be called from the dark to her fullness, then cued to begin returning to her dark state on a regular cycle. Those who agreed to call her must be faithful and well aware of pattern and rhythm.

Wind must be teamed with Cloud and Rain, and all reminded to come at the best season to clean the air and water Earth. But Wind should not always blow, so he must be encouraged to let Earth rest sometimes too. Rain would also need to be invited to leave with Cloud, as the last of Wind passed by, lest Earth become flooded.

These projects seemed overwhelming to most of the creatures. Who, for instance, was powerful enough to call Sun into rising each day?

Then Black-throated Sparrow agreed to sing for Rain to come in summer. He felt he could handle that. His tweet tweet introduction for his bell-like twittering call could beg for the monsoons--but someone else must call Rain in the winter. To take on that additional task was too much for Black-throated Sparrow's little voice.

Black-throated Sparrow's offering reminded the others that they could share the tasks which needed doing. That made everyone more comfortable about taking on a little individually, so together they could do a lot. Other sparrows said they too would help call in Summer Rain. Saguaro agreed to feed them his fruit at the time they would need extra strength to sing for Rain. Squirrels, who slept a good part of winter, thought they might dream up Winter Rain. They were willing to give it a shot, anyway. Rabbit, who also slept when it was coldest, vowed to help.

Bear offered to gather a few stars into his shape. Crab agreed to involve herself similarly. Others consented to rework the night sky and they split off from the rest of the group to begin their planning.

Creosote suggested she might flower in thanks for Summer Rain. Rabbitbrush agreed he would flower in thanksgiving for Winter Rain. Hummingbird offered to dazzle Rain with her colors and flight, reminding him not to flood Earth. Rainbow would be Rain's sign that he'd received Hummingbird's message.

Owl said he'd call out the departure time of Sun at Day's end, and the time of Sun's arrival at Night's end. Thrasher would help call Sun to rise, since that was such an important task. Rooster said he would too. Sparrow and Finch agreed to call from their roosting spots in thankful celebration of Sun's arrival and departure. Quail agreed to call goodbye to Sun when his last light glowed on the horizon, but preferred not to greet the dawn. Rabbit declared she would dance each morning when she left her nest as her thanks to Sun for his appearance.

Calling for Moon was perhaps the most complex task, and a whole team of plants and animals agreed to assist with that. Datura promised to demonstrate Moon's path of increase and decrease with the opening and closing of her pure white flowers. That prompted a number of cacti to do the same. They would open and close their snowy blossoms only at Night, for Moon's benefit. Their flowers' fragrance would be an incense offering to her alone.

Screech Owl and Mockingbird promised to call during Moon's fullness to remind her to begin shrinking again. Bat pledged his sonar to pull Moon out of her completely dark phase and once again into the light. These plants and animals had to be utterly committed and well organized because they had to guide Moon through such a variety of faces and be willing to work Day and Night.

Coyote agreed to spread any message the others asked and to broadcast the news, so long as he might include a little "personal opinion" in his reports.

Before long, the seemingly insurmountable challenge of ordering Chaos had been subdivided into smaller, do-able duties--and it is only because the creatures faithfully continue their efforts that we have any order today.

So whenever you hear Coyote calling, thank him for spreading the news of that first meeting--and just ignore his complaints of enduring hunger now, because he agreed not to eat Rabbit on the meeting grounds then.

And thank tiny Black-throated Sparrow too--for being the very first to agree to take on a small part of the huge hassle of bringing order to Chaos.

His Very Nature is Drumming

It is said that Day and Night, the two primary creators, sat together plotting how to evoke the memories necessary to call their creations home.

"Many remember when they hear it," said Night. She was thinking of the thrum-thrumming of the drums once used by all people to call to Rain in ceremonies, and to talk to one another over great distances.

"Yes, " answered Day. He was thinking of the sound of thunder rolling across vast valleys, awe inspiring as it voiced the approach of Storm.

"Man first used hollow trees," Night continued. "The sound reverberated in the listeners, activating centers that caused memories. Perhaps they could not have said what they remembered, but they traveled to their deepest places and 'knew' once again, at least while the drumming continued."

"Storm bounced thunder off mountains and across valleys causing everyone to pause and remember. All then scurried on their way to avoid Storm's passage, but in the moment of their pausing, they too 'knew' where they came from," said Day.

"What could periodically make a noise like thunder to remind our creatures how to come home?" asked Night. "Could we make something whose very nature would be to drum?"

"On trees?" said Day.

"That would work in most places," said Night.

So the beginning of Northern Flicker was the tree, the tool he would drum upon. Day and Night made certain of his drumming by designing him to eat the insects he would hunt within the tree. They made his head and neck muscles powerful. His bill they elongated, like a chisel, so he could drive it with great force into the bark of the tree to search out his meals. These he would extract with his long tongue, tipped with sticky bristles. For those times when trees or the insects within them were not enough to satisfy Flicker, he could also conveniently eat ants from the ground at their holes with the very same sticky tongue. Short, stocky wings were made to carry Flicker from tree to tree and from ground to tree so that he might feed. Night placed a crescent of new Moon black on every breast and scattered black spots over the bird's belly from the crescent on down. She also painted black stripes on each one's brown back and upper wing. Day gave each a white rump.

Because of his task and the need of creation to be remembering, Northern Flicker was spread across all of North America. In the East, Northern Flicker wore the yellow risen Sun under his wings and tail, a red crescent on the back of his neck and a black moustache. To the West, Northern Flicker wore the red setting Sun under his wings and tail, and a red moustache.

But in the desert, where there were fewer trees, Northern Flicker's design was modified so that he would nest in and eat from Saguaro cactus. He could also eat the fruit of Saguaro's flower, as did so many other desert animals. The desert Flicker was given the hottest yellow mid-afternoon Sun to wear under each wing, a red moustache and the name "Gilded." He was a bit smaller and lighter in color than the other Flickers, but drummed just as loudly on his cactus as the others did on their trees.

Day and Night liked this drummer so well that they made many smaller woodpeckers of other varieties and colors. Their thrumming was not so loud as Flicker's, for they were not as powerful, but their rapping also reminded listeners of the way home. For the thickest forests, Day and

Night produced woodpeckers larger than Flicker's twelve inches. These had larger voices to go with their larger size, so their drumming would carry through the densest stands of trees.

It was Flicker that began it all, however. He was the first of the woodpeckers and the most widespread. It was his design excellence that encouraged the formation of all the rest.

Together, the woodpeckers drum the way home.

Cloud Boy Messes With the Wrong Bee

It is said that there was once a time when Cloud Boy played regularly with any insects he could get his cloud hands on. He was always grasping for grasshoppers, darting after dragonflies, batting at butterflies and buffeting bees. He particularly liked bees--Carpenter Bees. Whenever you see wisps of clouds straggling down towards Earth, or dragging against mountains, or hovering as fog over streams and ponds, you know Cloud Boy and his friends are looking for bugs.

Now, Carpenter Bees were favorites because they were big, noisy and slow, like Bumble Bees. Like Bumble Bees, they ate nectar and gathered pollen from flowers. Like Bumble Bees, they were solitary. They did not build hives and live in colonies, like Honey Bee, who protected herself with large numbers of her kind.

They differed from Bumble Bees because their abdomens were black and shiny, while Bumble Bees had yellow, hairy abdomens. Another difference was Bumble Bees liked to burrow in the ground to lay their eggs. Carpenter Bees burrowed too, but in wood. Cloud Boy never knew where Bumble Bee might choose to build a nest, but Carpenter Bee holes could be easily seen in old cottonwood stumps and nesting sites were used over and over again--generation after generation. Then too, Mrs. Carpenter Bee was very noisy as she worked. Her buzzing could be heard from a distance as she cleaned tunnels, chewed new passageways, or made individual egg cells she sealed off with chewed-wood walls. While she worked, the stump-nest vibrated with her noisy song, so finding

43

Carpenter Bee holes and hanging around for a while at the right time of year guaranteed Cloud Boy and his friends a little fun. They loved trying to catch the black bee in their hands, much to Carpenter Bee's displeasure.

One May day, Cloud Boy was scouting out a Cottonwood forest near a river. He saw a round, black, buzzing blob bobbling before a hole bored into a tree stump. He knew Mr. Carpenter Bee courted Mrs. Carpenter Bee with this peculiar bobbling dance. He also knew the male bee would bounce around the nest his mate was preparing, guarding his territory from all encroachers. Cloud Boy knew the guard duty was buzzy bluff, for Mr. Carpenter Bee had no stinger. Mrs. Carpenter Bee did, but she seldom got really mad and was nowhere in sight.

That's because she was deep in a hole making bee bread loaves of pollen and nectar, laying one egg next to each loaf she made. She finished by closing each loaf and egg off with a thin, papery wall. It took lots of effort and she became more and more agitated as she worked. She was usually pretty good natured, but the stress of her responsibility was beginning to show. She buzzed more and more loudly as she worked, fretting about how much remained to be done and how she hoped she was provisioning her children with enough food for them to grow stronger than any other Carpenter Bee.

Deep in her dark tunnel, she had no idea her mate was sparring with Cloud Boy. Mr. Carpenter Bee dodged and buzzed ferociously. He darted through Cloud Boy's misty fingers. Again and again he butted his black head against Cloud Boy, until his face turned as white as the cloud he fought. When he tired, as Cloud Boy knew he would, he was snatched from flight and wrapped in a dewy, wet fist. There he protested until he was too soggy to buzz or fly any longer.

It was at this moment that Mrs. Carpenter Bee emerged from her nest. She witnessed her husband's capture and heard him spluttering in Cloud Boy's foggy grasp. She was in no mood for any adolescent interference in her family's business. Mustering up her meanest buzz, she dashed at Cloud Boy, nailing him with her stinger as hard as she could. Cloud Boy yelped and dropped his captive, then fled to the treetops. There he rubbed against the leaves to sooth his wound and shot nasty little lightning bolts at Mrs. Carpenter Bee. She retreated victoriously to her stump to continue her bread making, completely ignoring Cloud Boy's temper tantrum.

Mr. Carpenter Bee sighed with relief, mopped his now white brow with a foreleg, then used his back legs to scrape moisture from his wings. A minute in a ray of sunlight, and he was good to go again, sounding just as fierce as ever, bobbling around the nest entrance impressively. In fact, he was even more impressive than before, for his white face gave him the look of a painted warrior.

Up in the treetops, Cloud Boy pouted, privately vowing never to play with bees again. As the sun rose higher, so did he. He left behind the cottonwoods and the river and went to play with Butterfly, soaring nearby.

Butterfly had no stinger.

Two Coontails

It is said that there was once a time when Day and Night, the two primary creators, had not yet made Rattlesnake. But they had already made Antelope Squirrel, Rock Squirrel, Round-tailed Ground Squirrel, Pocket Gopher, Pocket Mouse, Kangaroo Rat, Deer Mouse, Woodrat, Cactus Mouse, House Mouse, Cotton Rat, Western Harvest Mouse--well--all the rodents, really. That was the problem, you see. Lots and lots of gnawing-everything-skittering-everywhere rodents and not enough of those creatures who ate them. The desert was becoming overrun with the furry things. Plants couldn't recover, even when Monsoon rains were good. Bird and reptile nests were robbed too. Order and balance needed to be restored. So Rattlesnake was made.

Rattlesnakes didn't lay eggs, so they had no nests rats could raid. Rattlesnake young were born live. They all had venom, even newborns. They were the perfect rodent eliminator. Because there were varieties of rodents in varieties of environments, varieties of Rattlesnake were necessary. This story tells how two of those came to be.

Day and Night experimented with venoms. They experimented with size. They played around with coloring and the arrangement of scales. They were particularly pleased with those snakes that boldly displayed their Creator's colors in their tails, the black of Night and white of Day. These were collectively known as "Coontails," after Raccoon's hindmost striped part--with, of course, the addition of a rattle. Two members of the "Coontails" were Diamondback and Mojave.

Mojave was mostly made for hunting flat areas with scattered mesquite trees and Creosote bushes. Three feet long, he loved Creosote so strongly that he took on a greenish tinge the better to mingle with Creosote foliage. He was fierce and quick, a specialist in the smaller rodents and reptiles encamped around the base of Creosote.

"We've made your venom especially powerful," Day informed Mojave. "Since your prey is small and fast, your venom must be fast acting. Your toxin will affect the nerves of those you bite, stopping their breathing and paralyzing them in moments."

Mojave nodded.

"Because you're smaller," Night added, "your young will get a head start in life. You'll give birth in July and August. Your earlier start will protect your offspring from the competition of Diamondback's."

The Creators then turned to the bigger, bulkier of the Coontails, Diamondback.

"You are built for power rather than speed," began Day. "You've also been given a tolerance for great variety in homesites. You can be found in mountains as well as plains, rocky as well as sandy soils, and arid scrubland as well as dense river bottoms."

A full six feet in length, Diamondback raised his head high above his coiled body and hissed to show he understood.

"Your size is imposing," Day smiled. "You may prey on rabbits as well as smaller rodents. Although your venom is deadly, your foods are a little slower, like you. You don't need Mojave's extra-strength poison."

"You'll give birth later in the summer and fall," declared Night. "Your species' size and power will be all your children need to make their way in the world."

Diamondback nodded.

"Welcome," the Creators bowed to their creations. The snakes returned the salutations regally, then turned to one another.

"I am born when the days are longest," declared the Mojave Coontail. "I will show my preference for Day." So saying he wriggled and heaved until he'd split his skin. In his efforts, he widened the white stripes of his tail to twice that of the black. Now the white of Day dominated the black of Night, just as in the days his offspring would be born.

"That's good," agreed Diamondback. "I like it. I'll keep my striping evenly black and white because I'm born when Day and Night rule equally, or very nearly so."

"Did you see that?" whispered Night to Day.

"I did," said Day in astonishment.

"You just never know what they're going to come up with, do you?" asked Night.

"Absolutely not," agreed Day. "That's what happens when you allow creativity to abound within your creation," he sighed. "You just never know."

Volcano Leaves His Mark

It is said that there was once a time when Earth told Volcano he would soon be extinct.

"The time for fiery mountain building is past," she said. "Time to cool my crust and provide footholds for more life-forms to flourish. Day and Night (the two primary creative forces) have ordered it. Sun agrees. I do too. It won't mean the end of you. The magnificent mountain you've built will remain. But we'll dress it with plants and animals for our entertainment. Every now and then, we may call on you to rumble and shake. Perhaps an occasional belch of lava and rock, but we want quiet, for the most part. We want your mountain to become a nursery for life other than rock."

Volcano wasn't surprised. He had noticed he had less energy for spewing rock and lava from his mountaintop. Lava tubes were harder to form. Perhaps it would be good to retire before he embarrassed himself with a misfire. Perhaps occasional comebacks to surprise and shake folks up would be fun. Certainly less demanding.

"Sounds fine to me," said Volcano, "but I would like to leave my mark on some of the life forms you want to come live on my mountain."

"Like what?" asked Earth warily. She had seen Volcano leave his mark on trees. They were nothing but cinders when Volcano was finished, and that was not what she had in mind as decoration for his slopes.

"Let me mark a few things with my fire," pleaded Volcano.

"No way," declared Earth. "Your fire would burn anything you touched."

"Yes way," coaxed Volcano. "I want my glory days to be remembered. You could give me something I could toast, but not crisp, singe but not ashify."

"Like what?" asked Earth.

"I don't know. Something that can approach my heat, then get away under its own power, maybe? Ask around. I bet some creatures would be interested in adding red to their color scheme. I could send a flare or two in their direction, brand them slightly, then they could go on their way."

"Well...," said Earth.

"It could work! I'd be careful," said Volcano.

"I'll ask around," said Earth doubtfully.

Amazing as it sounds, there were a few birds that volunteered to be marked by Volcano. They figured they could fly close enough to his flares to be colored red, but still fly away before becoming crisped. They were that eager to dress in red. Cardinal, Flycatcher, House Finch and Tanager wanted to be red. Their wives thought they were crazy.

"Don't go," begged Mrs. Cardinal. "It's just your foolish pride pushing you to do this."

"It's perfectly safe, my dear. Follow behind me, if you want. You'll get some color too, perhaps."

"We're paired for life," cringed Mrs. Cardinal, "so I suppose I will follow, but at a distance. I hope you know what you're doing."

Mrs. Flycatcher also chose to follow at a distance. She was not so interested in sharing her husband's fate, however, as attending the barbecue she felt sure would be the result of a sudden flare appearing in an airy atmosphere teeming with bugs. No doubt she could eat well while her vain husband sought to turn red.

Mrs. Tanager and Mrs. House Finch said, "You're on your own, Bucko," to their spouses and refused to even attend the ceremony. "Such idiocy," chirped Mrs. House Finch. "You'll never blend in to your environment again," warned Mrs. Tanager. But their husbands were determined.

Mr. and Mrs. Turkey Vulture watched and listened to the debate. They were thinking barbecue too, just like Mrs. Flycatcher, but they weren't drooling for bugs. They figured to be around in case one of the male birds made a tiny misflight and wound up broiled to perfection rather than simply red.

On the fateful day Volcano had agreed to flare, the birds all gathered near the crater. The vultures perched on the edge, certain that would be the best place from which to pluck any birds blasted from the sky. The Cardinals wheeled overhead, Mrs. Cardinal staying in the rear by at least half a mile. The Flycatchers made quick darting flights toward the crater. He planned to dash toward the flaring gasses the moment they shot up. She planned to snatch bees and dragonflies the moment they were well done. Mr. Tanager flew alone. Mr. House Finch did too, but much more slowly. He was the smallest and the most timid. He was having second thoughts.

Volcano gathered up steam and began to rumble. Curious, the Vultures leaned over to look into the crater. "So what does Volcano look like when he's erupt...," started Mr. Turkey Vulture, but he never finished his question, for at that moment a blob of lava shot past the Vultures, scalding them as they stared into Volcano. The stink of their own burned feathers and flesh was all they could smell. Their featherless, red heads and necks were proof of their attendance at the barbecue of their own flesh.

Mr. Cardinal and Mr. Tanager both flew into the flare--into and through--as fast as they could. They both emerged red from lores to tail. Except Cardinal was burnt black around his face, a bit of ash he never could rinse off. Mrs. Cardinal did get some glare-burn. The radiant red of the flare made her begin to glow. Mr. Flycatcher relied a smidge too much on his amazing ability to dart and dodge the volcanic fires. He zig-zagged through the flames so closely that he did indeed turn a glorious red on his head and belly, but he miscalculated the direction of one particular flare and it wrapped around his face, back and tail, blackening them forever. Mrs. Flycatcher was just darting skyward after a damselfly as the flare erupted. Her flanks took on a glow. Mr. House Finch was bringing up the cautious rear, and only his chest and face singed--that is until he felt the heating of those feathers and turned tail to flee, exposing his butt to the energy.

Now Tanager was Summer Tanager. He wanted a name change to reflect his new state. Flycatcher did too. He chose Vermilion Flycatcher to describe his new look, conveniently ignoring the sooty, blackened half of his body. Ahhh, vanity.

Volcano looked over the birds he'd marked, the volunteers and the accidental volunteers. He was satisfied. They were satisfied too. Only Mr. and Mrs. Turkey Vulture were dissatisfied. They could smell the barbecue, but couldn't eat it.

Volcano, after reviewing his work, was content to subside. His marked birds were some of the first to decorate his mountain's slopes, the foremost of many plants and animals to call the mountain home. Day and Night were pleased

The Little People

It is said that there was once a time when Little People inhabited wetlands. It was rare to come across these folk when traveling across country, but wandering storytellers always had lore of these tiny man-like creatures to spice up their tales.

The Little People lived in burrows and possessed one of two temperaments. They were either healers or tricksters. Meetings between Man and Little Man might prove beneficial, if Man was in need, or very ill. But, when Man was not respectful, Little Man might play tricks which would prove the downfall of Man.

Water, of course, is necessary to all life. When Man considered Water sacred, he acknowledged this relationship between himself and other creatures and never possessed or controlled Water to his own ends. But with time, Man forgot and sought to dominate others. One sure way to accomplish this, was to control Water.

When Man possessed the Water Places, he modified them, cutting them off from animals. The Water sites had to be abandoned. They found Water in the wild places Man had not yet tamed, or they died.

The Little People were deprived of their homes. They never forgot their relationship with other creatures. They were stealthy and might have cohabited the water holes with Man for a while, but they chose to migrate with other creatures to new sources of Water. Yet, they still hoped to open Man's eyes once again to the sacred.

As Man's concept of sacredness narrowed, he lost his ability to even see the Little People. Little Folk realized Man was blinded by his own mindset and could see only what he expected to see.

Man believed he controlled not only Water, but Mystery. Watching the light of Mystery leave Man's eyes, Little People knew they had to resort to forms Man could still see with his darkening vision. Forms that allowed them to travel quickly from one Water source to another.

They requested an audience with Day and Night, the two primary creators, to discuss a new form for themselves.

"Man is mostly Water," Day said. "How could he forget it was sacred?"

"Man is losing his vision," responded the Little People. "He can't see the sacred in himself, so he can't see it around himself either."

"Unbelievable," whispered Night, and she began to weep.

"How could such forgetting even begin?" wondered Day. He took Night's hand.

"You have our permission to seek a new form," declared Day. "I suggest you request aid from Water and the other elements. They are all components of Man. Earth is especially close to all her creatures and will help you reach Man before he withdraws further."

So the Little People called The Elements together, Earth, Fire (Sun), Air (Wind) and Water. A sense of peril permeated their debates.

Water gave her moisture with no worry as to the form it took. She did ask that the new creature keep her company wherever she might be found, however.

Sun contributed his energy in his unchanging golden color for the creature's belly and flank.

Wind argued for an agent of flight to flit from one Water site to another. One he could lift and carry in its travels.

Earth contributed green for its back, matching the plants around places of flowing Water, where the creature would try to communicate with Man. In honor of Day and Night, white and black would show in its wings.

The Little People merely asked to remain little.

In this manner, Lesser Goldfinch was made. Early spring finds him feeding in great numbers at Cottonwood's blossoms and newly sprouting leaves. Thistle and Seep-willow also provide Lesser Goldfinch with food in season.

Always Lesser Goldfinch sports near the wetlands. Always he chatters and calls out to Man--the Little People's new form for reminding Man of the sacredness within and around him.

The Creation of Quail Plant:
also known as Salt Heliotrope

It is said that there was once a time when Rain had filled the basin, then evaporated in Sun's rays so many times that the mud flats around the diminishing waters developed a higher than normal salt content. Most plants couldn't contend with the saline, though the water tempted seeds to sprout. Seedlings shriveled rather than thrived and there was no protection for the creatures that crept to the water's edge to drink from the brackish pond. Lizards were cornered by Roadrunner at the shoreline. Hawks plucked rabbits off the mud as they lapped their fill. The hunted didn't want to leave their waterhole, but there seemed no alternative. Quail, who was used to calling incessantly to his brood to warn them of danger and assure them of his guarding presence, volunteered to call again and again until he caught the ears of Day and Night, the two primary creators. Once he had done that, he would present the problem of cover at the waterhole to them, asking their assistance in providing some protection to the small animals needing to drink there in safety.

"He-low-o, he-low-o, he-low-o," called Quail, throwing his head back and using his chest muscles to project his voice. "He-low-o, he-low-o, he-low-o."

Quail proved himself the model of endurance that day. He sang his hellos from the hillside near the waterhole from dawn to almost dusk. It took all that time for Day and Night to hear him over the Apache Cicadas they were designing. Their ears were ringing so badly, they had to eventually take a break and leave the shady Cottonwood trees for the well-lit uplands.

"Good grief!" said Night, when they had put some distance between themselves and the noisy insects.

"What?" asked Day.

"I said," began Night, increasing the volume of her voice to minor shouting, "are you sure we're doing the right thing here? I almost can't hear myself think."

"I know," Day shouted back. "But remember, we've designed these bugs to reach adulthood only every three years, so it'll be that long before we have to listen to the eggs resulting from this mating frenzy again. Besides, they are food for so many other animals."

"I suppose," said Night doubtfully, not shouting quite so loudly, for their heads were clearing of Cicada cacophony.

"Did you hear that?" asked Day, looking away in the distance, toward Sun sinking against the horizon.

"What?" asked Night.

"There," said Day. "Isn't that Quail calling?"

"Oh, now I hear it," said Night. "Yes, I believe it is Quail. He must be settling down to sleep."

"I don't think so," said Day. "He's calling too often and loudly to be singing Sun to rest. It might be something else. Let's check it out."

So Day and Night approached the waterhole and spotted Quail up on his rocky perch.

"What is it?" asked Day. "We heard you from clear over there. Is something wrong that you're not clucking to your family and settling down to sleep? It's about that time."

"He-low-o," called Quail one last time. "I've been calling for hours, trying to get your attention."

"Why?" asked Night

"It's the waterhole," said Quail. "The soil around it is too salty for plants to live. We have no cover when we come to drink. I'm speaking on behalf of all of us small

57

animals that have to risk coming out in the open to drink when those who hunt us are nearby and watching."

"It is a risk," sympathized Night.

"By the tracks in the mud, I see it is a great risk," agreed Day.

"Why don't you turn in now," suggested Night. "You've worked hard today to tell us of this danger," she added. "Let us see what we can come up with tonight to remedy the situation and give you better cover when you come to drink at dawn."

Day and Night spent the dark hours listening to the Cicadas call in the distance and working to design a plant that would tolerate more salt in the soil. They settled on a flowering forb of the "forget-me-not" family. It seemed an appropriate tribute to Quail's persistence.

They designed paired coiling clusters of small, white, five-lobed flowers. The center of each flower wore a cheery yellow, a color favored by Day, until they'd been pollinated. Then they turned a lovely deep purple, a color favored by Night. The flowers were tubular to hold nectar for attracting many bees and butterflies. These would ensure the flowers would be fertilized and produce seed.

"A plant living on the edge needs all the help it can get to reproduce," said Day, waxing the leaves to protect them from Sun's burning rays.

"A plant living on the edge provides an opening for other life forms to gain footing too," commented Night, running mud from the water's edge through her fingers. "And since it's only about a foot tall, it will protect the smaller creatures coming to drink, but not those larger animals that hunt them.

"I like the flowers," said Day, as they sat back on their haunches to inspect their creation. "I like the way the flowers seem to glow in Moon's light."

58

"I like how the clusters are paired," said Night. "One for you; one for me. Mirror images."

"Let's call it Quail Plant," said Day. "Quail inspired it and the seeds that develop are ones he will delight to eat."

"Let's also call it Salt Heliotrope," said Night. "It's ability to tolerate salt makes it cutting edge among plant-life and its curved clusters of flowers look just like the arch Sun makes as he cuts through Sky."

"OK--but I bet Quail likes my name best," pouted Day.

"But Sun, who made the salt, will like my name best," declared Night.

"Are you absolutely sure we did the right thing?" she added, after a pause.

"In making Quail Plant?" asked Day.

"No, in making that Cicada racket," she answered, listening to them clamoring in the distant forest.

"Well, maybe we could make them give it a rest periodically," agreed Day.

When morning arrived and the small animals gathered to drink their fill from the cover of the new plants at the shoreline, they didn't care what they were called. They were just grateful for it's presence. Quail was a hero.

And later, when the seed developed into the four segmented nut Quail loved to eat, he didn't care what it was called either, though he accepted his tribute like the singing pro he was.

How Thrasher Got His Curved Bill

It is said that there was once a time when Thrasher's bill was as straight as a Woodpecker's. Long and powerful. Earth made it that way, but it was still rather warm and she had no water handy in which to dip his bill to harden it. Consequently, Earth warned Thrasher it was best not to use it roughly for a few seasons, in order to let it harden slowly.

"The more you use it, the more friction you'll create. The more friction, the hotter it will get. The hotter it is, the more flexible it will become. So don't overdo it!" lectured Earth.

Although his bill was not yet hard, Thrasher's head already was, and he was not about to be told what to do. His was a loud, brazen, bully-ish personality. What he lacked in colorful plumage, he made up for in colorful character. Light brownish-greyish in color, he was camouflaged against Earth's soils, which was a good thing, for Earth made Thrasher in such a way that Thrasher would often prefer running across the ground to flying. She made him to blend in with the dirt. But Earth feared perhaps she'd added a bit too much boldness and a dash too little brains, so that this bird recipe was one she would hesitate about repeating. Thrasher would never "blend in." With his mindset, he would always "stand out."

"I know how to be about my own business, thank you very much," Thrasher said to Earth, admiring his shadow's profile at his feet.

"Don't get sassy with me," she replied. "And if you make a mess of your beak, don't come back here because I'll just say, 'I told you so.'"

"I'm off," he declared, supremely confident as he took leave of his creator.

"I'll say," Earth shot back, shaking her head and wondering how long it would take before he got himself in trouble.

Thrasher strutted across the desert floor at top speed, listening and mimicking the sounds he heard until he developed a song that burbled boldly, like a rushing brook. His call was a brassy, "Riddit-Wit. Riddit, Riddit. Riddit-Wit." He tried to be first up and loudest every morning. Both his song and his call were vocalized boisterously, full of mimicry and mayhem. He demanded to be noticed.

And "noticed" he was.

Cactus wren had started nest building in a fine cholla cactus when Thrasher decided he liked the location too. When Cactus wren protested Thrasher's rearranging the twigs of the nest to his own liking, Thrasher whipped Wren with his bill and bullied the smaller bird into flying away.

Thrasher's mate was just like him in every way. Together they threshed the stones and sand for insects, lifting small rocks to look underneath. When they saw other birds feeding, they rushed over to grab their share, chasing the first birds off. They fed their own chicks until they were large enough to fend for themselves, then ran them off, thrashing them with their bills until the young got the picture and fled away, bruised. No gentle leave taking there!

All the while, they forgot that they had been warned about not using their bills carelessly until they had hardened. With the lifestyle they led, their long, straight bills did not stand a chance of remaining that way. Although at first they did not notice, other animals did.

"What's with the curve?" asked Cactus wren.

"What curve?" asked Thrasher.

"The curve in your bill," answered Cactus wren. "I must admit, I like the change if it means you won't be able to poke me so hard or dig up the ground where I like to hunt bugs. You plow everything up so much the bugs all leave. My best territories are now disaster areas, thanks to you."

"Bug off," was Thrasher's neighborly response.

He flew off to find his wife.

"Guess what Cactus wren just said," he called out when he saw her, perching on the cholla quills she pecked amongst for insects. "Hey, yours is. Is mine?"

"My what and your what?" answered his wife, continuing to snip gnats off the cholla.

"Your bill and my bill. Cactus wren said mine was curving. Is it? Now that I look at you closely, I can see that yours is. Is mine?"

"Oh no, it is bending. And mine is too, you say?"

"Yes, quite a sickle-shaped snoz you've got there, dear. You blew it. Earth told us this might happen if we weren't careful."

"We blew it. Yours is dented too. Just as dented as mine."

"No way."

"Yes way."

"Couldn't be."

"Could too."

They flew to a puddle to inspect their reflections and prove each other wrong.

"Look at that. Mine is as bad as yours. I was so proud of my lovely bill. Can we bend it back, you suppose?"

"Perhaps so," his wife chortled thoughtfully. "We could supervise each other until we each bent it straight again."

"Let's certainly try," said Thrasher.

Just then both birds noticed waterboatmen beetles sporting in the puddle they used as a mirror.

"Mine," declared Thrasher, dashing into the puddle and thrashing the water in chase of the beetles.

"Mine too. You can't have them all," squealed his wife, diving in after him.

The beetles darted.

The birds thrashed.

The water cooled their bills.

The bills hardened.

There was nothing to be done about it after that. The bills were now permanently curved.

As all Thrasher's bills have been ever since--to this very day.

Plan B and Disposable Wings

It is said that there was once a time before termites knew how to fly. Then, as now, they were socially inclined. They lived in colonies underground or in dead wood. Each colony consisted of a king and queen, soldiers and workers. Then, as now, they ate the cellulose of plants and dung. Some specialized in eating Palo Verde wood. Others chose to eat dried grasses, but all ate cellulose. Then, as now, this dietary preference was extremely helpful to their world. If it were not for their recycling of plant fiber, which did not decay readily in the arid desert air, Earth would soon be knee-deep in plant litter and poop. There would be no room for sprouting plants, no returning of nutrients to the soil, and no animals dependent upon plants for food. Then, as now, the service they provided was essential. But then they never flew, and now they do. When the time is right. When all is ready. When Rain knocks on their door.

Termite flight came about due to overcrowding. Overcrowding came about because Day and Night, the two primary creators, had not foreseen such a need for the insects they'd designed to live in individual colonies. Termites were built for walking. They walked to work to hunt and chew up cellulose. They walked to feed it to the king and queen. They walked to tend the eggs the queen laid. They walked to fight off invaders. They walked--well, you get the picture. For what did they need to fly?

But picture this: some of the eggs grow into new queens and kings who want to find mates for themselves and move out to start their own colonies. Picture them walking off to do that. They don't get too far just walking, do they? Neither the girls or guys get to meet anyone from "out of town." None of the couples get far down the road before they need to build a home for those new eggs about to arrive. So how much food can there be for all those newlyweds needing to set up housekeeping? Not much, if their parent king and queen have anything to say about it. How many generations of healthy termites can develop when new kings and queens are also brothers and sisters. Got the picture? So did Day and Night. Eventually. Complaints about starving termites in some places, and fields of dead plants and poop overwhelming folks in other places helped clue the Creators in. They began to see there was a problem; a flaw in Plan A.

They called a conference to develop Plan B.

Day and Sun sat in the back. They had to admit: they didn't know much. Termites stayed pretty much away from them. Termites liked dark places. They were Night's issue. Day and Sun would be supportive, but not actively involved. They played chess.

Night asked Earth to help. Wind volunteered. He was pretty much into everything anyway as Breath. Termite royalty participated through Wind (Breath) because to actually attend the meeting, they would have had to walk. Earth asked for Rain. She figured Rain made everything easier in a desert. Rain agreed to attend intermittently. That would have to be enough.

"I accept the blame," said Night. "I made Termite to be a homebody. I forgot the colony would grow and need to replicate itself in other places. Who has ideas? Wind, you're well-traveled, fast-paced too. What say you?"

"You know how I like to blow things around," began Wind. "I scatter smaller creatures exceedingly well. If I can hurry birds along, seeds across the ground, Cloud amongst Sky's reaches, I'm sure I could muster up Breeze enough for Termite, at least while the new kings and queens were hunting new homes." He paused. "Wait, King Termite says he's not too eager to be tumbled along to new locales. Too much risk of injury."

"Perhaps Rain could soften my surface, making me slick," suggested Earth. "Then Termite would slip along more easily.

"What about mud?" Night asked. "That could bog Termite down."

"What if Termite flew?" asked Wind. "I specialize in flying things."

"Without a doubt," answered Night, "but Termite doesn't like to roam far from home."

"Termite agrees that's true," said Wind, listening for more instruction. "But perhaps only new kings and queens would fly."

"That could work," agreed Night.

"Until they moved underground or into trees," inserted Day, proving he was listening even as he challenged Sun's chess skills. "Remember? That's why we made them walk everywhere. They're hardly ever out and about except to start new colonies."

"Termite says maybe 'throw-away-wings' would be the thing. Wings that could be taken off when royal pairs had arrived in new neighborhoods," relayed Wind.

"Break-away wings," repeated Wind thoughtfully.

"Maybe," said Night.

"Definitely," said Day, taking Sun's pawn.

"I thought you were just going to be supportive," teased Night.

"I am being supportive," insisted Day.

Someone, I forget who, pointed out that if each colony's exodus could be coordinated with everyone else's, queens could meet and choose kings who were not also their brothers. Interbreeding would be less likely. New colonies would be healthier.

"What will signal the young royals to take flight?" asked Sun, distracted by the loss of another pawn.

"Rain," announced Earth. She had been waiting for a way to involve Rain in the whole process. She was always looking for a reason to bring Rain to her desert.

"Do you agree?" Night called to Rain.

"Sure, why not?" Rain answered from afar.

So it was decided. Only potential kings and queens sprouted wings in their final transition to adulthood. Only kings and queens responded to Rain's appearances in late spring and summer. At Rain's signal, they filled the air, exiting from all their species' colonies at once. Hometowns could at last mingle in the mating game. Once they'd paired and mated, the royal couples took up housekeeping far away from their original homes, as far as Wind and their wings had taken them. Best of all, their wings were removable. They just broke them off when they were done with them and lived the rest of their lives together, happily home-bound. Termite heaven.

And since their brief travels carried them into new territories and new food supplies, dead plant matter and poop got recycled more efficiently. Everyone else's heaven.

Plan B works now, as Plan A did not then. Because now Termites fly.

How Redtails Learned to Dance

It is said that there was a time when Redtailed Hawks were not able to produce chicks and rear them to adulthood. They built a nest, laid eggs, but something happened again and again to make the nest fail. Once a freezing storm killed the eggs while the father and mother hawk hunted. Another time a drought meant so little prey was available that the chicks starved before they could fledge and leave the nest. The next year a fox found its way to the nesting ledge when the parents were gone stretching their wings. Their losses were noticed by the two primary creators, Day and Night.

"Bad luck, that's all," said Day. He watched the male and female hawks soar in a blue, blue sky.

"Yes, bad luck," agreed Night. "But I'm not sure that's the only reason." She watched the male stoop and dive to a lower altitude.

"Meaning what?" asked Day.

"Meaning that perhaps they don't work as well together as they might. If they did things a little differently, they might have better success raising young."

"I'm not sure I'm ready to start telling them what to change, are you? We made them--I grant you that, but I don't know how it is to raise baby hawks, or even fly like one," answered Day.

"No, that would be a mistake. We agreed not to tell anything we made how to live, rather to let them discover and develop their own skills and preferences. That allows them to grow beyond anything even we could plan or envision. It's been a wise choice on our part. Time and again we've been surprised by the originality of our creation. No, I don't mean edicts. I was thinking more along the lines of new challenges."

"Haven't they challenges enough? Challenges are killing off their hatchlings now. How can more challenges help?" asked Day. He watched the female hawk fly after and out-maneuver a ground squirrel. "Just watch how they can fly," he continued admiringly. "We sure did that right, didn't we?"

"Absolutely," replied Night.

They watched the hawks in silence.

"I wonder," said Day thoughtfully. "Could they be invited to prove their compatibility to one another, and to us? Could we start a contest as a challenge? What if we asked them to use their flight skills to give us a sample of how well they can match one another on the wing?"

"That would certainly teach them to work together better," agreed Night. "It might help them do the same at the nest site. Let's try it."

They invited only three raptor pairs to the competition, Northern Harrier, Cooper's Hawk and Redtailed Hawk. The displays had to take place in the air. That was the only requirement. The hawks were given a week to come up with a dance and practice it. On the appointed day, everyone gathered in silence before Day and Night.

The harriers went first. The female soared to over 1000 feet, while the male danced around her, making U-shaped dives, then cartwheeling, making sharp, chipping calls at the same time.

The Cooper's went next. They stayed at lower altitudes, but again, the male did most of the maneuvering. He flew like a butterfly, with deep wingbeats, rising up and down, as if riding waves of air. Both male and female spread their tail feathers wide and flashed their white undersides. They too called distinctively as they flew.

69

The Redtails went last. They screamed back and forth to one another, soaring high, though not as high as the harriers. They dove together and when the female leveled off, the male flew above her with his feet dangling downward. Then, suddenly, the female flipped upside down in flight, grasping talons briefly with her mate. They broke away to soar again, screaming back and forth as before. Then they joined the Northern Harriers and the Coopers hawks, perched before Day and Night.

Day could hardly contain his delight. He clapped and pranced gleefully.

"Magnificent," he shouted. "I've never seen such an aerial show before. You were all glorious. I can't decide who was best. You've all shown great skill."

Night was quieter, but couldn't stop smiling. She bowed to all the birds before her.

"Truly wonderful," she pronounced. "The coordination of calling and wingbeats was incredible. You were all so beautiful in the air, I want to cry. I never dreamed your dances could be so stunning. Harriers: what heights you achieved. Coopers: I loved the tail displays--so creative. And Redtails, how did you ever come up with that mid-air flip together? I too can't pick a winner."

"You are all winners," declared Day. "Each with your own unique courtship dance. Everyone watching will be as filled with wonder as we were. Congratulations. May you all dance forever."

All the birds departed, pleased and proud, each pair was privately convinced they'd done the best. And in their own ways, each had.

But perhaps the Redtails did the best at learning teamwork. Their offspring became the most numerous and widespread of all the hawks.

Must have been the mid-air flip that did it.

Weather War

It is said that there was once a time when Sun and Rain battled for control of the sky. Rain had the advantage. He pelted Earth until the soil was saturated.

Sun grew tired of never seeing Earth. He was thoroughly sick of seeing the backside of Cloud all day. When Rain ignored his requests for a change of view, Sun got angry. He flung his rays with greater intensity, trying to punch a hole in Cloud to see below.

The increased heat caused even more Cloud to form and the storm increased in violence. But the turmoil did have the effect Sun sought, eventually. The more turbulence, the swifter the air currents propelling the storm--and gaps developed in the cloud cover, providing Sun the viewing ports he desired.

Seeing a little success, he continued throwing rays into Cloud, attempting to toss his light all the way down to Earth. Rain liquefied many of the rays, turning them into an enormous Rainbow.

Sun refused to surrender.

As Cloud moved on the warming air currents, more thin spots developed in the damp dome he clamped over Earth. Sun cast rays at the weak spots and got some through as scattered light. As they hit Earth, Fiddleneck sprang up in response. The plants sported arched clusters of tiny yellow flowers, marking the splatter of Sun's liquid rays before Rain could separate them into all Rainbow's colors.

Where Sun saw a hole in Cloud, he threw rays that reached Earth without interference--until Cloud saw what was going on and closed the hole. These briefly unobstructed rays hit Earth and bounced off as Bladderpod Mustard and Golden Poppy. Their brightly gilded, four-petaled faces showed the full color of Sun's rays, but also the effect of Cloud's closing the hole before too many rays had come through, for the flowers had only four petals.

As Wind increased and revealed blue sky for Sun's pleasure, whole waves of light reached Earth. Where they splashed into valleys, they burst up as Desert Marigolds. Myriad petals rimmed their faces, showing the multiple rays that had called them forth from Earth.

Where the waves of light hit low mountain slopes, Brittlebush leapt up. The spray from the waves bounced so high that many yellow-rayed (petaled) flowers bloomed high above the foliage of the plant, the product of Sun's power minus Cloud's influence.

These flowers were some of the very first created by Sun's scorching temperamental attacks on Rain and Cloud. Flowers of other colors, the blues and purples, the oranges and reds of Rainbow, fell to Earth more leisurely. Cloud continued to move along, shedding refracted rays into fields to become Mallows, Lupines, Owl Clovers, Pepperweed, Paperflower, Palo Verde flower, Ironwood blossom, Hedgehog and Cholla blossom, and all the legions of other flowering plants of the desert.

"Wow," said Wind.

"Ecstasy," said Earth.

"Cool," said Cloud.

"Righteous," said Rain.

"Superb," said Sun.

The spoils of weather war were enjoyed by all.

How Palo Verde Turned Green

It is said that once there was a time when Palo Verde was not green. Oh, he had green leaves, designed as they are today, compound, with a string of leaflets. He grew as high as he does today, about 40 feet. His twigs were dense and those on his lowest branches swept the ground around the tree's trunk on windy days, just as they do today. But in those times, the bark of Palo Verde was brown--as brown as Mesquite's, though not so rough and scaly as Mesquite's. In those days, Palo Verde was not terribly unusual, as trees go.

He did, however, have a most unusual friend.

In a desert, most birds and animals dress predominantly in drab tones of brown and beige, with perhaps an occasional grayish-tan thrown in for variety. In this way they can blend in with the sand and stone of their home and find safety in camouflage.

There was one tiny resident, however, who persisted in dressing in iridescent green and could only blend in around the flowering plants it loved to visit for nectar, where it resembled the green leaves.

Hummingbird, with her glistening emerald wings, back and tail, was very obvious perching in Palo Verde's low branches, where she was too large to hide behind the leaflets and too glowingly green against the tree's brown bark to be camouflaged. Nevertheless, she continually perched in Palo Verde's lowest branches to rest after humming her way through nearby Chuparosa's red, tubular flowers, where she would lick nectar reserves from the blossoms' depths.

Hummingbird loved to chat, and Palo Verde was her willing, captive audience. She told him of dewy bells of Lupine, golden filamented Saguaro blossoms that powdered her face yellow, the delight of darting through meadows of globe mallow, the fun of dodging raindrops, and how it felt to blast into the wind at top speed.

Palo Verde listened in wonder and watched as she sported through his branches looking for the tiny insects that hid amongst his leaves, or hovered in his shade to give flight demonstrations and aerobatic pointers he would never be able to use. He just enjoyed her company. Her visit was a bright spot in his day.

One morning, after a particularly sumptuous breakfast of Owl Clover nectar, Hummingbird settled onto her favorite low branch and burst into cheerful conversation.

"Good morning to you kind friend," Hummingbird announced. "The new day is begun and a cool dew remains on all the flowers' faces, bathing me as I drink my fill. The sky is a glorious blue and the breeze is gentle," as if Palo Verde really needed to hear a weather report to know what the morning was like.

"It is a good morning, Friend Hummingbird. How goes the construction of your nest?"

"I've just spotted Spider's web in your branches over there. Excuse me while I go steal some of her thread for the weaving of the very nest you mentioned, which, by the way, is near completion and none too soon, for my eggs are ready to lay. Two, I do believe, and let me tell you, this flying for three makes the fine art of hovering tough!"

"I can only imagine," chuckled Palo Verde. "You're excused for now, but do come back and visit for a while. I was hoping you might do me a favor and take a message from me to Ironwood Tree farther down the hill. I've been noticing that her blossoms are not so bright a lavender as last year and I was wondering if she is feeling alright."

"I've been there once already today, despite the early hour. Her flowers' nectar tastes just fine to me, and her blossoms are plentiful. She didn't mention feeling out of sorts, but I see what you mean about her color. It does seem a little pale compared to last year. I'll stop by and ask after her health as soon as I finish with Spider's web. Oops, must go. Spider's getting perturbed."

So saying, she darted away to her nest, hidden in some locale she wouldn't reveal, even to her friendly Palo Verde.

No sooner had she gone than Roadrunner slunk into the shadows beneath the Palo Verde Tree. Mottled brown, black and white, he blended in perfectly with the dappled sunlight speckling the tree's brown trunk.

"Wasn't that a hummingbird that just left?" asked Roadrunner.

"What hummingbird? answered Palo Verde, aware that Roadrunner would eat his friend if he could catch her.

"Never mind," wheezed Roadrunner, as nonchalantly as he could. "I think I'll just rest here for a while, perhaps even take a nap. Don't mind me." He clacked his large beak nervously.

"You won't bother me, but I might bother you. In a wind, my branches get to dancing and I scrape the ground underneath me. That would disturb your sleep, so you should go elsewhere to nap."

"It's not a problem now; there's not much breeze," said Roadrunner in his silkiest voice. "I think I'll risk it."

"Suit yourself," replied Palo Verde. "But you can't say I didn't warn you."

Palo Verde tried to keep his concern from showing in his voice, for he hated to think of what would happen the next time Hummingbird came to visit and took her

75

habitual low perch, not knowing Roadrunner waited nearby intending to make a snack of her.

He thought and thought how he could warn her in time, but his voice was small when the wind was mild, and today he could not make himself heard by Hummingbird until she was sitting in his branches. He despaired as he waited for her to return with news about Ironwood.

Soon he heard the buzzing sound that indicated her approach. Sure enough, she headed straight for her usual perch. Roadrunner heard her too and tensed to pounce as soon as she landed.

At that moment, the moment before Hummingbird alighted, Palo Verde turned green. Perhaps it was his intense desire to hide his friend. Perhaps it happened because he chose to reveal her enemy lurking in his shadows. In any case, his fear for his regular visitor's well-being erupted in a strange popping sound that started at his trunk and spread into a chorus of squeaks as it moved to his twigs, turning him from brown to green. The rending racket startled Hummingbird away from her intended landing site, and spooked Roadrunner's meal plans right out of his head.

With a strangled squawk, Roadrunner dashed away from the tree's base, out into the open. He took one look to verify the strange new color of the tree he had been using to conceal his whereabouts, and fled away at top speed, too unnerved to wait around for an explanation.

Hummingbird, on the other hand, was all curiosity over her friend's shift in color schemes, and completely approved his choice.

"What happened? What was that noise? Oh, how fabulous you look!" clicked Hummingbird. "I love your new color. It matches me perfectly." She hovered, flaring her tail as she examined the tree from every conceivable angle.

76

"I don't know what happened; don't know what that noise was; thanks; and I guess I do match you now," Palo Verde responded as he went down the roster of her comments.

"I was scared for you, what with Roadrunner hiding in my shadows. Could I have been so concerned about hiding you that I turned a color to make that easier?"

"I don't know. A tiny hummingbird like me must know when a mystery is bigger than I am, and should remain unsolved. If a large creature such as yourself cannot find the answer, I know I won't either. But if you did change colors for me, there is one thing I do know. It is no mystery that you have a great heart, Palo Verde, and a better friend will never be found."

So saying, she settled down on her usual perch, now remarkably green, and launched into the details of health and wellness she had recently heard from Ironwood saying, "Now, as to the paler look of her blossoms this year...."

The Omen

It is said that there was once a time when Day and Night, the two primary creators, worried together as they hastened to fashion their newest creation. They wanted it to be ready for the change of seasons.

"I don't know why we didn't think of it sooner," Day said as he tipped the antennae with white.

"Winter's cold numbs us all," answered Night. "Almost everything we've made that lives through and beyond that season sleeps more and moves less during Winter. It's no wonder our thoughts did too."

"Still," said Day, "these insects are special favorites of mine. I so enjoy designing the color patterns and watching their fragile flight. We've made something quite unique in them, you know. Butterflies have a delicate strength."

"I know how you enjoy them," smiled Night, shaping the wings with raggedy edges. She infused them with darkness, something not quite black. "They'll need that to soak up any warmth from Sun as Winter progresses. I'm fond of them too," she added. "That's why I insisted that similar creatures fly during my realm--moths. They may need reminding from this one we're making now."

"You're right," said Day. "Your moths die in the cold winds of Winter, just as the butterflies. Moth larvae will need to be shown how to fly too."

Concentrating, he carefully placed two small white crescents on the leading edge of the deep twilight-colored forewing.

"Nice touch," appraised Night.

"Thanks," answered Day. "I thought it needed something to draw the eye of those young caterpillars that will be hatching in Spring with no clue to what they are capable of or what they will become. This will be the creature that calls their attention to the skies and their own future.

"Good point," nodded Night. "In fact, I'd say it needs more. Give it more light to make it stand out."

Day painted a margin on the trailing edge of the wings in yellowish-white.

"Since this butterfly will survive through Winter to remind all butterfly larvae what they can become, what do you say we put blue water droplets at the edge of the darkness, just before your light border? They will tell Winter the time for snow is past--to let Water be liquid again."

"Do it," Day agreed. "It will be a sign to more than just Winter that his season is ending. Even with your color influence in the majority of its wing, it will not be able to gather enough solar heat to fly in the worst of Winter's clutches," he continued. "What do you think about having it slow and sleep as so many other animals do to survive? Then it can come out in the earliest days of warmer weather."

"Makes sense to me," Night said. "Where will it shelter?"

"In the leaves its caterpillars like to eat?" suggested Day.

"They will be on the ground, under the snow. The butterfly needs better protection than that."

"How about under the bark of the trees the butterfly larvae like to eat?" asked Day.

"That could work," nodded Night. "Especially if the butterflies enjoy feeding on sap more than flowers. Then they would be predisposed to being on the bark and could slip into it's niches at the first heavy frost."

"Do it," Day said once again.

"Mourning Cloak flies," announced the hunter when he returned to his hut with his portion of the deer carcass. The doe had been weak with starvation; the winter too long for them as well. No fat, little flesh. He sighed, looking into his children's thin, lethargic faces. Perhaps the marrow would see them through.

"That means Winter is turning," he announced assuringly. "Soon there will be plenty of food. Just a little longer. A little longer and we shall greet Spring. Mourning Cloak flies to give us hope."

His daughter smiled.

Spiny Lizard's Homecoming

It is said that there was once a time when Desert Spiny Lizard faced weathering a storm without even the smallest clue as to where to seek shelter.

He was homeless because he'd battled for his life earlier in the afternoon and had barely escaped.

Active during daytime hours, he hunted bugs, small lizards and fruiting plants for food. The armored tank of the lizard family, he was stocky, short-tailed, light brown over all, and covered with large pointed scales, some of which were flecked with golds and dark browns. His squatty legs carried his bulk low to the ground, but he refused to keep a low profile. His habit was to do pushups almost constantly, raising his six-inch long torso twice his height, the better to scout for food and females. Pushups showed his blue side markings and neck patch to greatest advantage for impressing lady lizards. Black shoulder patches gave him the appearance of a collar. He knew he was impressive and wanted everyone else to know too. But showing off had cost him.

That morning he'd impressed more than just ladies. He'd caught the attention of Roadrunner. The tall sprinter of desert birds had dashed over to the rock where he was sunning and snapped him up. The pushups did pay off, though, because Roadrunner's quick grab was not sure and Spiny Lizard pushed off the bird's beak as she tried to swallow him, free-falling back into the rocks below.

You should have seen the desperate game of hide and seek that began then. Spiny Lizard raced around amongst the boulders with Roadrunner in hot pursuit. Such scrambling, such jousting with her bill, such reckless dashing under rocks. For all her quickness, Roadrunner was bested by Spiny Lizard's use of his terrain. He could scurry through the stones better than she and he decided the issue when he thrust his way into the heart of a patch of prickly pear and didn't budge, no matter how she tossed sand with her bill or darted around trying to spook him into the open. She had to give up, but she did not do so willingly. Spiny Lizard was so scared it was hours before he dared peek out from his lair. Then he cautiously departed.

The race for his life had cost him his home, though. He found himself in unfamiliar territory. He would have to find new hunting grounds for cactus fruit and arthropods. He'd have to find new ground squirrel holes to dart into for cover.

To top things off, a storm was brewing.

The afternoon sky was boiling with clouds. Rain announced his intentions with thunder and lightning. Afraid to be caught in a deluge without cover, Spiny Lizard raced back and forth in the dried seed pods beneath a huge palo verde tree, out of his mind with panic. His passage through the pods made such a racket he woke a snoozing woodrat. Normally a nocturnal critter, Woodrat heard the scampering lizard, plus the thunder and wind racing through the trees, and knew his nap was over.

Woodrat is also known as Packrat and if you know anything about his taste in homes, you know he glories in piles and heaps of sticks, stones and cholla bits, mixed in with paper, broken glass and whatever pretty trash he can find and drag to his abode.

No packrat ever thinks his house is just fine or quite big enough, thanks. Every packrat home can use an addition or three, and gets it on a continuous basis.

When Woodrat saw Spiny Lizard running laps beneath the palo verde tree in his derangement, he had to get involved.

"I say," he called from the midst of his eclectic heap. "What's the matter with you?"

This attention was enough to calm Spiny Lizard just a little. He slowed down enough to say, "I'm lost. I'm homeless. Rain's coming. I'll drown."

Woodrat laughed. "Not likely," he countered. "I've plenty of room. Stay as long as you like."

"Really?" asked Spiny Lizard.

"Why not?" Woodrat answered, enjoying his own magnanimity. "I've the space. You can help clean out some of my bug population. You're out by day, while I'm out by night. I see no problem, do you?"

Spiny Lizard didn't.

Thus began a cohabitation that continues to this day.

How Gila Monster Got His Colors

It is said that there was once a time when Gila Monster was totally black. Black as a moonless midnight. All his meditative excursions occurred at night, for black is not a color to wear on a sunny desert day. Not if your survival depends on staying cool. Every desert creature must find a way to stay cool. So Gila Monster was a creature of Night and Night only.

But he dreamed of Day.

Sometimes he told Owl, another creature of Night, about his dreams. Night did have its advantages, though.

"Jussst as well," he told Owl. "Makes it easier to find those nesssstling birds, rabbits and rats I like to eat. Everyone is home asssleep when I come calling. Just as well I only go out at night.

"Now eggs--eggsss are nice," he went on in his slow, lazy drawl while ambling back to his burrow. "Eggs don't go out by day. Quail eggsss--they're the best. But tortoise eggs--oh, yessss--now there's a treat. He flicked his black tongue to test the air for any scents in the night sands.

He wasn't really hungry; he had already fed once that night. In his youth, he could easily eat half his body weight every meal, but he was an adult now. Two feet long and with plenty of fat stored in his tail. His tail-fat would determine the comfort of his hibernation. He wouldn't starve this winter.

"Jussst as well," he told himself. "No young left in the nesssts by winter anyway. Everyone out and about. Too cold for us reptiles anyway. Might as well sleep. Jussst as well sssleep."

Lumbering into his burrow as dawn was breaking, he cleaned his grooved teeth with his formidable front claws. He couldn't inject his venom; he chewed it into his enemies and prey. His venom flowed down those grooves and it was necessary to keep them clean. Then he dropped his head to a pillow of sand, closed his eyes, and dreamed of Day.

Gila Monster's burrow was in the banks of an arroyo. Because the arroyo ran with water most rainstorms, the soil was a little damper there. That made digging borrows easier, and kept him cooler on hot summer days.

While Gila Monster slept and dreamed of Day, the afternoon winds began to increase and clouds formed over the mountains, gradually filling the sky.

Before long, Wind howled and drove clouds of dust in raging walls that scoured the desert with stinging, biting sand. Little clouds thundered and blundered together into one Cloud. Cloud became dark, bulging with moisture until it could hold no more. Cloud began flinging Rain into Wind, which fixed the dust to Earth again in great, muddy droplets that pounded the ground with such force, mist arose from the drenching. Wind's wall of dust became a wall of Water that beat against the Earth in torrents that could be heard approaching for sixty miles across the valley floor. The onslaught of Rain filled washes, gullies and arroyos to their brims, sweeping away trees and boulders, overwhelming any form of life in its way.

Despite the thunderous noise and thumping Earth when boulders danced like giants down his arroyo, Gila Monster had just ambled to his doorstep when the floodwaters reached the level of his burrow. As he stuck his nose out his door, the terrible tide wrenched him from his home into its watery embrace. He tumbled head over heels, bouncing off slower moving trees, scrambling to keep from being entangled in their rootballs and branches, where he

85

knew he would drown. Thrashed against stones, scraped by fine sand, forced to the top of the flow, where he would gasp a quick breath before being ripped down to the bottom again in a mighty eddy--time became timeless. Gila Monster mindlessly breathed when he could, held his breath when he must, and relaxed as he swept along in waters he could not escape.

Eventually, the constant pummeling stopped. He found himself right-side-up in a low pool which was gradually subsiding, even as he hauled his poor, mangled body out of the decreasing current. He was too exhausted and cold to slog through the fine silty mud to lift himself completely out of the water, but he made it to where he could push his nose above the muddy foam at the waterline to breathe. As the water receded, he felt it lapping against his bruises lower and lower on his body until just his tail was submerged, and finally, not even that.

Now, Sun broke through Cloud's blackness and warmed Earth. Gila Monster warmed too, until he could move enough to crawl out of the mud. Once free of its sticky, sucking hold, he dropped onto a rock above the flood line and slept.

He awoke at sunset, stiff and sore. Owl too was beginning to stir, readying for a night of hunting. He spied the huge lizard basking in Sun's last rays.

"Whoo, whoo, whoo are you?" asked Owl.

"Gila Monster," answered Gila Monster, wishing with all his might for a shorter name, for each battered muscle he moved--including those in his jaw--caused excruciating pain.

"That's a new look for you, isn't it?" asked Owl.

"What do you mean?" groaned Gila Monster.

"A little flowery and gaudy for my taste, but not without its appeal," allowed Owl.

"Whaaat?" asked Gila Monster, moaning as he lifted his horrendously heavy head to look down the length of his body. It was an amazing sight, one that caused him to look back toward the muddy remains of the pool he had crawled from to reach his rock. There he saw the reason for his changed appearance.

He had been deposited by the water's fury on a level plain, now a beach. Circling the small beach on three sides, stood a sweep of palo verde trees, past the full glory of their yellow season of blossom. Their spent, dried flowers had littered the ground, and these had blown and washed into the pool where the flood had released him. As the lapping water receded, these blossoms had been washed in rough, irregular bands along his back and tail, leaving him with a yellow, beaded patterning that had now dried in Sun's rays. His scales felt a little tight, with their new layer of color, but it didn't flake away as he moved. It seemed here to stay.

"Jussst as well," Gila Monster said to himself, for his self-inspection showed patches where his scales had been pumiced away and pink flesh showed through. These were protected now by the crusted yellow coating of flowers. "Probably bleed to death without it," Gila Monster reasoned.

"I'll bet," mumbled Owl as he preened, "that you don't absorb so much sunlight as you did when all black. That's why you could bask in the sun without getting uncomfortable just now. I do believe you've gotten your wish. You can go out in the daylight hours now--as long as it's not too hot, of course."

"That would be nice," droned Gila Monster, thinking of the new burrow he would have to dig tonight with his aching forelegs. "Time will tell."

Time did tell. Owl was right. Gila Monster began to frequent the daytime in the coolest hours, and got to see the myriads of creatures active during Day. He still continued to hunt on summer nights, however, for that's when his preferred victims could be found asleep in their beds. Each night, after eating, he would chat with Owl, if Owl had already eaten too and was perched high, preening in a tree.

"Jussst as well," drawled Gila Monster. "Nobody of Day wantsss to talk to me. They just run away. Too fassst for me. Jussst as well hunt and talk with you by Night."

"Mmmmpht," mumbled Owl, as he preened.

How Black-tailed Gnatcatcher Was Made

It is said that there was once a time when clouds of gnats overran the desert. Then the monsoon rains brought moisture, and the problem became overwhelmingly worse. Any animal with eyes, ears and wet nostrils was being driven mad. The warblers, verdins and hummingbirds were overworked. They tried to keep the number of gnats in check, but the task was impossible. The animals complained loudly, but Day and Night, who together created all things, were in constant debate with one another over whatever project they were currently working on--be it mountains, slugs, or flowers. Their ceaseless arguing drowned out the protestations of the animals from the desert. A gathering was held in a huge floodplain near the Gila River. Representatives of most of the desert animals attended.

Of course, the gnats attended too.

The animals had to roar to be heard over the gnats' incessant buzzing. The insects did their best to disrupt the proceedings. Nevertheless, despite having gnats enter their mouths as they talked, the necessity of keeping their eyes closed when not walking, and the heavy burden of buzzing and biting gnats in their ears, the poor animals did reach consensus on the need to demand help from Day and Night. The creators' over-providence in the gnat department would have to be pointed out to them. Then suggestions made as to how to remedy the situation, and the expectation conveyed that relief should be quick in coming--like yesterday, for instance. They elected Verdin their spokesperson. Small sized, he would appear humble enough. Enduring by temperament, he would persist long enough. Restlessly energetic, he would be quick enough.

So Verdin set off in search of Day and Night.

After traversing Earth to the farthest horizon, he finally found them at table, supping together on various wave-lengths of sunlight and starlight. True to form, they were arguing loudly.

"No, no, no," Day was saying. "Enough of your toads. I will not allow another variation on toads to mar the evening's quiet with their croaking."

"What's it to you?" snapped Night. "They hide during your part of the day and hunt and sing during mine. You don't need to have anything to do with them," she added.

"Precisely," accused Day. "They have your hours, your colors, and your moisture-loving nature. They have little of me in them. You already have so many varieties too. Enough is enough. No more unless you consent to a bright orange and yellow version," he countered.

"How could a spectacle like that possibly survive?" spat Night, her blood beginning to boil.

"That's my final offer," declared Day.

"I'll not have you controlling my creatures," seethed Night.

"I'll remind you, they're my creatures too," sneered Day.

"Ahem," said Verdin.

"A creature with my hours is mine."

"You can't make anything without at least some help from me, so it's mine too."

"Ahem," repeated Verdin.

"Why you...."

"Don't EVEN go there."

"AHEM," shouted Verdin, and began clicking incessantly until Day and Night stopped arguing with one another and turned to find the source of their disturbance.

"Verdin?" asked Day. "Is that you?"

"Of course it is," answered Night. "Though very far from home. What's the matter, Little One?"

"All the animals of the desert have compelled me to approach you with their request for assistance," began Verdin formally.

"What's that?" asked Day, not clear on what was being requested.

"HELP!" shouted Verdin. "We need help."

"Why?" asked Night, quite surprised at Verdin's tone. He was tiny on stature, but huge on insistence.

"Look at the desert. What do you see?" directed Verdin.

"A somewhat obscured view," said Day. "What is that? Fog?"

"Listen," ordered Verdin.

"Can't--I'm deafened by the croaking of innumerable toads," whined Day.

"Oh hush!" groaned Night. "You hear as well as I do, and I do hear something...." She paused to listen more intently. "Is that buzzing?"

"Exactly," persisted Verdin. "The buzzing of hordes of gnats--uncountable numbers of gnats--myriad clouds of myriad individual gnats--infinite numbers of...."

"A whole bunch of gnats. Got it!" urged Day.

"They got a little out of hand," marveled Night.

"I'll say," agreed Day.

"So what's to be done about it?" pushed Verdin. "I can't go back without some promise of relief."

"Of course not," chorused Day and Night, agreeing for the second time in ages.

"I'm exhausted," continued Verdin. "I can't keep up. It's a losing battle against the gnats. Warblers, hummingbirds, none of us get any rest. If we haven't thinned the numbers by now, we're not going to be able to, and my fellow gnat-eaters said to remind you that some of us are just about ready to migrate south for the winter, so they will not be available to help me much longer. I need another bird that's a permanent resident. One that's got a huge appetite for tiny insects. It has to specialize in tiny insects, or it won't do us any good."

"Absolutely, I'll get right on it," promised Day.

"Me too," agreed Night.

"Gotta be tiny," began Day.

"Long-tailed to act as a rudder in the hot air," added Night.

"Gotta be quick," added Day.

"And big on appetite," reminded Night.

"They should be full-time residents of the desert," said Day.

"Why not have them forage together all year, male and female? A double punch to the gnat population all the time," suggested Night.

"Sounds great," agreed Day, thoroughly involved in the process now.

"And to signify our collaboration in this emergency, let's stick to a color scheme that most represents our opposite natures, black and white."

"I like it," agreed Day. "We should work this quickly more often. Why not make it mostly gray, the combination of black and white. The long tail, though, should be black."

"Fine by me," shrugged Night, "but the tail should have white outer feathers to accentuate the length and represent your energy in this creative endeavor.

"Alrighty then," Day announced, pleased to apply the finishing touch.

Both breathed life into their creation, and Black-tailed Gnatcatcher was born.

"Now go see to that gnat problem," instructed Day.

"Verdin will be your guide," informed Night.

So Verdin returned to his desert home with a new partner in the efforts to control the gnats. Although the other animals were at first hard pressed to understand how any solution so small could be of much help, Black-tailed Gnatcatcher and his mate soon made believers of them all. They more than lived up to their name.

How Tortoise Was Made

It is said that once there was a time when Night and Day worked particularly well together. It happened that way, sometimes. New life would burst on the scene with incredible rapidity for an issue of time. Then there were whole eras during which very little new material was created. Perhaps these were epochs in which they were arguing over projects and little else was accomplished. No one really knew.

Just now, though, Earth was tired. Night and Day had been demanding. They fought, planned, collaborated, tossed around ideas, but the actual elements from which life was woven had to come from somewhere. Fire and air came from Sun, but Earth provided earth, water, and wood. Since Night and Day had been particularly creative in the eon just past, Earth was tired.

She napped.

She dreamed.

She dreamed of a cleft in a rocky hillside. It was about four feet tall and two feet wide. The ruggedness of the slope did much to conceal its presence. From a distance, shadow alone betrayed it and only during certain times of day. It opened to the east, warmed by the morning sun and shaded from the afternoon's cruelest heat. A long, low tunnel led back into the hillside six feet from the entrance.

Earth dreamed she looked into the cave. She dreamed she crept inside and curled around and around herself before settling down on the dusty, shale scattered floor.

She napped.

She dreamed.

She dreamed a creature that reflected her traits perfectly, slow moving, the color of the soil, low to the ground, steady, enduring, long-lived. She dreamed she gathered the dust and flakes of shale from the cave floor. She mixed these with the condensation from her breath that had gathered on the cave's ceiling. She molded a creature with four short, stumpy legs and a head on a thick, longish neck. It dried to a dull, flaky finish. Then she hefted a chunk of driftwood, deposited in the cave in some past millennium when ocean waves washed against the cave's entrance. She used rock to carve and smooth the wood to a circular, semi-glossy bowl. This she placed on top of her creature to protect its vulnerable body, which looked ready to crumble into the dust of which it was made. On its underside, she placed a wooden disk. She carved patterns into both bowl and disk in such a way as to remind anyone who looked at them to return to the center of their own life's circle. In those slow-stirring origins, answers would be found.

The creature lifted its head and moved its legs. It slowly lumbered across the cave.

Earth stretched and awakened. She crept from the cramped cave to stand in the sunlight of Day's afternoon. She couldn't remember why, but she felt deeply satisfied.

Earth stretched and awakened. Sun was shaking her. He said Day and Night were ready with their latest project and he and Earth were being called to help bring it into being. There would be no more rest for either one of them until Day and Night were appeased. Earth shrugged. Nothing new in that! Still, for some reason she couldn't fathom, she felt deeply satisfied.

Later, after sunset, when dark of Night breathed against the cave hidden in the rocky hillside, Tortoise awoke.

And later still, because Tortoise's origins were primarily of Earth and twice as deeply dreamed as any of the other creatures, she awoke from her slumber. She plodded laboriously from the cave's entrance—and entered the world.

The Origin of Cliffrose

It is said that there was once a time when a girl sat alone in a canyon near her home. In her silence, she heard Earth. Earth called her to come and dig in a certain spot not far from where she sat, not far from her home. She did as told and found a substantial deposit of clay. She understood immediately that she was a potter. This was her connection to her people, her life and her land. She took a sample of the clay and went to the camp of another clan, a day's walk from her own and apprenticed herself to a woman who lived there, renowned for her pottery. She did this without even going to her own home to inform her family. She did it because she knew. The old woman potter accepted her as apprentice. She did not ask about her family or what payment she could make for her lessons, food or board. She did not ask because she too knew.

So Rose, the young girl who heard Earth, stayed and learned her art. The potter sent word to Rose's family and kept the girl for the next three years. By that time Rose had married into the potter's clan and had a baby. Every day Rose came to the potter's home and helped with every aspect of pot manufacture. In three more years Rose had two more children, and was making her own pots. She was developing a name for herself with her distinctively colored paintings and symbols. With two potters in the village, the people had plenty to trade and they were visited by merchants who brought items from the south and took Rose's pots across country to places she had never seen and peoples she would never know.

Rose made each pot an individual. At the same time, each pot spoke of Rose, its maker. When dried corn was poured from baskets into giant storage pots, the song of the grain hitting fired clay was of Rose. When water was carried from the spring and poured into the beans for the day's meal, the splash of water and beans knocking against the sides of the pot spoke her name. Rose was part of every pot she ever made. Each pot celebrated Earth and Rose.

The children grew. Her son became a great runner. He carried messages from village to village. He was killed when a raiding party from the south attacked his settlement and carried off the harvest. Her daughter married and had twin girls. Her daughter's husband was blinded in a hunting accident. He was despondent at his inability to hunt and provide for his people. His despair affected everyone in the clan. It was tradition that only women were potters. He became Rose's first apprentice. He learned the patience to work the clay. Earth gave him hope and vocation too. Rose's youngest son grew to be a shaman. He heard Earth instruct him in how to heal his people of sickness through herbs and ceremony. He went to study with a healer in another village.

In time one of her granddaughters became her apprentice. The girl learned from both Rose and her father. She developed a whole new method of making platters with handles and her fame spread.

Another child came to Rose as an orphan. His family had traveled to a meeting where they had contracted a fever, killing all but him. As he returned to his village with neighbors, they camped near Rose's home and he spent a day watching her at work. He never left.

Her husband's sister's daughter visited and asked to be taught the family art. Eventually, she married the orphaned apprentice and they relocated closer to the great river in the south. They had many children, most of whom farmed agave, beans and corn.

Ten years after her husband's death, one of Rose's great-granddaughters came over to where Rose worked, to play with the clay. She was only five years old, but Rose had a feeling. She watched the girl become entranced with her play. She became Rose's final apprentice.

When Rose died she was buried with many honors and the feast given after the ceremony was attended by the whole village and many friends and family that had traveled from afar to pay their respects.

The next spring a plant sprouted over her resting place. Because he did not immediately recognize it, her son-in-law did not remove it when he tended her grave.

When it matured enough to bloom, it had five-petaled cream-colored flowers with a yellow center, a petal for each apprentice. The petals were connected in the golden center, Rose's spirit. When the seeds formed, they were attached to white plumes that looked very much like feathers and floated on the winds that scattered them, flying as her spirit had flown. The shrub grew to be 10 feet tall, with bark as loose and peeling as Rose's skin had looked in her last years. But the plant was evergreen, another attribute of her enduring spirit. The bark could be woven for sandals, rope and mats. The wood was good for making arrows. Deer browsed the leaves.

Because Rose had been buried below the cliff walls of the canyon where she had first heard Earth, the plant was named Cliffrose. Through it Rose continued to help her family and her people. Through it, her people remembered Rose, generation after generation.

How Funnel Weaver Got His Name

It is said that there was once a time when assorted spiders were discussing spinning and webs with one another--from a safe distance, of course. They gathered periodically to compare notes on insect movements and hatchings, creative snaring, night hunting versus daytime trapping, all to keep each other on their spiderish toes. A comparison of techniques for spinning, weaving and web building turned rather competitive, something not very unusual for this collection of kin. Each of them had different needs and lived in different habitats, but they still compared their skills and talents, as if they should all be alike, or at least flamboyant in their differences.

Tarantula went on so about the lovely silk lining he made for his burrow entrance, with just a few strands of web across the doorway to ensnare insects that might stumble across it. Simple, inconspicuous, easily repaired.

Wolf Spider thought the idea quite nice, as he had a burrow too, but he felt it a smart addition to add sticks or leaves to the lining and build out from the doorway. Consequently, his lining extended enough to make his burrow entrance more noticeable from above, though not to the ground-crawling insects he found delectable. Hapless insects that blundered by too closely were ensnared effectively, just as with Tarantula's model. More work to repair, yes it was, but worth it for the aesthetics.

Tarantula harumphed. "Dangerous aesthetics, if you ask me. Just asking for Tarantula Hawk to notice and pay a visit. Inconspicuous is best. I don't want to become Tarantula Hawk's prey."

Orb-Weaver laughed. "You call that aesthetics? Check out my web for aesthetics. Now that's design. That's planning. That's a thing of beauty, a work of art."

"Oh please," responded Labyrinth Spider. "I do everything you do and more. I'm just not the show-off you are. I build an orb-style web, then add a backdrop of silk-anchored debris under which I spin myself a hiding spot. And I do it all between two pads of a prickly pear, not out in the open for all to see, like you. Beauty, complexity--and modesty. Bet you can't top that!"

The last spider didn't know what to answer. He was smaller than Wolf Spider, but resembled him somewhat in appearance. He could weave a fine blanket web. It had no great style or pattern, but it covered the grasses in which he liked to hunt insects and it worked to ensnare them. Still, it seemed pretty unimpressive. He liked the concept of a burrow--really. It had appeal. He liked the design Orb-Weaver created so flawlessly. In envy of the others, he kept his silence and crept away.

Returning to his grassland web, he watched it billowing in Wind's breeze. He sighed.

"Moving air is my job. Why the deep sigh?" asked Wind.

Spider explained about the conference he'd just attended and how he envied the burrowing spiders their cave-like homes, yet admired the orb-weavers their lovely web design too. His own web seemed unimpressive when compared to the artistry of the others.

"It works, doesn't it?" asked Wind. "It catches your meals?"

"Yeah, but where's the flair, the style? I want something that makes a statement as well as being utilitarian."

"A web-burrow with style?" asked Wind.

"Yeah, something like that."

100

"Maybe I can help," Wind said thoughtfully.

He blew on Spider's web. It ruffled. He blew harder. It billowed. He blew harder. It ballooned, then began to tear.

"Clearly, I have nothing to work with here if you anchor it down in your usual manner," said Wind. "We'll have to think of a way for you to weave me something I can play with. I have an idea for a shape that might suit your needs, but I require an unattached web to work with."

Spider was catching on to the idea, and although a bit fearful for his personal safety, he had a suggestion.

"When I first left home I attached myself to a stick, let out a tether, and ballooned to a new location to set up my own web. How about my tethering myself to some grass now, then you blow gently enough to keep me aloft without breaking my tether and I'll spin you a web in mid-air you can then work into a shape?"

"I'm game," Wind responded.

The two discussed a plan, then experimented with air-flow and tether tension until the spider could hang suspended in mid-air and spin his unexciting blanket web to gently undulate in the carefully modulated breeze Wind blew steadily across it. The goal, of course, being to not tangle the web, or drop the spider, or break the tether. The tether was under ever more and more tension as Wind blew to keep the spider and a growing web wafting gently in his breeze. Not a moment of this was easy. It took supreme concentration from both Spider and Wind.

"Finished," called Spider as he wove the final strands of the blanket and cut it loose. He scurried back to the grass to which he was tethered in order to watch what came next.

In the exact instant Spider cut the web loose, Wind stopped blowing steadily and became a tiny whirlwind that snatched the web in mid-air and shaped it to resemble himself. Just as suddenly, Wind dropped the funnel-shaped web into the grass, where the spider waited and leaped to the task of tacking the whirlwind web down before it lost its shape. When finished, they both stood back to look at the cone-shaped web anchored narrow-end-down at the root of the grasses that supported it and held the wide part of the funnel open.

"Not too shabby," admired Wind.

"Incredible!" gasped Spider. "No other spider has anything like it."

"Try it on for size," suggested Wind.

Spider scuttled over the webbing and down into the vortex of the funnel, where he stationed himself to feel the vibrations of the web strands. Yes--even with this shape, it still communicated to him. He felt enclosed, almost like being in a burrow. He could feel the difference in vibrations where Wind ruffled strands, where grass scraped against silk, where...." A gnat struggled in the funnel-web and Spider dashed out to claim his prize.

After eating, Spider thanked Wind for his help with the remodeling. Wind admonished him to study the pattern and begin weaving it for himself, for he wasn't sure he could create it for Spider ever again. Spider saw the wisdom in that and immediately began educating himself so as to be able to spin the funnel-web alone next time.

"With a new web, you'll need a new name," said Wind. "I hereby change your name to Funnel Weaver, from this day henceforth," announced Wind imperiously to no one and everyone. "Now, I think I'll mosey off to casually mention news of the wondrous new web I've seen to the rest of the spiders."

Funnel Weaver chuckled. "Once again, then, I am in your debt. Not a single one of them can claim any web so marvelous as this one. I'll be the envy of all my kin." But Wind was already gone.

102

How Bat Learned to Listen

It is said that there was once a time when Mexican Free-Tail bats hunted by day. This was so long ago that swamps covered much of Earth. Horses were the size of small dogs and had three-toed feet. Over the eons, horses changed into the animals we know today, but bats changed very little. They look very much the same now as then, but some things have changed. They learned to listen.

Earth changed over the eons too. Swamps gave way to deserts in some areas. One desert came to be called the Sonoran. Here Night, one of the primary creators, spawned Moth, gave her mastery of the air, then invited Mexican Free-Tail Bat to thrive on her off-spring. Bat accepted. But Bat's eyes were not suited to hunting by night. A new strategy needed to be developed. This is the story of how that came about.

Bat was born into the highest dome of the warmest cave of the Sonoran desert. Around him crowded many other bat youngsters. Baby bats needed the warmest temperatures to grow quickly. Since warm air rises, the highest ceiling of the cave was given over to the infants. Mothers left their newborn bats jostling and shivering together, hanging upside down from their high perches. Each mother listened to her baby's voice and learned to find it when it called. She would nurse it, then leave to rest lower in the cave, or go out to hunt. Bat's mother knew his call and came periodically to feed, groom and comfort him.

The darkness of the cave accustomed the bats to the darkness of Night, but it was hard to see anything well enough outside to stalk it and snatch it from the air. Nevertheless, simply flying around with one's mouth open provided moths, beetles, and assorted other flying insects in good abundance. Moths were a special favorite, though, and they were hard to distinguish from other airborne edibles.

None of that interested Bat, however. His focus was nursing and growing, both of which he was accomplishing rather nicely.

As he grew, he began to become curious about his nursery. While most bats are quite content to be crowded and cramped into small quarters, he wanted to explore. To explore, he had to be willing to go alone, for the other bats of the nursery could not imagine life without jostling.

Bat began to crawl, using his thumbs and feet. He crept to less crowded parts of the cave. He would call his mother from there when he wanted to be fed. He moved farther and farther away from the other youngsters. Away from all the racket of everyone calling at once, he learned to hear his own voice. His mother worried about his anti-social tendencies, but she could find him so much more readily when he called to be nursed, that she did not try to correct him.

Alone, he began to play. He played with his voice. He made his voice high; he made his voice low. He played with the cave. He noticed that his voice sounded different in different parts of the cave. He learned to find parts of the cave by talking aloud and listening to what his voice sounded like. One day he noticed that when he called his mother for food, the more incessant he was, the more the sound of his voice changed as she approached him. He could almost see her coming just by listening to the changes in his voice. The more he practiced, the better he got at "seeing" her coming toward him. He began to take short flights in the cave, casting his voice off the walls to "see" where to land next. He no longer had to crawl around. He moved around so much, his mother marveled. Finally she asked about his mobility.

"This morning you were on the other side of the room. I find you here now, but last feeding you were in another room of the cave altogether. How are you getting from here to there so quickly? Why aren't your thumbs torn to shreds from crawling so far?"

"I'm flying," said Bat.

"Riiiight," replied Mother Bat.

"No, really. And this time, I heard you coming and met you halfway."

"No way," replied Mother Bat.

"Yes way," answered Bat and promptly gave a flight demonstration.

He explained to his mother how he had been learning to see by listening and no longer depended on the proximity of other bats to define his world.

"I'm getting quite good," Bat announced. "I can tell you have a moth-hair mustache from your last meal and a moth-wing stuck to your back."

His mother reached over with a wing to rub her mouth, then her back.

"You're right," she squeaked in amazement. "Show me how you could tell that in the dark."

So Bat began showing his mother what he'd discovered about throwing his voice, how higher frequencies and more rapid bursts of sound actually helped define the interior of the cave in great detail. With practice, she began to "see" him and learned to tell him apart from the others not only by his own unique voice, but also by his own unique face, which she began to be able to visualize with her voice.

"You're ready to go out to hunt tonight with me," Bat's mother said one evening. "You don't need my milk any more.

"I've been throwing my voice to hunt, thanks to you, and have been able to tell Moths from Beetles in Night's sky every night, not just nights with a full moon. I catch the bugs I want, not just anything that happens to be in my way. I know you don't mind that I'm sharing our talent with some friends. Not only do we now eat primarily moths, but we can be even more selective. We catch our moths from behind and bite off their abdomens, the juiciest part, letting the head, thorax and wings fall to the ground. Their pesky legs don't get caught in our throats anymore. All thanks to you.

"Tonight, just after sunset, start flittering around, exercising your wings. Everyone else will be doing the same thing. It's so exciting. I'll find you and we'll make your first exit from our cave together. Fly up and out of the entrance to a height of about 150 feet, using a spiraling flight pattern. You'll be swept along with the crowd, so it's not hard, just dramatic. Then, break off and head toward the horizon and the last of Sun's light. I'll give you some demonstrations and watch you catch your first moths. You'll find them quite delicious.

"Then I'll leave you to your own resources and cruise my usual hunting grounds. I cover nearly 50 miles a night, you know. You need not do that your first time out, though. Just keep practicing your air speed and distance. Eventually you'll fly nearly 60 mph and be ready for the 500 mile migration we make to escape the cold of winter. We like Mexico that time of year. You'll like it too. That trip's not until October, though, so you have time to build up your strength and stamina.

"The last thing you need to know is that I'll meet you back at the cave at sunrise. You really won't need my help, though, excellent flier that you are. Just follow the example of the other bats. We'll all congregate about a thousand feet

106

over the cave and begin plummeting down to our roosts. You'll take to it naturally, don't worry.

"I'm proud of you, son. Your knowledge has changed your community enormously, and I know you'll continue to be a blessing to our kind."

That night Bat made his debut in the world outside his cave, ate his first moths, and gained his independence from his mother.

His echolocation talents, learned as he played with his voice in his dark nursery, increased with maturity. He shared his skills freely with members of his colony, and eventually with all bats.

How Wire Lettuce got Teeth Marks

It is said that there was once a time when Wire Lettuce was anything but wiry. As a perennial, that is a plant with a life span longer than a year, he knew all the seasons of the desert--or so he thought.

He grew to two feet in height.

He knew how to ration his water use so that he had large leaves that cast impressive shade. He also blossomed extravagantly with plentiful lavender petaled flowers.

He was said to be stubborn--or perhaps proud, for he retained flowers and leaves throughout all the months of the year, whether those months had been wet or dry, hot or cold.

"How do you do it?" marveled Jackrabbit as he lounged in the shadow of the broad leaves. It was late afternoon and the cool spot under Wild Lettuce was great for hanging around and hiding from Sun.

"Do what?" asked Wild Lettuce.

"Stay so green," answered Jackrabbit. "Palo Verde tree has dropped his leaves. So has Ocotillo. It is too hot and dry for them, but you still have yours. What's your secret?"

"I decided when I was a seed that I would always shoot for the best," drawled Wild Lettuce. He puffed up just a smidgen. "I would be the best lettuce I could possibly be. I would never lack for anything. I learned from the smartest lettuce mentors. They taught me the places where water came close to Earth's surface and how to grow my roots to take advantage of that. They taught me to plan for droughts and budget my water, throughout the day and throughout the year. I learned from the best, but I was smart too. I kept things small at first, hoarding my resources of water and minerals until just the right time for investing in growth producing strategies. I worked hard. I raised what you see before you today from the bottom up, all by my own effort. Oh, I wanted to give up now and then. Remember the drought of two years ago? I was half my size at that time, and one summer day I just wasn't sure I could make it. But I didn't give up. I carefully monitored my water usage, checking every five minutes for water loss and sunburn. I didn't nap once all day, though I was sleepy--oh the heat zapped me like everyone else, but I didn't nod off. I stayed awake and watched my water reserves. I never gave in. That night the rains came. What a relief, but I'd been wise. I played my strengths exactly right, working root expansion to support branches and leaves in exactly the right ratio with careful timing of all my processes--and I outlasted the drought. That's what happens when you plan very carefully. That's what you can do when you've learned from the best and then taken their teaching one step farther."

"Wow," said Jackrabbit, a little sorry he'd asked.

"Discipline," said Wild Lettuce. "Knowledge and discipline is an unstoppable force. You can survive anything any season brings your way if you plan wisely and practice discipline."

"Sounds a little intense, don't you think?" asked Jackrabbit. "Don't you ever just have fun? Grow something a little crazy? Try something a little risky? Lose just a little control?"

"Not when solid growth is what you're after. Keep that goal before you at all times. Then you'll never lose your way. You'll never lose your leaves either," Wild Lettuce chuckled. He then rustled all of his very dramatically in the passing breeze.

"Sounds like you've got it covered," admitted Jackrabbit. "No surprises for you."

"I've seen and survived every season," reiterated Wild Lettuce. "And I did it with style."

"I've got to go now," said Jackrabbit. "Thanks for the advice."

Wild Lettuce just rattled his splendiferous leaves.

"Did you hear that?" Jackrabbit asked Wind when he got where Wild Lettuce couldn't hear.

"Seen and stylishly survived every season, huh?" said Wind thoughtfully. "I bet there's one he hasn't seen."

"What's that?" asked Jackrabbit.

"The Windy season."

Wind started to blow.

He blew through Day, he blew through Night. He blew from up and he blew from under. He blew to the right and he blew to the left. He blew behind and he blew before. He blew through all Wild Lettuce's planning and discipline. He left his mark on every growth strategy Wild Lettuce attempted. When he stopped, Wild Lettuce was Wire Lettuce, spindly, almost leafless, nearly flowerless. Those left to him showed jagged edges on the narrow leaves and the tips of the lavender flower petals. Wind's teeth marks. He'd taken a bite out of Wild Lettuce's pride and plans.

To this day Wire Lettuce never forgets the season he just couldn't plan for. He remains virtually leafless, but many branched. He dries out and looks like straw in a drought, giving him another of his names, Desert Straw. Give him a little rain, though, and he'll blossom any time of the year. Cautiously, sparsely, but stubbornly.

Snout Butterfly Dreaming

It is said that there was once a time before the Snout butterfly had a snout. How he came to have a snout is rather an unusual love story.

The American Snout has narrow front wings with a squared off apex and a scalloped margin, each sporting two orange patches on a brown background, with small white spots sprinkling the tips. The hind wings each have one large orange splotch on brown. When the wings are folded closed, the front wings can be tucked beneath the hind wings, which have a dead-leaf-look to their underside that helps to camouflage the resting butterfly. These features Snout butterfly always had, from the beginning, designed by Day and Night, the two primary creative forces, as they indulged in their "butterfly-stage" of creation. The snout, though, was not of their doing. The snout was a feature Snout Butterfly developed himself, with the aid of a good friend who helped him discover a feature uniquely his own amongst desert butterflies, as dear friends are often wont to do.

Snout Butterfly was a brush-footed butterfly. Day and Night installed this feature on a number of butterflies, not just the American Snout. Like all insects, butterflies have six legs and most walk through life using all six, but brush-footed butterflies are club-footed in the pair of legs closest to their head. That pair is usually shorter and full of sensitive hairs which are used to test and taste the flowers and plants upon which the butterfly alights, checking for the best nectar and the proper host plant upon which to lay the eggs--which will hatch into the caterpillars--which will pupate and become butterflies--well, you know that part of the story. Brush-feet, then, are additional mouth parts that help clue the butterfly in to his environment. American Snout's were unusually long. He used them as other brush-footed butterflies did. Until....

Another part of the story that you already know is the tale of how the caterpillar longs to become something more than what he is. He senses greater things for himself and dreams of flight while dragging his cumbersome bulk up and down stems, searching for leaves to chew into oblivion, adding even more bulk and cumbersomeness to his bloated body. Then, the magic of metamorphosis ensures that his dreams have not been in vain. The American Snout larva grazes on Desert Hackberry to absorb the formula that causes his transformation into a butterfly. But is that the end of his dreaming? I should say not.

"Come, Friend," called the flower, by means of color and aroma--and the butterfly came, first to several flowers on the Aster by the rock, then to one flower on the plant nearby, and finally to the flower who called from the Aster plant glistening with dew.

"At last," cheered the flower. "Well, what have you brought me?"

"Brought you?" asked the butterfly.

"A traveler should not arrive without a gift at the door of a friend like me," answered the daisy-like blossom, nodding her golden face fringed with delicate purple rays.

Butterfly paused.

"I have nothing," answered Butterfly. "You are the one with all the glory. Look at you shining in the sunlight. How I wish I had your colors, but they are denied me. How I wish I could make sweet nectar as you do, but I must settle for drinking it. How do you make such a miracle of flavor?"

Aster laughed. "You have pollen from the flowers around me. That is your gift. With that I will generate the seed with which to begin new plants with new flowers like me. As for the nectar? That is my gift to you. It is a mystery how I make it. I just do. How did you learn to fly?"

"I'm not sure," said Butterfly thoughtfully, trying to remember. "I guess I just do."

"Exactly," said Aster. "Those are just small pieces of the mystery. The mystery that's impossible to speak about, though we keep trying."

"What mystery?" asked Butterfly, drinking his fill of nectar and dipping his brush-footed forelimbs in dew with which to wash his face.

"The mystery of everything," responded Aster. "The mystery that made us and all the relationships between us, all the ways in which we need each other and feed each other."

Butterfly paused and pondered.

"You mean Day and Night?" Butterfly asked, thinking back to his birth and their two curious faces watching him start off in the world, eager to view the results of their collaborative efforts.

"Even before them," said Aster.

"What's before them?" wondered Butterfly.

"Mystery," declared Aster. "Haven't you heard that mystery is one? Then one made two. Two made three and three made countless thousands?"

"No," said Butterfly. "And what did the countless thousands make?" he teased.

"The remembrance of unity," answered Aster. "The heart of mystery."

Butterfly became still.

"That sounds like an endless trail," said Butterfly with amazement.

"There is no end to any of it," agreed Aster.

"How did you hear of it?" asked Butterfly, more in awe of his friend with each passing moment.

"I heard it while yet in the seed. I heard it while inside my bud. I hear it in the sunshine. I hear it in the wind from your wing beats. It comes with being still, of remaining in one spot as plants must do. It comes with having a given number of days. Even now the seeds are forming within me and as they mature, I will die. That is my contribution to the countless thousands."

"And your nectar," reminded Butterfly. "I am one of the countless thousands, right? That is your contribution to me, right?"

"As your pollen is your contribution to me," laughed Aster. "We are forever connected to one another through our gifts."

Butterfly remained still.

"How glad I am that we've met. None of the other flowers have spoken to me as you have. I might never have seen the beauty of your wisdom had you not called me 'friend' and chosen to share it with me. I can never thank you enough. I wish I could drink every part of you down as I swallow your nectar. Then we could be together forever."

"The same beauty you find in me is also in you. You can only see it in me because it is in you too. Whether you like what you see, or dislike it, matters little. It is always some part of yourself you are seeing. As you drink my nectar, you do drink the 'all' of me. We are together forever."

"How do you know?" asked Butterfly.

"Because of mystery," answered Aster. "And because you and I are part of the countless thousands, right? And what is made by the countless thousands?"

"The remembrance of unity," answered Butterfly. "I was paying attention."

"Clearly," agreed Aster.

Butterfly continued sitting still.

114

"How can I learn a flower's wisdom?" asked Butterfly. "It may be part of me, but I've sure forgotten it. "

"By sharing," said Aster. "You have wisdom I need to remember too."

What do I have that you want?" asked Butterfly.

"You are the part of me that knows how to fly," answered Aster.

Butterfly was stillness itself.

"How can I reach for more flower wisdom?" he asked.

"Just reach," laughed Aster delightedly.

Butterfly playfully reached out his brush-footed pair of legs. He reached as far as he could. He stretched and wobbled with his pantomimed grasping, grunting with his play-acting efforts. Aster laughed hysterically, but fell silent when Butterfly tried to bring his front legs down again to brush against Aster's face. He found his legs were stuck reaching forward for his dream of unity with Aster. Now his brush-footed pair of legs surrounded his proboscis, his long tongue. His legs made him look long-nosed. He was startled, but had no trouble walking on his other four legs. Now his front, sensory legs worked together with his proboscis, to reach into a flower's essence in rapturous ways he could never have previously imagined.

"In addition," said Aster, marveling at Butterfly's description of the sensations he was having through his nose, "your new look makes you appear even more like a dead leaf. Your nose adds a stem to your leaf-look. Now you can remain still even longer because you're camouflaged even better. Think how much longer we can converse, Friend."

And that is how American Snout Butterfly developed his snout and his ability to explore Aster wisdom better than any butterfly before or since--with the help of his friend, of course.

Gopher Snake Fake

It is said that there was once a time when Coyote watched Sonoran Gopher Snake watch a standoff between Rattlesnake and Cougar.

Surprised when Cougar jumped off the boulder behind which he slept, Rattlesnake coiled, raised the top half of his body, opened his mouth threateningly and rattled his tail, all in the flash of an instant. Cougar, though many times larger, with many more teeth too, flattened his ears, snarled an apology, and backed cautiously away.

"The victory of Littleness over Large in the struggle to survive," said Gopher Snake admiringly.

He already looked somewhat like Diamondback Rattler, he realized. Perhaps he could add to the illusion and use imitation to his advantage.

He practiced his hiss. By forcefully exhaling over his glottis, a portion of his throat, he could make a sound like the rattle of the Rattler, almost.

He coiled and raised the top half of his body. There, that wasn't hard. Then he blew out his cheeks and flattened his head, and darned if he didn't look like a venom-blessed Rattler, almost.

The final touch: the tail thing. He raised his hindmost part and shook it violently, but without rattles, the effect was hugely disappointing. But then, a stroke of brilliance. Rather than lifting his tail, as Rattlesnake did, he kept his against the ground and vibrated the tip so rapidly, a buzzing was produced that had the same effect as rattles, almost.

He tried out his new look on Quail, passing nearby.

116

Quail squawked and raced off without a second glance, screaming a warning to all his relations within hearing.

Gopher Snake was delighted.

Coyote approached and Gopher Snake did his best Defensive-Rattler imitation. Coyote pounced, grabbed Gopher Snake behind his head and killed him.

"The victory of the Informed over the Imitator in the struggle to survive," sneered Coyote, licking his chops.

Toad Song

"It is said that there was once a time when all Rains were equal. Morning Rains. Afternoon Rains. Evening Rains. Winter Rains. Summer Rains. All the same. Not in intensity, duration or total amounts of moisture delivered. They were the same in their capacity to nourish life on Earth.

"Then Day and Night, the two primary creators, discussed how the needs of life were really not equal. Spring was the season of greatest creativity, when life was bursting at the seams. Plants germinated, flowers produced seeds, animals bore young. Spring needed that something extra the other seasons didn't. But how to supply it? That was the question.

"Earth's soils varied greatly from one place to another. The patterns were established and caused huge diversity of life across the planet. Sun also had his pattern and so did Moon. They shed the light needed to quicken life according to their established orders.

"Water and Air were less fixed. They could be more flexible. Day and Night sought them for advice."

"So what?" yawned the newcomer, so new he was not quite tailless.

"Wait.

"So they agreed they could work together. Rain would be the delivery system. But they needed a Catalyst."

"What has this to do with me?" asked the younger.

"Wait.

"So the search for the Catalyst began. Many creatures were interviewed. Some just didn't want to be out during Rain. Mountain Lion, for instance, chose to hide in her den. Some agreed to contribute in part. Creosote, for instance, agreed to dispense a certain aroma. Many ingredients were indeed added to spring Rain, but nothing ignited it to become the elixir of life it was intended to be."

Still-Tailed burped. He licked his lips and sleepily narrowed his eyes. Experienced now, he chose not to ask. He pretended to listen while his elder rattled on and on.

"Wait," said the oldster, as if he'd heard his listener's thoughts.

Still-Tailed opened his eyes wide in amazement, then was distracted by a dragonfly.

"So Day and Night rested near this very waterhole.

"'We need Magic,' said Day.

"'I thought we'd have it by now,' shrugged Night. 'What are we missing?'

"'Nothing I can think of,' sighed Day.

"At that very moment, I croaked.'"

"What, you were there?" asked Still-Tailed.

"Indeed," said Tailless. "And that began a chorus of toad song around the water's edge that sparked inspiration in spring Rain, making it the most life-gifting of all seasonal Rains."

"Toad song," said Still-Tailed.

"Toad song," asserted Tailless.

They looked up at the growing towers of Cloud catching the last of Sun's rays and turning splendidly crimson in Sun's departing glory. Rain dimpled the waterhole.

"Braaaaawk," said Tailless.

"Braaaaawk," answered Still-Tailed, taking up the chorus just before the other toads joined in.

"Braaaaawk, braaaaawk, braaaaawk."

Night smiled and sighed. "You just can never tell where Magic lies," she said. "It always surprises. And always preludes beauty."

All in the Ear of the Listener

It is said that there was once a time a young White-crowned Sparrow perked up with curiosity at a strangely discordant birdsong bludgeoning his eardrums.

"Who is that bleating?" he asked the Abert's Towhee, who scratched in the dust beside him.

Towhee chuckled, then turned serious. "You'd do well to show more respect. That's the local male Loggerhead Shrike. I agree that his song seems grotesque to us, who sing with much more talent, but notice his gusto. He projects over a large area, which tells a female Shrike he's healthy. He couldn't care less what you and I think of his aria. He only hopes to attract a mate."

"But his sweet phrases clash so with the clicks and squeaks he croaks. How can any bird, even a female Shrike, find that attractive?" asked Sparrow.

"Ah, friend, a female's mind is a mystery," sighed Towhee. "Why do they do anything they do? Here now! Don't go out in the open to stare. Take care or you'll become his next meal and find yourself impaled on a thorn while he eats you, little by little."

Sparrow shuddered. "He sounds like a monster!"

"He is, to us. To his mate, he's the man-of-the-year. Peek around this bush and see how he sits on that branch so as to reflect the sun off his white chest. That makes him clearly visible to the girls. And that voice? Well, there's no accounting for taste."

"But what do you mean about his eating me little by little?" chirped Sparrow in fright.

Towhee turned and looked Sparrow directly in his eyes, speaking with deep authority, "I'm telling you right now, and you'd better never forget, Shrike is the only predatory songbird. He hunts folks like us, though he's not that much bigger than me. He eats insects, yes, and mice, yes, but also birds. Don't be fooled by his neat white, black and gray raiment. He is no gentleman. He's a killer. He has no talons, but he'll still catch you with his feet and deliver a death blow with his hooked beak. With that he can grasp your neck and sever your spinal cord. Then he hangs your lifeless carcass on the thorn of a palo verde tree or a barbed-wire fence, and snacks on you whenever he grows hungry--or feeds you to his girlfriend to impress her with his hunting skills--or drops your body parts into his squawking hatchlings' gullets. That's why he's known as The Butcher Bird. Never mock his song."

With that, Towhee turned away and scampered into the shade of a stand of creosotes, the twisting branches of which would thwart arial attacks.

A bug-eyed White-crowned Sparrow youth followed, terrified into silence.

"Keep up that awful singing," he thought to the Shrike. "I can't stand it, but at least I know where you are."

Winter Wren, King of the Birds

It is said that there was once a time when Winter Wren was known as King of the Birds. The Japanese even called him King of the Wind. Tough to believe--since this teeny, dark brown, mouse-like, smallest of all wrens who dashes hyperactively in and out of tiny cracks and caves in rocks, and darts beneath the thickest forest undergrowth in search of insects always holding his tail cocked skyward-- sure ain't kingly to look at. Dwarf of the Birds, perhaps. But King? Hardly.

He is the only wren who lives in both the Old and New Worlds. That's impressive.

Primarily a resident of conifer forests, he can withstand the worst of winter onslaughts--not a season known for its abundance of insects--by hunting down cocoons and larvae hidden under bark or leaves. That's not something most insectivores do. They leave, heading south for warmer, insect-friendly lands. So Winter Wren can endure. That's impressive.

Yet, he will travel, heading south to desert riparian forests some winters, just for a change of diet and scenery. He can be an adventurer too. That's impressive.

But Kingly?

Don't be fooled by size, Aesop warned. He said Winter Wren won his rank in a contest with the other birds. They had agreed that whoever could fly the highest would be crowned King of the Birds. Eagle flew highest, but when he achieved his maximum altitude, hitchhiking Winter Wren crept from beneath Eagle's wing and flew higher yet, proving brains could beat brawn. Okay--brains are impressive too.

But none of these is reason enough to be crowned King.

The real reason is revealed in his name, his scientific name. Known as Troglodytes troglodytes, he is the "cave dwelling recluse" times two. Twice as unafraid of the shadowlands as other would-be heroes, he dashes into the darkest, deepest places. There he finds food, with which he returns to the light.

To and fro he scurries. Into the sightless realms, back to the sunlight--endlessly, tirelessly journeying. Plucking the stuff of blackest Night, digesting it, then bringing it up to the light of Day.

Taking what's hidden below, up--to be seen and known.

> But which way is up?
> In the deepest pits of Hell,
> It can be difficult to tell.
> So when in travail,
> Watch Winter Wren's tail.
> It always points up.

That's why he's King of the Birds.
And King of the Wind.
Because he's King of Consciousness--and all that lies below.

Moon Incognito

It is said that there was once a time when Moon peeked over the horizon to find Cloud hanging there, low in the sky. Sun was set. Moon was full. Her rising called everyone's attention east.

"How funny, look!" Wind directed. "Moon has a hat."

"A sombrero," agreed Cactus Wren.

"Or a fedora," declared Saguaro.

"What's a fedora?" asked Woodrat.

"It's what that doesn't look like," announced Owl. "Anyone can see it's a lady's bonnet."

"Wait," Wind ordered and gave Cloud a few nudges. "Now what?"

"A baseball cap--Moon definitely wears a baseball cap," insisted Javelina, remembering one he'd found in a picnic ground he'd scavenged last fall.

"Oh good grief," Moon sighed.

"A topless hat," called Antelope Squirrel.

Everyone laughed, for indeed, Moon was rising above the layer of Cloud.

"Now she wears a headband," Wind announced, puffing away what had been the top of the "hat."

"No, it's a blindfold," called Night snake, just leaving her hole for the hunt.

"Glasses," said Kangaroo Rat, as Moon peeked through Cloud.

"Wish I could see," grumbled Cloud.

"To play this silly game?" Moon asked disdainfully.

"But you are playing," declared Wind. "You're absolutely vital."

"Yeah, I guess so," Cloud remembered, brightening visibly with Moon's honey-colored light.

"Unbelievable," Moon scoffed, but chuckled a little too.

"A collar," sang Thrasher.

"No, a mustache," yipped Coyote.

Everyone held their sides with laughter. Even Moon guffawed.

"Now she wear boots," Skunk insisted. "Silver boots."

It was true. Moon's light was no longer golden. She was white. She was risen beyond Cloud. The watchers dispersed, headed for bed or a night of activity.

"So they're finely finished?" said Moon, no longer the center of interest.

"Guess so," replied Cloud, a little regretfully.

"That was a blast," roared Wind. "Same time tomorrow?"

No one answered.

A couple weeks later, as Moon set in the west, she remembered the moment. All that was visible was her smile.

Ms. Cardinal Gets More Red

It is said that there was once a time when a young, female Cardinal talked to every morning's rising Sun. She called when the horizon first pinkened. She called when it turned orange. She called as Sun first peeked over Earth's edge, and kept calling until Sun cleared the place where Earth met Sky--now such a nice shade of blue. Then she went to breakfast.

"Why do you do that?" asked Curved-billed Thrasher, normally one of the first to begin the morning chorale. He thought it unlikely she claimed territory with her chip, chip, chipping. Typically, that would be male Cardinal's task, and he was not in sight. "Why are you up so very early and who are you talking to? No one's here but me."

"Who are you talking to?" countered Lady Cardinal. "Here so early each day. Are you worried I'm trying to be first to greet Sun? That I'll beat you out? Please, I want more than that!"

"I'm here announcing my presence," Thrasher answered. "I'm telling Thrashers from all over that this place is mine. I'm the bird to be reckoned with, if you're a Thrasher from around here."

"From the numbers I hear answering you," said Cardinal, "all Thrashers think they're the bird to be reckoned with in this part of the desert."

"Yes, well...they're just reporting in," explained Thrasher.

"Of course they are," remarked Cardinal, just a tad sarcastically.

"So why are you here?" asked Thrasher, to change the subject.

"To beseech Sun," said Cardinal.

"For what?"

"For something IMPORTANT."

"What?"

"You wouldn't understand."

"Try me."

"For fairness. Male Cardinal is far redder than I. Everyone notices him in a crowd. His black mask stands out so sharply against his head and chest. Everyone says so."

"I never have," said Thrasher. He looked just like his mate. All Curved-billed Thrashers looked pretty much alike. "So you're beseeching Sun because you're jealous of your brother?"

"I knew you wouldn't understand," sighed Cardinal.

"Well, what do you want?" asked Thrasher.

"More red," declared Cardinal. "I want my black bill to be red."

"Consider it DONE," announced Sun. And, indeed, Female Cardinal's bill was now red.

"Oh, thank you, thank you," she said, staring at her reflection in a puddle. "Now I'm pretty too," she exclaimed joyfully and flew away to show off her new look to her neighbors.

"How did you do that?" Thrasher asked Sun.

"All Cardinals are born with black bills," replied Sun. "As they mature, their bills turn red. My abracadabra was only a matter of timing."

"Well done," laughed Thrasher.

"Thanks," said Sun.

"But won't Male Cardinal's bill turn red too?" asked Thrasher.

"Even as we speak," replied Sun.

Thrasher laughed uproariously.

"And you were singing so much because...?" asked Sun.

"Because I'm the bird to be reckoned with in these parts," declared Thrasher.

"And the other Thrashers are answering back because...?" asked Sun.

"Oh, they're just reporting in," said Thrasher.

"Of course they are," said Sun.

127

Predicting Dickcissels

It is said that there was once a time when Day shook his head as he watched events unfolding on Earth. He turned to his partner-in-creation, Night, and said, "They're such a study of opposites."

"Who?" she asked, turning to see where he looked. Tracing his gaze, she focused in on the Sonoran Desert of Arizona, but she was not sure which creature had attracted his attention.

"That Dickcissel," answered Day, pointing to the bird he was observing. "They are so predictable, yet always surprising."

"How so?" asked Night. The bird he'd indicated seemed quite a normal example of the female of the species, so far as she could tell. At the moment, she perched on a dried flower, eating seed. Nothing unusual about that, Night thought.

"Think about it," Day went on. "Not just that one bird, but the whole species; most do just what we programmed them to do--except for those that don't. They all nest on the ground--except for those who nest in shrubs. Some females have yellow bellies, some don't. Some have yellow eyebrows, some don't. They breed in one prairie field in vast numbers one year, then don't show up at all the next. You can count on them to gather in flocks of hundreds to migrate together each fall--except for those who stick to themselves and stay put. They overwinter in Venezuela by the thousands, a plague on the farmers of that country--except for those who visit House Sparrows at seaside resorts in California or South Carolina instead. Look, it's fall migration, and this bird of the plains has one citizen scouting out Newfoundland, stopping only on account of the Atlantic Ocean, and another loner sunning in Arizona. Does anything else we've made display such a variety of behaviors? Does any other creature so delight in breaking its mold?"

Night giggled as she examined the sparrow-sized birds scattering over the northern and southern hemispheres, now that families were raised and fall migration the order of the day. Mature males looked like mini-Meadow Larks, a bird with whom they shared the prairie grasslands during the breeding season. They had a black bib on their breasts, yellow bellies, a reddish wing-patch, and yellow lines over their eyes. Female and young Dickcissels had no bibs and were variable as to the amounts of yellow they sported, just as Day had said. Still, she thought, they weren't all that hard to figure. They all ate seeds and insects and hatched from blue eggs. Was there another creature that showed more variability?

"You're forgetting about human beings, dear," she reminded her consort.

Day had no answer to that!

A Case of Mistaken Identity

It is said that there was once a time when Sun winced and closed his eyes to the glint of his reflected rays off the faces of Desert Marigolds that were sprinkled across the Sonoran Desert floor, busily blossoming with glee in the aftermath of Rain's visit.

"Wind," he hollered from his heights. "Do something. It's blinding."

"What would you have me do?" asked Wind, surveying the glistening specks with admiration. He thought the flowers seemed adorned with diamonds, and liked the effect. "They simply reflect your light and glory. They can hardly be blamed for that. They can't help it." Wind figured a little ego stroking would sooth Sun's mood.

"Blow harder and dry the plants off. Rain has had his dance with Earth. Now it's my time and the wet flowers hurt my eyes."

"I would if I could," Wind laughed, seeing Sun's mistaken assumption. "But the blame's not Rain's. It's more your own."

"Explain," Sun ordered--something quite typical for him, being somewhat overawed with himself on account of his importance to all life on Earth. He readily forgot he was no more important, really, than any of the other elementals. Perhaps it was because he spent so much time above it all. Usually, the others simply tolerated his overrating of himself. It wasn't worth the effort of arguing. But this time Wind was delighting in turning Sun's complaint back on himself.

"It isn't Rain that shines on the flowers below," he explained. "It's a small beetle. It's shaped like a drop of dew, though, so your mistake is understandable."

"No insect can sparkle like Rain," insisted Sun.

"This one does," declared Wind, "though you'll never turn his twinkle into Rainbow. I dare you to try. His light's echo is simply a mirror, a mirror of your face."

Upon a second, painful, examination, Sun noticed the "drops" did slowly move; some even took flight. Wind brought one piloting his currents up for Sun's closer inspection. The beetle's elytra, the shell coverings over the wings, flashed a stunning metallic gray. It was, indeed, a perfect mirror.

"I see," said Sun, once again turning away his burning eyes. "How did they get so shiny?"

"That is your doing," insisted Wind.

"Explain," Sun ordered, but with less authority this time.

"They live and feed only on blossoms of the sunflower family of plants. See? It is all your own fault. As larvae, they grow within the flower parts, sipping sap. As adults, they eat yellow pollen. How can they help but glisten when you, Sun, are responsible for their origin, housing, and food?"

"I had no idea," Sun marveled.

"You frequently don't," Wind muttered.

"What?" Sun asked companionably.

"Nothing," Wind answered.

"You know," Sun said thoughtfully, "they are kind of nice, aren't they? I am rather fond of them, after all. Remarkable sparks off the old Helios, don't you agree?"

"Yes," Wind concurred, chuckling. "Quite."

So, having been introduced, Shining Flower Beetle flew back to his Desert Marigold.

Typically Towhee

It is said that there was once a time when a towhee lost a leg. He didn't misplace it. It was torn from his body at the hip by an attacking falcon. Not much of a meal for the hunter, but Towhee escaped and lived.

"If that can be called 'living,'" said Uncle Towhee upon learning his nephew's fate. "Towhees scratch. We have always scratched. We do our two-footed shuffle in the dust to find seed. How can he eat when he can't scratch? How can he be Towhee without doing the shuffle?"

Crippled Towhee hopped. It is "typically towhee" to hop. But he wobbled and stumbled, catching himself with his wing on his legless side. Airborne he was fine. Flight was no problem. But landing....

That was a problem.

That was a disaster.

A crash in the dirt every time.

But while down there, with his face in the soil, he noticed seed. So he sat up and ate. Then he hopped again. Stumbled again. Used his wing as a crutch on his crippled side again. Noticed seed again. Ate again. Flew again. Crashed onto a branch and clung on with one foot again, and again, and again. Until he learned how to balance, on one leg, not two.

He joined his fellows in the dirt. He watched while they scratched. He saw the seed first, and wasted no energy in shuff-ling. He was not "typically towhee," but he lived.

"He's not doing it right," said Uncle. "He's not one of us."

But after he hung upside down from the dried, seedcoated face of a common sunflower, ate his fill, and flew off to land, one-legged, in the brush beneath a mesquite tree, all without falter--no one listened to Uncle.

They stopped thinking of Towhee as maimed or Not Typically Towhee.

He was just Towhee.

The Naming of Night Snake

It is said that there was once a time when Night slept...and slept...and slept. This left Day in charge--all the time. Let me tell you--things really got hot! No one knew when to sleep and when to venture forth. Owls grew hungry perched in their roosting trees, waiting for Night to come so they could hunt. Butterflies and birds of Day got so tired of flying they were falling out of the sky. They didn't know when to rest. Turkey Vulture couldn't keep up with his workload. Trees and flowers began to bloat with gasses they normally released when Night fell. They were overwhelmed with processing sunshine in the endless Day. Since Night never came to cool things off, Day's temperatures grew higher and higher until Earth itself panted like Coyote after outrunning the victims of his latest skullduggery.

"Someone needs to find Night," gasped Cougar. She had given up prowling because of the heat and refused to move beyond the shade provided by Mesquite tree until Night returned.

"Who, whoo knows where to find her?" asked Owl from the branches over Cougar's head. "I know her ways when she's here, but not when she's not. I wouldn't know where to begin to look."

"Why? Why would she leave us?" wailed Phainopepla, a black, crested bird normally perched in the very top of Mesquite's twigs, but not today. Today he hid from Sun in the shaded inner branches of the tree.

"We can concern ourselves with that once we've found her," answered Cougar. "We need to find her first to beg her to come back."

"Do you suppose she was offended?" asked Phainopepla, continuing his line of thought. "I, for one, did take her for granted. I wear her favorite color, but am active during Day. I always sleep through Night's presence and never thanked her for the relief she brought."

"Me neither," said Cardinal, another bird hiding within Mesquite's sheltering shade.

"Not me," said Owl. "Night is my time for hunting and flying about. I have never been ungrateful to her or taken her for granted."

"Me neither," hissed a small voice from Mesquite's roots. No one above heard him.

"I have a hard time believing all the other creatures who move by Night have done any differently than I have toward her," continued Owl. "Besides, she doesn't impress me as the sort to be put off by the forgetfulness of Day creatures."

"I wouldn't think so either," hissed the soft voice from below. Again, no one heard.

"I still feel guilty," said Phainopepla sadly.

"Who cares?" huffed Cougar. "What's needed is action. We must find her and beg her to reappear."

"But where to look?" reiterated Owl.

"Exactly," said Cougar.

"Raven once told me that Condor told him that Night dwells beyond the western mountains when Day has control of Sky."

"Rumors," said Cougar. "Would you go in chase of a rumor?"

"No," admitted Phainopepla, "but maybe Condor would go."

"And where is Condor?" challenged Cougar.

"Exactly," said Owl.

"I'll go," volunteered the small voice from below, but again, no one heard. So its owner departed, leaving the rest to their debate.

The small voice belonged to a small snake. He was less than two feet long. He was light gray with black spots and a black eyeline. But who could see those when he was underground? Just now, that's where he was--and going deeper.

He had once upon a time explored his burrow, borrowed from a lizard he'd once upon a time eaten, to a system of tunnels once upon a time dug by who knows what underground creatures--then abandoned. Many times he'd worried he was lost in the dark, subterranean spaces forever, but he'd eventually followed the maze to the bedchambers of the snoring queen of darkness, Night. He watched in wonder a few minutes, then, feeling like an intruder, he crept back through the labyrinth of tunnels to his own doorway to the upper world under Mesquite's roots. There he had squinted in Day's light and awaited Night's arising, when he would bestir himself to hunt, just like Owl.

Now he hurried along, following the maze in his memory, hoping to find the same bedchamber as before. He was hours in the darkest recesses of Earth. His memory sometimes led him astray, but he merely looped back and took another path, trusting that he could once again find his way to the sleeping queen. No one had come this way since his last journey, and that was so long ago that little remained in the way of scent to lead him along. But he had a feeling, and blind turns did not deter him from it.

Finally, the tunnel began to widen. He caught a faint whiff of his own scent too. This was where he had watched Night for some time as she slept; he was sure of it. Pausing to listen, he could hear her breathing.

"Hello," he called softly, hissing as he cautiously slithered closer.

His answer was a snore.

"Hello," he called a little louder, creeping a little closer.

Nothing.

"HELLO," he yelled, as loud as he could. And for good measure he grabbed hold of some of the shadows Night had wrapped around herself, grasping firmly with his teeth and tugging with all his might.

"Who's there?" he was relieved to hear Night call.

"One of your subjects," he answered. "One of those who depend on your arrival for our feeding. I speak on behalf of us all, however, for even those creatures who hunt and eat by Day are oppressed now by his endless light and heat. You have slept too long and we suffer for it."

"How long have I slept?"

"Too long," said the snake.

"I'll come immediately," said Night. "I'm so sorry for my tardiness. Obviously, I can't rely on Day to awaken me when it's my watch. Would you take on the task?"

"I suppose I could," conceded the snake as they moved through the tunnels toward Earth's surface. "After all, I do know the way."

"Very good," sighed Night. "I'm most grateful. You're not just one of my subjects, but my most loyal one as well."

Night and the snake arrived at the entrance to the upper world together, but as Night arose to the cheers of all living creatures, she saw that the snake held back. He shunned the fanfare that greeted Night and she understood. She promised all who heralded her arrival to never oversleep again. One of their number would faithfully awaken her, but she refused to say who.

137

Later, when the small snake finally left his burrow, he found Night sitting on a nearby boulder, waiting for him.

"I wanted a moment with you," she whispered, mindful not to wake Phainopepla. "To thank you again and to give the acclaim you refuse from your fellow creatures."

"That's not necessary," began the snake.

"I know, but I want to leave you with a sign of my special favor. After all, you are the one who will wake me daily so we no longer have such an imbalance of Day's reign ever again. It'll be a small token of my regard, just between the two of us."

"OK," agreed the snake, and Night marked a black trident on the back of his neck.

"There, a symbol to remind us that you alone are the one destined to goad me into wakefulness. You alone are my sacred serpent. From now on, you're to be called Night Snake."

So the pact was finalized.

Night never overslept again.

And she always precedes Night Snake from his hole--when no one is looking--so none is the wiser about where she sleeps or who wakes her.

Walkingstick's Origin

It is said that there was once a time when quiet energies wanted to take form. They spoke to Moon, assuming that Sun was too active and fiery of nature to understand their needs. They whispered in her ear of slow-moving, hidden things. They began in her new phase, when she was at her darkest. Each night they whispered their dreams until she was at her fullest, the phase where she punctuated the desert night with moonglow and creation's shadow.

"We would move most slowly, hardly faster than you through the night sky. We would move primarily at night, the world of your dominion. We would be mostly unseen. There, but not there. We do not want the limelight. Give us the talent to blend in rather than stand out. Let us hide. Let us whisper rather than scream, the smallest voice in Earth's noisy playground."

So it went, night after night, while Moon built herself rounder and fuller. Until she finally heard what was gently speaking to her, and knew what they wanted. She considered what she'd heard. She dreamed about it.

Then, in the days when she and Sun both occupied the sky at the same time, she discussed it with him. Together they approached Day and Night.

"There is room for more 'slow,'" Night allowed.

"There is fun to be had in making something 'there, but not there,'" mused Day.

So the quiet energies gathered to be molded into creatures.

One of the first to emerge was Walkingstick.

She was "there, but not there," because she matched so well the tree branch on which she stood. She even developed a gentle swaying to imitate a twig rocking in the breeze.

Her eggs she dropped one by one to the leaf-littered ground, where they resembled seeds--"there, but not there" again.

She moved verrrry slowly, so as not to attract attention, and wisely chose the nighttime for most activity, when there were fewest awake to see.

If discovered, she stiffened and dropped immediately to the ground, where she looked like a broken twig, fallen from the branch. She would lay still the entire day until nightfall brought her even more anonymity. Then she arose and crept back to her tree.

She never said a thing.

The quiet energies nodded respectfully.

"We are pleased," they whispered to Moon.

"So am I," Moon answered.

Everything is Prairie Falcon

It is said that there was once a time when all The People met to discuss the journey ahead and how they would remember who they were and to whom they were related, even after they had separated into many smaller groups to spread over the Earth. How would they remember the connection between Earth and Sky? A symbol, they decided. So they cast about for which symbol they could all agree upon.

The gathering was led by their shaman. He told them there would always be Wise Ones amongst them. These would function as reminders. Studying their ways would lead to the realization of interrelatedness, the memory of community. That Humans were connections between Earth and Sky.

"Lightning," said some. Streams of light from Heaven to Earth. They could symbolize those moments of instantaneous awareness of oneness. Etched into rock, they could mark places where this vision had come to The People, letting everyone know these were sacred places.

"Mountains," said others. Clearly, they reached from Earth to Sky. They could mark known territory and beckon travelers home to themselves.

"Home," said still others. Each hearth in each home could act as the altar which connected Sky Sun's fire to the heart's center on Earth, relationships.

"Trees," suggested some. Not only did they anchor in Earth and obviously reach up to Sky, but their roots penetrated the Underworld. These should be the symbol to remind all People.

The calumet, insisted one group. The sacred pipe burned tobacco from Earth, sending it skyward as smoke, carrying the prayers of The People to the realm of Spirit. This should be the symbol chosen.

The Shaman had fallen silent after his initial suggestion, listening while each group stated its case. He watched several children leave their families and collect together on the edge of the forest surrounding the meeting place. Unnoticed by the crowd, he joined them.

The four children, who had tired of their elders haggling, watched as Prairie Falcon dropped down from her nest in the high cliffs nearby. She floated over the grasses of the meadow before them until she came upon a careless ground squirrel sitting atop his burrow. She twisted in flight to snatch the squirrel before it could perceive its danger and carried it back to the cliff to feed her young.

"Prairie Falcon connects Earth to Sky," stated one boy.

"She feeds her Sky Children with creatures from the Underworld," agreed the other.

"She's the color of dry grass and flies to the mountaintop," said one of the girls. "Both Earth and Sky are her elements."

"Anything could be the symbol of that connection," the last girl said.

"Indeed," smiled the Shaman. "Everything is. Earth and Sky are one and the same."

He faced them. "You four are the Seers of your Peoples." He touched each one on the crown of their heads with his right hand. "Tomorrow we go in our different directions. Hold on to what you've seen today. Remember for us all, as long as you breathe."

To Know By Heart

It is said that there was once a time when Yellow Starthistle languished for friendship in the farm fields of the New World. But not for long.

Originating in the Old World, native to Eurasia, this bushy, yellow-flowered thistle was a favorite of Honey Bee. The plant made its home on the edges of fields Humans cultivated for grains and fodder for farm animals. It thrived there for centuries, invading crops of alfalfa as they grew, and got harvested with it too. Thus began its long distance travels.

Yellow Starthistle never intended to stray far. Most certainly not out of reach of Honey Bee, its dearest friend and readiest pollinator.

Starthistle had always been content to add little by little to its terrain with each passing year. It produced seed that was of two sorts, with pappus and without. The seed without fell to the soil at the base of the plant. Pappus, the tufts of fluff giving wings to seeds, was short, stiff, and not very flight-worthy on Starthistle. It was better suited to latching its barbs onto clothing, and animal fur to hitch a ride to new ground. Man and Man's animals served as transportation. Yellow Starthistle's expansion was steady and slow, from one farm field to the next.

It's true, the seed-eating birds adored Yellow Starthistle very nearly as much as Honey Bee and stripped seed from dead flower heads, spilling some aside, but Man must take the credit for making Yellow Starthistle into a star-traveler.

Alfalfa was the currency of Spain's conquest of New World lands--at least from the vantage of Conquistador and Colonial livestock. Seed shipped overseas to be cultivated abroad fueled the expansion of Spanish armies and missions, the establishment of ranches and mines, the founding of villages and cities. Seed from home for the domestic livestock from home. But the seed stock was not pure, for Yellow Starthistle seed made the journey too. Not by Man's intention. But, there it was, in Chile, sometime in the 1600's. In alfalfa fields. Without Honey Bee, its peerless pollinator.

Then Honey Bee made the journey too. Never had she intended the trip. Certainly not out of reach of Yellow Starthistle. But her tendency to fertilize crops while making golden honey made her precious to People. They brought her with them too.

She actually beat Starthistle to North America. She landed on the east coast of the new lands and thrived so nicely on the new varieties of flowers, that she grew wild and swarmed west to the Rockies, outpacing the Colonists' expansion by far.

There, though, she stopped. The great wall of mountain was too much for her to cross. For that, she must await the beekeepers. Eventually, they came. She crossed the mountains with them, because gold had been discovered in California. Her gold was in demand there now too.

Gold extraction required livestock, of course. They dragged the wagon and plow. What fed the miner's mule, the rancher's cattle? Alfalfa, Chilean Clover. First cultivated in California in 1851, all seed came from Chile until 1903, so Gold Rush demand for alfalfa was fed by seed from Chile. Farmers complained the alfalfa seed was contaminated with weed seed. Ah, yes--Yellow Starthistle.

They knew each other at first sight. They knew each other by heart. The yellow thistle of Eurasia and the champion pollinator, together again. Honey Bee preferred her old friend over the flowers native to her new home, and pollinated Starthistle first.

The natural bond begun on other continents ensured Yellow Starthistle's conquest of California, and many other parts of the West.

As to Honey Bee, her gold has proved the most enduring, in California, or anywhere else.

144

The Errors of Youth

It is said there was once a time when newly fledged Starlings and Gila Woodpeckers sat on a post together, screeching at the top of their lungs and flapping wings unused to flight. Juxtaposing positions with one another, they were like juvenile thugs on a street corner, taunting the world passing by below. The noisy alliance was watched by two Gilded Flickers, also members of the woodpecker family.

"I thought you said Starlings were enemies because they raid woodpecker holes. They toss out eggs and nesting grasses, then steal the cavity for their own nests," said the younger Flicker to his parent.

"Absolutely," was the elder's response. "Starlings are not from here. Their bills are not good for making holes, like ours are. The best they can do is stick their beaks into a hole, then open their mouth to pry bark from trees or open holes in dirt while hunting bugs. So they steal our holes to nest in our Saguaro cactus."

"Where are they from?"

"Someplace called Europe, so I heard. They were brought in cages across the ocean to New York City and released in Central Park by a Human who liked Shakespeare and wanted the birds he named in his plays to be part of the New World too."

"I don't know what any of that means," said the young Flicker.

"I don't either. It's just part of Starling lore, which is easy to overhear, because they always chatter."

"I look just like you, and the Gila's look like their parents, but the Starlings' kids are brown, not the shiny black/green/purple of their moms and dads."

"Another sign of their bad breeding," declared the older Flicker. "But by winter they will all look alike."

Just then one of the young Starlings imitated the scream of a Red-tailed Hawk and the juvenile Flicker ducked for cover. His parent smiled and said, "Be careful what you say in front of them. They will steal the words from your mouth as quickly as your home. They mimic everything, quite shamelessly."

"If they're so awful, why are the Gila Woodpeckers associating with them?" asked young Flicker, while sipping nectar from a Saguaro blossom.

"See that Saguaro over there?" asked Gilded Flicker. "They all were born and grew up there as neighbors. They don't know any better. It's all about the company you keep."

Coyote's Journey Home

It is said that there was once a time when Coyote sat beneath a mesquite tree, hanging his head in pain. Although he had survived the bite of the diamondback rattler he'd surprised under a creosote while investigating a series of rodent holes, he would not survive the infection in the necrotic flesh left as the bite's aftermath. Head swollen to thrice its normal size, drooling from a mouth he could no longer close, skull throbbing with a pain that nearly blinded him, he could not eat or drink. Alone, he knew his death was upon him. Remembering the den of his birth, he chose to make one last trip home. There he would die.

He'd been born on the side of a mountain, north of the city, in a region where humans ranched cattle, retired, or lived scattered across the desert in small communities from which they commuted to jobs in the city. There were abundant open lands to wander and nights to sing through. When grown, he'd left his family pack, seeking independence and his own hunting grounds. In the five years since his departure, he'd not returned once. But he'd found new coyote clans, mated, raised several litters, had many adventures. Now, unable to hunt, too sick to run, he was abandoned to meet his fate alone. Slowly, weakly, he walked to meet it.

As he drew nigh his birthplace, his confusion increased. People were much more in evidence than he recalled. Whole neighborhoods of them had sprouted in the desert in his absence. Trails were now paved. Roads were so well traveled, he had difficulty making his way without being seen, but since his time was short, he did not have the option of traveling only at night. He dragged himself the

147

last mile past huge earth-moving machines busy plundering the dry riverbed for sand and gravel for the expressway under construction so the city might sprawl ever onward.

Finally he came to the spot he was sure he'd once lived, but nothing was as he remembered. There was a familiar hill, dimpled with houses, but the mountain that should have been next to it, the one that had held his family's den, was gone. Reduced to a low hill, it now housed a gated community whose yards were paved with the crushed rock blasted from the hillside now existing only in Coyote's memory.

A dog barked from the yard behind the block wall he stumbled against, seeking a bit of shade. He already smelled of death, so his presence was apparent to this creature--the closest he would come to a relative, in this place--the closest he could come to a remembered home. He collapsed against the cool wall and sank to the dirt. Curling slightly, gently resting his bulbous head on his front leg, he sighed.

Closing his pus-filled eyes, he finished his journey home.

Crazy

It is said that there was once a time when Rabbit hunkered over a piece of fruit, munching quite contentedly. Quail saw him and wanted some for herself.

"Share, share, please. Share, share," she clucked as she strolled cautiously toward Rabbit. She was not sure of his mood and hesitated to rush right in, though the fruit looked very ripe and yummy. She took a zig-zaggy course to reach her goal, attempting to appear coy and inoffensive.

Rabbit said nothing. As she neared, he sprang straight up, almost a foot high. This startled Quail so much she dashed into a creosote bush for cover, cackling frantically. Rabbit continued chewing his fruit.

Calming, Quail approached again.

"Share, share," she urged as she sauntered over. "Please, share, share," she clucked cajolingly.

Once again, Rabbit said nothing. When she was just close enough to stretch out her neck and peck the cactus fruit, he leaped high as he could once again.

Quail spooked and ran, screeching, for the safety of the creosote. There she gathered her wits, and assailed Rabbit in anger.

"What's that all about?" she cackled, disconcerted. "What's the matter with you, anyway?"

Rabbit said nothing. Just continued eating.

Quail strode nearer again. She didn't say anything this time, just crept cautiously closer. Once again, when she was just about to help herself to a bite of juicy fruit, Rabbit launched into the air and she bolted for the brush, screaming all the way.

"That's enough!" she shrieked. "You're completely crazy. I don't have to put up with this. You're nuts, a lunatic, out of your mind, bonkers, crazy, crazy, crazy," and she ran away, utterly discombobulated.

Rabbit chuckled as he nibbled his uncontested booty.

"Crazy like a fox," he mumbled, with his mouth full.

The Social Genius

It is said that there was once a time when sparrows flocked only with those of their own species during the winter months.

In the north, while on their breeding grounds, they worked in pairs to raise young. Once that enormous task was accomplished, the pairs broke up, and each species formed flocks, the better to protect themselves from predators as they migrated, and find food resources they'd all find palatable. Then, when established on their wintering grounds, they kept that philosophy, seeing no reason to change.

But then came Brewer's Sparrow.

The Brewer's that chose to winter in the Sonoran desert picked it because they liked open spaces. They liked dry climates. They liked scrub environments. Let's face it, they loved deserts. They bred on the flats of the sage-lands of the Great Basin desert. There they nested on the ground, or in nests built in low bushes, always less than five feet off the ground. These birds never dreamed of high places. They dreamed exceptionally, though, horizontally.

By this, I mean they were remarkably egalitarian. They gathered with any and all sparrow flocks, buzzing and chattering in joyous fellowship with no regard to species. They even flocked with Towhees.

Non-Brewer's were initially shocked and confused to find these strangers joining their ranks and prattling away as if they were old friends. They tried to leave and regroup amongst their own kind, but companionable Brewer's accompanied them every time.

Eventually, the other sparrow tribes decided the need to eat far outweighed the matter of with whom one ate. The Brewer's simply wore them down with their complete lack of regard for appearance or rank.

This is the reason we find wintering flocks of sparrows harboring a number of sparrow species in our Sonoran desert after fall migration. And why every sparrow gathering seems to be a party.

Brewer's Sparrows will simply have it no other way.

Warning

It is said that there was once a time when a Thrasher youth explored leaf litter beneath a palo verde tree. Using his bill, the bird swept through bits of yellow blossoms fallen from the branches, seeking caterpillars and other edibles. His mother watched discreetly from a branch above. Only yesterday she'd been shoving food into her son's mouth while he skittered around, following her as she ran over the ground or flew into bushes and trees, endlessly begging to be fed. This was how they learned, she knew: learned to fly, forage, keep an eye out for predators, to imitate their parents and thus learn life skills. Today she went one step further. She left him alone to fend for himself the whole morning, slipping away while he played in the shade under the palo verde. He was worried at first when he missed her, but now he worked through the decaying blossoms looking for something to eat, not realizing she was watching over him nearby. He was nowhere near ready to be totally left to his own devices, but she would see him there soon.

In an open, sunny area just beyond the tree's shadow, Round-tailed Ground Squirrel was foot-drumming. She thumped her left hind leg rapidly on the ground, staring malevolently at something Mother Thrasher didn't immediately see, but she didn't have to.

"Quick," she screeched. "Into the tree. Come to me."

Her startled offspring instantly dashed to her side, both relieved to see her again and frightened by her warning.

153

"What's wrong?" he gasped.

"Squirrel is threatening someone," Mother Thrasher replied.

Together they watched the female rodent thump the ground, run a few feet, thump again, move off a little farther, and thump again.

"What's she doing?" asked Thrasher.

"She must have babies in her burrow," replied his mother. "She is warning there's a snake nearby, perhaps hoping to draw it away from her children. You must always be alert to such warnings," she continued, "for a snake will eat you as readily as baby squirrels given the opportunity. And listen for squirrels barking too, for that is the way they warn of danger from above. Hawks and falcons love Thrasher flesh as much as that of ground squirrels."

As if to demonstrate, another Round-tailed dashed to her drumming sister. After spotting the creature causing the consternation, she stood erect on her hind legs and chirped a high squeaky bark.

Thrasher shuddered. He was thin, not quite adult-sized, and his feathers not developed fully--a gawky Thrasher teenager. He realized just how much he didn't know.

"Now that's unusual," Mother Thrasher mused aloud. "One squirrel warning of danger on high, the other from below. What could that mean?"

Both birds worked their way through palo verde branches, attempting to see what the squirrels saw.

Nearby a boy sat on a smooth rock. He totally ignored the squirrels and their distress over his presence. His attention was given to plucking burrs from his shoelaces and socks, whimpering as they pricked his fingertips. When he was finished, he got up and left.

"A Human," said Mother Thrasher. "Of course. What other creature has the capacity to threaten us from every direction? Oddly enough," she added, "no other has its ability to extend us grace, either. The question always is, which will it be this time?"

The squirrels fell silent and returned to their burrows. The thrashers returned to foraging.

Seasonal Diet

It is said that there was once a time when Old House Sparrow sat with a covey of younger birds. Not all were House Sparrows, but all were "of a feather" in that they were small seed-eaters. He was advising them against letting their stomachs cause them to rush into feeding situations they'd not reconnoitered first.

They were clustered together in a hackberry bush in noisy rehashment of their busy day, a prelude to sleep. Roosting together brought them a measure of warmth and safety in weathering winter nights. The change of the season provided the topic for this particular lecture. He hoped the lesson would not be lost on them.

"Always look before you leap into a field of grass seed," he told his audience of first year sparrows, finches and goldfinches. "And be aware of the season, for that will have a great deal to do with which predators you must watch for."

"How so?" mewed a tiny female goldfinch.

"You already know to scatter when quail and doves sound the alarm. You learned that or you would not be here. They fear the hawk and falcon all year long and always warn us when they are sighted, but not so with one predator."

"Who?" asked a sleepy White-crowned Sparrow, newly arrived in migration from northern snows.

"One who likes reptiles best. Oh, he does snap up baby quail too and baby anythings he finds helpless in their nests. But reptiles are his special delight. Once baby quail have grown, they're too big for his cruel, hooked bill, and guardian quail and doves pay him no heed as he crouches next to a stone or within a bush. They no longer care for his appetites, but you had better.

For with the coming of winter, the reptiles sleep, and you become his food for the season."

"I know who, I know," said Costa's Hummingbird, perching high in the hackberry bush. He hated dragging out a story and always came to the point quickly, something Old Sparrow did not appreciate as the storyteller of the moment.

"Nicknamed 'Snake-Eater,' I have seen him snatch a snake from a sunny snooze, whip it against the very rock upon which it was resting, breaking its bones, then gulp it down and run off with the tail hanging out because the snake was too big to swallow all at once," continued Old Sparrow.

"Yes, but..." interrupted the tiny hummer.

"What kind of snake?" asked a finch, turning pale with fear.

"A Rattlesnake," answered Old Sparrow, slowly and dramatically.

"How long did the snake's tail hang out? Did he eat the rattles too?" squeaked another House Sparrow.

"Three hours--and yes."

A communal shudder quivered the hackberry.

"So be ever vigilant," Old Sparrow began in closing. "Keep a watch for...."

"Look out!" cried Costa's, just as pandemonium struck.

Roadrunner leapt from beneath a nearby creosote bush to snap at the lowest perched sparrow, which happened to be Old Sparrow. The screaming stopped when Roadrunner slammed his prey against the ground, then gobbled it down in one swallow.

The shocked seed-eaters shivered in the higher perches to which they'd scattered.

"Roadrunner," said Roadrunner, smiling smugly. "Keep watch for Roadrunner."

"Class dismissed," he cooed over his shoulder, as he sauntered away.

Pronghorn Antelope, Wind Racer

It is said that there was once a time when Wind raced over the prairie and set the grasses to dancing. He wove in and out of the long leaves, raked open the flowering stalks, and cast pollen about so grass seed might form. Low shrubs and bushes hid within the grasses, plants like Globe Mallow and Buckwheat, but they were not what Wind delighted in. His pleasure was in making the grasses roar as he passed. Their leaves and seed stalks set up such a clatter, they sounded like the surf dashing against the sandy shore on the edge of an ocean. Making waves in water was his first desire, but making waves in fields of grass was a close second. This had everything to do with the vastness of perspective available on those playgrounds. He could watch the billows he formed in water and grass flow for miles and miles across enormous vistas. Such sights made him feel powerful--but also lonely--for he raced alone.

Many animals made the grasslands their home. Some were huge grazing beasts. Some were tiny mice and grasshoppers. None could match Wind in speed and endurance. Wind began to imagine himself a partner. Someone fast. Someone sleek. Someone with a competitive spirit, who loved to race. Someone who wouldn't eat all his precious grass. There were already creatures enough who did that. Beyond these parameters he simply could not envision. He needed help, he realized, if his speedster companion was to take form.

So he stormed off over the horizon to find the land of twilight, the place where Day and Night, the two primary creators, met to converse. There he made his request. Day and Night took Wind's ideas, added their own, and before long Pronghorn Antelope stepped from the shadows into the sunny prairie.

Wind was impressed by the creature's beauty. He stood about three feet tall at the shoulder and was five feet in length. His body was tan, the color of dried grass. His rump, belly and sides were white. Two white splotches marked the front of his neck. His nose, cheek and horns were black. Four slender legs ended in an ungulate's hooves.

The horns were quite unique. They consisted of two bony projections from his skull, covered with a matted, hair-like, black coating. His horns were about a foot in length, each gently curving backward, except for one tine, which pointed ahead, and gave the animal its name.

"You'll be glad to learn he doesn't eat much grass," Day said to Wind. "Only new grass sprouts interest him. The diet he prefers is one for browsers, not grazers. He thrives on forbes and shrubs such as Globe Mallow."

Day and Night were especially proud of two features. Pronghorn had hairs on his white rump that he could raise up, flashing a signal to start the race. Additionally, Pronghorn dropped his horns' sheaths each winter, "throwing down the gauntlet," as an annual challenge to Wind.

Female Pronghorn looked the same, minus the black markings on nose and cheek. She was smaller in size. Her horns were either absent altogether, or shorter, and did not branch. Like her mate, she too could challenge Wind by shedding her horns' sheaths and start races with her white rump.

"But, how fast are they?" Wind asked.

In answer, the Pronghorns blasted across the prairie with a bounding gait called stouting, another challenge to Wind. Wind couldn't ignore their insolence and whipped over the mesa to catch up. On and on they raced, dashing just ahead of Wind. Twenty-five, forty-five, even fifty-five miles per hour, and they still outdistanced him. He would have to come up with his best performance to beat these sprinters. Wind howled with frustration and delight. Day and Night had handed him the competitor of his dreams, and then some.

The races began in earnest. Sometimes Wind won. Usually Pronghorn won. But Wind changed his strategy. He crept up on Pronghorn in the smallest breeze, then blasted away with gale force, catching his opposition by surprise. Now Wind always won.

Angry, Pronghorn went to Day and Night.

"Wind cheats," he complained. "He sneaks up on us without moving the grasses, so we don't know he's there. Then he whips ahead and outruns us. We need to see him coming from far away. We need to spot the slightest shifting in the stance of grasses, in plenty of time to flash a start to the race and dart away."

So Day and Night modified Pronghorn Antelopes' eyes. They enlarged them and set them far back and higher on their heads. With their new eyes, Pronghorn could see three hundred and twenty degrees of their vast horizon. Their newly enhanced vision allowed them to see grasses starting to stir in small breezes from miles away, forewarning them of Wind's approach. The playing field was leveled. Sometimes Wind won. Sometimes Pronghorn. Competition was keen. The racing intense.

Pronghorn Antelope, the fastest animal on Earth over long distances, was the perfect competitor for Wind. Neither Pronghorn nor Wind tires of the game.

Nor do the grasses tire of roaring their approval, whoever wins.

Relatives and Other Embarrassments

It is said that there was once a time when White-throated Swift dipped a little lower in flight than usual and flew into Sun's setting a bit longer than usual. Meanwhile, Lesser Nighthawk glided a little higher than his norm and started out when the sky held more light than usual, so the two birds shared a word or two in the twilight hours of a summer's eve.

"It isn't easy being a Goatsucker," sighed Nighthawk.

"It's not such a flattering name," agreed Swift.

"Nor is it correct," wailed Nighthawk. "None of us nurse on goats. Humans tagged us with that nasty rumor, as if they knew all."

"Still, the name stuck?" asked Swift.

"It did," admitted Nighthawk. "Not that our family doesn't have its peculiarities."

"Like what?" asked Swift, darting spastically in flight, mouth open, scooping insects from the cooling air. Nighthawk's flight was smoother, silent, but just as aerobatic as he snatched bugs into his great, open mouth. His behavior seemed absolutely normal to Swift.

"I have this cousin," began Nighthawk. "He's a Poorwill," he continued, as if that was explanation enough.

"So?" said Swift.

"Well, he nests on the ground," Nighthawk ventured. "And perches on a branch lengthwise rather than across it..."

"Oh my," interrupted Swift. "That is odd. I never perch except in the rocky crags above, where I nest and sleep. Nor would I ever nest on the ground."

"No, that's not what's odd," hastened Nighthawk. "I do that too."

"Oh," said Swift, hesitantly. "I see," he muttered, with a strange roll of his eyes, a sure sign he did not.

"My cousin eats bugs," Nighthawk began again.

"What's so odd about that?" said Swift, again interrupting.

"Well," said Nighthawk, beginning to get defensive. "Listen long enough for me to tell you."

"It's time for me to be off, so be quick about it, will you?" huffed Swift.

"He hunts from the ground," Nighthawk said quickly. "He looks up for passing bugs and flies up to get them as they pass by, then lands again to wait for another."

"You mean he doesn't scoop bugs from the air in flight?"

"Not like us."

"Strange," conceded Swift.

"And he doesn't always migrate like most birds do," added Nighthawk. "I leave and go south in winter, but he stays, hides under a rock and hibernates. A bird that hibernates. Have you ever heard of such a thing? How embarrassing!"

"Well," Swift drawled slowly, indicative of offense. "As I said, I'm quite partial to rocks. And, depending on food supply, I don't always migrate either. I sleep away cold days too, when bugs are not plentiful. Perhaps I don't sleep as long and deeply as your cousin, but I can relate." He ascended to his high altitude dormitory for the night, without another word.

"Oh," replied Nighthawk, abashed.

Later, after Moonrise, Nighthawk spotted Cousin Poorwill sitting in a dirt road, waiting for dinner to arrive.

"Hello down there," called Nighthawk.

"Who? Me?" answered his cousin. "So, I'm not too weird for you to talk to anymore?"

"Turns out you're surprisingly normal," answered Nighthawk, sucking a moth down his throat. "Shockingly so."

162

Listening to Green Fly

It is said that there was once a time when Green Fly lit on the paw of Coyote pup and began to dance. He rotated his wings in amazing ways. The left one he lifted up away from his back and to his left. The right one he pressed tightly against his back, then he walked forward three paces and diagonally ten. Puppy watched in wonder.

"What is he doing?" the canine asked from where he rested in the sun.

His mother watched from the mouth of the den set into the hillside.

"He's just talking to you," she answered.

"Is he going to bite me?" asked the pup.

"No, this fly is only interested in plants, not your blood," she replied.

Green Fly was five millimeters in length and a bright spring green in color. Each of his two transparent wings sported a black dot. His wings were never still for long. They buzzed when he flew, but even sitting at rest, he was continually exercising them, twisting and turning them at odd angles.

"What's he saying?" asked Pup.

"I don't know," his mother answered. "Perhaps he's greeting you. Perhaps he's giving you advice. It's hard to say."

"Does anyone understand his language?" wondered Pup.

"Perhaps another Green Fly would; I can only guess," replied Coyote.

"Why talk when no one can understand?" asked Pup.

"Everyone wants to be heard," replied the mother. "And Green Fly is short lived, so he must hurry. In a month's time, you will not see these flies anymore. It will be another year before you observe them signaling to you, when the eggs of this generation will have hatched and matured into a spotted-wing acrobat like the one you watch today."

"How sad to live such a short time," remarked Pup.

"None of us knows how long we will live," answered Coyote. "We simply live in the best way we know how. The best way for a coyote is not the same as the best way for a green fly. Perhaps he's telling you that."

"He keeps sticking his left wing off to his left side. It's as if he's pointing in that direction. Perhaps he's telling me I will find something if I go look there."

"Maybe," his mother answered. She continued to watch as her puppy trotted across the slope in front of the den, headed left. "I wouldn't be at all surprised if adventure awaits you to the left."

"It must," Pup confirmed. "Green Fly just flew in that direction."

"Be back in time for dinner," Coyote called.

The Larger View

It is said that there was once a time when Harris hawk flew in to perch on the top of Saguaro. He surveyed the surroundings, for he was new to the area. Creosote, who spread his branches ten feet away, noticed the newcomer and spoke to him in welcome.

"Greetings," spoke the plant, from the midst of his resinous leaves, glistening in the sun.

"Hello," answered the dark hawk, after the briefest of glances down. He adjusted himself on his prickly peak and continued to scan the horizon.

"You're new, yes?" asked Creosote.

"Yes," was the monosyllabic response.

"From afar?" continued Creosote.

"Yes," answered Hawk.

"Why have you come?" asked the rooted one.

"To find a new home," answered the creature of flight.

"What can you see from up there?" asked Creosote.

With that, Harris hawk began to describe everything he could see in the most wonderful detail. Creosote was speechless and mesmerized. It seemed the hawk saw everything that moved, and all that remained unmoved. He told of the colors of far distant mountains and the creepings of ants in the hill beside Saguaro. It was wonderful what he saw from his high station. Then he told of lands he'd seen on his journey to that very Saguaro top, since leaving the land of his birth. Creosote was shocked because the initial words from the red-shouldered bird had been so few. Clearly this creature spoke from his passion for life and flying.

"Oh, how I wish I could see all that," sighed Creosote. "But I'm grounded and will never reach the heights you can."

Hawk looked at Creosote in surprise. It had never occurred to him that plants dreamed of larger perspectives. He began to consider how Creosote might be assisted to a higher view. He ruffled his feathers, the better to think.

"You are long lived, I'm told," he began. "Even longer than Saguaro."

"Yes," answered Creosote. "But how does that help?"

"You have time," said Hawk, "whereas I do not. It's a good thing I can fly to high places, for I don't have time to grow into them. You, on the other hand, can drape a limb over the young saguaro at your side, and wait for it to grow up high enough to raise your one branch until you can see distant horizons with it."

"It might work," mused Creosote. "It just might."

"Good luck," Hawk encouraged. "Wish I could know how it turns out, but that is not my fortune."

Indeed, it took fifty years before one of Creosote's branches, hooked over a small saguaro with the help of Wind, was carried aloft to its highest point by the cactus's growth. It was held securely between one of Saguaro's mighty arms and its body.

"And I'm the only one of my kind who can see the far mountains," finished Creosote, ending his story to Milkweed, who'd wrapped herself over and under half of his limbs.

"I want to see too," she declared.

"You don't have the time to rise to high places like I did," soothed Creosote.

"She doesn't need it," hummed Saguaro, as a breeze buzzed over his prickly, green skin. "She can climb up my body under her own power, just as she's crept throughout your own."

"That high?" wondered Milkweed. "It might work. It just might."

With a few years of steady effort and climbing on Milkweed's part, Saguaro supported yet another plant's larger vision of the world.

Three rooted companions, who now shared the perspective of a once-perched hawk, long vanished from Earth.

The Election of Dawn's Herald

It is said that there was once a time when birds vied for the position of Dawn's Herald. Different regions picked different birds, but in the Sonoran Desert, the two finalists were Mockingbird and Curved-billed Thrasher. Day and Night were amused by the competition. Neither of the two primary creators felt their comings and goings needed to be announced. Most of their creation agreed with them. After all, it was not likely the obvious and inevitable would escape anyone's notice for long. But the birds were keen on the competition, and what started as entertainment ended in a hotly contested battle between songsters. Mockingbird and Curved-billed Thrasher belonged to the same bird family, the Mimidae, but blood was was not thicker than winning this title.

Rumors flew faster than Wind: Mockingbird's children were hooligans and bore young indiscriminately-- Curved-billed Thrasher had once taken a bribe from Cactus Wren; tales surfaced with little regard for truth or relevancy. An election day was declared and both birds sang their hearts out everywhere around the desert, campaigning for the honor of serving as Dawn's Herald. Since only the birds took the cause seriously, they would be the only voters. They picked their representatives, who agreed to gather at South Mountain, near Phoenix, Arizona, on election day to cast their voice ballots.

"I am first to sing each morning," Mockingbird claimed. "No one sings louder than I. Sun tells me he follows the direction of my voice, lest he get lost and fail to arrive."

"My voice is no less in volume," contended Thrasher, "and is much more melodious. I am first to sing each morning, because I have been silent all Night. Mockingbird is bound to be first singer in the morning when he never shuts up--Day or Night. But after driving everyone crazy and sleepless, should he also take credit for calling Sun to rise? I think not. Vote for your right to sleep in peace. Vote for me."

The debate continued right up to election day. As the bird representatives gathered to vote, they were met by both candidates, still loudly singing their own virtues. Golden Eagle agreed to call out the names of each bird species so their representative could voice his vote, each in kind. For formality's sake, Mockingbird and Thrasher voted first--for themselves, of course. Thrasher flew to a nearby cholla where he perched amongst the thorns. He hoped voters would presume his stance to be symbolic of his capacity to endure. Mockingbird left the gathering once his vote was cast.

One by one Eagle screamed for the next vote. One by one each bird species' representative answered. Mockingbird had a decisive lead.

Then Horned Owl held out his wings to signal for silence, and Eagle paused the roll call. But the voice voting continued. Turkey Vulture, who had been circling above, policing the voting process, landed on a mesquite tree, spooking Mockingbird from his hiding place. No more would Mockingbird be imitating other bird species and voting for himself.

Curved-billed Thrasher won.

Even today, he is first to herald the dawn.

Unless Mockingbird beats him to it on account of singing all Night.

The True Home of Screech and Burrowing Owl

It is said that there was once a time when Screech Owl lived underground. He flew through the Earth as he now flies through Wind. He loved gemstones and watched over them where they were hidden in the soil. In those days of his Underworld past, he was known as a Gnome, one of a family of creatures that stood only about seven inches tall and loved the dark. They lived in tunnels and caves underground, but for all the lack of light in their world, they had a great deal within. They were very wise and good-natured, quite the pranksters, and well-known in the underworld for their dancing and ability to get along with other creatures. They hunted the jewels they adored by mining them in their tunnels, tapping with tiny pickaxes-- tap, tap, tap, tappitty--tap, tap, tap, tappitty. They were also very curious creatures, but none more so than the Gnomes with wings. They could simply travel faster than their brethren, almost as fast as their imaginations. So when they heard stories from Tortoise and Antelope Squirrel about the world above, their inquisitive natures began to lead them off down this new path of discovery. They just had to see this Upperworld for themselves. They were cautious enough, however, that they chose one of their number to be the first to make the journey, to pave the way for the rest.

Antelope Squirrel was about the same size as First Gnome, so he guided the creature of the dark through his winding tunnels to an entrance beneath protective Creosote's twisting branches, where they could enter the world of light unobserved. Antelope Squirrel crept from his hole, peering through Creosote's leaves for any danger.

First Gnome followed, but Sun's light blinded him so severely that he screeched in pain. He screeched and screeched, never adjusting to the light, as Antelope Squirrel had expected. Desperate to conceal the whereabouts of his burrow from possible predators, Antelope Squirrel finally pushed the squealing Gnome back underground, where he did eventually cease his wailing.

"Well, that certainly went smoothly," panted Antelope Squirrel sarcastically. He was winded from pushing the flailing, screaming Gnome down the tunnel several feet until darkness spared the poor creature's eyes.

"I'm sorry," apologized First Gnome. "I never imagined it would be so awful." His eyes streamed tears. "I guess that's the end of that dream. Gnomes will never be able to tolerate Sun's light. We'll never mingle with the creatures of the Upperworld, only those who live in both, as you do."

"I'm sorry too," said Antelope Squirrel, contrite now for his earlier sarcasm. He didn't doubt First Gnome's pain. He was actually more shocked and embarrassed than anything else. "I really thought your eyes could adjust. Mine do. I have to blink a few times when I first come out, but then I'm OK."

"Mine didn't ever recover. I was totally blind. And even worse--the burning and pain never stopped," assured First Gnome. He started considering options. He hated to give up his dream and the dream of his people. "I wonder if I can shield my eyes somehow. Maybe there's another way I can see the Upperworld."

"Can you hide your eyes with your wings?" asked Antelope Squirrel.

First Gnome tucked in his neck and hunched his shoulders and wings to cover his eyes. Then he slowly progressed toward the tunnel's doorway. He stood there a few moments, gazing out of squinty eyes through his feathers and the additional shielding of Creosote's leaves. His eyes watered, but he wasn't in pain. He saw enough to convince him of the worthiness of his cause. He watched Coyote trot by. He saw Man tending his distant fields of crops; he saw Centipede undulate past. This convinced him that wonders abounded above, and he had to find a way to open this world up to all Gnomes.

He crept back to where Antelope Squirrel waited in the dark tunnel.

"I could see if I covered my eyes," he reported, "but it's not much use to me if I can't fly around in the daylight."

"You could walk," suggested Antelope Squirrel.

"Not fast enough," said First Gnome. "I'm used to flying. I can't move very quickly if I've got to hold my wings over my eyes. It's too awkward."

"What then?" asked Antelope Squirrel. "How else can you protect your eyes? What else have you got that you can see through, but will block enough light that your eyes don't burn?"

"I wonder," said First Gnome as he reached into his pack. He pulled out two stones he had mined from Earth earlier in the week. They were two pieces of lovely amber. He placed them over his eyes, where they fit perfectly, and walked to the tunnel's entrance. The Upperworld now had a golden glow to it, but he could see without pain. He turned and came back to Antelope Squirrel.

"These work fine out in the light, but I can't see you in the dark now. Here I'm blind."

First Gnome tried to remove the amber so he could see without light again, but they wouldn't come off.

"Oh no," said Antelope Squirrel. "How will you go back to your friends? How will you tell them what you've seen or go back to live with them again?"

"It looks like I can't," admitted First Gnome. "You'll have to tell them for me. My desire to see this new world has prevented me from ever going back. Tell them about the amber. Tell them if they use it, they can't return to the Underworld. Maybe, though, some of them will choose to join me in exile and help me explore this new world. I hope so, at any rate. I don't want to be here alone."

Antelope Squirrel scampered back to the other Gnomes while First Gnome explored the Upperworld, staying close enough to the hole so as to watch for Antelope Squirrel to come back.

He spoke with Black-throated Sparrow, who told him about flying through air and demonstrated his technique. First Gnome gave it a shot and found it similar to flying underground, so before long he was practicing takeoffs and landings like a pro.

"You fly very well," Black-throated Sparrow twittered. "Much more swiftly than I," he admitted begrudgingly. "But your eyes--they're...well, strange. Almost hypnotizing. They remind me of Horned Owl's."

"My eyes are the result of living in the Underworld," First Gnome told him. "Because of them, I can't go back."

"What happened?" asked Black-throated Sparrow.

But just then Antelope Squirrel appeared. He told First Gnome he'd discussed his dilemma with his village and they had all chosen to come to the Upperworld with him. They were even now searching for amber to cover their own eyes and expected to join him in the time it took a Palo Verde tree seed to sprout and grow roots three inches long. Some other Gnomes without wings wanted to come too. They were outfitting their eyes with amber in order to do so. They would band together and make their own way in the Upperworld, living as Antelope Squirrel did, partly underground and partly above. First Gnome waited for them all to arrive. Black-throated Sparrow did not. He was a little unnerved by the whole amber-eye-thing.

First Gnome experienced his first twilight, night, and dawning while he waited. Antelope Squirrel explained the drama as evening fell, to the best of his ability, but he knew experience would be the best teacher. He curled up to nap while his friend practiced getting about in his new world.

First Gnome continued to practice his flight skills. He found the night to be kind on his eyes; light from stars and Moon was just enough for him to see and his ears helped guide him as well, for he listened to Wind in trees, crickets crawling through sand and mice skittering through dry grass. That was almost better than seeing. Best of all, though, was twilight and dawning. That lighting was perfect for his vision's comfort. Full daylight was still a bit difficult, even with the amber shades, so he decided to sleep by day, fly about by night, waking just often enough to see who was moving about in the Sun's rays, thus satisfying his curiosity about his new neighbors.

Antelope Squirrel awoke at First Gnome's first dawn and said, "What are you going to call yourself?"

"What do you mean?" asked First Gnome.

"Well, you're not really a Gnome anymore. Gnomes live underground and you can't see there now, so you're stuck in the Upperworld forever. You need a new name to go with a new world."

"I guess that's true," acknowledged First Gnome. "I hadn't thought about it, but I can't be a Gnome ever again, so it is time for a new name. Black-throated Sparrow said my eyes were like Horned Owl's. Do you think so?"

"Yeah," Antelope Squirrel nodded, then shuddered. "He'd eat me if he could, which I hope you'll never do, but there is a resemblance. You could pass for an owl."

"Rest assured, you're too big for me to hunt," chuckled First Gnome. "I promise to stick to small rodents, moths and scorpions; will that suit you?"

"Perfectly," sighed Antelope Squirrel, pleased he would not be losing his friend now that he lived in the Upperworld. Then he laughed. "I can't forget how you bellowed when you first saw light. I never knew you could screech so loudly. Call yourself Screech Owl. That suits you."

"Embarrassing, but true," admitted First Gnome. So the name stuck.

When his village arrived, shortly thereafter, he introduced them to the name and the new world at the same time.

One family of winged-Gnomes chose not to leave the Underworld completely. They agreed to live in burrows, yet still flew with Screech Owls at night. Their legs grew longer, since they spent more time walking. They developed their own language. They retained their Gnomish proclivity for dancing and intelligence. They even got along with Man, though many wild animals found that difficult. Their name was Burrowing Owl.

Those who stayed with First Gnome used a number of sounds to communicate with one another, but their main call, heard often during full-Moon-nights and their favorite hours--those of twilight and predawn--was an imitation of the noise they made underground while mining the gems they so loved and which now covered their eyes. The tap, tap, tap, tappitty of their picks in their mines was now their call. Other creatures thought it sounded like a stone bouncing downhill, but Screech Owls knew otherwise.

Screech Owls also retained their intelligence and phenomenal ability to get along with other creatures, including Man. They began stopping by to visit at dusk or dawn, and nesting in Saguaro cavities near Man's homes. They still danced too, bobbing and weaving to tunes they alone heard as they spoke with Man.

Gnomes these owls could never again become, but Gnome-like they remained--in memory of the Underworld, their first home.

From Pod to Prongs

It is said that there was once a time when Unicorn Plant longed to travel. Being a plant was such a stationary existence. Oh, sometimes his leaves and branches bobbled in a breeze, but that was all the moving around he could manage. He envied Rabbit. He envied Hawk. He envied Bumble Bee. He envied Skunk--sometimes. All these could roam where they chose. He could only watch.

He wanted to speak with Day and Night, the two primary creators, to see if he might not change his lifestyle and become more mobile, but he couldn't even seek them out without help. He was forced to ask Wind to lend his energy to the cause, which Wind was glad to do. An afternoon of Wind's gusting about brought Unicorn Plant the answer his heart desired. Day and Night would meet with him.

Now, Unicorn Plant was named for the seed pod he produced. The purple/pink flowers he sported were an inch and a half long, and nearly an inch wide. They were a showy, tube-like creation with four lobes and a yellow runway showing bees just where the pollen was stored, for efficient fertilization. This lack of subtlety ensured there would always be lots of seed pods in season. The pods were pretty dramatic too. They were often a foot long, very hairy and sticky, and curved like a scimitar, thick at the base, but pointed at the tip. These would dry, burst, and scatter an abundance of crinkly seeds. Before breaking apart, though, the pods were long, horn-like affairs which reminded someone of the mythical horse's, hence the name.

Upon the arrival of Day and Night, greetings were exchanged; then they got to the business at hand. When it came to making changes in creatures, Night tended toward conservatism. She hated to radically alter anything once the original pattern was established. She worried over whether modifications might ruin the creature's fit into the rest of its world. She had a reputation for trying to talk complainers into changing their perceptions about themselves rather than their actual physical selves. Day tended to just say "no." He was a tad protective of his authority figure status. Nevertheless, he had come, hadn't he? Unicorn Plant knew what he would be up against in this conference with his creators. Wind had coached him.

"I want to move," Unicorn Plant pleaded. "It's so boring being rooted to one spot. All I can see from here is all I'll ever see. How about some wings like hummingbirds, or feet like a centipede?"

True to form, Night placated by reminding Unicorn Plant of his lovely blossoms and distinctive seeds and pods. He was already one of the hairiest plants around, rivaling (sort of) the mammals who munched his seed pods so appreciatively. How would they eat if he was off strolling around and they couldn't find him. Didn't they leave enough pods to dry and drop seed for the following summer's generation? How could he callously abandon them to dry, stick-in-the-throat grasses and bursage?

Unicorn Plant countered with: "But if I had wings, I could scatter my own seed much wider and farther, making more plants for mice and squirrels to nibble."

Also true to form, Day said, "Forget the wings. There's more to flying than wings and you're not cut out for it. Just do the job you were made for and be glad you're alive. You've already got the advantage of flowers with their own landing strip to guide in the critters whose wings you so admire. I say, leave the wings on the bees and stop dreaming. We put a lot of effort into designing you, but you don't seem to appreciate that, do you?"

Night soothed Day by reminding him that he didn't know what it meant to be rooted while longing to see the world. Probably they had made Unicorn Plant too intelligent and sensitive for planthood. They owed it to him to work out their differences, to at least hear his concerns.

Unicorn Plant nodded.

Day sighed. "Fine, but wings are out, and the roots stay. Maybe your seeds could be attached to puffy things so they'd fly," he suggested. "Then they could still scatter far and wide. Part of you'd travel. You'd like that, wouldn't you?"

"I guess I'd like knowing my seeds get to roam, even if I don't," acquiesced the plant. "If that's the best you can do."

"Why can't you just talk to Wind? He knows of far off places. Ask the insects and birds that visit your flowers about the sights they've seen," Day backstepped.

"It's not the same," Unicorn Plant pouted.

"No, it's not," Night agreed. "But your seeds and pods are so unique I'd hate to totally redesign them. The pods give you your name, after all. Why don't we think how to modify them a little less drastically. Your seeds are too heavy and oily to fly. They're so singularly black and wrinkled as they are. What a shame to lose that for the sake of forcing flight on them. Surely we can move them around some other way."

"How?" asked Day and Unicorn Plant in unison.

"I don't know," Night replied. "Can't you tweak the pods for travel?" she asked Day. "If they were stronger, they could blow around in the breeze before splitting open and spread the seed that way."

Day liked "tweaking," actually. He started to see possibilities. "We could reinforce the structure under the pod's fleshy coating with a hard fiber. Something woody perhaps."

178

"Too heavy to blow on a breeze," Wind inserted. "That'd take a real storm."

Everyone turned to stare at him.

"Well, it would," he insisted. "I know I wasn't asked my advice, but isn't it better coming now than after you've screwed up?"

"If he's going to be part of the plan," Night allowed, "he should be part of the planning."

Wind winked conspiratorially at Unicorn Plant. "Beef up the pods," he suggested, "but leave me out of spreading them. Then weight isn't an issue."

"If you're out of the plan, you're out of the planning," announced Day.

"Oh, come on," groaned Wind. "You're stuck here. You need my input. What about burrs?"

"I like the seeds as they are," Night stated flatly. "NO burrs."

"We could make the pod the burr," Wind said.

"We?" Day countered.

"Okay, you," Wind answered. "I forgot--'If I'm out of the plan, I'm out of the planning.' I'm gone." He winked at Unicorn Plant as he left.

"It'd be an awfully large and heavy burr," Night thought aloud.

"For the usual small, multiple stickers," agreed Day. "But how about if the pod's reinforcement held the seeds, and split when the pod dried and burst. After the pod's flesh fell away, you'd be left with a woody interior, split open to spill the seeds, and two-pronged, curved, pointed tips. Work those tips toward each other, and we've got pinchers Scorpion would envy. When that seed case fastens onto a passing animal, it'll carry seed off everywhere. Not just seeds, but pods would be well traveled. No wings, no feet, but grappling hooks the like of which no other plant

179

has. What do you say to that?" Day leaned close to Unicorn Plant in his eagerness to make the changes.

"It's still unique," encouraged Night. "Though once the pod's wood ruptures, the twin prongs take away from that 'unicorn horn appearance.' Perhaps you'd consider a name change too?"

"To what?" asked Unicorn Plant.

"How about Devil's Claw," moaned Bighorn Sheep, already sporting an ankle bracelet of two pods.

"Works for me," the creators assented.

"Me too," agreed Wind.

"You still here?" asked Day.

"Looked like you were finished, so I thought I'd drop by to chat with Devil's Claw here," Wind parried.

"We are finished," said Night. "We'll be leaving now."

"We played that well," said Night to Day as they left. "We didn't do wings or feet."

"Stayed true to the original idea," agreed Day.

"We played that well," said Wind to the plant, as they watched their creators leave.

"I still wish I could do the roving," sighed Devil's Claw, "but I'll settle for part of me getting the grand tour, if not all of me."

"Hey, you got Day and Night to make adjustments, and you're still named for your novel seed pods," reminded Wind.

"There is that," agreed Devil's Claw. "There is that."

Tropical Buckeye's Covenant

It is said that once there was a time when the People forgot that life and death were not separate, but one and the same. They saw existence as a struggle, a struggle to maintain life and avoid death. Methods and modes beyond number were developed to keep the people alive and deny death, no matter what the quality of life. Fear of dying guided their decisions, their understanding of life and what it might be for. One thing they knew...life was to be maintained at all costs.

Some of the People began to question just what was meant by "life," but the predominant way of thinking was that life was anti-death and death was anti-life. Even thinking about death was not considered life-enhancing or healthy. That was negative thinking, and negativity was not "good." It was "bad." It was not possible for "bad" to be of any "good." It was always bad. The People were locked into "either/or" thinking. They had forgotten the oneness of all things.

Night reflected upon this situation. As part of the feminine creative force, she helped birth and destroy creation. She knew increase and decrease to be two halves of one circle of life. She wondered aloud how to symbolize this to the People in order to help them understand.

Day heard her musings and concurred that symbols should be made. He suggested they might consult with creatures already available to find those who would agree to portray the truth of the oneness of life and death.

One of the first to agree to reflect this truth to the People was a butterfly.

"I already demonstrate this in my transformation from one form to another," Butterfly reminded his creators.

"I die to my caterpillar self so as to become a butterfly. I'd be happy to be remade in a form that better symbolizes life's continuity."

"I'll help where I can," Day said, "but Night, you and Butterfly take the lead in this project. Night, you are darkness, and death is associated with black and darkness. Lead on, my lady. Lead on faithful Butterfly."

So the remodeling began.

Night removed the bright colors from the butterfly's wings, leaving him black as herself. Butterfly was a little startled by the change, but suddenly remembered that he had a role in his recreation too.

"I recommend four marks," the butterfly said. "The marks shall represent the four directions that comprise the circle of life--north, south, east and west. They can also represent the four seasons of a annual cycle."

"Agreed," said Night. "What color?"

"How about red?" asked Butterfly.

"Great! One of my personal favorites," said Day enthusiastically.

"Where?" Night asked, chuckling at his eagerness.

"How about the top of the fore wings?" Day said thoughtfully.

"Good," said Night.

Day marked four red marks on the black fore wings of Butterfly, near the top, two on each side. They looked like quotation marks enclosing the insect's body.

"Next let's consider circles, two on the hind wings and one on the fore wings, each representing the circle of life. The six circles together can depict the four directions--plus two-- up and down. And let's have shadings of dark blue within each circle to represent the stirrings of new life over Water," Night thought aloud.

"Lovely," agreed the butterfly.

"Indeed," chorused Day.

182

"Now red and green ripples at the edges of my wings to represent the path of life through all these directions," suggested Butterfly.

Day etched in the requested markings and stood back to admire their work.

"Stunning," he announced in wonder.

"Beautiful," Night agreed.

"Leave the underside of my wings a mottled jumble of browns," continued Butterfly. He alone remembered there was another side of his wings that needed marking. "That way when the people look at me with my wings closed, they'll think me quite plain and dull. Then, when I open my wings they'll be all the more astounded."

"Very smart," agreed Night.

She and Day added the tones of Earth to the underside of Butterfly's wings.

"I thank you, Butterfly, for offering yourself as the People's reminder that death holds the promise of continued life and that it is, therefore, nothing to fear. Once they make peace with their own deaths, they will be able to live life more fully. You are the beautiful symbol of that truth."

"It is my privilege," bowed Butterfly, now Tropical Buckeye Butterfly. Away he flew to sip monkeyflower blossoms and work his magic in the hearts of the People.

"One of our finest," said Day as he watched Butterfly go.

"But certainly not our last," reminded Night, and the two turned to the next creative venture.

Tropical Buckeye is one of the creatures with whom we share the desert, a constant reminder of the relationship of life and death.

How Ruby-Crowned Kinglet Broke Winter

It is said that there was once a time when Winter held sway over the pine forest. All hope of Spring's return froze and powdered like the dusting snow, blown away in the next gust of wind to moan through the frosted conifer needles.

The desert lands to the south were warming. Sun coaxed buds on tree limbs, and annuals lifted first leaves above the soil in search of light. But the mountainous north remained firmly in Winter's grip. The pine forests and all within them despaired. Endurance leaked away.

Sun tried to shed light into the forest, to remind everyone that warmer weather would come, a message of promise and cheer, but snow-bearing clouds marched relentlessly across the surface of Earth, snagging on the mountains for days on end. Very little sunlight broke through. What did was too lost in the freezing atmosphere to hint of any warmth.

Sun sensed the mood of despondency enfolding the forest and sought a messenger who could penetrate Winter's fastness with a morsel of hope for those within.

Kinglet, an olive-grey bird with two white wing bars and an incomplete white eye ring, hovered at the yellowish flowering catkins of cottonwood trees. Only four inches long, when he hovered, plucking small insects attracted to the tree's blossoms, he seemed so like a hummingbird that Sun had to take a second look to identify the tiny bird.

Having recognized Kinglet, Sun considered his attributes, deciding whether he had what it took to infiltrate Winter's realm to the north. Kinglet was so small he was likely not to attract Winter's attention. Not only that, but Kinglet bred in pine forests, spending only Winter's months in the mesquite

184

and cottonwood forests of the desert waterways. He would be heading north soon anyway, to stake out a territory and find a mate. He was perfect for carrying a message from Sun, but what form should it take?

Sun confronted Kinglet and asked his assistance.

"I don't like cold, snowy Winter," rattled Kinglet in short bursts, sounding very much like a sewing machine. "That's why I'm here. How could I survive?"

"You would need extra energy," conceded Sun thoughtfully. "I've plenty of that and could surely give you some."

He touched Kinglet on the top of his head and kept his ray there until Kinglet's crown grew red with heat.

"Ouch," squealed Kinglet, squirming away from Sun's burning ray. He scratched his head to conceal the reddened feathers.

"Sorry," apologized Sun, "but how do you feel? Any stronger?"

Kinglet felt so jazzed he could not sit still. He flitted from branch to branch, unable to perch and converse for any length of time. He couldn't seem to stop flitting his wings and darting from branch to branch and tree to tree. Amazed at the change, he reported that he felt ready to fly to the northern tundra, if need be.

Sun chuckled, then hid behind a flowing cadre of clouds to test Kinglet's newly acquired energy. Kinglet cooled a tad in the temperature drop, but, following Sun's instructions, he focused on the red spot in the center-top of his head, and found a reserve of Sun's heat that helped him stay warm. He quickly learned to rejuvenate by plugging into his own private heat lamp.

"Totally, totally, totally grand," burst Kinglet, exposing his red cap with pride.

"Now your name must be changed to reflect your new markings. How about Ruby-Crowned Kinglet? And, we still need to craft a message--something small so as not to overburden you in your journey, but obvious enough to inspire hope in all who observe you." Sun examined the tiny soon-to-be-interloper.

Tiny yellow claws caught his attention.

"Why are your feet yellow?" Sun asked.

Ruby-Crowned Kinglet looked down. "Oh, must have brushed them up against the Cottonwood flowers while I hovered grabbing gnats."

"The golden pollen on your feet can be the sign you deliver to the creatures locked in Winter that southern climes are already in blossom and soon north shall be delivered too."

"That's certainly no burden," shrugged Ruby-Crowned Kinglet. "So be it."

And it was.

Ruby-Crowned Kinglet zipped northward, pausing only to sip dew from leaves and tiny insects from the air.

When he reached his frozen breeding grounds, the Ponderosa Pine on which he alighted noticed Kinglet's coating of foot pollen and asked its source. Hearing Winter's hold had already been broken in the lowlands, the tree reported the good news to his neighbors with every breeze sighing in his boughs. Word spread--of Spring's approach and Ruby-Crowned Kinglet's new heat source. The wonder of it must have shattered Winter's confidence, or so the forest creatures surmised later, for that very same day the cloudy skies delivered rain rather than snow and sleet, causing Ponderosa Pine to dream of running sap and golden sunlight.

Hearing Ruby-Crowned Kinglet sing his territorial song, his notice to Sun that the message of Spring was delivered and all was well, Sun nodded approval.

Clouds still hugged the mountains for now, but not for long. Spring was on its way.

How Coachwhip Got His Tail and Name

It is said that there was a time when Coachwhip had a completely ordinary tail. It was no different than the reddish-brown-rest-of-him, certainly no matter of distinction. But then, it never occurred to Coachwhip that his tail should be a matter of distinction.

Rattlesnake--now there was a snake with a fine and wondrous tail. Coachwhip didn't envy Rattlesnake, though, for Coachwhip had far finer and more wondrous speed than Rattlesnake. Rattlesnake needed his tail to warn away danger. Rattlesnake needed his venomous bite to paralyze his prey and defend himself from enemies. Rattlesnake was big and bulky, and had to hunt at night, for daytime temperatures were too much for him. In contrast, Coachwhip was a svelte snake, infinitely faster, and needed neither Rattlesnake's tail nor venom to make his way in the world. His lightning speed allowed him to outrun his prey. His sleek shape let him climb trees. His ability to endure higher temperatures let him hunt by day, when he could hunt by sight as well as smell. No, he envied Rattlesnake not at all. Let Rattlesnake have the notoriety of a special tail.

But Fate had different plans.

One day Coachwhip climbed a mesquite tree to reach a nest he saw swaying in the lower branches. Coachwhip liked eating baby birds, and he climbed hoping the Verdin babies were home in their ball-shaped nest with its side entrance.

After casing the nest, he decided they must have recently fledged and were gone practicing their flying skills

and learning to pluck bugs off tree leaves in order to fend
for themselves one day. Their scent was still very strong in
their tiny cave of a nest, but no one was home.
Disappointed, he slowly slithered over the branches and to
the trunk of the tree.

Now, one of the hazards of hunting by day is that
plenty of other hunters are out then too. Coachwhip was
spotted by two Harris hawks perched in a nearby saguaro.
They watched him make his way down the tree's trunk.
Just as he reached the ground, one hawk struck with its
talons. The bird's sharp claws grasped mostly thin air, for
Coachwhip had seen the shadow of the stooping hawk
approach and zipped toward a gopher hole under a nearby
creosote bush. His tail, though, did not avoid the razor-like
talons. It was split in two as the hawk tried to snatch him
up before he could dash down the gopher hole.

Just as the first hawk was foiled, the second hawk
struck. Harris hawks frequently hunt together, one flushing
the prey for the other. Coachwhip never saw the second
hawk coming, and felt his tail caught up once again, this
time in the beak of the dark brown hunter.

Halfway down the hole, he strained to hold on to
roots so as not to be pulled back out to a certain death.
Coachwhip thrashed and fought with all his might. He felt
his tail shredding even more in the savage tug-of-war, but a
flip-flop-jerk maneuver, plus the slipperiness of his own
blood, caused the hawk to lose its hold, and Coachwhip
made good his escape down the burrow.

Thankfully, it was empty. There he waited out the
day, slipping in and out of shock, until night fell and he felt
sure the hawks would be gone. The long strips of his
shredded tail began to bleed again as soon as he moved.
Blood and soil mixed to cover the raw flesh of each strip.
Scales still covered one side of each tether-like strip, but
Coachwhip could not think how he would staunch the flow

of blood when each sandy inch he slithered along raked his wounds open again. Since the last seven inches of his tail were shredded, you can imagine his pain when he tried to move.

He was weak from blood loss. In despair, he crawled to the cover of a large rock, thinking it would perhaps offer some shade during the day ahead, the day he would surely die.

"What or who is blocking my door?" a thin, dry voice complained from somewhere beneath the snake. Coachwhip was too exhausted to answer. He felt something against his side, tickling in its attempt to push him out of the way. Then, surrendering to his greater weight and size, it tunneled below him to exit its burrow.

With an upheaval of the sand along his flank, Coachwhip watched Giant Hairy Scorpion crawl into the open. At the same time the arachnid turned to inspect his rearranged doorstep and saw the snake stretched alongside the rock. Even in the dark, he knew the snake was in trouble, for he could see the snake's uncharacteristically limp muscles. When a prod of his pincered pedipalps produced no response in the reptile, Giant Hairy Scorpion went on a tour of inspection. He traveled the length of the snake to its head.

"What's up with you? What happened? Why aren't you moving?" asked Scorpion in a scratchy voice that creaked like the sand he strode across.

"Too weak," moaned Coachwhip. With that he slipped into unconsciousness.

"Must be BAD," muttered Scorpion, retracing his steps down the snake's length and continuing on to his tail. "Ooooh, there's the damage. What a mess! Look at those long, dangling ribbons of scales and flesh, oozing with muddy blood. Gross! Wonder how this happened? Well, whatever the cause, if I want my burrow back, I'm going to

189

have to get this snake out of here. That means dressing this wound so Snake stops bleeding and heals. But how?"

Giant Hairy Scorpion carefully scratched the top of his head with the tip of his tail. How, indeed?

Using his pincers, he gently untangled the mangled scraps of Coachwhip's tail. The snake moaned and inadvertently twitched his tail, causing an involuntary hissing, unconscious as he was. Scorpion waited for the snake to relax again, then he restraightened the fragments of tail, taking each to its full length. This time, Coachwhip remained still.

Next Scorpion tried to figure how he could bind all the ribbons of flesh and scales together. They would have to be bound together, somehow, in order to heal in one piece.

"Creosote resin," Scorpion thought aloud. "Maybe I can chew up some of that and use it to hold the tail together." After asking Creosote for fresh resin and getting permission to use all he wanted, Scorpion chewed what he needed from the plant's green leaves and spit it into Coachwhip's wounds. There it mingled with the blood and sand and could not hold the wet, blackened strips of flesh together.

In desperation, Scorpion grasped two strips of tail in his pincers and wound them together. They held. Inspired, he remembered the bird nest he found the summer before, blown from a tree by the high winds and pelting rain of a storm. He remembered how the grasses had been woven together so well that the nest kept its form long after it hit the ground. He decided to try weaving the strips of Coachwhip's tail together. It might look strange, but it would give him a chance to heal--a chance he wouldn't have otherwise.

After some experimentation, Scorpion developed a method of passing the strips of tail over and under one another, braiding the pieces together. Afterward, he chewed creosote resin and caulked the seams of his creation until the bleeding stopped.

By this time, dawn was silvering the horizon, and Scorpion was so tired he could hardly work his pincers. He had to rest. Final inspection of his handiwork could wait.

Throughout the day both snake and scorpion slept as if dead, hugging the shade of the rock. When Sun erased the shade in his march across the sky, the snake and scorpion both groggily awoke and moved around the rock to the new shady spot.

Twilight caused Scorpion to begin his customary waking ritual, stretching his legs and claws, arching his tail, all in preparation for a night of active hunting. As he stirred, he noticed that Coachwhip no longer blocked the entrance to his burrow.

"Thank goodness for that!" he exclaimed. "I don't like camping out in the open. I'm just lucky no enemy spotted me today." He examined his patient, still sleeping. The tail was thinner than it had been, not surprising with all the trauma it had seen, but the resined edges were smooth, and now blackened with dried blood. It was holding well, and looked quite nice, actually. Giant Hairy Scorpion was rather pleased with himself. "Not bad work at all, in the dark of night and faced with an emergency." Satisfied, he scuttled off for a well-deserved meal.

It was not until the next morning that Coachwhip began to stir and show some intention of taking his leave. Stiff and sore, he slithered his head around to examine his tail. It still throbbed, but looked quite novel. He liked it. It hurt terribly, but when he carefully lifted it from the desert floor, it all held together, something he hardly dared hope for.

Giant Hairy Scorpion had already returned from his night's hunt and gone to bed before the sun rose. He heard the rasp of the snake's scales as he moved on the sand. He stuck his head out of his burrow and said, "Don't do too much right away. Take it slowly. Give it another day or two to knit, and I think you'll be fine."

"It's beautiful work," marveled Coachwhip.

"Yes, it is," agreed Scorpion, "so don't mess it up."

"I won't. But how can I thank you?" Coachwhip flicked his tongue as he spoke.

"Just don't eat me," answered Scorpion.

"Deal," announced Coachwhip.

Coachwhip was as good as his word.

His tail healed into a wonderful braided pattern, etched in black. All his descendents inherited the pattern as a reminder to watch out for Harris hawks hunting in pairs.

Much later, when Man and Horse came to the desert, Man noticed the snake's tail pattern resembled his own braided horse whips and called the snake "Coachwhip."

This is how Coachwhip got his tail--and how his tail got him his name.

How Blue and Yellow Palo Verde Were Made

It is said that there was once a time when rising Moon and setting Sun glared at each other from their respective horizons.

"They're at it again," quipped Wind, unwinding after a busy afternoon of dust devilling.

"What's it over this time?" Creosote asked his old friend.

"Moon says Sun got too much say in designing Palo Verde. She's mad she wasn't consulted," Wind shrugged.

"How do you hear all this gossip?" marveled Creosote. "I'd know nothin' short of nothin' if I didn't know you."

"Ohhhh, I get around," Wind answered with playful evasiveness. "It comes of not having roots."

"Point taken," sighed Creosote. "So lay the whole story on me, why don't cha?"

"Well," said Wind conspiratorially, "the way I heard it--and I got it from Cloud, who heard it from Rain, who heard it from Earth, who heard the whole thing as Palo Verde was first being planted in her--Day and Night were keen on making a new beetle. Don't ask me why; I think we've enough of them already, but...some weird name...what was it? Oh, yeah, Bruchid, I think. A Bruchid beetle hatchling needed something to eat and Day wanted to let it eat the seeds of a new variety of tree, so he and Sun started working on Palo Verde."

"What about Night?" asked Creosote. "Doesn't she get ticked off when something new gets made and she doesn't get any input?"

"Oh, she was right there," Wind replied. "My guess is she was a little distracted. She likes to go with black beetles, but Day talked her into allowing bright colors. Some varieties are part-black, though, and I think she was busy focusing on how to paint them. Day called over Sun to help with Palo Verde, but Night forgot to call Moon."

"Usually those two ladies stick together," observed Creosote.

"I know. But, like I said, I think Night was still working on the beetles and didn't realize how far along Day and Sun had gotten in developing Palo Verde," continued Wind. "She didn't notice what was going on until they were almost done."

"What had they done?" asked Creosote. "Had they left anything up to Night?"

"Not much, though she did give it her approval. It was only afterwards, when Moon heard Palo Verde was being planted and confronted Night, that she had second thoughts and insisted they all have another go at it."

"What do you mean 'another go' if Palo Verde was already finished?" asked Creosote.

"Moon, with Night's backing, insisted they start over on another Palo Verde."

"What about the Palo Verde already in the ground?" asked Creosote.

"They let that remain. They made a whole new kind altogether," explained Wind.

"Two Palo Verdes?" asked Creosote.

"Two varieties, yeah," answered Wind. "The first kind is a darker green. You've heard how they made it so most of the tree is green and can use Sun's light to make food even without leaves, like in the dead of winter, or times of drought?"

"I heard it just now," said Creosote.

194

"Well," said Wind, amazed at how thoroughly his friend was left out of the information loop, "in addition, the first kind grows tall quickly. It's located along water drainages for the greater dampness there. It lives around forty years or so...."

"Is that all?" interrupted long-lived Creosote.

"That's it," replied Wind. "Most importantly, and I think this is where Moon got so upset, the flower is entirely Sun's design. It has five petals, with one being larger than the rest. All the petals are bright-Sun-soaked-yellow and the largest also sports bright orange spots. Moon was fit to be tied until they all agreed to make another tree, very much like the first one, but with noticeable differences."

"Like what?" prompted Creosote, eager to hear more about these newcomer trees.

"The second tree is more drought resistant," Wind went on. "It doesn't get quite as tall and grows much more slowly. That means it can inhabit hillsides rather than just washes. Its water needs are less. Then too, " he said, as Creosote nodded to indicate his continuing interest, "it's not as dark a green as the first one, as if the color drained from the flower somehow went into the bark."

"How so?" wondered Creosote.

"I'm told Moon insisted on a flower that was the same shape as the first Palo Verde's, but a duller yellow, and that the larger petal be pure white, like her in her glory," said Wind.

"Sounds pretty," said Creosote. "Though I've never regretted that my flowers are all yellow."

"Yeah," chuckled Wind. "Wonder where Moon was when you were made!"

Creosote shrugged.

"Anyway," Wind sighed, "the second tree lives longer too--over a hundred years. It also blooms a little later than the first Palo Verde, in deference to the first tree's place in creation. "

"I can't wait to meet them," said Creosote.

"You will soon, I'm sure," said Wind. "They're being planted all over the desert."

"Are both kinds just called Palo Verde?" asked Creosote.

"The first is now Blue Palo Verde and the second is Yellow. I think they'll both answer to Palo Verde, though."

"So why is Moon still peeved with Sun?" asked Creosote. "She got her new tree."

"It's the principle of the thing," shrugged Wind. "She still can't believe they made Blue Palo Verde without her."

"But isn't that Night's fault too?" asked Creosote. "Why isn't Moon mad at Night?"

"I guess they worked it out," said Wind. "Besides, Night's her superior. Sun's her peer. Which would you prefer?" he continued. "To have 'issues' with, your superior or your peer?"

"Point taken," admitted Creosote. "Better to have 'issues' with a peer. Much safer."

"I don't think Sun will forget her next time," Wind grinned.

"Or Night either," added Creosote.

"Hush, she'll hear us," whispered Wind, watching Moon trail across the sky towards them.

"Mum's the word," murmured Creosote, settling down to sleep.

A Black-headed Grosbeak's Motherly Advice

It is said that there was once a time when a mother Black-headed Grosbeak was preparing to depart for her species' wintering grounds in Mexico. Her mate had already been gone two weeks. He assisted diligently in rearing the young until late July, when adult males flew south to establish territories in warmer forests. Now was her turn to go. In a week or so, her first-year son would follow, with all the other youngsters of his kind.

The breeding season just past had been rough. Only one of her three offspring had survived. He was growing up quite nicely and already knew where to find food and how to fend for himself passably well. He was beginning to develop his song too, which would have a great deal to do with his ability to attract females in another year. Until then, he would first need to survive the trip south, traveling on her verbal instructions alone, since she would not be there to guide him. Her kind had migrated this way since the beginning. First the males, then the females, lastly the young. Clearly, each year's fledglings were more ready than their parents ever thought to travel alone, but since he was her one and only this year, she was more anxious than usual that she fill him in on everything he would need to know to make it to Mexico and through the winter to his adulthood.

After telling him which route to take, which landmarks to watch for, where seeds and insects were likely to be found as he crossed the deserts, she began to coach him on the forests of Mexico, completely unknown territory to him, and the insect food he should seek there for his continuing healthy development into maturity.

197

"Right now you look very much like me," she began, pointing with her beak toward their reflections in the bird bath upon which they both stood. "You have my head striping, brown back and wings. But by next spring you'll have your father's appearance. You'll have his fine black head and orange neck, chest and flanks. Your wings and back will turn black like his. You already have white in your wings and tail, as he and I do. The underside of your wings is already dull yellow, and your flanks are showing some orange, but you must finish your transformation in Mexico. That's where you'll find and eat an abundance of one particular insect that will ensure you mature to the perfect male specimen you are meant to be. This will be impossible, though, if you don't eat the proper diet. Do you understand?"

Her son nodded nervously. There had been so much information to memorize in the last few days that he was feeling brain-drained. What if he forgot the landmarks that would guide him to the home in the desert where seed and water was available, where he could stay a week and build up fat and strength to continue the trip south? What if he got lost in the city where his mother had told him he should look for a golf course where there was a pond with plenty of beetles, dragonflies and other insects? And what the heck was a golf course anyway? Now he had to eat a particular bug too?

"You'll find them in the forests of Mexico," his mother continued. "They migrate just before we do, so you'll be sure to find them there. It is from them that we derive strength, for they fly every bit as far and as well as we do. It is from them that males like you develop your black markings, the white speckles in your tails, the gorgeous orange of your chest and belly, and the bright yellow of your under wing matches the yellow of their under wing. You will owe much to them and the gifts they give you. Always be grateful as you hunt and eat them. Do you understand?"

"I guess I understand that I have to eat them and be grateful," responded her juvenile off-spring. "But I'm not at all sure what they look like other than being orange, black, white and yellow."

"Oh, of course," laughed his mother. "I've been so intent on lecturing you on a proper diet for developing young males that I forgot to tell you what sort of insect to watch for. They are regal. We call them the 'king of the butterflies.' You'll recognize them by their black heads and bodies--spotted all over with white. Their orange wings are edged in black--black once again spotted with white. Their wings are veined in black both above and below, and their under wings, as I said before, are largely yellow. For many birds, they are poisonous, but for us...well, they make us what we are. They are the very essence of our being. They are commonly known as Monarchs."

"A butterfly," reiterated the young Black-headed Grosbeak.

"Yes," answered his mother. "They fly south in good numbers. They flock in the forests of central Mexico. I'll see you there," she comforted her fidgety son. "We'll eat them together," she promised.

She preened his head one last time, sighed, then lifted off from the bird bath.

"See you in Mexico," she called. "Remember what I've told you."

"I will," he answered, more hopeful than certain. "Watch for me," he added.

"I will," she responded. Then she was gone.

He watched her fly out of sight and thought nervously of when he must follow.

"Oh noooo," he moaned, staring into the empty sky where she'd been. "I forgot to ask what a golf course is!"

Caution Ignored

It is said that there was once a time when lizards were choosing their color schemes and behaviors, deciding how they would be different from one another, each species adding something to the creation threads Day and Night had conjured for them.

Those creation threads were, of course, the same that Night wove continuously into the tapestry of life, but such was the magic with which the threads were endowed, that a great deal of choice remained to individual creatures. They could modify their own creation threads in wonderful and surprising ways. They often consulted with one another to decide who would be this way as opposed to that way, who would have this trait as compared to that trait.

With this in mind, the "Prowl and Pause" group of lizards met to discuss how they would continue to divide colorations, territories and behaviors in order to create more species. They were called Prowl and Pause because they practiced that style of hunting. They crept along, head swinging from side to side to look for prey, darting to snatch anything they might be able to eat, but pausing frequently to watch for danger and get their bearings within their hunting grounds. They all had great speed and long, slender tails. Two lizards with this hunting style were Whiptail and Zebra-tail. They lived in the same sorts of environments, so it was natural they should discuss options for further development with one another and give some regard to each other's advice.... Or not.

Whiptail and Zebra-tail had both opted for detachable tails. Roadrunner enjoyed snacking on lizards, and often spotted Whiptail and Zebra-tail as they hunted during the coolness of morning. Having tails that were easily broken off their bodies allowed both lizards to escape, while their squirming ex-tails diverted Roadrunner from making a meal of the rest of their bodies. Then they would grow new tails to replace the ones lost to Roadrunner. Whiptail's tail was a lovely blue in youth, turning more gray as he matured. Zebra-tail chose a tail banded in black and white, striped like a zebra. Both tails were quite long and dramatic, but Zebra-tail's was more strikingly obvious because of his color scheme. He loved showing it off. His tail was a matter of pride for him and he flaunted it as he ran from his enemies, waving it like a flag in their faces, then dashing away to hide.

Whiptail saw Zebra-tail taunting Roadrunner one day and feared for his friend's life. He was sure Zebra-tail had gone crazy. Why tempt fate?

"Because I can," was Zebra-tail's casual response.

"But it's dangerous! It's asking for trouble," squeaked Whiptail.

"Exactly," winked Zebra-tail. "Admit it now, you love seeing Roadrunner get frustrated too."

"Well, sure, what self-respecting lizard wouldn't? But what about your life-span? Seems to me you're looking to shorten it considerably by playing such pranks on every lizard's dreaded Enemy."

"I'll just zip away," Zebra-tail promised.

"Roadrunner's pretty zippy too," reminded Whiptail.

"Not so zippy as I," bragged Zebra-tail.

Whiptail shook his head. The folds in the skin of his neck stretched and refolded with each head-wag. Still concerned, he fell silent.

Zebra-tail winked again, crept away--paused--slithered ahead--paused again--dashed for some shade--paused.... Well, you get the picture.

What else could Whiptail do but simply watch him go?

Two days later Whiptail came across the X-shaped tracks of his mortal Enemy in the sand. Roadrunner had been by this way, and his scent still lingered, so Whiptail was on the alert more so than ever. He paused often to reconnoiter the trail.

He gulped when he saw what Roadrunner must have also seen--Zebra-tail's prints and scent were also in the smooth sand. Warily Whiptail continued to track the two of them.

A breeze whispered in the creosote, raining white puff-ball seeds to the desert floor. Whiptail ignored their pelting and followed the tracks of his friend and their mutual Enemy.

At one point, Roadrunner's prints got erratic, then left the trail. Zebra-tail's prints just disappeared.

"Oh no," whined Whiptail. "He wagged that tail one time too many."

"Ouch! Get off me," came a muffled voice from beneath his belly.

Jumping to the side in alarm, Whiptail gasped in relief as Zebra-tail poked a well camouflaged head out from under the sand.

"Is the coast clear?" he asked.

"I think so," Whiptail whispered, pausing to scan the trail.

"That was a close one," admitted Zebra-tail as he emerged from hiding.

"Too close," frowned Whiptail, when he saw Zebra-tail's tail-less state. "That looks sore."

"It is, but soon it will heal," Zebra-tail said as he turned to examine his raw behind. "We've both lost tails before."

"You more than I," scolded Whiptail. "You ask for it with that silly tail-wagging routine of yours."

"Adds excitement to life," winked Zebra-tail coolly. "Catch ya later."

"Hope it's me and not Roadrunner that you catch up to!" called Whiptail as he watched his friend amble off--pause--slither on--pause--dart ahead--pause.... Well, you get the picture.

"What would be the fun in that?" teased Zebra-tail, casting one last wink over his shoulder.

Restoration

It is said that there was once a time when heavy winter rains inspired a thick growth of grass in the springtime, along with abundant flowers and desert herbs. Trees such as Palo Verde and Ironwood dressed in fresh greenery and blossomed vigorously. But Rain is often fickle, and did not maintain her presence throughout the spring or summer. The grasses and other annuals withered and dried to crisp, brittle ghosts. Gusting fiery winds stripped plants of leaves, blossoms and seed. Palo Verde lost his leaves and resorted to using only his green branches and twigs to convert sunshine into the food he needed to remain alive. He rattled like a hundred rattlesnakes in every whoosh of wind, for all that clung to his twigs were dried seed pods. The world hesitated to move, or even to breathe under the relentless burden of the summer drought.

Eventually, the seed pods split and cast his seed to the ground where they were gathered and eaten hungrily by many desert animals.

One, Antelope Squirrel, stuffed his cheeks to ten times their normal size. Then, having much more than he could possibly eat just then, he dashed about scratching small holes in the earth, burying a few seeds in each one. As squirrels do, he stored Palo Verde's seeds for the time when food would be scarce. Then Antelope Squirrel would return to fill his belly on his hidden treasure. Again and again, Antelope Squirrel hastily gathered Palo Verde's hard, black, tear-drop shaped seed until his cheeks were bursting. Then he darted under that bursage, beneath this root, next to that rock--scratch, scratch, scratching himself a

204

storage room for his food supply, burying it to hide it from others, five or six seeds at a time.

But, of course, Antelope Squirrel was not so secretive as he hoped. Thrasher watched him. So did Round-tailed Ground Squirrel and Cottontail Rabbit. They saw where Antelope Squirrel hid some of his seeds and robbed him as soon as his back was turned.

Antelope Squirrel sometimes outsmarted himself, though. He hid his seed so well that he forgot where they were. Some of his storage rooms remained hidden, as the drought and heat progressed. Hidden, not just from others, but from Antelope Squirrel too.

Summer winds thrashed and roiled. They managed to build up clouds, which managed to rumble with thunder, and split with lightning, but which never managed to bring the showers for which Earth thirsted. The desert waited.

Then, one afternoon lightning struck Palo Verde. His great trunk was severed and his limbs crashed to the ground. Flames flickered in the dried grasses at his roots for a moment or two, before bursting into a tidal wave of fire that raced up the gully, feeding on dead plants and leaves from Palo Verde and other trees lining the dry watercourse. The wall of fire swallowed everything in its path. Antelope Squirrel ran for his life. In the aftermath, only smoking ashes and the skeletal remains of trees stood against the horizon. The blackened world held not one sign of life. Palo Verde was dead. Silence ruled.

And then, finally, Rain. Finally, she decided to show up. Finally, she gave Earth a belated drink. She fell in a great, soaking drizzle, easing closed the cracks in the achingly dry soil, gathering in shallow depressions in puddles, trickling in tiny streamlets between creosote and bursage. Soaking, soaking, soaking.

Some of those depressions in which Rain puddled were the remains of the holes in which Antelope Squirrel had buried and then forgotten his store of Palo Verde seeds. Within a few days of Rain's tardy appearance, they sprouted. Five or six seedlings here, five or six more there. A new forest of Palo Verde trees was in the making, courtesy of Antelope Squirrel. Unbeknownst to him, he helped restore Palo Verde to the gully stripped of life by the fire. It turns out, he was an agent of renewal as he emptied his cheeks into his hiding places--though he never planned for anything beyond his own belly.

How Black Phoebe Came to be Black

It is said that at one time Black Phoebe was as white as snow. In fact, she was called Snow Phoebe because she hunted for spring's first insects over streams still partly frozen, dipping to nab bugs off the surface of open pools in the thinning ice. She liked the colder temperatures and this was a good thing, for the earth seldom warmed enough to entirely melt the ice except at the lowest elevations. Thus, she was camouflaged by the snow she so resembled.

This was long before Man had fire. Man ate his foods raw and slept huddled with others of his kind in order to stay warm during the long nights. Eventually, though, when fire was stolen from the Storm Clouds' games with lightning, it did not take Man long to become careless with it and start great wind-swept fires. One such fire leaped out of Man's camp as he slept, igniting the grasses of the prairies and burning up into the mountains. Every sort of animal and person fled before it, for the smoke warned of its coming by day and the light of its flames by night.

Snow Phoebe and her mate lived near a stream and perched on low branches over its icy banks, watching for prey to come to the water's surface. They did not know of the immense fire burning at the flanks of the mountain containing their stream until they began to smell smoke and great numbers of animals began to splash through the waters they patrolled, fleeing up the mountainside to outrun the fire.

Most just thrashed through the stream and kept going, but some noticed Snow Phoebe and paused long enough to advise her of the approaching doom.

"Hurry, hurry, run, run," said the deer, her fawn slipping on the mossy stones beneath the water as they crossed the stream. "The fire is coming, burning everything in its path. You must run. You must flee."

Smaller folk showed up too. Tiny chickadees dashed through the trees overhead.

"The ashes are coming. The ashes are choking. Everything that can run or fly is coughing and retreating. The poor plants cannot move and are roasted where they root. Weep for them and fly away for yourself. The fire pities no one. If it catches you, you're done."

Phoebe looked up, most uncharacteristically, for she typically looked down to scan the water's surface for her food. She saw the billowing smoke the wind was bringing her way. She looked at the nest on the steep cliff to one side of her stream. She had finished it only the day before. Already she had laid two eggs.

"I can't go," Phoebe answered the Chickadees, who darted frantically in the trees awaiting her answer. "I have family."

"You'll be toasted; you'll be roasted," they responded as they dashed away.

Phoebe and her mate consulted. They had to risk staying with their nest. Perhaps it was high enough on the rocky cliff that it would not be burned. Perhaps the stream they hunted each day would help them by holding the flames at bay.

The smoke thickened, the flames drew close.

Phoebe stationed herself on her nest to protect her eggs from the hot sparks and ash that shot at them from burning trees and blew at them on the hot, sucking wind. Her mate perched on a tiny ledge nearby, tucking his bill beneath his wing in order to breathe.

The fire tried to suffocate the two birds, but it could not cross the stream to the cliff which was their home. The wind was hot and dried their eyes.

"Don't watch," called Phoebe's mate. "Close your eyes until it's passed."

The fire could not burn them, but it still tried to bury them in ash. In this the fire was successful, but the pair of birds did not startle from their places. They hunkered down and waited out the heat which singed their feathers.

Eventually, the fire passed and the wind died and became a cooling breeze. Phoebe's mate stirred first and opened his eyes to the newly blackened world around him. Below his perch he could see the hordes of flies which were hatching in the stream's shallows, warmed by the fire.

Quick as a thought, he left his perch with a sharp snap of his wings and snipped a fly just rising from the water's surface to bring to his mate where she sat, still tucked into their nest.

The flutter of his wings announced his presence and she opened her eyes to an astounding sight.

Her once white partner was now completely covered in black soot, all except for his white belly. That he had just dipped in the stream as he hunted the fly he now offered her.

"Look at you! I hardly recognized you," she gasped, not forgetting to accept the fly.

"Look at yourself!" he answered, for she too was black from head to tail, except for her belly, which had been shielded from the ashes by the nest she refused to abandon.

And from that day to this, Snow Phoebe has been known as Black Phoebe, with only a white belly to remind her that she once loved the snow. For after the fire, she favored the warm and humid places of lower elevations, where she could hide in the shadows of trees and bushes. But she still perches on low branches over a pond or stream, snacking on the bugs that rise to the water's surface. She still protects her nest too, just as persistently as she did in her first, snowy home.

How Creosote Found Companionship

It is said that once the desert was populated by Creosote and only by Creosote. Being the perennial plant best suited for enduring droughts has its advantages. Because he could survive two years without rain, he was first to establish himself in new regions of hot, arid land. Yes, being an expert at desert survival gave Creosote an edge other life forms lacked, but it also set him apart, making him lonely. He blossomed yellow-rayed flowers that mirrored Sun, but no insects came to pollinate them, so no seed formed. He expanded his range by producing new shoots from the outer edge of his root crown. Eventually, he was surrounded by clones of himself. His flowers, which were the means of propagation for most plants, just withered and fell to the ground where they blew hither and yon at his base when Wind gusted by.

Wind might have been a pleasant diversion, but Wind never stayed long enough to provide much companionship. He was always on his way somewhere else. Sometimes quickly, sometimes dallying a bit, but ever on his way elsewhere. So well traveled was he.

"Diversity of companions must come naturally for him," thought Creosote. "I'll ask his advice on how to broaden my circle of friends."

Wind began increasing his speed by late afternoon and noticed Creosote creaking and groaning in his gusts. Creosote seemed to be attempting to get his attention.

"Why all the moaning?" asked Wind as he circled Creosote in a dust devil.

"If you were me, rooted to one spot century after century, surrounded only by relatives who've had nothing new to say for century after century, how would you find new companions?

"Okaaaay, I understand all the moaning now," quipped Wind, "but I confess that your question confounds me. I just don't know how to answer you. I've never had such a problem. I will keep your question in mind as I travel, however, and ask those I come across to see what they suggest. Will that do for now?"

"I suppose it has to, but I thank you for your help and look forward to your return," replied Creosote politely, though he had hoped for a little more conversation in the present moment. That was not to be, for the dust devil broke down and Wind was off and away.

But not for long. Within a few minutes, Wind was back.

"I was just over to the pond beyond the hill and spoke to Amoeba in its muddy water. It said to just divide and there'd be two of you. Then you'd have someone to talk to." Pausing, Wind looked around at the clones Creosote had already created and said, "Oh yeah, that was a part of your problem, wasn't it? I guess Amoeba has less need of sparkling conversation than you. Well, I'm off to ask someone else."

Creosote shivered with laughter as Wind sped away. "Oh yeah," he repeated, "that was part of my problem." Then he looked at the monotonous view of himself stretching clear to the horizon--and sighed.

The following day Wind was back again.

"I have something to discuss with you," began Wind. "I'm not sure what you'll think, for it might seem a little severe."

"What?" asked Creosote, curious as to what Wind meant by "severe."

"Well, I spoke with Cottonwood over by the river on the other side of the mountains that you can just barely see if you move over.... Oh yeah, you can't move.

"Well anyway, Cottonwood was full of webworms. Webs nearly covered some of her branches, and those webs were filled with caterpillars that were eating her leaves. She said that it did take some of her strength, but she felt it was worth the extra effort on her part, for she enjoyed hearing the caterpillars voices calling to one another. She said after they were gone, she would sprout new leaves, so the pruning was not really so hard to endure. She rather liked that she was part of them now, and part of the moths they would become.

"In addition, she said many birds visited her branches to eat the caterpillars. Some of those, like the cuckoo, are from lands far to the south, and their stories of their travels fascinate her. She, like you, is rooted to one spot, so she grows tall, and has quite a height advantage over you, but...I digress. Her height matters little to you.

"She said she's allowed bees to move into a hollow broken limb, and woodpeckers nest in her trunk. Everything from hawks to hummingbirds nest in her branches and javelina and deer spend hot afternoons in her shade.

"In short, she said to offer something of yourself to feed or house others. She said that if you grant refuge to others, you will always have company. She is not from the desert, but she said it worked by the river and perhaps it might work for you too.

"Could that be an answer to your question? I don't have leaves and can't imagine letting someone eat them, but you are obviously the strongest living thing in the desert. You're the only one here! Maybe you could do as Cottonwood does."

212

"Perhaps," said Creosote thoughtfully. "Let me consider what she has to say."

"Of course," said Wind. "I'd have to take my time with such an idea too. Let me know what you decide, though. Cottonwood is interested in your story, now. And so are others."

"Who?" asked Creosote.

"Oh, just others," was Wind's elusive response. "I did ask around, you know."

So saying, he swept away dramatically, pushing a dust storm before him.

Creosote looked at the wide expanse, populated with one clone of himself after another.

Sun set.

Sun rose.

Sun set again.

And rose again.

"Wind," whispered Creosote, for the afternoon blanched in a breathless oppressive heat.

An eddy formed in the slow moving air currents, stirring the spaces around Creosote to give him a larger voice in Wind's increasing speed. Soon a dust devil whirled around Creosote and he creaked and groaned loudly.

"Who should I invite?" asked Creosote. "To take refuge, I mean."

"Ahem. Funny you should ask," answered Wind, ignoring the momentousness of Creosote's decision. "I was approached, actually, by a gnat-sort of creature that is currently homeless. She needs a place for her eggs and must lay them somewhere they can eat well when they hatch. I told her I couldn't answer for you, of course. But I would get back to her with your decision. She's awfully small. I would think her eggs must be too. I can't imagine her larvae could eat too much. But that's easy for me to say."

"Well, I could meet her, I suppose. We could see what could be worked out. When could that be arranged?"

"She's not much of a long distance traveler, but I think I could blow her here in a day or so. Shall I head out now?" asked Wind.

"Yes, do," answered Creosote. Wind left immediately.

When he returned, tiny Midge buzzed to alight on Creosote's branch. After introductions, Wind fell off so Creosote could hear the insect's explanation of her offspring's life cycle.

"I won't be remaining with you," she explained. "My life is almost over, but my egg will hatch and the red grub will need to feed in order to develop into an adult like myself. It would provide you with companionship for a little while. I would lay my egg on the end of your branch, so the grub could eat from your growth bud. I'm not from the desert, though, so I don't know whether the grub can survive here."

"Perhaps I can think of something to help," said Creosote.

"Very well; I leave it to you," said Midge, and deposited her egg on the end of one of Creosote's branches. Then she buzzed away to die, her mission accomplished.

"Wow, that was quick. Not much companionship there," commented Wind.

"I live thousands of years. I guess I can't expect much companionship from such a short-lived gnat. Still, her offspring is here for the tending, and it will leave me its eggs, and so on and so on for the whole of my life."

"Oh yeah," Wind blew, covering the egg with a layer of dust. "You have plenty of time to develop relationships-- generations of them. Me too, actually. I just never usually stay around long enough to do so. You're forcing me to make some now, though, as I help you out."

214

"You have been a helpful friend to me," said Creosote gratefully.

"Tell me that after the grub hatches," responded Wind, gathering his wisps and preparing to leave. "I'll check back soon to see how you're doing."

"Later," said Creosote.

Before long a red grub hatched from Midge's egg, just as she had said. Wind was there to watch. Wind and Creosote greeted the grub, but it wasted no time in burrowing into Creosote's terminal bud.

"Wow, that was quick," repeated Wind. "Not much companionship there."

Creosote was disappointed, but then began to notice the tingling in his bud and that the grub was quietly communicating to him there.

"I don't hear anything," Wind said, when Creosote told him.

"Nevertheless, I feel it," Creosote answered. "I think I'm going to build a gall to protect and house it."

"Whatever you say," said Wind. "This is all getting way too domestic for me. I'll check back with you later."

"Okay," said Creosote, already envisioning the reddish-brown, spherical, woolly gall he would build in honor of his first guest.

As time passed, Wind brought more and more refugees to Creosote's branches. Before long Creosote had a grasshopper that ate from his leaves, and his alone. Soon it took on the look of his body and was well camouflaged. A katydid followed suit. Creosote was pleased to have them chirping in his branches and copying his color scheme.

Lac insects soon scaled some of his branches, sucking sugars from his flesh.

Wind brought twenty different kinds of desert bees, all of whom designed their life cycle to feed on Creosote's blossoms exclusively. Now his flowers were fertilized and

215

his seed formed white fuzzy balls which broke into five sections as they aged. Now Creosote could propagate by seed, just as other plants did.

Creosote's roots exuded a substance that kept some plants from sprouting near him, but Wind blew enriched sands to his base which cactus seed could sprout in and find shady protection from the worst of Sun's summer heat. Mammillaria and many annuals took refuge there. Creosote was their nurse plant.

With the plants and insects, came the rodents and reptiles. These burrowed at the base of Creosote, enriching the soil even more and stirring the soil for his roots.

Birds came to pluck insects off his branches and rabbits nibbled his twigs.

With the plants and animals, came Man, who used Creosote's resin as glue and drank a tea from his leaves as a healing tonic.

The desert was no longer full of Creosote and only Creosote. Creosote, with the help of Wind, had seen to that.

How Red-faced Warbler Turned Red

It is said that there was once a time when three different kinds of male wood-warblers were bragging and showing off before one another. Each said he was Night's favorite warbler. Night had a special place in her heart for warblers. She enjoyed their busy ways, and their lovely songs sung to accompany her departures and arrivals. She never thought they sang to accompany Day's departures and arrivals. No way. She was quite sure the warblers sang only for her departures and arrivals.

Because they were favored, the warblers were marked in distinctive ways with Night's favorite color, black. Each was unique. The three male warblers boisterously compared and contrasted their traits and black markings in their efforts to prove who was the most handsome, daring and bold.

"I am the biggest," announced Painted Redstart. "I am therefore the best and best loved."

"Size isn't everything," chirped Wilson's Warbler. "I may be smallest, but that makes me the most special. Small is most endearing."

"And I...," began the third warbler.

"...am just in the middle," finished the other two in chorus.

The three paused their argument in order to flit around in the fir tree in which they perched. They competed in snipping up insects from cones and foliage, thereby displaying their prowess at hunting.

"Time's up," announced Painted Redstart, flashing his white-edged black tail. Since he was biggest, he assumed the leadership role. "I caught six gnats during our break. What about the two of you?"

"I caught plenty, rest assured, plenty," said the third warbler, flitting around uncomfortably.

"Oh I'm sure," smirked Wilson's Warbler, puffing up his little chest and darting at Painted Redstart in blustery bursts. "I got eight, so there! Smaller is faster too."

"So? I fly the farthest when I migrate, so I'm the strongest," said Painted Redstart.

"No farther than I," said the third warbler. "I've seen you in the mountains of my winter home in Central America.

"I winter there too," chimed in Wilson's Warbler, "but not in the highest mountains. I'm just passing through this region now. I prefer lower altitudes and water drainages. The air there is thicker and more of a challenge to fly through."

"Oh give me a break," said Painted Redstart disgustedly. "Everyone knows exertion at higher altitudes is much more difficult. This other fellow and I have it tougher than you."

"How would you know for sure?" responded Wilson's Warbler snidely. "Since this rarefied atmosphere you two inhabit deprives your brains of oxygen."

"I've heard all I can take," shouted Painted Redstart, running Wilson's Warbler into the next tree.

The third warbler chuckled nervously, aware he was not exactly coming off well in this contest between male egos.

"I'm the best because I'm the handsomest," declared Painted Redstart. "I have the most black, so Night's favor lies with me. You have almost no black," he went on to Wilson's Warbler, "and neither do you," he said to the third warbler. "My black's like a cape flowing down my back and over my shoulders. Add to that my white wing-bars, and

218

red belly and I am clearly the most astoundingly handsome. Compared to me, you two are quite dull."

"Handsome is as handsome does," cast back Wilson's Warbler, from the neighboring tree.

"What does that mean?" asked Painted Redstart of the third warbler.

"Beats me," said the mostly gray and white third warbler, hoping the conversation would divert away from color schemes, for he had none of Day's bright colors.

"It means Night can slop loads of black on any warbler she cares nothing about--that's easy," said Wilson's Warbler. "It's the most meticulous applications that prove her love. Yes, I'm greenish backed, the rest mostly yellow, but Night left her marking on me in the form of a perfectly round black cap. It takes a great deal of time and attention to draw a perfect circle. His black spot is more like a smear," he said of the third warbler's markings. "A little cap that messily oozed down his cheeks and ran out before covering the back of his neck."

At this, the third warbler was so embarrassed and angry, his face and chest turned a bright red. Every bit as red as Painted Redstart's belly. He joined his larger companion in chasing cocky Wilson's Warbler over the ridge and down into his preferred creek-side habitat, obnoxious thing that he was.

"Hey, you should get mad more often," observed Painted Redstart, when they finished running off their mutual irritant. "You're quite the stud now, though not so studdly as I, of course."

Looking at his reflection in the creek, Red-faced Warbler had to agree. He was much more impressive red-faced, even more so than Painted Redstart, though he wisely kept that opinion to himself.

Ever since, Red-faced Warbler has offset his gray and white mundanity with a very red face and breast.

Against all that bright red, Night's gift of a ragged black hat and ear muffs is infinitely more striking. Proof, so far as he is concerned, that Red-faced Warbler is Night's favorite.

How Phainopepla Was Made

"That's ridiculous!" scoffed Day. "Of course you are represented in the creatures that are active during the time of my rule. What of the creatures of the dark? Am I represented in their colors? What about Bat?"

"Bat is often black, I admit," answered Night, "but most of the creatures who prowl during my rule are not like him. Their colors are more often lighter. My color, black, is under-represented, both during the day and the night. I want to have a presence. Any time of the day or night. Every time of the day or night. I want to be represented too. Look at the numbers of creatures that carry your colors, red and yellow. Need I remind you about the warblers? You left your sign quite plentifully in their plumage. I want equal time."

"Wait now, many warblers have some black in them too."

It is said that during the time of creation, when choices were made about just what was being created...what its role would be...what it would look/sound/act like, the fighting between Day and Night could go on and on and on. In fact, it is amazing such great variety of life finally came to pass, for the two argued about nearly everything.

Sun and Moon were the subjects of some of the earliest arguments, with Moon being a concession, of sorts, to Day's demand that Sun's light be remembered at night. However, Day had to allow Night to have deep, mysterious caves and the bottom darks of the oceans in return for Moon's reflected light. Not only that, but once created, Moon showed a definite preference for Night and

221

supported Night in most arguments, disregarding Day's role in her creation. Sun, however, stuck quite loyally by Day.

"I want a completely black song bird."

"You already have Blackbirds."

"Only some of those are entirely black. Most are marked with your colors too."

"You agreed to that!"

"I know, but you have Cardinal. I want a black Cardinal in return."

"But that would be copying form. And you have Cardinal's face," Day blustered. "Besides, Cardinal's mate is not so bright as he. I was less flamboyant with her."

"So what? She's not black, is she? Now THAT would have been a real compromise on your part. No, I want a black Cardinal. I like the form. It bears repeating."

"Crest and all?"

"Crest and all."

"Oh, alright. But I get his eye. He gets a red eye. And so does his mate. I insist."

"Whatever," spat Night, thinking privately that eye-color was probably a small price to pay for getting her black Cardinal.

"And his mate...."

"Oh, here it comes," drawled Night querulously, knowing the real bartering was about to begin.

"His mate..." began Day.

"Will have the same form. I insist," ended Night.

"Oh alright!" groaned Day. "Now let me have some say. His mate will be yellow."

"No way. You already have her eye. She should be the color of the horizon when you first come dawning. Why not make her gray?"

Day thought for a moment. A combination of Day and Night. And she WOULD have a red eye, after all. "OK," he agreed, pausing pointedly to pout.

"One last touch," interrupted Moon, glad Day and Night seemed close to agreement.

So saying, she shot moonbeams into both black Cardinal and his gray mate, leaving spots of white light on their wings, bright in the male, duller in the female.

"Now you have a bird representing Night," intoned Moon, "with a bit of me there too."

"Agreed," shrugged Night, secretly admiring Moon's enhancement.

"Agreed," shrugged Day, secretly admiring Moon's enhancement.

"But it needs its own name," said Sun, secretly jealous of Moon's enhancement. "Call it Phainopepla."

"Say what?" gasped Moon, shocked Sun would even consider attaching such an odd name to any new creature, much less one that carried her light.

"Whatever!" affirmed both Day and Night, happy for an end to this particular argument.

"And it should eat red mistletoe berries, fruit of MY light. RED, like the color of it's eyes," said Sun, smirking at Moon.

"Fine," said Day.

"Fine," said Night.

"Fine," glowered Moon.

Survival Strategies Every Reakirt's Blue Larvae Should Know

It is said that there was once a time when caterpillars didn't know how to become butterflies. There was concern that there would never be any butterflies to flutter to flowers and fill the world with their beauty. Day and Night, the two primary creators, discussed the problem and carefully planned different paths to adulthood for different caterpillars. When they had finished, they called on each species individually to give them guidance. Here is what Day reported to the Reakirt's Blue hatchlings he and Night had deposited on host plants as eggs.

"The world is full of peril, if you're a Reakirt's Blue butterfly larvae. Let's face it; there are wasps and flies that would just love to lay their eggs on your tender flesh so their young can hatch and eat you alive as they develop into adults, guaranteeing that you won't. If you want to survive to fly, here's what you have to do.

"When you hatched, you found yourself on a plant that's a member of the pea family, right? You started eating buds and leaves and now you're green and fat and starting to get large enough to be interesting to critters that would like to have you for lunch--or dinner--or snack--whatever. Unless you're really sluggish, you've probably noticed there are ants that climb your host plant too. They look for insects to eat, insects like you. Still, you can use their presence to your advantage.

"You have a honey pot. It's down close to your rump. When the ants start to crawl on you--and they will crawl on you--you just ooze some juice out of your honey

224

pot. The ants will eat it and decide they like you. If they like you, they let you live.

"But more importantly, if the ants like you, they'll also protect you. They'll run off any wasp or fly that is trying to lay her eggs on you. They'll also keep other insects and spiders at bay. Ants can be your friends. Just don't run out of honey.

"What happens if a wasp finds you and there's no ants around? Good question. Here's what you do.

"On the eighth segment of your caterpillar body-- yes, count them--you do have an eighth--no, start at your head. There. That's where you'll find your everscible tubercles, sometimes known as everscible tentacles. You've never heard of either one? Well, you still have them. They are fleshy, bulging, bulbous things you can push up out of your body when you are in danger. When you stick them up, they will give off chemicals the ants will smell and come rushing to help you. The chemicals also make them mad. It's a very good thing to have angry ants coming when you need to be saved from wasps. The ants will tend you the whole of your caterpillar career. Just don't run out of honey.

"After your last molt as a caterpillar, you'll be ready to pupate. That's the stage of huge transformation which turns you into a butterfly. What you need to do now is leave your host plant. I know--it's hard to imagine--but do it. Crawl to the ground and find the nest of the ants who have been tending you. Crawl into their underground tunnels, but not real far, and let nature take its course. You'll pupate without having to know how. Trust me. The ants will find you and touch you and turn you and continue to tend you. For Pete's sake, don't run out of honey.

"It's important to note that I told you not to climb too far into their tunnels. There's a good reason why. As an adult butterfly, you don't have a honey pot. Now the ants have no reason to like you and every reason to eat you. When you emerge from your pupal stage, you have only a minute or two to flee the ants' nest and make it to the upper world of flowers. When you reach the surface, crawl a safe distance away and pump up your wings. No--don't pump up your wings when you're still underground. Keep your priorities straight.

"Once you're a butterfly, you'll enjoy sipping nectar from the many wonderful blossoms you'll spot from the air. Be aware, spiders and praying mantises will be waiting for you on those very same blossoms. Birds will be watching for you in flight. They mean you only harm. Stay away. It's dangerous, but the nectar is worth it.

"Remember, as a butterfly, you're on your own, kid. The ants won't help you then. Good luck."

Mother Owl's Question

It is said that there was once a time when six great horned owls sat in a huge, ancient palo verde tree which contained several enormous clumps of mistletoe in addition to the owl family. They watched evening falling. Night, one of the two primary creators, approached to converse with them.

"Greetings, my Advocates," Night began. She bowed and bobbed in owl fashion as she stopped before them. "I see you have nested very successfully this season and have four beautiful offspring to train in your fine art of hunting," she acknowledged, in praise of the two adults. To the fledglings she said, "You are fortunate to have two such mighty hunters as your parents to provide for you and teach you their skills. I am sure you will learn your lessons well and will have young of your own one day to glide silently through my skies, stalking prey in my domain."

The juvenile owls fidgeted nervously and fluffed their feathers. They knew from their parents' statuesque, attentive pose--ears erect, golden-gaze fixed--that this visitor was greatly respected by both and deserved their regard as well.

"I have come to warn you," continued Night, "that there is a band of humans at the waterhole you frequent to hunt. I have been following them and listening around their fires as they ready for sleep. They are afraid of the dark and all my creatures. They especially fear owls."

"Who, who, who are we to cause them fear?" asked Father Owl.

"Who, who, who have we ever harmed among them?" asked Mother Owl.

227

"I can't say I understand it myself," said Night. "But I think it has something to do with your eyes. They are so intense," she continued. "They seem to see more than what's before them. Perhaps the humans think you can see right through them.

"Or, perhaps it is your call," Night continued. "You were made to question, and perhaps that causes them doubt. They may think your 'Who?' asks 'Who will die next?' I heard them talking as they prepared their evening meal. They think your appearance forecasts death, their own or a family member's. I worry they may harm you if they see you by Day or notice you moving in my depths. Hunt carefully until they pass. Take your young to other hunting grounds to hone their skills."

"Is their fear so powerful that we should be turned away from our lands?" asked Father Owl.

"I am advising that," nodded Night.

"Are they so different from us?" asked Mother Owl. "Does death come always for us but only occasionally for them, and only if WE announce it first?"

"Of course not," answered Night. "Death comes for everything Day and I have created. There is no exception. Without it there is no renewal."

"Then when they hear us call, 'Who, who, who?'" Owl remarked, "why don't they answer us, 'Death comes for me and everyone I know...perhaps right now--perhaps not. Now, Owl, tell me something I DON'T already know!'

"Isn't that a better way to understand us, Night?" Owl finished.

"Perhaps I shall ask them," smiled Night, bowing her leave, in owl fashion. "I do believe I'll ask them."

To Beret or Not to Beret

It is said that there was once a time when Black-tailed Gnatcatchers all looked alike. There was no way to tell which was male and which female. They knew immediately, but no one else did. Friendly and chatty, they called to one another as they roved from Hackberry to Whitethorn to Palo Verde, picking small insects and spiders from the branches of their thorny hosts. Flicking their long tails, they darted, in perpetual motion, tic-ticking and cheeh-cheehing every other breath.

A mere five inches long, most of which was black tail edged in white, their tiny bodies were grey above and white beneath. Since both sexes were usually not far apart, built their nest together, shared egg incubation and fed youngsters together, they could not be differentiated by duty or display.

"I embarrass myself constantly," said Hackberry, concealer of this year's nest.

"Me too," agreed Mesquite. "I'm grateful for their ministrations; where would I be without them snacking on what's snacking on me? But I hesitate to thank them, at least by name. Even with a fifty-fifty chance of getting it right, I'm on record as one hundred percent wrong. She or he? He or she? I can't tell. Who's that on the nest now?"

"She?" guessed Hackberry.

"He," said the bird.

"And there you have it!" said Wind, entertaining himself by blowing around a cloud of gnats hovering over the center of the wash where Mesquite tree and Hackberry

229

resided. "A perfect example of our problem." He looked straight at the tiny bird.

Staring steadily back, without blinking once, Black-tailed Gnatcatcher adjusted himself on the nest and said, "What do you want me to do about it? Cheeh."

"Cheeh, cheeh," his mate called back from the Palo Verde across the wash.

"Wear a feather askew on your left wing," suggested Mesquite.

"I have to fly, you know," male Black-tailed Gnatcatcher answered.

"Hold a leaf in your mouth," suggested Hackberry.

"I have to eat, you know," said Gnatcatcher. "Cheeh, cheeh."

"Tic-tic cheeh, cheeh," his mate answered from a Catclaw Acacia twenty feet away.

"Why don't you let her sit on the nest all the time? Then we'd know who was who," said Wind.

"She needs to eat too," Gnatcatcher said. "Tic-tic cheeh."

"Cheeh," his mate answered, perched just above him in Hackberry.

He left the nest, and she settled over the eggs. He then went to Mesquite, perched on a scrap of bark on the tree's trunk and, with his bill, reached behind it. He tore off a bit of Shadow from behind the bark, where Sun never shined, crammed it on his head and said, "Well?"

"That helps," approved Mesquite.

"Now I can tell you apart," agreed Hackberry.

"Bravo," said Wind. "You look like you're wearing a beret." (He had wintered in France.)

230

"Very handsome, dear," assured his spouse. "Cheeh, cheeh."

"Fine, but it comes off in the fall," announced male Black-tailed Gnatcatcher. "Cheeh."

"But why?" asked Mesquite.

"Wanna keep you guessing at least part of the year," answered Gnatcatcher. "Otherwise, where's the fun for me?"

So ever since, male Black-tailed Gnatcatchers wear black caps to go with their black tails during breeding season, but the rest of the year, they persist in confusing their desert hosts.

Much to their everlasting delight.

And their hosts' everlasting chagrin.

Defend the Young

It is said that there was once a time when Wind watched a small herd of javelina moving single file through the grassland, heading north, to a drier, desert terrain. The heavy sow leading the band of travelers could not know the land before her had little water. She did not know where they might bed down to hide from the hot sun. She did know she smelled no scent markings from other javelinas as she led her followers through the prickly pear they browsed. The land was harsh, but unclaimed. With any luck, Mountain Lion would not bother tracking them so far north and would continue to hunt the hill country in the humid south, where javelinas were more abundant.

Her mane on her shoulders and back bristled as she remembered her last litter, lost to big cats the winter before. That was when she left the larger herd. One last rub of her head on the back of the dominant male, scent-marking herself from the gland over his tail. The herd of forty was diminished by seven more when she turned aside. They seemed inconsequential as they trotted away. Only one or two watched them leave.

The small troop, also known as collared peccaries, bonded by scent-marking themselves again and again in their greetings. They grunted and squealed to each other as they fed on roots and cactus. They marked their trail with their oily scent so any strays might find the troop's path. They bedded down together to rest, rooting out shallow basins where they lay side by side.

There was safety in numbers and two sows were pregnant, including the leader. When the babies were born, they would be covered with a reddish, bristly coat of hairs, and black manes. Only a pound in weight, they would grow quickly and take on the gray adult coloring, with a lighter patch over the neck and shoulders, at three months. There were two males, but they were young and only about thirty pounds. The two pregnant sows were closer to forty. A two-year-old female and her three youngsters, all under six months old, made up the rest of their assemblage.

Wind wondered if the newcomers would survive. He watched them move through the saddle connecting two low peaks. Just as they began their descent into the next valley, Sun pushed an ember-red sliver of his roundness over the horizon, setting light and shadow into play on Earth. Heat accompanied him. The peccaries would soon need shade and rest. Wind stirred into action.

He spotted an arroyo at the base of the very hills the javelinas crested. It had steep walls, and he knew by the cottonwood trees that lined it that water was beneath the sand's surface. He coasted down to the trees before turning uphill again, carrying the scent of water to the lead female. Her eyesight was poor, but she smelled the trees and turned toward them.

"And," whispered Wind in her ear, "there's a number of caves in the banks where you may rest out the day."

As the peccaries drew closer, the sow began looking for shelter, but the youngest saw a cave first and scampered up to it. It was large and well shaded, but occupied.

The largest rattlesnake she'd ever seen was coiled beside a stone in the cave's entrance. It headed straight for her. She squealed in terror.

Instantly every javelina rushed to her aid. Wind watched in awe as the adults attacked the rattlesnake, biting with their tusks, gnashing their teeth in fury. In seconds, the reptile lay dead. The cave was theirs. Their youngest was safe.

These strangers will be just fine, Wind thought. They will survive. They protect their young.

He left the peccaries to their sleep.

233

From Black to Blue

It is said that there was once a time when Night, Wind and Moon sat planning the arrangement of stars in a patch of the sky. The design was to be simple, but no easy task to accomplish. That's why they were practicing.

Night wanted the stars set in rows stretching straight across the sky, from horizon to horizon. Wind would blow them into place once Night made them from her darkest core, and after Moon had redirected Sun's light to ignite them. But this took great finesse on everyone's part, so they practiced intently in the sand of a dune. Night held a handful of sand; Moon lit the particles til they glowed. Then Wind blew carefully across the sand, combing it with his breath.

They were somewhat successful.

But not especially so.

Still, the surface of the sand did look as if it had been brushed. There were straight, even, hills and dales.

Which suddenly shuddered and heaved aside, even while Night, Wind and Moon watched in amazement and consternation. For the sand Night held contained a metamorphosing beetle. The beetle wormed through the Moon-glowing sand, pretty much blinded by such overabundance of light, to come face to face with Wind, Moon, and one of the two primary creators, Night. Everyone stared. No one said anything. About an inch long, the beetle's shell was not quite hardened, and he was feeling very small and vulnerable.

"Boo," said Wind.

At which the beetle fell over on his back, further disrupting Wind's artistry in sand. He appeared dead. Not a leg jerked. Not an antenna quivered.

The star makers waited, holding absolutely still, keeping absolutely silent.

And eventually, the faker came 'round. The beetle got up, thinking the danger was past, so there was no further need to play dead. While upside down, though, his shell had hardened, and now his back was pebbled with grains of sand, in lovely, straight rows. Not only that, but his original color, black, was now oozing with Moon glow, giving him a blue-gray cast. He looked around.

Yikes! The "Big Three" were still there staring at him. He guessed another dead-bug flop would be overacting, so he just stood there.

(Pregnant pause.)

Then they were all laughing uproariously. Beetle wound up on his back again, this time waving his legs in hysterical laughter. Night guffawed til tears rolled down her cheeks. Moon doubled up in giggles til she was half her usual self, and Wind couldn't catch his breath.

"Forget the star layout I planned," gasped Night. "If a beetle can destroy everything on a small scale, imagine the mess we could make cosmically. We'll come up with something else."

"You don't hear me complaining," Wind sighed with relief. "That took too much breath control for my comfort."

"Keep the Moon glow," Moon told the beetle. "It looks rather good on you. Seems to be solidifying somewhat too. Is it?"

"I think so. Seems waxy," replied the beetle.

"It will help you retain water," assured Moon. "Helpful in a desert."

"Goodbye Ghost Beetle," chuckled Night as she strolled away. "Nice meeting you."

Ghost Beetle bowed and strode away over the sand to scavenge his evening meal.

Labyrinth

It is said that there was once a time when a juvenile White-crowned Sparrow sat perched in a swaying creosote bush, watching in amazement the spectacle before him. Born the previous spring, the six-month old bird knew all about snakes. Hatched in southern Canada, he'd seen the local rattler catch and eat his nestmate, who had been first to fledge, but too clumsy of flight to escape the snake after becoming stranded on the forest floor. Still, he'd never seen a sight like this.

It was his first Fall south. Everything in the Sonoran Desert was so different from his birthplace. Mourning Doves were not new to him, but Gambol's Quails were, and so were Cactus Wrens and Curved-billed Thrashers. All of these were tailing a five-foot Diamondback Rattlesnake across a patch of open sand between a stand of Globe Mallow and a clump of creosote. The snake ignored them entirely, but the birds kept pace with the rattler, from a healthy distance. Quails clucked, wrens screeched, thrashers babbled, all to draw attention to this unwelcome visitor. They walked behind until the reptile slithered into the creosote forest, at which point the smaller birds took to the branches to keep an eye on this enemy. The larger birds hung back, not wanting to head where the walking and escape weren't easy.

A House Sparrow perched next to the White-crowned, nervously chattering at the snake. He turned to the shocked and silent youngster from up north.

"That's one snake won't surprise any of us," he announced. "Anyone can see that invader in our territory, with all of us calling the alarm and following on his tail."

"Yes, I can see that," White-crowned said, nodding. "I've never watched such a parade, but it's not one I'll soon forget! I feel safer knowing so many are on guard for all the rest of us. But where's he going?"

The two sparrows watched the rattler apparently abandon all sense of direction within the creosote patch. The direct path across the sand turned into a crazy back-and-forth-over-and-around course, followed by every inch of the snake's long body, without hurry, and with complete focus. There was no short-cut.

"I can't see anything making him do that," reported House Sparrow. "Can you?"

"No."

"I've seen a labyrinth before," said House Sparrow. "People walked in on a straight path, but then the route became full of twists and turns until they reached a central garden, with benches to sit and rest. It never made any sense to me, but Rattlesnake reminds me of them. Perhaps there's a labyrinth we can't see, but he can?" Sparrow wondered.

"Maybe," White-crowned sparrow answered doubtfully.

After many loopings, the snake came to the other side of the creosote thicket and headed straight to a cholla, beneath which a packrat had built a large midden. He entered a hole.

After the snake was out of sight, silence reigned. Birds held their peace, waiting. There was a rustling within the packrat nest. Then all was quiet again.

"Guess we won't see that snake til next month," said House Sparrow. "That was a big packrat that lived in there. He'll take that long to digest."

"So he did see a labyrinth," mused White-crowned sparrow. "One of smell instead of sight."

"I suppose so," agreed House Sparrow. "He smelled the rat's trail, made as he ran around hunting seed and cactus last night, and followed every inch of it back to his nest, no matter how wild and crazy the path got."

"I couldn't see he had any goal, but he did," marveled White-crowned. "Maybe the shortest path to what you want isn't always a straight line."

The Edge of Night

It is said there was once a time when Night, one of the two primary creators, stole up upon young Cottontail, crouched beneath a bursage and shivering with fear. She noticed the rabbit's right ear was torn at the tip and flopped over.

"Rest now, little one," she breathed soothingly. "I will cover you in darkness and hide you from your enemies."

Cottontail snuggled down into her shallow, dusty bed and sighed deeply, ending with a whimper.

Night deepened the twilight, continuing to enfold the wild, wounded baby.

"What happened, my pet?" she asked gently.

"My mother is dead," gasped the shaking youngster. "She flushed from the creosote where we both hid and the hawk grabbed her. She screamed when his talons cut her. Then she was quiet. He tore her apart in front of me. I smelled her blood and warm flesh. I could not move. I could not stop watching."

"She died well, little one. She died saving you."

"But as I crept away, Coyote saw me and gave chase. My mother could not help me then, as I darted through cactus to get away. My ear caught on a thorn and tore, but I did not cry out. Coyote never found where I squatted in the prickly pear pads."

"Your mother taught you how to run. She taught you where to hide. Because of her teachings you did not yelp when your ear was torn, so Coyote never found you. All creatures die, little one. What matters is how you live. Your mother had the heart of the mountain lion, though the form of a rabbit. You have that too."

"How so?" asked Cottontail.

"You are wise, quick, and passionate," assured Night. "I see that very clearly."

"My mother was too," spat Cottontail, "and she is still dead!"

"All creatures die, little one," repeated Night fondly.

"Now that my mother's gone, where can I be safe?" sobbed Cottontail.

"Safety is an illusion," Night said with a tiny smile.

"Then I will stay strong with running, and eat greens to stay healthy and never get old and weak."

"Eternal youth is illusion too," sighed Night. "Still, preserve health as best you can."

"For what?" wailed Cottontail.

"For your children," answered Night. "For your passion, for your lion's heart, for Life."

"So what? That's not enough," gasped Cottontail, utterly heartsick.

At that moment, Sun, who had already slipped below the horizon, ignited the western clouds with the glory of his setting. Colors of salmon, midnight blue, gossamer orange-gold, flashed together for a minute to turn the world pink, before fading to grey and silver-black in Night's arms. Night and Cottontail watched, spellbound, love-struck.

"It is enough," acknowledged Cottontail.

"Indeed it is," replied Night.

The End of Silence

It is said that there was once a time when Roadrunners were silent.

They were born into the Cuckoo family of birds, a disreputable start. Weirdness began at the toes, which in Cuckoos meant two facing forward and two facing backward. (Everyone knows a proper bird's foot has three toes facing forward and one pointing behind. How else would you know if it was coming or going? I'm told Cuckoos don't know either.) Add the fact that many Cuckoos accidently leave their eggs in other birds nests to be raised by those other birds and you can see how reputations might start. Roadrunners generally don't do that, except to other Roadrunners, but if they were to start tomorrow, no one would be surprised.

All Cuckoos can fly, but Roadrunners forget how after about fifteen feet, so they took up walking or sprinting to get from place to place. In all fairness, they are a little large to fly too far, being about two feet in length and cursed with a bad hairdo that cuts down on aerodynamics considerably. Nevertheless, at a top speed of 15 MPH, they outrun even Whiptail Lizards, so they manage to eat.

Another thing that helps the eating is that pretty much anything smaller than they are is fair game. They eat cactus fruit, baby quail, snakes, small flying birds and large flying insects which they jump straight up and snatch in mid-air. If the prey has not had the grace to die of shock instantly, Roadrunners beat all heck out of whatever they've got in their bill against a rock until it stops moving. Then they whack it once or twice more for good measure and good tenderizing. Everything is so much easier to swallow after the spine has been shattered.

Because of their size and forgetfulness at flying, it was decided by Day and Night, the two primary creators, that Roadrunners would not have to migrate. They could stay put. Other Cuckoos have to migrate because they can fly between North and South America, a distinct advantage because there are a couple of large bodies of water to cross. Roadrunners don't have to stay put, so long as they can walk there, which accounts for them being sighted in places like Kansas and Louisiana. What other reason could there be for being sighted in Kansas or Louisiana?

The point is, though, that all these travels and even the staying puts, were all done silently. Prey items were disappointed because they would have appreciated the warning, but Roadrunner parents were delighted.

All that changed, however, one morning, when Roadrunner kids were sitting in their nest, a little bored, frankly, waiting for Mom and Dad to deliver breakfast. One spontaneously bill-clacked for no apparent reason and without a bit of foreshadowing. You know how siblings are. Within five minutes they were all doing it and when Mom and Dad got home, they thought a bee hive had moved into the tree holding the nest because the whole place was buzzing. They quickly shoved the meals down the kids' throats to shut them up, but it didn't work for long. The kids kept buzzing, so the parents kept shoveling food. This is known as harassment.

It was only a matter of time before the kids came up with other sounds, including a cooing, not unlike a dove's, unless you're a dove. They thought it was a cool secret code, so secret even they didn't know what it meant. The racket around the nest was pretty extreme by now, and could be heard by other nearby Roadrunner kids, who took up the habit and drove their parents crazy too.

To retaliate, the parents began whining before feeding the kids and pretty soon the kids expected chow whenever they heard the whine. When they got a little bigger, they tried to race each other toward the whining, to be the first to get the food from Mom or Dad. Eventually, parent Roadrunners whined to draw the kids away from the nest and out into the desert, where they lost them amongst the creosote bushes at the earliest possible moment, usually adolescence. It didn't take long for all Roadrunner parents to learn this behavior, called positive reinforcement.

By this time, everyone knew Roadrunners could talk, though no one was ready to call it singing. Other Cuckoos were so embarrassed by their cousins' strange vocalizations and pathetic family dynamics, they begged Day and Night to not have to associate with them and moved away from the desert. The Yellow-billed Cuckoos stayed, but only along the rivers and only for a couple of months. They migrated to Argentina as soon as their own kids could fly. They'd have gone farther south, but they ran out of land.

Desert lizards wished Roadrunners would leave too, even if only for Louisiana, but no such luck.

Sara Orangetips and the Fire of Life

"It is said that there was once a time when our people were traveling north, in search of a new home. As you will learn, winter is one of Rain's seasons in our desert, but in that winter, Rain did not visit the land. We had only the cactus to slake our thirst. We survived, but we did not thrive. We needed more food and a better variety to keep up our strength for the journey. Some of us grew weak and fell behind. Many newborns were lost because their mothers' bodies could not provide nourishment. Still, Rain refused to come and renew Earth.

"We plodded on.

"Nights were so long and cold. Freezing, dry Wind screamed up the canyons all through the darkest hours, swirling dust up our snouts and down our throats. We prayed for sunrise so we might warm ourselves. But Wind brought no Rain.

"Our people despaired.

"'Have we come here to die?' they asked.

"'Will winter never end?' asked others.

"'Is there no refuge for us?' asked those not too weary to speak.

"Still, we plodded on. Quivering with exhaustion, step by step, we traveled into the unknown.

"Then our scouts brought word the lands ahead were so withered by drought and ravaged by frosts, even the cactus blackened and died.

"'Where can we go?' people asked.

"'What will we eat now?' said others.

"'Will winter never end?' wept those too weary to walk further. Which included all of us.

"The leaders talked together.

"'We rest here,' they announced, trying to hide their fear and dispel panic.

"We collapsed in the dust. Too footsore for panic.

"In the morning, we awoke to clouds of butterflies shimmering above us. Some even landed on us. They were white-winged, but the tips of their front wings were fire-red, edged in black. They were points of sunshine flickering up the slopes of the arroyo in which we slept.

"'Who are they?' our people asked.

"'Where did they come from?' others said.

"'What does this mean?' some asked in wonder.

"'Winter's dead. Winter's dead,' sang Thrasher to our astonished folk, his voice thundering off the canyon walls. 'Sara Orangetips fly. See the Fire of Life in their wings?' he asked us. 'The flames and the charring? They carry our promise that Spring's coming, and always will, so long as they fly. Winter's dead. Winter's dead. Sara Orangetips fly.'

"By day's end, Rain came calling," finished the huge boar, sipping delicately from the pool of water forming in the pit he'd just dug in the gravel for himself and the two month-old reds that accompanied him. They wobbled down the steep edge of the crater to cool their hooves.

"All that because you asked what kind of butterfly that was?" whispered one young javelina to his twin.

"You know Gramps," murmured the other, winking knowingly.

A Word of Advice

It is said that there was once a time when young House Finch was preparing to leave home to establish his own territory. Millions, or so it seemed, of his well-wishing relatives flocked in the Whitethorn Acacia upon which he stood, greeting the dawn and one another and screaming advice, so as to be heard over everyone else. He perched quietly, shell-shocked by all the noise and the momentousness of the morning.

He was not quite wearing adult colors. They would be his come fall, but he'd announced his intention to move and he was not backing down. He could fly well enough, though he tired somewhat easily. He figured he would build his strength and skill gradually. He already fed himself, though his youngest nest-mate still begged from their parents. He knew deep in his heart that he needed more trees in his life, and he was determined to go find them.

"You're so young," screeched his aunt on his mother's side, fluttering just above his head to catch his ear. "Always watch out for Kestrel. Kestrel always watches out for you!" Then she was lost in the restless, shifting, mass of fidgeting finches addressing him. He knew a response was unnecessary and utterly useless in the turmoil.

"Birds of a feather... his mother squealed as she plowed past him, shoving aside his sister to perch nearby. "Look for a girl from a good family," she yelled before toppling off the twig too weak to support her weight.

"Oh, Mother," he sighed, resigned.

"When angry, count to ten," called his sister.

Why didn't she ever? he thought.

"Bathe daily," yelled his grandmother on his father's side as she struggled to hover nearby. "Personal hygiene is the key to success," she assured.

"It's the early bird..." his grandfather bellowed before being drowned out by other voices.

"Work hard and make me proud, son," called his father from a perch somewhere above.

"Fight fire with fire," twittered his second cousin, once removed.

"Do as you're told," bawled his uncle.

"Don't count your seed before you've gathered it," hollered a neighbor.

"Set a little seed aside each day," screamed a stranger.

"Find a mentor."

"Don't leave the flock."

"Follow your dreams," shrieked his brother, like he would know.

"Get a higher education. Sit at the top of every tree," said someone lost within the crowd.

Closing his eyes, House Finch took flight and flew all the way to the stand of Cottonwoods four backyards away and across the street. The voices of his youth could not be heard here, but the trees had no need of ears. They witnessed the whole thing and they were quite amused.

"One more piece of advice?" asked Cottonwood, leaves shivering with laughter.

"Do I have a choice?" groaned House Finch.

"Find those who know they don't know. Converse there," smiled Cottonwood.

"After breakfast," said House Finch thoughtfully.

Follow the Sugar

It is said that there was once a time when Western Bluebird rested after a morning of foraging. It was his first winter. He was in a land very different from where he'd been born. He paused in reverie.

In his birthplace, he'd hatched in a nesting hole in a tree bordering a meadow. He and his nestmates were tended by two busy parents, who shoveled insects down the gaping maws of their young from dawn to dusk. Father had a red breast and white belly. His back was also rusty. But his head, neck, wings and tail were a bright, glorious blue. Sky blue. Mother was grayer where her mate was blue, but her wing flashed just as resplendently as his with speck-of-the-heavens blue.

Bugs, bugs, and more bugs. That was the totality of his early menu. But that was the totality of his need. Protein, protein and more protein. Building feathers was only possible with protein. Once that was accomplished, there was crowding, flapping, perching, pecking, waiting to be fed at the doorstep, then a nearby limb, then really flying to the ground and back up again in search of his own bugs. Next there were colder nights, fewer bugs and the urge to leave all he'd known. He left his home forest with many fellow bluebirds, but when they stopped wandering south, small bands scattered around territory quite foreign to him. What was on the menu here?

"Follow the sugar," called a three year old female. She streaked off into the desert.

What did that mean?

Five bluebirds flew off to cottonwood trees lining a watercourse. He followed her.

She dashed into a clump of mistletoe, ignoring the Phainopepla perched just above. He was guarding the stash of mistletoe, hoping food would attract a mate, and it usually did. Gray all over, where he was black, the crested pair of silky flycatchers called phainopeplas claimed mistletoed trees for the berries they produced. But now they had more competition for those berries.

Phainopepla fled when first-winter Bluebird joined three-winter female in her clump.

She hungrily snapped mistletoe berries, tiny and red, from the sticklike branches erupting from a branch on a mesquite tree. He did too. The berries were juicy and sweet.

Mistletoe, a semi-parasitic plant, fed off the water and nutrients produced by the tree, but it also made its own food with its own chlorophyll. Some mistletoe bore female flower parts, some bore male. Winter was its season for blossoming and fruiting. Tiny aromatic flowers became tiny red berries, a great favorite with many birds. Birds spread the plant by wiping their beaks on branches after a sticky meal, or in their scat left on tree limbs. Desert mistletoe grew on most legume producing trees: palo verde, mesquite, catclaw and other acacia, and even invaded non-legume creosote on occasion.

First winter male Bluebird dropped down into a large mistletoe bunching from a creosote bush. He gobbled berries. Yuck! They were sour. He shuddered, disgusted.

"Follow the sugar," female Bluebird repeated, chortling at the expression on his face. "Mesquite's is sweet, acacia's quite meet, palo verde's no treat, and creosote's like dirty feet," she chanted. "And that's the mystery of mistletoe," she added. Then she flew to another mesquite tree burdened with mistletoe and continued to stuff herself.

He stopped reminiscing and looked around for his self-appointed guide through these wintering grounds. He knew he'd found his wintering companion and future mate.

"Follow the sugar," he sang as he flew.

The Small and the Mighty

It is said that there was once a time when Night, the feminine half of the two primary creators, strolled through the desert under a full moon. The evening was cool, but it was spring, and days were warm, warm enough that early annuals had flowered and gone to seed. As they dried, their limbs became brittle and their burrs hardened. Night sighed as she stepped through the growth covering her chosen path.

"Look at my slippers. How will I ever get them clean?"

They do brush off," promised Slender Pectocarya, notorious for her small crescent-shaped burrs. "But would you mind doing that elsewhere? I'm really trying for new territory next spring. How about that hillside over there? Wouldn't my tiny, white flowers be a wonderful carpet for its lower slopes next February? Provided we have plentiful winter rains, of course. If you could just pluck off my burrs over there, I'd be ever so grateful."

"If you're going over that way," added Filaree, "how about dropping off a few of my seeds too?" He hooked a few of his corkscrew-shaped seed pods to Night's shoes. In the next rain, moisture would cause the corkscrew to unwind, pushing the seed into the ground.

Bigelow bluegrass seed covered Night's footwear too. "On your way, before you reach the hill, how about sprinkling some of my seed under the creosote bushes? Yes, the thickest ones, just there, where my sprouts will be well shaded and better watered in the lowlands. My whole life is spent in six weeks of late winter-early spring, so your help in seeing next year's seed to good soil is much appreciated."

Night bent low, over a patch of plants only an inch high. Some branched, but many had just a single, erect stem. Tiny, red flowers clung to the plants, no bigger than a pinprick in size, and blood red. Tiny seeds, two per flower, dropped to the sandy soil below the plants, almost microscopic, but powerful, for the plants they became dominated the small plot of sandy soil. Their greens were soft to the touch. No burrs. No stickers.

"I'm so small," Sand Pygmyweed answered Night's unspoken question. "I have Wind and Rain to scatter my seed. I remain a tender carpet beneath your feet rather than a hitchhiker upon them."

"So tiny, were it not for your numbers, you'd go unnoticed," said Night in amazement. "How brave of you to maintain such vulnerability," she added, stroking the supple stems.

"Not really," answered Sand Pygmyweed modestly. "Like all life, I'm here only for a short while. Formed of Air, Earth, Fire, and Water: I'm no better, no worse, than any other.

"Wisely and well spoken," said Night. "You have knowledge many have yet to learn. Even though minute in size, you are mighty in soul."

Embarrassed, Sand Pygmyweed blushed. The entire patch looked pinkish surrounded by the other plants touched by rising Sun.

And to this day, each year's Sand Pygmyweeds redden at the deep, genetic memory of Night's praise, while humbly maturing their seed for the next generation, which they will never see.

A Mother's Secrets

It is said that there was once a time when Cottontail was seen busily digging beneath a creosote bush.

"Why are you doing that?" asked Young Goldfinch, perched in the highest branches of the same creosote. Born earlier in the spring, she still was not too young to know the cottontails bedded down each night in hiding spots fashioned by thickets of anything from bursage to cholla. They snoozed in quiet concealment, without rearranging the soil.

Cottontail ignored her, intent on her burrow building.

Mother goldfinch spoke up from the midst of the rest of the goldfinch clan clustered in constant conversation in a mesquite tree nearby. Little Goldfinch didn't know how her mother could have heard her question to Cottontail over the chatter of the rest of her family, but she'd been surprised often before by her mother's ability to hear her children over the crowd.

"It's time for nest-building," she told her daughter.

Visions of young Goldfinch's own recently departed nest came to mind, along with images of rabbits flying into trees to build nests like hers. She burst out laughing.

"Cottontails build nests?"

"Mommas do. Cottontail's nest is underground, a warm and safe cave for her babies," continued Mother Goldfinch. "A mother's job is to find a secure home for her little ones, where they can grow up undisturbed, in secret, away from those hunters who'd harm them. As I did for you," she added. "So when momma cottontails have their babies, they dig a nest. That's the only time Desert Cottontails bother with a burrow."

"Well, I hunt seed, not rabbits," declared Girl Goldfinch, "but I can see Cottontail plain as the branch I'm sitting on. Her nest's not much of a secret."

Cottontail glared at the birds above her. "Not with your lot around," she huffed. She pouted as she re-filled the hole where she'd been working on and off for several days. "No home is safe with your family around, telling everything they know, and then some, to anyone who'll listen." Exasperated, she hopped toward a dense stand of creosote on a nearby hillside, searching for another nest-site. The goldfinches fell silent as they watched her white puff-tail bounce out of sight.

"Ooops," sighed Daughter Goldfinch. "I'd have liked to watch baby bunnies grow. I'm sorry I gave away her nest."

"I'm betting she's going to dig again right over there where the bushes are thickest. You watch. You'll see her again, and her babies too," Momma predicted.

Two days later Little Goldfinch spied Cottontail collecting grasses and small sticks in her mouth as she browsed the edges of the creosote patch. She wasn't eating the grass, just filling her cheeks, bopping back into the shadow of the bushes with her collection.

"Is that for the nest?" she asked her mother discreetly, careful to mask her question in the mewing calls of her relatives so none but her mother would hear.

"I'm sure it is," Mother answered. "I'm told she also pulls hairs from her chest and belly to line the nest with something soft for her babies. As I did for you," she added. She looked down her own belly, at her brood patch, the area of thickened skin from which she'd plucked her downy feathers when making her nest. In doing so, she'd lined her nest and bared her warm skin, the better to incubate her eggs.

I didn't know that's where those feathers came from, thought Daughter Goldfinch, remembering her days as a nestling. There were the times her parents sheltered her and her naked nestmates from rain and cold with their bodies. Times the adults were harried trying to bring seed and aphids to their growing youngsters often enough to keep away starvation. Times they warned of predators and flew to decoy bushes to hide the nest's location from prying eyes. She realized just how hard they'd worked. Even to the point of plucking their own feathers to soften the nest.

Now Cottontail was lining her nest. Her work of rabbit-rearing was about to begin.

Young Goldfinch watched Cottontail sneak in and out of her creosote forest, but never followed to find the nest. She watched in surprise when Cottontail climbed a tree stump to get a higher view of the area, looking for anyone too interested in what she was doing, and quickly averted her eyes when the rabbit glanced her way. Weeks later, as she watched three baby rabbits leave their nest for the first time for rough and tumble play between the bushes, she never told a soul.

She didn't know about being a mother yet, but she knew the importance of keeping a mother's secrets. Those, she vowed, she'd never reveal again.

The Confidence Keeper

It is said that there was once a time when Day and Night, the two primary creators, sat together under a Mesquite tree, consulting over a need they sensed in their creation.

"A better than average intellect is a must," Day was saying, "to ensure enough understanding."

"A strong heart, too," said Night, "to ensure courage in listening. Such knowledge can be a heavy burden."

"Raven is certainly one of the smartest," continued Day.

"But also one of the most garrulous," reminded Night. "A marvelous mind, but one that could not refrain from using the knowledge to his own ends. He lacks the discretion necessary. His sense of fun is legendary, so he could keep from becoming depressed by others darkest secrets, but is he trustworthy enough? I think not. Raven is not naturally given to silence, especially if the telling of a tale will benefit him some way."

Day sighed. He thought. "There's Owl," he suggested. "A creature of your realm; one who sees well in the dark. With a reputation for wisdom," he added, after a pause.

"Yes, I too thought of Owl," Night responded. That one is wise, no doubt. Smart too. Those are not always the same," she reminded. "He travels in silence by night, so he's available to listen when others gather to talk before nodding off in sleep. His reputation as a harbinger of death has fortified him against the pain, griefs and worries others might share with him. He could keep still regarding what he was told. Yet, something's bothering me about asking him. I can't put my finger on it."

"He's trustworthy," said Day.

"Undoubtedly," agreed Night.

"Perhaps, though, he's not wise enough," Day said, thinking aloud.

"What do you mean?" prompted Night.

"It's Owl's nature to make an answer," Day continued. "He's compelled to find a solution, and tell it. He gives advice even when not asked for it. He's too directive."

Both Day and Night held their counsel for a time, resting in the peace and calm of the moment.

"Perhaps that's what bothers me about him," Night admitted. "The thing I couldn't put my finger on. There are sorrows that can't be told and silences that should not be broken. It is, sometimes, not respectful of another's travails to have all their answers."

"Thinking you have their answers is one thing; telling them is another, and Owl can't refrain from fixing. He can't conceive of being wrong. He doesn't just listen. He can't, because he's so sure he knows the remedy." Day fell silent.

"Perhaps no one should hold the position. Were we wrong? Should any creature be a repository for such secrets? Who can be trusted to know, but not manipulate? Who can be trusted to listen, but not advise. Who?"

At that moment, Bobcat paced stealthily downhill, past their shade tree, padding softly through the sand of the dry wash in front of them. Before moving out of sight at a bend in the drainage's bed, he cast a look over his shoulder at his creators. It was calm, without fear, unimpressed with their status, but alert, vigilant and knowing.

Day and Night watched him depart in silence.

"As furtive as he is, I'm sure he heard more than we think," said Day.

"More than we or any other creature can guess," concurred Night. "He would overhear and know secrets others don't even intend to confide.

"He's usually solitary," said Day.

"Normally silent," said Night.

"Shall we ask him now?" asked Day.

"No, wait a bit. Didn't you want to discuss a new nebula too?" remembered Night.

"Oh, right," recalled Day. "And then we'll ask him."

Water Dancing

It is said that there was once a time when Hummingbird paused to rest on a stone at the edge of a trickle of Water leaking from the side of a shaded canyon. He bowed deeply to dip the tip of his beak in the flow, drinking to fill his void. At the conclusion of each sip, he savored the elixir for a moment, then wagged his head to and fro, bobbing in time to some melody in his mind.

Nearby a shaft of Sun's light brightened the canyon's shade by slipping through a gash in the opposite wall to puddle on a Globe mallow that appeared to grow from the rock itself, but which had secretly tapped into the same moisture Earth served up to Hummingbird.

A Hairstreak butterfly hovered over the mallow's flowers, waiting for a female to arrive with whom he might mate. His four wings were mostly gray, but his hind wings were marked with a black spot in a patch of orange and two black and white tails, one very short, the other longer.

Since there were no other Hairstreak's abroad, this one's attention was free to wander and he couldn't help but notice Hummingbird sashaying after each swallow. After a minute of watching, he skipped down to the canyon wall where it wept Water from its depths and took a sip for himself. The fluid was warm and delicious. Minerals dissolved in the water renewed him. The strength of liquid stone fortified him. He felt goooood.

Now Hairstreak understood Hummingbird's dance to be the only appropriate response to such a wondrous dram. His tails began quivering and his hind wings rubbed together so oddly that Hummingbird laughed out loud.

"Your top looks like your bottom and your bottom like your top," he reported to the gyrating butterfly. "I can't tell if your coming or going."

Indeed, the orange spots on the butterfly's hind wings did resemble eyes and the tails were like antennae.

Hairstreak and Hummingbird both rumbaed with joy, revitalized by their drinks. They compared moves and laughed at each other's antics.

Although this occasion was the first of Hairstreak's ventures into dance, it was hardly the last. In fact, Hairstreak butterflies are now well known as displayers of great joy in life by the excited rubbing of their hind wings. This you may be privileged to see as they visit flowers for nectar.

But if you are very lucky, you may find them dancing in the company of hummingbirds in wet-walled canyons. And if this should be the case, stop and listen. If you are very quiet, you may hear butterfly and hummingbird laughter echoing through the gorge, invading your heart.

A Change of Coloring

It is said that there was once a time when Day and Night sat listening to complaints. Curved-billed Thrasher was telling his experience with Tarantula Hawk.

He'd been minding his own business, sipping and munching soggy cactus fruit where it'd fallen after Wind had stripped it from a prickly pear in a pre-Rain hyper-dash across the desert floor. It had been on the ground a while, sitting in the warm sun, wet from the recent rain. It was fermenting.

A number of other creatures shared the meal, Tortoise, Cactus Wren, a variety of bees and wasps. Everyone ate hungrily until they were full, or groggy, whichever came first.

The larval stages of tarantula hawks feed on spiders, but adults are nectarivorous, so they were one species of wasp feeding with the others. They drank so much they were having trouble flying. They stumbled along, buzzing their wings, but going nowhere.

Thrasher was feeling dizzy too and had the misfortune of stepping on a female tarantula hawk as she perched on a stick, attempting a take-off. Extremely irritated, she rewarded him with a sting. Her one-third inch long stinger was reputed to do the worst damage of any other desert insect's. Thrasher, instantly paralyzed with pain, couldn't argue the point. He screamed a whole non-stop minute, then escaped under the cactus, squeezing between thorny pads, as far from the fruit as he could hide.

Now he stood before Day and Night, complaining of the unwarranted viciousness of her attack and requesting action be taken so this might never happen again.

A male tarantula hawk stood nearby, standing in for the offending female and representing his species. He introduced himself to Day and Night.

"Where is the subject of this complaint?" asked Day, surprised the wasp wasn't there to plead her own case as a matter of self-defense.

"She's not able to be here, Honorable Creators, for...." began the male wasp, before being interrupted by Thrasher.

"Because with a stinger like hers, she doesn't have to care what anyone thinks of her. She doesn't need to respect authority, even yours," declared the wounded bird to Day and Night.

"Calm down, Bird," soothed Night. "You've had your say. Now it's his turn." She turned to the wasp. "You were saying?" she prompted. "Where is the accused?"

"Gone, My Lady," stated the shiny black, two-inch long insect, drawing himself up to look bigger beside the seven-inch tall Thrasher. "She...."

"Won't accept the consequences of her behavior," announced Thrasher.

"Silence," roared Day, then added more quietly, "or you'll face the consequences."

A humbled Thrasher crouched low to the ground in submission.

"Go on," Night told the wasp.

"She fell victim herself, that day, to one she could not protect herself from, regardless of her stinger. Proving our species should not have ours removed," continued the spider wasp in a pleading tone. "Lest our females be in greater peril. Not to mention our young who rely on their mothers' stingers for food."

Thrasher raised his eye-brow in disbelief, but kept quiet. Day looked amazed. Night said, "Who bested her?"

"Roadrunner dashed into the feast and made short work of many of the drunken insects, crushing them and gobbling them down before they could defend themselves," admitted Male Tarantula Hawk.

"Impressive," muttered Day to Night under his breath, so Tarantula Hawk could not hear.

"Indeed," answered Night in a whisper.

"Your females will not be punished by removing their stingers," she assured the Defense, "but we shall agree to make changes to help prevent accidents such as yours," she nodded to Thrasher.

"Hardly an accident," growled Curved-billed Thrasher quietly, so only the defending wasp could hear, but Day looked his way with a glare, so Thrasher said no more.

"We'll color your species differently as a warning to other creatures to avoid you. That will keep away many potential predators. For the rest, you'll still have your stinger," and with that, Night deferred to Day. He answered by turning the male wasp's wings a bright reddish-orange, a color of warning that happened to be one of his favorites, a product of his fiery personality.

"How will that help?" pouted Thrasher. "He's not the one with the stinger."

"The whole species carries this color now," answered Day. "So watch for it," he added. "Especially when eating overly ripened fruit."

"And you," he turned to stare at Male Tarantula Hawk. "Learn to sip only so much as still allows you to fly. That too is your defense. Don't be stupid and feast yourself to the point you lose it."

With that, Day and Night declared the matter closed.

The Original Down Jacket

It is said that there was once a time before Earth knew seasons. The temperature was always moderate, or even a little warm, the perfect nursery for new life. Needless to say, the first winter came as quite a shock. Every creature was forced to adjust and find some manner of keeping warm. Hot springs became popular hangouts. Sun-warmed rocks were perches for everyone in mid-afternoon. Nights were hardest for all. Then, whether on branch or in burrow, sleepers kept company and snuggled for warmth in numbers.

Birds found shelter in old nests, amongst leaves or even in the holes of rodents, but still shivered in chill winter winds. Some found a way to depress their usual temperature of a hundred or more by slipping into a torpor during the night's coldest hours. This left them vulnerable to those who hunted by dark, but because they were so immobile, if well hidden by the shelter they'd chosen, most escaped with their lives--so long as the temperatures didn't drop too low.

Morning found every bird out seeking food. Fat reserves and calories from daily foraging kept them alive in the cold.

It was the quail that discovered another way to keep warm.

Cactus Wren darted about chasing seed from Desert Broom, which was blowing to gather under Creosote Bush's feet. He noticed a handful of Gambol's Quail dashing about on a similar mission, looking three times their normal size.

"How have you gotten so fat?" he squawked, most indiscreetly. "Where did you find so much food?"

"We are as hungry as you," answered a male Quail. "Our search for seed is as endless as yours."

"But you are as big around as you are tall. There's much more to you now than when I noticed you last. All of your band is bulging. What's up with that? Is marching better for collecting seed? Is that why you prefer that to flying?"

A male Quail paused disdainfully. He thought little of Cactus Wren, so prone to thieving and a solitary lifestyle when not raising chicks. And such chicks! Virtually helpless until a couple of weeks old. His own offspring were far more capable fresh from the egg. The two birds had little in common. Except the cold.

"We are puffed up to stay warm," Quail told Cactus Wren, a little condescendingly. He hurried to catch up with the rest of his flock, for they were feeding and he was not. He clucked sociably with his friends and scratched the ground with them, attempting to ignore the lone wren, who had flown in to continue his line of questioning.

"What do you mean?" asked the speckled Wren. "How does that keep you warm?"

"Fluffing our undercoat of tiny, downy feathers traps air underneath, which we warm and wear like insulation," explained Quail. "That's why we look so much bigger and rounder. We're not fatter, just fluffed. You try it," he suggested.

Cactus Wren did. He found it a real help against the chilly winter weather. Being completely unable to keep quiet about any news, he spread the word until all the birds

263

were doing it. As he told the story, though, all the credit for discovery was his.

"What a blowhard," Quail said when Cactus Wren's version of the down coat story got back to him.

"What else can you expect from such a social misfit?" replied a nearby quail hen. "He has so few friends he lied to gain some. But quail will never be in that number," she promised.

"At least more birds know how to stay warm," said Male Quail. "Our breakthrough has spread from our community to all winged ones. What does fame matter when lives are being saved?"

So now, every winter finds all birds wearing down jackets. Due to Quail's generosity and Cactus Wren's bragging.

Sparrow Send Off

It is said that there was once a time when sparrows who wintered in the desert were simply here one day and gone the next. They departed for breeding grounds in other lands silently, without fanfare. The flocks they'd formed during the darkest days of the year simply crumbled. Individuals took off when they were strong enough to travel in order to find mates on their summer turf, there spending a frantic-paced season nest building, egg tending, young feeding and giving flying lessons until a new generation of sparrows was able to see to their own livelihoods. Yet this behavior seemed so wrong, so very wrong. Not the proper way to tie up friendships formed while flocking. No way to start another round of chick-rearing. Something was lacking. It just wasn't sparrowish, some birds felt.

Winter, being the season free of the tasks of bringing up young sparrows, was the time for rest and relaxation. Flocks formed naturally as experienced travelers discussed changes in the area from last year, which faces were new and whose offspring were the best looking. Newcomers learned where to find water, the best wild seed, the most protection from predators, and met new species they'd never seen on their birthing grounds. A few sparrow species shared some of the same habitat in both seasonal homes and knew each other slightly from summering together, but much better after winter get-togethers. Brewers and White-crowned sparrows were in this category. While south, they associated with each other in large, mixed flocks, feeding together, hanging out at the water tank together, chittering sociably, watching for potential dangers, and roosting together in bushes for warmth on cold nights. Then, come spring, they went their several ways.

"We need a way to celebrate and close out the season," Brewer's Sparrow insisted. He was a chatty and personable soul. Always the first to greet everyone in fall, he hated the communal habit of leaving without any goodbye. "We should announce our departure to our friends. That way, those who are ready to leave can travel together and those who are not will at least know we're heading out. It's safer to move north together rather than separately.

"I've made some good buddies amongst the White-crowned crowd too. I enjoy spending warm afternoons scratching in the dust for grass seed with them. They are full of stories of lands farther north than I'll ever fly. I think they look so regal with their black and white head-striping and they're so much bigger than us. They make us look good just by standing near us."

"Speak for yourself," laughed his listener, also a Brewer's. "I feel scrawnier standing next to their bulk, but I have made some good friends too. Among the Sage and Chipping sparrows, as well. I miss them when they go. They always seem to push off before we do."

"And we never get to say 'goodbye'--exactly what I'm complaining about."

"So what's the fix? What are you suggesting?"

"How about a post-vacation, pre-nuptial party? A way to say goodbye to the single life, any kind of social life, and pleasures with no responsibilities. A last hoorah before mating and driving ourselves crazy providing for kids."

"A party?"

"Or parties."

"Who's invited?"

"Everyone."

"How will we spread the word?"

"Call it from every bush and tree, all day long. Every time you're not actually eating and drinking. We'll pick a spot and call everyone to show up there."

The two of them started their busy, trilling-buzzy calls in their best announcement voices, and before long five or six more Brewer's sparrows joined their ranks. They chattered on about migration paths, waterhole and weather predictions, rumors mostly. Other sparrows came by, hearing the commotion, and before long the entire leeward side of a gently wooded hill swarmed with sparrows, Brewers buzzing, White-crowns twiddling and assorted other voices adding to the chorus, including House Finches, Abert's Towhees and a squawking Cactus Wren. It turned out everyone was looking for an excuse to indulge in a little jubilation before the hard work ahead. Females as well as males.

The palo verde trees were in bloom, though downsizing the show from their peak of glory, and caterpillars crawled amongst the yellow petals still on tree limbs or blowing across the ground in every breeze. These impressed none but the Cactus Wren, who did pause long enough to eat the larvae, then review the birds' travel plans--just out of curiosity. He was already where he would live his entire life. The sparrows, though, ignored the crawlies and kept right on talking. Loudly. From every creosote, budding cholla and blossomed palo verde. It was impossible to think. No one waited to get a word in edgewise; there was no edgewise. The party went on for days, wrapping up only so the revelers could rest at night. There wasn't any one spot where everyone gathered. Any place there was a little shade, a little companionship, a little sunshine, would do. After two weeks of insane socializing, one morning the desert was minus the calls of the White-crowns. They had all left for northern forests and tundra.

Brewers still congregated, but their numbers dwindled too, the pull of their beloved sagebrush-filled breeding grounds impossible to ignore. Soon all the sparrows had migrated and the desert seemed starkly silent without them.

With the next winter's influx of northern sparrows, the commitment was renewed to gather for a season-closing, post-vacation, pre-nuptial fling to which all were invited.

Every spring since then is noisy with their gossip until all are on their way, stirred by awakening hormones and carried by the winds they start up with their incessant chattering and fanfare. So satisfyingly sparrowish.

Admit it, you wondered why spring is always so windy, didn't you?

Tortoise Gets a New Diet

It is said that there was once a time when Tortoise turned, with a mouth full of cholla quills, and said, "You know what? I could really use a change of diet."

"What sort of change?" asked Earth.

"Not that I'm complaining," said Tortoise, "but I do eat loads of thorny-type foods, due to a lack of anything else. Cactus is nice...lots of moisture and what not. And grasses are good too, until they get a little old and tough in the parching desert breeze. At that point, the seeds can sort of stick in my craw, but--hey, I realize this ain't a jungle. Plants in the desert do sort of tend toward thorniness. Still, it would be so nice to have a bite of something that just slid right down, something leafy and green. And flowers-- flowers would be nice. Flowers and leafy greens," she sighed. "Yeah, that's the ticket."

"Have you thought about moving to a jungle?" Earth suggested.

"At my rate of travel?" asked Tortoise.

"I see your point," said Earth. "I rather like leaves too," she added. "But those kinds of plants like to grow in wetter places than the desert. Perhaps, though, the banks and beds of watercourses could provide enough moisture for the herbs you're dreaming up. Would that foraging ground be alright with you?"

"You bet," Tortoise responded enthusiastically. I hang out in those sorts of places anyway. I prefer them for digging my burrows and laying eggs. Arroyos and washes are my favorite places."

"Will you settle for something less than lavish?" Earth asked.

"Meaning?" Tortoise responded.

"Meaning that I will probably have to stick to smaller leaves and blossoms than you were perhaps hoping. Anything too large will just lose water too quickly to survive."

"I understand," nodded Tortoise. "I'd just be grateful if they had no thorns."

"Then I'll see what I can do," promised Earth. "Variety is good."

"And thornless even better," reminded Tortoise.

"Got it," chuckled Earth.

Tortoise crawled into her burrow to avoid the afternoon heat. The days were getting shorter and the nights somewhat cooler, so she knew her season for active feeding and strolling around the desert was coming to an end. Still, she was a little surprised to wake up from her early October afternoon nap--the following May. By this time she was hungry enough to settle for thorns, but she remembered Earth's promise and departed her burrow with high hopes.

"Helloooo," called Tortoise upon emerging from her hibernation home. "Create anything new while I was gone? she asked optimistically.

"Something with leaves and flowers maybe?" questioned Earth a little distractedly, for she was overseeing Saguaro and the ripening of its fruit for the benefit of many desert animals.

"That's the agreement I remember," assured Tortoise.

"I came up with some modifications," said Earth. "With the help of Sun, Rain and Wind. Take a look in that wash over there."

Tortoise ambled down a gentle slope to a strange new plant that sprawled along the sandy floor of the wash. It had tiny white flowers with maroon in the center. Quite lovely, really. Nearly microscopic, but lovely. The leaflets were small as well, and oblong in shape, with not a single thorn to be seen. She took a bite. The thick, white, sticky sap was slightly bitter, but quite an improvement over Prickly Pear.

After eating one of the plant's foot long stems, she said, "You've outdone yourself. This is truly delicious. The flowers are so small, yet pleasant to look at and more pleasant to munch. I can't thank you enough."

Earth looked at the plant Tortoise paused before. "That's Rattlesnake Weed, just one of the new ones," she smiled conspiratorially. "There are two more, so keep looking."

Tortoise continued her breakfasting stroll through the gravelled streambed, now empty of any water. She entered the shade of Palo Verde where he anchored an island of Giant Bursage and Hackberry to the floor of the wash. There Javalina had dug into the gravel, scouring a shallow pit which pooled with an inch of water. Evidently the wash had run with water the previous week and the sands beneath the dry surface harbored moisture. Tortoise drank her fill.

The sunny bank of the island beyond Palo Verde held a great stone. Rooted in the dirt alongside the rock was another plant Tortoise had not seen before. It had tiny blossoms, yellow as the sun, and pea-shaped, for this plant was a legume, meaning it formed pods for fostering its maturing seeds. It's gray-green leaves were pinnately compound, as were Palo Verde's, typical for legumes. Tortoise stretched out her neck and took a taste. The leaves were hairy, but not thorny. She feasted on pods, leaves and stems from the ground-covering foliage.

"I see you've found Desert Lotus," applauded Earth. "One more to go."

Tortoise, reptile that she was, was beginning to heat up in the desert sun. She headed for the shade of a nearby Hackberry bush.

The lowest branches of the Hackberry were stripped of leaves, leaving an open spot for another plant to root and grow within the protective Hackberry branches. Tortoise didn't recognize it. The stems were rather sticky and branched in U-shaped junctions--quite unusual. The leaves were larger than Snakeweed or Desert Lotus, to Tortoise's great delight. They were tortoise-bite-sized, and most looked three-toed--if she thought of the leaf as a footprint. It had flowers too. These were nearly an inch across, shaped like a funnel, mostly white, but with a pale, pink 5-pointed star traced within. Lovely. And tempting too. She took a bite. She swallowed. A tortoise fantasy!

"You did it!" exclaimed Earth. "In a single morning you found all three. I bet Rain you couldn't find them all in one day, but I just lost. That's Wishbone bush, by the way. I hope you noticed the relatively large leaves and the fact that the stems are floppy and easy for you to reach."

"I sure did and can't thank you enough for my new foods. They are wonderful. Tasty, juicy, and no stickers! A dream come true."

"Oh, I had fun," assured Earth. "I like making variety. Variety is good."

"And thornless even better," reminded Tortoise.
Earth laughed.

Scrub Jay, The First Questioner

It is said that there was once a time when no one questioned anything. Day and Night continued creating one new life form after another, and all was harmony. Then came Scrub Jay.

"Blue," Day said. "That's a good compromise color, and not one we've overused, I think."

"Agreed," said Night. She was satisfied, for blue reminded her of both Earth, in her waters, and Sky, in his daytime appearance. Night suggested a gray back and belly to assist Scrub Jay in blending into the shadows of the scrub oak forest this bird would call his summer home.

"Why not a white bib too?" added Day. "A raggedy edged one perhaps."

Day and Night stood back to review their work. He was quite striking in appearance. Blue always is. But then they watched Scrub Jay in action, and what they saw did not exactly enthrall them.

Their newest creature was given to thievery, often robbing nests of eggs or very young birds, or dipping into stores of food put up by woodpeckers. He bobbed his head oddly too, for no apparent reason. At the same time, he was quite meticulous, wiping his bill habitually on his perch after swallowing a morsel of food or drinking from a stream. Other times...just because. To drink, he would tilt his beak straight up to the sky to roll the water down his throat. Then wipe, wipe, wipe--to clean his bill. None of these eccentricities had been planned into his pattern when Day and Night were debating his creation. They were at a loss as to how these peculiarities had developed.

Worst of all was Scrub Jay's raucous, screechy call, sounding like an accusatory, questioning "See?", drawled out as an obnoxious, "Seeeee? Seeeee?" Scrub Jay called it constantly, as if doubtful of his creators' credentials.

"I'm not sure I appreciate his attitude," huffed Night. "Gratitude is not one of his traits."

"Not exactly," agreed Day, "but I have to admire his moxie, nevertheless. Perhaps it's not such a bad idea to have some creatures question our handiwork. Nothing ever changes unless we query ourselves occasionally and make revisions due to that self-doubting. Let's keep Scrub Jay as he is, to remind us to stop now and then and question our work, our values, the way we view what we're creating here. It'll keep us on our toes and much more flexible in our ways."

Night rethought her position. "OK," she agreed. "But why stop with one 'questioner'?"

"Yes.... Why?" asked Day. Immediately they began to plan Phainopepla as the black and white asker of "Why?" from the tops of mesquite and ironwood trees.

"And who...who?" asked Night, already envisioning the "questioner" she would make to hunt throughout her dark domain.

Thus began the creation of a number of specialists, created to question and bring doubt to mind in all listeners, for Day and Night knew the importance of some occasional second guessing. A crack in the facade of omniscience, allowing wisdom to sneak through.

Ahhh, the blessed questioners.

How Verdin Got His Colors

It is said that there was once a day, after shining for eons of similar days, that the Sun thought to look over the face of the Earth, seeking his closest relative.

"Every day I shed light which the Earth takes and makes into new creatures. Surely one of them shows my attributes and can be called my kin. I am so far away from all Earth Mother's activity down there that I need to see myself in at least one creature. All of them resemble her. They are obviously made of her substance. But where is mine? If I can find kin among them, I'll have reason to keep shining my light on her. But what is the use of my efforts if none of the life on Earth even resembles me?"

A passing Cloud heard the Sun's musings. Without taking its eyes from the shadow it was playfully casting over the landscapes below, it made a suggestion.

"You are hot, so hot you make me rise from the waters of Earth below, but were I to approach closer, I know I would disappear. So I stay only this high and no higher. Look in the hottest places for your closest relative among those below.

"Then too, you are high above the Earth. None is higher than you in the day sky. You should look for your closest relative among the creatures who can leave the earth to approach you, but not fly so high as to be able to challenge your authority.

"Additionally, you are always in motion. You never stop walking across the sky. I have seen that some of the life below is slow and lazy, but much is not. Your close relative will be found among those who never rest during the day, just as you do not."

Sun considered Cloud's suggestions and thought Cloud's assessment practical and accurate. Sun was always hot, always high over Earth and always moving.

Surely his closest relative on Earth would show those attributes.

He would begin his search where Cloud suggested, in the hottest places on Earth, in a creature that could rise above the Earth, but not so high as to challenge his authority, and in a creature that was in constant motion all day.

He discovered quickly that the hottest places on Earth were deserts and the hottest of these had fewer varieties of life than other parts of the planet. One desert seemed a good balance between hot temperatures and enough occupants that his search for kin would be successful.

In this desert, a huge Saguaro cactus lifted its limbs to the sky...high, but not so high as to challenge his authority. It withstood his heat, was not too high, but it did not move except for a gentle rocking in a steady wind, and that was hardly enough to qualify as his close kin.

He watched an eagle, golden in Sun's light, circling on widespread wings over the desert below. Higher and higher it rose on the air currents and its own strength. It could not come up as high as Sun, but it approached much higher than Saguaro had done and, frankly, Sun worried. He thought Eagle must envy his high status and did not trust kin such as this to remember its place and not challenge him. Eagle would not qualify as close kin for it could not be trusted.

"Eagle is a bird, though," Sun reflected. "My kin will be found among birds, for birds can fly and approach me. But perhaps a bird that only flies as high as Saguaro can reach would be best. That is high enough, but not so high as to displease me."

276

So Sun focused on the birds of Earth below, in the desert that held the Saguaro.

He was so intent on his search that Earth parched in his mid-day radiance and heat waves rose to obscure his vision.

Nevertheless, in amongst the green foliage of a thorny acacia, he noticed a gray creature bobbing on the very tip of a branch, scouring it for tiny insects to eat. Having snatched a morsel, it was off to a new branch, dancing between the leaflets, seeking a new snack with eager beak and dashing demeanor.

Tiny it was...not a challenge to his authority at all, and it never seemed to fly higher than the trees, which meant not higher than Saguaro could reach.

Always in motion it was...never pausing in its busy-ness, never napping, ever flitting, industrious as he in every way.

Even in the worst heat of the day it seemed undaunted.

"Surely, this creature is one of my own," said Sun.

He reached out to grab it in its constant fluttering flight. He wanted to bring it closer for a better look, tiny as it was. He grasped it at its shoulders.

"Ouch," wailed the little bird, ticking aloud in its distress.

"Oh, hold still for just a moment and let me look," said Sun. "I won't be long. I'm looking for a close relative and you may just be the one I seek."

"So what?" replied the bird. "What if I am close kin? I don't care. Just set me free so I can eat. And do hurry up about it. I can smell my feathers burning."

"What is your name?" asked Sun.

"Verdin," answered the bird. "Now, let gooooo."

By this time Sun could smell feathers burning too. It was not a delightful smell, so he did let go.

277

"Verdin," announced Sun, "is obviously close kin, for he flew, he loved heat, and he hated to sit still even long enough for me to make his acquaintance."

And that's why to this day Verdin has a face turned yellow from looking Sun in the eye, and red scorch marks on his shoulders, where Sun was holding him. These mark him as Sun's closest relative on Earth.

Satisfied with his findings, Sun decided to continue to send Earth light each day for making more creatures. She was providing them with his attributes too.

The Evolution of Cochineal

It is said that in the time when the quiet, cryptic energies approached Moon for her assistance in appearing on Earth's surface, there was much discussion about how these things should come to pass. Moon consulted with Sun, naturally, and that done, all the other elementals were soon involved. "There, but not there," became the theme of not only the quiet energies; it was also the next big creative push. It took on nearly festival proportions, quite out of character with the energies seeking manifestation. Reclusive by nature, they hated being examined and consulted by Day and Night, Sun and Moon, Earth and Sky, Wind and Water, and the other elements. Realizing this, Day made a decision.

"Let's come up with ideas that fit our theme and then we'll ask for the energy to come forward that wants to play that role. Our wild committee meetings are scaring the bashful energies away. Let's spare them involvement until we have some specific plans in hand--what do you say?" he asked.

"Good idea," said Night. The rest concurred, except Water, who felt the energies themselves might provide some insight into what their final forms should be and should have input in the process from the beginning.

"We won't be keeping them out of the planning process entirely," said Day. "When we are creating the new creature, the energy will have its say--completely. But to have them waiting while the rest of us loudmouths throw around ideas and possibilities is just wearing them out. I can tell some wish they'd never asked Moon for help."

"It **is** chaotic right now," agreed Water. "OK. We'll wait to bring the quiet energies on board until after we've hammered out a few ideas."

The energies gratefully left the field to the elementals and the boisterous discussion continued. Fire suggested hiding energies of different colors in unlikely places. Sun immediately chimed in his approval and Day, not surprisingly, agreed. Light was important to these three and they liked the thought of hiding it where others would least expect it. The rest were intrigued and said they'd help when called upon.

Red was one of the first colors they worked with, as it was a favorite of Day, Sun and Fire. Fire said he considered it the biggest of all colors, and that it should reside in the smallest of all creatures. Everyone loved the idea. It was time to bring in the quiet energy that wanted to participate in the project. One volunteered and the process of form building began.

They chose, after further discussion, to make an insect. Cochineal, a name that means "scarlet-colored" was made of males, who were small and winged so that they could fly around to find mates--and females, who stayed in one place and laid eggs. The place where the females would stay was on prickly pear pads. They remained with their mouths pressed against the cacti's green skin, sucking plant juices for food. For protection, they formed a white, waxy matter which covered their bodies and made the prickly pear pad look patchy. It was the females that hid the color red under the wax. They were about a quarter inch long and when engorged with prickly pear juice, they turned a bright red.

There was a crowding problem, however, which the quiet energy solved by suggesting that when the eggs hatched beneath the stationary female, all the young ought to have the power of motion. While in their crawler stage,

280

they would move to the edge of the prickly pear pad of their birth and shoot out a wax filament and catch the breeze to float them to a new pad. This would give the females the chance to fly too, though only briefly. When they became adults, they'd latch onto the pad of their choice for the duration of their lives. The suggestions were accepted.

Red was hidden most inconspicuously, since it couldn't be seen unless the white wax was peeled away to reveal the insect below. The quiet energy loved the anonymity--but agreed that since red was the biggest color, it must have a time for notoriety, if only for the sake of Sun, Fire and Day.

That season for show, when red would come busting out all over, was determined by another creature--humans. When they harvested the cochineal, dried them, crushed them and mixed them with a fixing agent, red burst out of dyed textiles and foods. No longer hidden, red was glorious. The Aztecs were producing the dye when the Spanish came to the New World. The Spaniards liked it so well they imported the cochineal/prickly pear combination to other parts of the world to farm it. Michelangelo bought some for his paintings. It became the red in British Redcoats, Canadian Mounted police uniforms, Hussar breeches, the Turks' Fez and even the first American flag's red stripes. So much red from so tiny a source. Red so very much "there" after an insect-hidden phase of "not there."

Everyone loved the irony.

Palo Verde Webber's Insubordination

It is said that there was once a time when Palo Verde Webber argued with Day and Night, the two primary creators. This was astounding for a number of reasons. One was that Palo Verde Webber was so tiny in size. Barely a quarter inch long and blending in with the blossoms of his host, the Foothills Palo Verde tree, he was hardly noticeable at all. The webbing he stretched about in the ends of branches in spring revealed his presence, but muffled his voice even more than his diminutive size. It may have been a communal shout that first got the attention of the royals, but once that was accomplished, they found themselves quarreling with a very determined creature. A light yellow-green in color, the caterpillar web-spinner owned a face no larger than the head of a pin, but managed to state his case boldly and occupy the Creators for most of a morning listening to his quarrel.

Palo Verde Webber wanted to fly. It was in his genes. He just knew it. He would not take "no" for an answer. He insisted. He begged. He had rights. He would not just go away.

Day and Night began arguing patiently, but wound up exasperated. Day threatened to eliminate the tiny larvae completely, but Night and a good many birds disagreed. The birds spoke up in behalf of their food stuff, unwilling to see such easy meals zapped into oblivion. Night advised level-headedness rather than deleting a creation from the diversity of life already formed. She reminded Day that Palo Verde Webber was an indispensable member of his community, though regrettably unruly and disrespectful of his sources.

"Then you handle this debate," Day announced. He stalked away huffily to be amused by Wind, who spun in circles in the distance, juggling clods of dried grasses and measuring how high he could whip a funnel of dust into the air.

"That can't be good," clicked Verdin, the tiny, grey bird that benefited from Palo Verde Webber hatchings each spring. He scoured Palo Verde branches for the little tidbits he loved so much and couldn't imagine how anything so puny and vulnerable would risk Day's anger and possible removal from his own diet. Verdin would miss the tasty, little fellow.

"You must understand, dear Webber," Night continued, "you will fly. It's your destiny. You'll be a tiny, brown moth one day, and soon too. You'll fly all you want then. That's why you feel it's in your genes. It is, but you must wait. All things in time."

So saying, she left, refusing to hear any more argument.

"I can't believe your impudence," stated Cardinal.

"You're lucky to be alive," wheezed Gnatcatcher.

Palo Verde tree was more sympathetic. Besides, he preferred spending less time hosting hordes of Palo Verde Webbers. Their webs sometimes got so thick they killed the new growth at the end of his twigs. If they flew away as larvae, he'd have to feed them less, and that was agreeable to him.

"I'm sorry you couldn't convince them," he said to the irate wiggler. "You certainly deserve to follow your calling, just as soon as you're convinced of it, and you're obviously obsessed with flight. I know they've said you must wait, but isn't there some way you could take to the air now? Just to show them? Think about it. Maybe there's some way you can fly without wings."

Well that got Palo Verde Webber thinking.

The next morning Palo Verde stirred in the quickening breeze of a new day.

"I like your new look," whooshed Wind in passing.

"What?" asked Palo Verde. Then he saw it himself. Nearly every branch was festooned with a gossamer streamer, six feet or more in length. At the end of each, billowing on Wind's breeze, was a tiny adventurer in the process of leaving the tree that had been home, tethered for the moment, but still in flight. Palo Verde Webber was flying.

When the birds reported the news, Night laughed, and even Day nodded respectfully.

"Who'd have guessed?" asked Day appreciatively.

"Isn't that the point?" Night answered merrily. "We give everyone some freedom and oh, how they run with it."

Jojoba Hallelujah

It is said that there was once a time when the Jojobas began to fret about reproduction. Day and Night, the two primary creators, made the bush very long-lived, upwards of 150 years and more, so the concern did not immediately present itself. They also made the plant in male and female form. Each was covered with oval, grey-green, inch-long, leathery leaves. Leaves were paired on both sexes' branches. Both sexes were necessary to produce acorn-like seeds on the female's branches, the only fruit of their labor and their sole hope of procreation. Male and female both flowered in the winter. The male produced plenty of pollen, but the flowers on the female were tipped upside down, facing the ground. Very few insects seemed able to efficiently drag the male's pollen to the female's flowers to pollinate them, so very few seed-nuts ever formed. Those that did were eaten by animals. Rabbits, pocket mice and squirrels all delighted in them, and none were left to germinate a new generation of Jojoba.

Around the time of their 179th birthday, Male Jojoba grew concerned.

"Perhaps there's something wrong with your flowers," he called to his wife, rooted six feet away in the rocky hillside above a small desert spring.

"There's nothing wrong with my flowers," huffed Female Jojoba. "I've made nuts often enough to know I can do it. The squirrels know it too. That's why they watch for fruit ripening each summer and eat all I produce. I just need to make more, so a few get past their jaws and bellies. Perhaps you aren't producing enough pollen," she suggested.

"There's nothing wrong with my pollen count," retorted Male Jojoba. "I make plenty. You've seen the golden leggings the bees have when they leave my flowers. I don't know why they can't seem to deliver it to you. I still say there's something wrong with your flowers."

"I make plenty of flowers. You can see that for yourself. I make them the only way I know how. If there's anything wrong, we need to talk to Day and Night to seek revisions. Maybe that's what we should do. Get their help," responded Female Jojoba.

"You know how long it takes to get an audience with them. As plants, we pretty much have to wait for one of them to stroll by so we can ask to get on the agenda."

"Maybe not," breathed Wind. He could not help but overhear the Jojoba as he warmed in the sunlight over the spring and rose up the crease in the desert's skin that formed a small gully above the waterhole. "I can search out Day and Night for you. I have no roots to limit me."

As he eddied in the warming air currents, he noticed Male Jojoba's pollen wafting on his breeze.

"Hold on," said Wind excitedly. "What have we here? Maybe we don't need Day and Night. We may be able to do this ourselves."

"How?" asked Male Jojoba. Then he noticed the small golden cloud lifting from his branches toward Female Jojoba. "Oh, I see," he said enthusiastically. He began trembling in the passing gusts, attempting to shake more pollen into the air.

Female Jojoba saw their intent and she began cheering it on.

"Come on," she sang out. "A little higher, a little harder." They all watched the pollen cloud approach her.

Wind exhaled more forcefully. Male Jojoba shook harder in the heating currents swirling around him.

Antelope Squirrel, departing his burrow to bask in the sun, quickly caught on to what Wind and the Jojobas were attempting. He knew he'd benefit by having more seed-nuts, so he skipped up the slope, just under the misting pollen, blowing with all his might every few hops.

"Come on, Wind," he gasped. "We can do it. Don't give up. Lift it higher, higher," he chanted as he watched the sulphur fog creep toward Female Jojoba. "You did it! It's there," he announced as the pollen wafted between her branches.

"Hooray," Male Jojoba burst out.

"Finally," Wind huffed and puffed.

"I can feel it," affirmed Female Jojoba.

Both the Jojobas were so delighted they raised their leaves upward to applaud Wind's efforts. In so doing, little whirlwinds formed around the base of the leaves, the very spot the flowers resided, pulling pollen up into the blossoms and fertilizing them.

"Keep doing that," called Wind. "Keep your leaves up," he commanded. "It creates an updraft."

Both Jojobas did exactly that and reproduction has never been a problem for them since.

Bighorn Sheep's Customizing

It is said that there was once a time when Day and Night, the two primary creators, strolled to the meeting place Night had prearranged with Desert Bighorn Sheep. Night informed Day that Bighorn had approached her with a special request and asked to discuss it with them both. It seemed, she reported, that Bighorn wanted to swim.

"What?" roared Day. He well remembered the extra time and energy he and Night had put into the sheep's creation, especially the ram. They had been weeks designing the creature. His coat was tan, with white gracing the underbelly, muzzle, eye-patches, rump and backside of each leg. Hooves were jet black. He was already very handsome, really.

Forming the mouth so early in the game had proven to be a mistake, though. As soon as he could speak, Bighorn requested huge horns. His mate could have small ones, but as the ram, he wanted something impressive. Day and Night designed brown, curving structures larger than the ewe's. But Bighorn wanted more.

"Larger," he snorted.

Day and Night went larger.

"Bigger," the ram insisted.

Night stretched the horns into a double curve.

"More," said Bighorn.

"Now you're getting ridiculous," Day said through clenched teeth.

"Not at all," insisted Bighorn. "The size of my horns, in addition to my weight and age, will determine my dominance in mating. The girls need to see something incredible. The guys need to be intimidated. More."

Night added mass. "We really must stop here," she told Bighorn. "Now your horns weigh as much as all the rest of your skeleton combined. We can't increase them further."

Bighorn stood. But couldn't lift his head.

"Lotta good your keen eyesight does you now," scoffed Day. "Or your ability to skip twenty feet through the air from one tiny ledge to another in your mountain home. You won't be going anywhere."

Bighorn grunted, but refused to accept smaller horns.

"Let's rethink the design of the rest of him," suggested Night. "What if we rework the tendons?"

Day enlarged the tendon that ran from the sheep's skull to the spine. That allowed Bighorn to pivot his head better and bulking up the muscles in the neck and back soon had him lifting his head.

"He'll crush his skull if he fights as he is," mulled Night.

"Double up on the bone," said Day. They did. Experimentation proved the two-layered skull was tougher still with the addition of boney struts between the two thicknesses.

"Now you're talking," enthused Bighorn. "With these changes I can head-butt at a speed of twenty miles per hour. And I can fight for a whole day and night against a challenging ram. You'll both get to watch me battle for the babes," he bragged.

Night found him amusing, but Day was irritated.

"We've already spent five times as much energy creating you as Pronghorn," Day reckoned on his fingers. "You've demanded more design upgrades than any other creature we've made. Enough is enough. Get out there on your cliffs and make a go of it."

"You betcha," answered Bighorn confidently, not the least overawed.

"Not even a 'thanks,'" griped Day as Bighorn Sheep scampered off.

"No, someone that imposing finds humility difficult," Night sighed.

"He'd better not want any more custom designing," blurted Day.

"What else could he possibly want?" asked Night

And here they both were again, off to meet with Bighorn once more, because now he'd decided he wanted to swim.

"A desert mammal, drinking water only every two or three days--and he wants to swim?" Day fumed and stomped.

Night turned away so Day couldn't see her smirk.

"Here we are," she announced as they came in sight of a waterhole between high cliffs Bighorn loved to scale.

There the beast was, swimming through the still waters like he was born to it. He climbed out, shook off, and grinned, pleased with himself and his joke.

"Oh, he can already swim," giggled Night. "My bad."

"You will pay for this," Day promised, laughing despite himself. "You will both pay for this."

How Yellowthroat Got His Call

It is said that once there was a time before birds had learned individual songs in accordance with their species' ways. They experimented with assorted calls and songs in an attempt to find something they liked the sound of, for they knew they would be expected to pick a pattern of notes distinctive to their own kind so that Earth and Sun would always be able to tell them apart, even if they were hidden from sight by foliage.

It is also said that at that time, the world was a cacophony far exceeding anything known today, for every bird was in a hurry to find the best songs and claim them for its own species, so the improvisation continued both day and night. The patience of the other animals was quite tested to the max. Sleep was impossible for everyone, and as the birds were the only ones that had any stake in the matter, the other animals (mammals in particular, for they got most crabby when deprived of sleep) grumbled and griped. Nevertheless, progress was being made, as one species of bird after another found its song and officially filed to claim it with Earth and Sun.

About midway through the process of assigning birds their songs, Common Yellowthroat and his mate were contemplating nesting sites in the cattails of the cienega they called home. In actuality, she was much more interested in the matter than he, for she would take charge of construction, but he consulted with her and remained nearby while she tested first this spot, then that, until she found a clump of grasses hanging over the waters of the spring that could support her handiwork.

Meanwhile, he occupied himself with showing off: reminding her of his handsome appearance and physical prowess by lofting himself into the air, then dropping rapidly, while she pretended to watch.

Understand, please, that Common Yellowthroats do not normally aspire to high places. Typically, they like to hide in the reeds along waterways and glean water-plants of insects, seldom even rising to the tops of those same reeds, much less the twenty foot height that he was now scaling in order to show off. He deemed this necessary, though, in order to impress his mate. So much the better if it caught the eye and interest of any unattached ladies, for it was always delightful to have the attention of as many ladies as possible in any given moment.

He was confident of his good looks. His black mask, edged above in white, he knew, was very unusual and appealing to the ladies. His yellow throat and breast contrasted smartly with his greenish back and white belly. But good looks weren't always enough, and he had already learned that outrageous behaviors helped to draw the ladies' attention. Hence the atypical high flying.

Unaccustomed as he was to such heights, he had to admit that once at the top of his flight pattern, looking down left him insecure, causing his confidence to quake so that his voice became a spluttering that was unique, but not profoundly impressive. It's distinctive quavering, though, did draw his wife's focus away from home building and caused her some amusement at his posturing.

While she returned to busily sorting through construction materials, she watched her mate's antics and chuckled. She inwardly acknowledged his boldness at flying so high. At the same time, she was also well aware of his discomfort with heights and knew this caused his stuttering and rapid descent. Somewhat teasingly she suggested he claim the strange sound he was uttering for those occasions when he found himself at the height of passion.

"Your aerial dance and call are certainly singular and quite commanding," she chirped encouragingly. "Why not claim that song for your own?"

Pleased to have her attention, he decided to do exactly that.

"Great idea! That will be my song for the heights, but I also need one for the reeds, a more everyday variety of call. It will let you know where I am as I forage and also let other birds know this is our territory, so they will have to go elsewhere to nest and hunt. What sound shall I make for that?"

She knew this decision hung heavy on his mind. It was, really, at least as important as nest building this season, for an answer was expected, and soon. While they were not the last couple to choose their calls, they were far from the first either, and future generations of Yellowthroats would certainly be affected by whatever calls they chose--or the lack thereof.

She paused to listen to the hullabaloo around her. It was a clamor of sounds, not unlike an elementary school's band warming up for practice--almost frightening. Still, she picked out a bit of a tune from the chaos and tried to point it out to her husband.

"That's a rather nice bit of melody there; do you hear that?"

"Hear what?"

"Hear that. No, wait. Now--there it is again. Hear that?"

"Hear what?"

"That ditty.... There--that ditty."

"Which ditty? Which ditty? Which ditty?" he cried in frustration.

And that is how Common Yellowthroat learned and claimed his "common" call, a saying memorized and passed down from that generation of Yellowthroats to those of this very day.

That, along with his "height of passion" call are two of the ways Yellowthroats identify themselves to each other, to other birds, and to Earth and Sun.

Irruption

It is said that once Sun looked at Earth and noticed that beetles were swarming over portions of the Sonoran desert. Those beetles were an inch or two long and had orange-colored heads and upper thoraxes. The larger part of their bodies was black. They could lift their black wing-covers and take flight. They buzzed along, finding conglomerations of their own kind where they would alight and seek mates. Scorpion weed was their food of choice, and wherever there was a stand of this spring annual growing, the beetles were climbing amongst the branches, denuding them of leaves and blossoms. The females were larger than the males. As the beetles mated, linking their abdomens together for extended periods of time--even overnight, the females continued to eat by day, and rest by night, the males hanging from their bodies like ornaments.

Sun admired the snappy colors of the beetle. "What are you called?" he asked, as one flew by.

"Arizona Blister Beetle," was the hasty answer.

"Why the 'blister' part of your name?"

"Because my blood can raise blisters on bare human skin if I'm crushed or held." Then it flew off, too intent on finding other beetles to pause for further conversation.

"There are so many," mused Sun to himself. "Too many, I'm sure. Look how they swarm over the purple flowers and strip them of blossom, seed and leaves. Surely these plants will not survive this onslaught. How will they produce enough seed for another generation? Next spring will be bare of these particular flowers."

"Earth," spoke Sun. "I have a matter to discuss with you. Do you see those blister beetles?"

294

"Yes," muttered Earth, allowing herself a slight distraction from the weaving she never ceased creating, the tapestry of life.

"They are incredible this season, an extravagant eruption. Look how many there are. Is this a good thing? They are destroying the scorpion weed and mating so profusely that their numbers will be even greater next year. What will they eat then? They are quite impressive to look at, that I'll admit, but I rather like the flower too. I want to see it next year sprinkled across the desert, but at this rate, there will be no seed left to sprout next spring."

"There are things you do not know. There are things you do not see. I have woven these beetles into a whole network of living things. Nothing stands alone. Nothing is free of the constraints of the weaving itself," was Earth's response.

Sun reflected on the tapestry Earth worked. "Explain," he requested.

Earth paused. Her face was blank, her mind searching. "How to begin? How to begin?" she pondered. "It is such an enormously interconnected story, but perhaps a small part will do.

"Do you see that swarm of Arizona Blister Beetles there?"

"Exactly my point," answered Sun. "See what they are doing to the scorpion weed?"

"Yes, but that stand of scorpion weed is past its prime. What you see being eaten is all that is left of a gathering of plants that sprang up and produced seed earlier this spring. That seed from the older plants has already fallen to the soil where it is being secreted for the next rain of winter to awaken. Look there, and over there. There are other scorpion weed plants too thinly scattered to attract the attention of any swarms of beetles. They will reproduce unhindered. The beetles thin the scorpion weed, but no more than that. To destroy all the scorpion weed would mean their own destruction.

"Then too, although the beetles are mating prodigiously and will lay many eggs this season, when the eggs hatch in the soil where they have been laid, the larvae must find the nest of a solitary bee in order to develop into an adult Arizona Blister Beetle. The larvae must feed on the bee larvae and bee bread in the nest's chambers to mature. Because the spring flowers have been plentiful this year, this has also been a good year for the solitary bees. The beetle larvae will find some of those nests, but not all. Most will find nothing and die. It is all tied together in what I weave. Even I do not know all the connections because life makes its own connections as soon as life is given. Some I have intended, but the weaving makes more and more in the process of being woven. There is more here than can be seen. I trust in that. You must do the same."

"You won't be overrun with blister beetles next spring?"

"Their numbers will be held in check," chuckled Earth, continuing to weave.

"Have I any say in all this?" asked Sun, still not certain he could trust the weaving's process.

"The major role, I would say," assured Earth. "Without your light none of it would exist. I cannot weave in the dark."

"True," shrugged Sun thoughtfully.

"Absolutely true," soothed Earth, taking up a new color.

The Trouble with Ground Squirrels

It is said that there was once a time when Day and Night, the two primary creators, accomplished the task of making three desert ground squirrels in one day. Perhaps it was because they rushed that difficulties arose.

Day chose a warm, spring day for the creative endeavor, when winter-rain-encouraged flora sprouted everywhere. He hoped that would give the squirrels the best possible start in the world, since they would be plant eaters. Night gave a special dispensation, of sorts, by agreeing that all three squirrels could be diurnal, creatures of the daytime hours rather than hers. She let Day take charge of gathering the energies they would use in making the squirrels.

The desert had very few large trees, so ground squirrels were not made for climbing. They were given strong front claws to dig burrows for hibernating through the cold winter and for hiding from the hot desert sun in summer. In addition, their ears were set back on their heads, and were not as large as other squirrels. This kept dirt out of their ears while crawling through underground tunnels.

The largest was Rock squirrel. As large as his tree-climbing cousins, and weighing in at one and a half pounds, he sported a large bushy tail, eight inches in length. He was grey in color, but speckled to help camouflage him amongst the stony canyons in which he lived.

The other two were smaller in size. They were six inches long with three additional inches of tail. They weighed about 7 ounces each.

One, Round-tailed Ground Squirrel, looked like a miniature prairie dog, sandy brown all over except for his black-tipped tail. He blended perfectly with the soil of the desert flatlands in which he liked to burrow. He fancied communal life, just like prairie dogs. He was the only ground squirrel that did.

The last created was Harris's Antelope Squirrel. He looked something like a chipmunk. A white stripe ran down the length of his brown body on each of his sides. He carried his black, frizzy tail arched over his back. His belly and chest were white. He shared territory with Round-tailed Ground Squirrel, but also used rockier soil for his home and food gathering.

The first thing each squirrel did when released was climb a mesquite tree and begin nibbling the new growth of leaves.

Night looked at Day.

"Do you see that?" she asked. "How did that happen?"

"Yes, and--I don't know," answered Day.

"I thought they couldn't climb trees," commented Night.

"Maybe I forgot to mention that to them," mused Day.

They watched Rock Squirrel eat prickly pear fruit and buds. Then he raided a quail nest for eggs and ate three beetles.

"I thought he was supposed to eat only plants," Night pointed out.

"I thought so too," was all Day could answer. "But I guarantee Round-tailed Ground Squirrel was made to eat greens exclusively: spring flowers, cactus buds, and sprouting grasses when tender and young."

They watched him munch on ocotillo flowers, then devour a dead nestling fallen from a palo verde.

"What is going on?" insisted Night.

"I must have used faulty ingredients," swore Day.

They saw Harris' Antelope Squirrel stalk and kill a mouse.

"So much for Plan A," Night sighed dramatically.

"I can't imagine what went wrong," insisted Day. "I mixed everything the way we discussed."

"It's almost as if you forgot Obedience Salts," Night said, deep in thought.

"I didn't, though," Day declared. "I used up the last of it, so I put making more on the 'TO DO' list. But now that you mention it, I do recall stretching it to make it last between the three squirrels."

"Why am I thinking that's not good news?" asked Night.

"Incidentally," Day admitted. "There was very little left for the last squirrel--the Antelope model."

Night groaned.

They watched the ground squirrels cavorting over the countryside, thieving cactus fruits and seed from birds and packrat middens. And they bred like--well, very efficiently, with the younger generations no easier to live with than their elders.

"Look at that one there," demanded Night.

Harris' Antelope Squirrel sprawled spread-eagle in cool dust shaded by a creosote, radiating indolence and self-satisfaction. He was messy too, insisting on littering around his burrow with the remains of stolen cactus fruit.

"You'd think he owned the place," said Night, gritting her teeth.

"Or made himself," agreed Day.

"At least they'll all den up for the winter to hibernate," Night remembered. "We'll have a little peace then."

"Theoretically," said Day uncertainly.

"Oh no," moaned Night. "You're not sure?"

As it turned out, Rock Squirrel did disappear for all but the warmest winter days. Round-tailed Ground Squirrel took a thorough, communal, seasonal nap. Antelope Squirrel, though, was awake all year. He was active in the heat of summer and cool of winter. Being last made and least salted, he was most deficient in obedience and a perfect reminder of what could happen when ingredients ran low and projects got rushed.

"He was your endeavor," Night accused. "Antelope squirrel's personality is not my doing. You're the one who made him so contrary."

"I know," admitted Day. "I should have been more careful. I wanted him as my own and wound up with a creature nearly opposite of what I planned."

Hmmm, thought Night. Maybe he IS my creature after all.

How White-Winged Dove Came to Meet Lightning

It is said that there was once a time when the dove we now call White-Winged was only gray. Naturally, he was known simply as Gray Dove. The condition that brought about the name change happened rather suddenly, and is not common knowledge. That's because the characters controlling this story live rather higher up than most of Earth creatures dare to look when violent storms shred the peace, so events transpired unnoticed except by a few. Coyote knows. Figures, doesn't it? That canine seems to be involved in any and everything, directly or indirectly, due to his skulking, secretive ways. Although he is a witness, and cause, of all that transpired, it's a tale he tells infrequently. He worries he may still be punished and so, quite uncharacteristically, he doesn't brag of his exploits. There really is little doubt he could not fare as well as White-Wing did. But I digress. This story is not about Coyote, but the victim of Coyote's transgression.

First, you should know that all doves are special favorites of Rain Cloud's. Not the white, fluffy, harmless Wind-blown puffs that skate across the fair blue sky and pleasure the eye. I mean the water laden, blackish-brownish, bulging monstrosities that bludgeon Earth, created by Wind and Water's rage. Rain Cloud's powerful forces dominate whatever scene he happens upon. He demands that all life pause and pay him homage. So everyone stops and takes cover to hide from Rain Cloud's wrath. They remain frozen, except for their quivering, until he passes. Those who disobey risk injury or death by Lightning Bolt, product of Wind's tempest among Water's torrential raindrops high over Earth. Edicts from Wind, Water and Rain Cloud are not to be ignored.

But from the beginning, the doves have walked a fine line between respect and disregard for Rain Cloud's demands, and thus gained his begrudging admiration. They do stop all activity, but they do not hide. Whether by intentional design, or stupidity, they often sit right out in the open and endure Rain Cloud's pummeling. I've always assumed doves figured the region was so gray with Rain Cloud's stormy authority that they would blend right in and go unnoticed, wherever they paused, whether on the end of a tree limb, or even right on the ground. The point is, though, they still pause and give homage to the power around them. They just don't hide from it.

So there Gray Doves were, colored as the clouds above them, enduring the pelting rain, huddled on the ground in an open field, half obedient to Rain Cloud's commands.

Along came Coyote, completely disobedient and showing total disregard for Rain Cloud's authority. He trotted between creosote bushes and saguaro cactuses, getting drenched and muddy, but Rain Cloud was too busy to see. It was very dangerous, but Coyote expected to take advantage of the other creatures who cowered and quaked beneath Rain Cloud's awesome jurisdiction, too distracted to notice his stealthy approach. Surely an easy meal might be had at the expense of a rabbit hidden away under a bursage. Coyote trespassed across Gray Dove's open field.

The multitude of Gray Doves exploded into flight with a roaring of wings that rivaled Rain Cloud's thunder and drew his attention. He didn't see Coyote, the cause of the uproar, but he instantly struck the Gray Doves with Lightning. There was crackling, intense heat, and a smell of charred feathers. Because they were airborne, the birds survived, but they were stunned and forever changed.

302

They dropped back to Earth with fire-red feet, burned by the lightning they'd trod in the sky. They also had black wing-tips and a black crescent on each cheek, crisped courtesy of Lightning. The intense white light of Rain Cloud's punishment remained locked in a stripe across each wing and quivered in the end of each dove's tail feathers. Even when they perched, the white of Lightning's strike was still visible in their wings, a constant reminder of their crime and conviction. Rain Cloud was sorry, but did not repent of his punishment. Even his favorites must obey his orders, at least somewhat.

In the chaos, Coyote withdrew cautiously to the cover of a dense copse of mesquite trees lest the now White-winged Doves declare him the perpetrator of their misfortune. But they were too traumatized to name names. Coyote got off. Once again, he suffered not the least little bit for his shenanigans. He could not have survived a Lightning strike if he'd gotten his just desserts, you know. Since he's grounded by four paws, he'd be forever stilled from all life's activities by Rain Cloud's revenge. Perhaps it's just as well he got off. He does have a few redeeming qualities, after all. There was the time he saved Horned Lizard from the wildfire by running with that reptile's mouth clamped tight on his tail. It was quite accidental, of course, but fortuitous for Horned Lizard.

But that's another story--one about Coyote--and this one's about White-Winged Dove.

Horned Lizard Finds Kin

It is said that there was once a time when Flat Lizard approached Sun for a word. No other lizard had ever approached Sun before. Flat Lizard knew he was not like other lizards, and because of his presence, Sun now knew that too.

"I am your kin," announced Flat Lizard, earning a mighty laugh from Sun.

Surely the creature was deranged, so Sun turned his face away and ignored it. But Flat Lizard followed Sun across Sky, continuing to ask for an audience again and again-- the live-long day--leaving off only when Sun finally set, ragged tempered from Flat Lizard's constant begging and ridiculous assertions.

Flat Lizard slowly plodded back to the sands of Earth, undaunted in determination, but hungry. He needed to refill his stomach with the ants he loved eating. In fact, ants were nearly all he ever ate, stalking them as they harvested seasonal seeds in long queues, lapping them up, toad-like, with his sticky tongue. Because ants are mostly made of chitin, a hard polymer exoskeleton, they were not much nutrition for Flat Lizard. He had to eat many ants to sustain himself. Because of this, his stomach was larger than most lizards, taking up more than ten percent of his total mass. And because of this, Flat Lizard was not built for speed. So, after spending all day with Sun, he slowly plodded back to the sands of Earth, where he partially buried himself and gobbled down the ants that filed by him, hoping they'd remain oblivious to his presence, for were they to swarm, they could cause him great harm.

Before falling asleep, Flat Lizard reconsidered his claim against Sun. He was different! He was flat, whereas other lizards were more rounded in girth. This helped him soak up Sun's energy faster than others each morning, helping him activate his body to hunt another ant trail or hide from his enemies.

Coyote fit in that later category. Coyote loved to catch Flat Lizard in the open--loved to have him for a snack. Flat Lizard was able to squeeze the vessels in his neck so as to increase the blood pressure in his eyes. He only used this defense in the direst of circumstances, but when he did, bloody fluids shot from his eyes and irritated Coyote's eyes and nose, convincing him to find another munchie. Flat Lizard didn't know anyone else that could do that.

His tail was shorter than other lizards; he was slower and flatter than other lizards; he could shoot blood from his eyes. He was different! He was Sun's. He knew it right down to the fringed scales on his side. But he still had to convince Sun.

With the next morning's dawning, Flat Lizard was there in the east. Instead of "good morning," he greeted the orb with "I am your kin," and again followed Sun on his journey across the heavens, importuning every step of the way for some sign of acknowledgement and blessing.

This day, Sun did not laugh at Flat Lizard's suggestion of relationship. He was too weary of his companionship to be amused. His ploy for the day was to continue to ignore the reptile, however useless that had proven the day prior. Still, Sun felt the rebel could surely not hold out another whole day. The creature's endurance would fail, leaving him free to continue his journey in spectacular silence. No one could tolerate his heat and light for two whole days in a row! He continued his march across Sky.

305

Wind knew of Flat Lizard's quest. He gazed up often to watch the obviously mismatched pair cross the blue expanse. Flat Lizard looked like a tiny black spot against Sun's fiery face. Though he knew to stay out of it, Wind couldn't help but lend a gust of air to help lift the lizard along his way from time to time.

Flat Lizard was feeling the effects of his petitioning. He was starving. There were no ants on his path following Sun, and he had to wait until evening to satisfy his hunger. And his thirst. There was no thirst he had ever known like that gained by dogging Sun in his travels. Yet that need too must wait for nightfall. Flat Lizard plodded on, fueled by his determination alone. The time passed with Flat Lizard pleading for attention and Sun spurning him--again, the live-long day--with the lizard's requests sounding weaker and weaker and coming more and more infrequently. By Sunset, the two were marching in silence.

Sun departed, smug in his belief he would travel alone the next day.

Flat Lizard left to return to Earth for food, water and rest. His feet were burnt and bloody and he was exhausted. But, still determined. As Sun's offspring, how could he be otherwise?

The third morning, Sun peeked cautiously over the horizon to hear, "I am your kin," and he succumbed. He could not take another day of Flat Lizard's company. That and the fact that he was becoming begrudgingly respectful of this crazy critter accompanying him. He listened to Flat Lizard's argument. Whether kin or not, he had to admire the wee one's spunk. For that, if no other reason, he was willing to mark the beast as his own.

He started at the tail.

"Here I'll singe the steps I take to climb out of the east each dawn, steps you have taken as well."

Next was the lizard's back.

306

"Here I'll draw the open Sky in the shape of an oval. Across that Sky I'll show a pole, with hand and foot holds on either side, showing how we have both ascended the heavens.

My journey will end at your head. End of Day. How shall I show that?" He paused to speculate.

All this time, Flat Lizard remained mute. He made no comment upon Sun's choice of mural or its placement. It was a little uncomfortable getting scorched, but he was overwhelmed by his good fortune. Sun was finally validating his identity as one of his own.

"I know," said Sun. He took soil and baked it into thorns, four of the largest of which he put on the back of Flat Lizard's skull. The rest he scattered on the sides of his head.

"There," and he stepped back to observe the full effect of his artwork. "Your crown," he said approvingly, "turned backwards to give the appearance of my last rays, casting behind me over Earth as I depart. A royal crown," he added, for he knew that would please Flat Lizard.

"I humbly thank you," Flat Lizard bowed, finally breaking his silence.

"I humbly acknowledge our kinship," bowed Sun.

Wind watched it all, impressed.

"Now I need another name," said Flat Lizard. "One that reflects my heritage."

"You're regal," said Sun. "And horned. How about Regal Horned Lizard?"

"Fine," agreed the recently exonerated dreamer, and they went off to get approval for the new name from Day and Night, the two primary creators. Only Regal Horned Lizard returned, for Sun continued his own journey alone.

"How did it go?" asked Wind. "Do you get to keep the new name? Congratulations, by the way. I've never seen another wear Sun down like that."

"Thanks," bowed Horned Lizard. "We are kin."

Wind started, then smiled. After all he had just witnessed, he was not about to argue. "Pleased to meet you, kin," he bowed.

"Same goes for me," laughed Earth.

"And me," burbled Water.

In this way, Horned Lizard's trek was truly concluded--with all the elementals acknowledging him as their own.

In this way, Horned Lizard was the first--but definitely not the last--to discover his kinship with everything.

The Adoption of Regal Horned Lizard

It is said that there was once a time when Day approached Night and asked, "Have you seen it?"

Day and Night were the two primary creators, so there was little they had not seen that was found upon Earth. Night was bemused.

"Seen what?" she answered.

"I must say, I like this leeway we left our creatures. It's amazing the deviations they manage to come up with," Day said, smiling and shaking his head in wonder.

"Who are you referring to?" asked Night.

"One of the lizards we made."

"Which one?"

"The one that's flatter than most.

"Well, what's it like now?"

"Like it's new name, actually. It's now called Horned Lizard."

"We've used horns before."

"Yes, but not like this. Sun and Horned Lizard worked together to create a particular effect and I think it rather striking. You'd like it too."

"Describe it."

"Well, I already said it started as the lizard we made flatter than most. Do you remember?" asked Day.

"I do," said Night. "It was to enable it to collect warmth from Sun faster than other lizards. We put a fringe of scales on the edges too, as I recall. It mostly eats Harvester Ants, right?"

"Yes, that's the one," said Day. "Evidently, it decided to pursue that affinity for solar energy several steps farther."

"How so?"

"It asked Sun to adopt it."

"Adopt it?" asked Night, surprised.

"So I'm told."

"By whom?"

"By Sun. He says the lizard insisted on their kinship, said he knew it right to his very scales. He petitioned again and again, nearly driving Sun crazy, until Sun agreed to adopt him. Sun even came with Horned Lizard to see me and seek the new name."

"How are horns a sign of Sun's acceptance?"

"It's not just the horns, but how they are placed. Sun also burned the pattern of his own journey on the lizard's back. The short tail has black hash-marks which look like the steps Sun climbs out of the East each morning. On the back is a blackened oval within which paired hand and foot holds ascend to the lizard's head. There you see his crown, for he wears the horns Sun made him like the rays of light Sun casts back upon Earth as he sets, ten of them, in all. The four largest horns are directly on the back of the lizard's head."

"So the pattern on the lizard's back is egg-shaped?" asked Night.

"Encased in an egg shape, representing Sun's path across Earth," answered Day.

"Perhaps it represents not just Sun's journey, but Horned Lizard's as well."

"I hadn't thought of that," pondered Day. "Perhaps--perhaps."

"I must see this Regal Horned Lizard," declared Night. "One could not make such a journey and remain the same."

"Perhaps not," agreed Day. "Probably not."

Hornworm Goes Underground

It is said that there was once a time when a fat, green, four-inch-long caterpillar walked along the branches of Desert Tobacco, strolling and munching, munching and strolling--until all the leaves were eaten and most of the white, trumpet-shaped blossoms too.

"Now what?" asked Desert Tobacco. "You've left nothing of me except some of my bigger branches. You'll finally have to leave and find another poor plant to stuff down your gullet. I can't wait to see you shuffle off into the sunset."

"Burp," said the caterpillar, beginning to stretch along a leafless stem, settling down for a nap. He looked just like the green stalk he grasp tightly with his stubby legs. Camouflaged to perfection, a snooze was just the thing to add to his agenda.

"No wait!" moaned Tobacco. "You can't stop now. Keep those ridiculous little legs moving that flabby bulk on down the road. You're disgustingly fat. I can't even hold you up any more. And what's with the horn on your butt, anyway?

"That's my name--don't wear it out," yawned the caterpillar.

"What?" hooted Tobacco.

"That sticker is what gives me my name. I'm Hornworm," said the caterpillar, smacking his lips as he meditated on the delicious meal eaten at Desert Tobacco's expense. "Very good, by the way."

"What?" asked Tobacco, extremely disgusted.

"You're really very good--good to eat, that is," smiled Hornworm.

"Oh, I'm so glad. So very, verrry glad," oozed Tobacco Plant--and he really was--oozing, that is, because

Hornworm had cut away so much plant material that tobacco juices flowed from his wounds.

"Me too," sighed Hornworm contentedly.

"Nooooo. Don't sleep. No loitering. No siestas allowed," bellowed Desert Tobacco, but to no avail. Hornworm merely posed his branch-imitating pose and held still as a statue, deaf to Tobacco's laments.

But there was one creature who heard Desert Tobacco-- sort of. A Gilded Flicker smelled the scent of tobacco on the air and came to investigate the reason for the aroma. He was not fooled by Hornworm's masquerade. He tried to snatch Hornworm off Tobacco's stem and nearly succeeded.

"Ouch," screamed Hornworm, rising up and thrashing to and fro with the front half of his body. Only his hind legs held him to his plant host, but they were tenacious. Gilded Flicker could not dislodge him. Hornworm discharged a green fluid from his back end, completely disgusting Desert Tobacco--and confusing Gilded Flicker. Nevertheless, Gilded Flicker refused to leave off pecking at the caterpillar that seemed impossibly connected to Tobacco.

"Couldn't have happened to a nicer guy," cheered Desert Tobacco. "I'm so sorry. So very, verrry sorry."

"Yeah, right!" muttered Hornworm through clenched mandibles, as he hung on for dear life.

"Let go," a voice called.

"What?" asked Desert Tobacco.

"Hmmph?" asked Hornworm.

"Drop to the ground and hide in the loose soil," said Earth. "I'll conceal and heal you," she promised. "And when I'm finished, you'll fly better than the bird that's beating you up."

"Whose side are you on?" pouted Tobacco.

"Hush," scolded Earth. "You'll sprout leaves again and come back better than ever."

Being without options, Hornworm did as he was told. Contrary to his own instinct, he let go of Desert

312

Tobacco, tumbled to the ground and hurriedly burrowed into the soil. Flicker stabbed his bill into the earth, tossing leaf litter like salad, but he couldn't find the juicy morsel he sought. Hornworm made good his escape. Even after he no longer heard Flicker thrusting his beak into the soil, he squirmed his much deflated body into the dark depths of Earth. He had lost lots of fluid, but there was nothing to be done about that now. At first, hiding was his goal, but as the afternoon wore on, something just felt right about staying where he was.

He felt sleepy, very sleepy. Since he had certainly not gotten the nap he'd been craving when he was above ground, he decided to rest for a while underground. That was the last thing he remembered....

Until he woke up later--much later. He had no idea how long he'd been asleep, but he found himself in a casing of unknown origin. It was brittle, though, so with a few hunches of his shoulders, it split open. Even so, it was still very dark. Then he remembered that he'd crawled underground to escape a bird. Earth still held him in her grasp--and what was it she'd promised? Something about flight?

He dug his way to the surface and tumbled out into the light of day.

"Told you," said Earth.

"What?" asked Desert Tobacco, working to sprout spring leaves.

"I was talking to Sphinx Moth," explained Earth. "You probably remember him as Hornworm."

"That?" squealed Tobacco. "That ugly thing?"

"He just emerged," encouraged Earth. "Give him a moment to collect himself and stretch his wings."

Sphinx Moth took her advice, a little disoriented by his new persona. He uncrumpled four wings and shook the last of the sand from his fine, long legs. Next he unrolled his proboscis, his long mouthpiece, which he knew would be great for poking into the depths of flowers in search of nectar. He didn't know how he knew that--he just did. With a thrumming of his wings, he took flight.

"Hurrah!" praised Earth.

"I'm awed," said Desert Tobacco. "So very, verrry awed."

"Yeah, right!" responded Sphinx Moth, to hide his own wonder at his transformation.

"No--really," assured Tobacco. "Impressive. Very verrry impressive."

Sphinx Moth darted from flower to flower, dancing with hummingbirds.

"You fly as well as we do," they marveled.

"Better than any old Flicker," agreed Sphinx Moth.

"Told you," Earth reminded him, pleased with herself.

"Thanks for your help," Sphinx Moth said gratefully.

"Forever and always," Earth assured him.

Later, as evening fell, another Sphinx Moth hovered over Desert Tobacco.

"What now?" he asked.

Hold still," said Sphinx Moth, "while I lay my eggs on your leaves."

"Oh noooo," groaned Desert Tobacco.

"Here we go again," laughed Earth.

And that is how Hornworm learned to burrow into Earth in order to learn to fly like a hummingbird--and to leave Desert Tobacco alone long enough to resprout the leaves and flowers necessary to assure future generations of Hornworms their green munchies.

How Raven Lost His Stealth

It is said that there was once a time when Raven flew as stealthily as Owl. He flew in absolute silence. The day came, however, when the wisdom of this was called into question, and Day and Night, the two primary creators, were willingly held accountable.

One day their presence at a meeting in a nearby meadow was requested by Costa's Hummingbird, on behalf of many animals of the desert. Day and Night believed in staying involved with their creations and were willing to revisit decisions made at any point along their path of production. They'd heard all was not well between Raven and the others. They expected to hear complaints about him. They were prepared to consider modifications in their design. Raven, they were told, had been invited, but refused to attend.

Day and Night took positions in the middle of the field. They were surrounded by their offspring. These had already been debating what should be done, even before Day and Night's arrival.

"He has quite the reputation," Anna's hummingbird said in a squeaky, insect-like voice. "He's a known thief. He's robbed my nest before out of sheer meanness. My young couldn't have been more than half a mouthful for him."

"I lose children every year too," accused Mockingbird. "I demand something be done about it."

"It would help," Day whispered to Night," if Mockingbird refrained from so much public rabble-rousing in the vicinity of his nest. He's certainly not helping his nestlings to remain hidden."

"I know," Night answered, but her heart still went out to Mockingbird. "There are others who rob nests of helpless

315

youngsters just as regularly as Raven, but he is also good-sized and not easily driven off by the parents. It's always painful to lose children and the investment they represent in the future."

"True," Day murmured, but he still felt Mockingbird bore some responsibility for his loss.

They returned their full attention to the rest of the delegation confronting them.

"He's not just a thief. He's also a prankster. He makes off with my prettiest baubles, collected at great risk to myself. They mean nothing to him, but everything to me. If I place a bit of shiny glass or metal in just the right position on my house so that it is the envy of every other packrat in the neighborhood, I can be sure Raven will sneak off with it. Just because he likes teasing me, he shows me where he stows it, but it's always out of my reach. I'm sick of working so hard on home improvements only to have them disappear when I turn my back," a rodent complained.

"Worse still," said Mule deer. "Raven is smart. I watched two sitting in a tree together one winter. Below their tree was the frozen carcass of one of my kind. They pretended to be preening one another, but I could hear words passing between them. Raven can make more than thirty different sounds, you know. They communicate way too well, if you ask me. I watched those two leave the tree, and one hung around to guard the remains from other scavengers while the other went in search of Coyote. He actually led Coyote back to the deer. Both Ravens watched Coyote rip into the frozen meat. He tore them passage into the carcass and they fed when he left. It was horrible to see."

"I'm sure it was," soothed Night. "It might have been you under that tree."

Mule deer shuddered.

"You can't condemn Raven for being intelligent enough to take advantage of Coyote's greater strength," declared Day. He was feeling a little defensive of Raven now, having heard nothing but blame placed on the big, black, heavy-beaked bird.

"But his vocabulary can rival Man's," insisted Mule deer. "And when two or more gather together, there's no telling the trouble they'll brew. He's so canny at knowing where his next supply of carrion will come from, even Man associates him with death. Raven is well known to haunt Man's battlefields, just waiting to pick out the eyes of the dead and dying."

Eagle gasped, then continued, "I'm reminded of when I saw him doing just that to fish stranded in an evaporating pool of water. I was shocked."

Day leaned toward Night. "I'm detecting some jealousy here," he said quietly. "Raven is bright. He can speak quite fluently with his kind and take action as a gang. He's also big and a strong flier. That's intimidating, but I see nothing wrong with it. I can't see punishing him for being smart and capable. Why don't I ask them what they suggest as a solution?"

"They feel unable to defend against Raven," Night responded. "Their anger and fear is such that they won't be reasonable. Any solution they recommend will be extreme. Better that we come up with an answer of our own."

Day nodded. "That's good advice. Let me buy us some time for consulting. I also want to speak with Raven."

"Agreed," said Night.

"We will consider all we've heard," Day announced loudly. "We promise to make changes, but we need to talk about just what to do. A week is all we ask. Give us a week to come up with a plan."

There were mutters and moans, but the animals left the matter in the hands of their creators.

Day and Night then sought out Raven. They found him hounding Hawk in flight, trying to steal the rabbit she clutched in her talons. He was not happy to stop long enough to discuss his fate.

"You are the subject of much debate among the other animals," began Night. "You had better deal with us now."

317

Raven left Hawk alone and told Day and Night he'd meet them by a small stream below. Raven chattered and cawed all the way to the cottonwood trees in the drainage. Day and Night couldn't tell what he said, but after they summarized the charges against Raven, he said not one word. He simply glanced into the trees around his perch. While they'd talked, dozens of other ravens had flown silently into the glade. Now they presented a united front against their creators. They were a little ominous, even for Day and Night.

"Are you trying to bully me into letting you off?" shouted Day. "Do you think you can scare me with your numbers like you frighten the others?"

"You've pulled one too many tricks," Night glowered. "You will not intimidate us. From now on, you will be noisy in flight. Never again will you sneak up on anything. Whether you're talking together or not, everyone will hear you coming."

Day agreed. It seemed just to him.

"We don't care," Raven told them, then spoke his own language to the other birds. They took flight haughtily with a great whooshing of wings. Surprised, they faltered. Then they departed, the whole clan, acting as if nothing had happened.

"You will care," Day answered. "You will."

"They already do," Night assured him. "But they'll never let us see that."

So, Raven continues to be smart. He's still a thug. He's still big, black and powerfully beaked. He's still strong in flight. But he no longer has stealth. The whoosh, whoosh, whoosh of his flight ever reveals his presence and helps protect other animals from his thievery and trickery.

Day and Night helped even the odds, and because of Raven's attitude, they were delighted to do so.

318

How Pillbug Got His Name

It is said that there was once a time when Pillbug knew nothing about conglobulating. Day and Night, the two primary creators, made him and his kind with plenty of unique features. Most of Pillbug's fellow crustaceans lived in water, but he lived on land. Most land-based animals breathed with lungs, but Pillbug retained his crustacean gills and needed moist, dark places to live in because of that. He was not an insect, but was eaten by birds and lizards who typically dined on insects.

A half-inch-long scavenger and burrower, Pillbug ate dead and decaying plant and animal matter, thus fertilizing and aerating the soil. He specialized in recycling and replenishing.

He lived in family burrows, mated primarily in spring, and his mate nurtured several rounds of eggs each year in brood sacs on her underside. There they hatched into tiny look-a-likes of their parents. Mother continued to carry her hatchlings until they molted and became too large to be transported. Pillbug parents busily gathered food for their young each night until they'd grown up and made their own burrows. Pillbug cities could be revealed by moving a log or rock. Light scattered all residents, however. Moist, undisturbed darkness was Pillbug's preferred home.

Molting was accomplished in two stages, first the back half of Pillbug's body, then the front half. This shedding of the old crusty body-shield allowed a growing youngster more room in a newly forming, larger crusty shield. Eating the old shell provided protein. The molting half was differently colored than the non-molting half, giving Pillbug an odd two-toned effect when growing.

So, Pillbug already had plenty of distinctive personality traits. He didn't need another.

Still, on the day the teacher turned over a stone to show his young pupil the creatures underneath it, the child prodded the crustaceans until they rolled tightly into balls to protect their softer undersides.

"Pillbugs," he pronounced with glee.

"Conglobulating Pillbugs," asserted the teacher.

"Conglobulating?" asked Curve-billed Thrasher, who watched hungrily from a perch on a tree limb overhead.

"If you say so," answered Cactus Wren, also awaiting the moment the Humans left so he could eat.

"No, he said so," responded Curve-billed Thrasher, indicating the man by pointing with his bill.

"Yeah. Well--leave it to Humans," Cactus Wren said, shaking his head. "They will make up the most ridiculous words!"

Lupine to the Rescue

It is said there was once a time when the bees so were frantic trying to pollinate all the spring flowers of the desert that they were beside themselves.

"I'm so behind schedule," buzzed Bee One to Bee Two.

"The workload this year is unbeelieveable," agreed the second.

"My wings are worn to nubs," complained a third.

"And who knows how many millions of flowers we have left to pollinate?" asked a fourth.

Bees One and Two were already on their way back to the hive with their balls of golden pollen carefully glued to their third and hindmost pair of legs. Bee Three answered though.

"Exactly," she said.

"Exactly what?" asked Bee Four, burrowing whole-bodied into a hedgehog's purple blossom.

"The point is," answered Bee Three, "that we can't tell whether or not some bee has been to a blossom before us, stolen the nectar we'd love to sip and already pollinated the flower. It would be nice if we could tell before landing, so we wouldn't waste our time."

Bee Four was off to some nice creosote blossoms, pasting pollen busily to her hind legs. "Sure would," she responded.

"Would what?" asked Bee Five, just arriving to burrow into the hedgehog blossom Bee Four had just left.

"It would be nice if you could tell that I've already been to that flower before you wasted your time landing on it," answered Bee Four.

"Sure would," sighed Bee Five disappointedly, leaving the hedgehog blossom to begin work on the flaming orange flowers of a nearby ocotillo.

"But who'd give us that kind of break?" asked Bee Three, lifting off with a full load of pollen and turning toward the hive.

"Me. I'll help," spoke up Lupine.

"How?" asked Bees Four and Five.

"How what?" asked Bees One and Two, just returned from the hive.

"Oh never mind," said Bee Four distractedly, with a trace of impatience.

"I'll tell you when I have it figured out," Lupine promised Bee One and Bee Two.

Now, Lupine was a favorite of the bees, but he displayed his blue, pea-like flowers in an upside down ice cream cone-shaped cluster that bloomed from the bottom up. More often than not, the lower, larger blossoms were visited by the bees, and the smaller ones toward the cone's pointed, highest tip went unvisited when they finally bloomed. Lupine's thinking was that if he had some means of letting the bees know his lower blossoms were already fertilized, they might work up the cluster and sip from the smaller, higher flowers, fertilizing them too. That would guarantee an increase in the seed pods he produced and a better chance of making lots of new Lupine plants next spring. Helping the bees find his unfertilized flowers made good sense to him.

Lupine was a little on the short side. He grew to be about a foot tall, and was often smaller when the rains had not been plentiful. Consequently, his overall view of things was limited. But Lupine had a relative nearby, also a member of the Pea or Legume Family. Palo Verde grew to thirty feet tall. He too produced seedpods. His overall view of things was quite nice, thank you. Lupine called to his cousin, the tree, on the very next gust of wind.

"Palo Verde. Look over the hills for an answer to my question."

"And your question would be...?" asked Palo Verde.

"Can you see any way that I could let the bees know which of my flowers is already fertilized, so they don't visit them again and again and miss the ones that still need their help?"

"That's a question of a tall order; too tall for me. Why don't you ask Sun? No one's taller than he is."

Lupine adjusted his five-fingered leaves to gather Sun's rays more efficiently.

"Good idea," he answered Palo Verde.

"Oh Suuuun," called Lupine. "I would like a word with you. That's all right. Stay there. If you come closer, I'll burn up. I just have a question."

"I wasn't going to come any closer," chuckled Sun. "What do you want?"

"From way up there, is it possible to see a solution to my problem? I want to know how to tell the bees which of my blossoms have already been visited and fertilized, and which have not."

"Why don't you hang a sign on each flower, then change the sign after a bee fertilizes the flower," suggested Sun.

"How would I do that?" asked Lupine.

"Let's see. Your flower has an upper petal, the banner, and lower petals called a keel. How about if I put a drop of yellow sunshine on your banner. It can direct the bees to pollinate your flower. After they've done that, I'll darken the color on the banner to a sunburn red. Tell the bees to visit the flowers with yellow spots, and they will know no other bee has been there before them."

"Yellow and red on a blue background," thought Lupine. He looked his banners over carefully. "I guess that could work. How about you place the yellow dot righhhht there?"

"There it is," said Sun, placing the drop of sunshine he wrung from a ray.

"There what is?" asked Bee Three, returning from the hive.

"The answer to your request," said Lupine.

"What request?" asked Bee Three. "I like the new look, by the way."

"Funny you should mention that," said Lupine. "Let me tell you what Sun has done for us."

And that is how Lupine helped show the bees which of his flowers they had already fertilized, and which still needed their visits.

The Race

It is said that there was once a time when Sharp-shinned and Cooper's hawks competed to see who flew fastest. They were similar in appearance and lifestyles. Woodland hawks who took avian prey, they were fashioned for a life of darting amongst trees. No one knew which would be fastest in long open stretches.

Cooper's Hawks had longer tails and claimed greater speed because of it. Sharp-shinned were slightly smaller and declared themselves faster because of it. The females of both species were the largest, so to rule out size as a factor, Cooper's hawks demanded one of their males fly against a female Sharp-shinned. To rule out the longer tail as a factor, the Sharp-shinned hawks insisted the stakes be raised by flying in a high wind, where a longer tail might become a liability by being harder to control. They chose to fly when Wind gathered Cloud together to pelt Earth with hard Rain. Flying could not be more difficult than at such a moment. Rarely was it attempted, and never for long distances. The chosen path was one that started in a huge mesquite tree. The competitors would fly from that to the fattest, darkest, most threatening Cloud, and back to the same mesquite tree. The winner would end the controversy over which had the greater speed forever.

The day was chosen and many animals gathered to watch. No one perched or crouched in the mesquite tree so that none could accuse them of affecting the race in any way. Only the male Cooper's, who represented his kind, and the female Sharpy, who represented hers, sat together on one great branch. They stretched their wings and adjusted their weight. Neither was relaxed enough to preen. They watched Great Horned Owl, who with a twist of his head would indicate the cloud they would dash toward and who with a nod to Gilded Flicker would start the race with the woodpecker's pounding on a hollow mesquite log. High above the scene, Turkey Vulture sailed in a space he hoped would be above the worst of Wind, but beneath Cloud, so he could oversee the contestants as they reached their turning point and headed back to Earth. They all waited for Wind.

True to form, the summer afternoon heated Air. Clouds formed and collected in crowds, building high towers that blackened with dense rain. Wind picked up and started moving monstrous clouds ponderously across the sky. Earth added dust to the mix to give Wind gritty form. The limbs of the tree in which the hawks perched began to shuffle, then to toss wildly. The birds moved their wings away from their bodies, prepared for flight, and fought to remain perched as Wind tugged at them. They watched Owl through the dust that splattered against their tree in gusts. When he deemed the danger greatest, Owl twisted his head toward the lowest Cloud, grayish-black with the water it held. Then he nodded to Flicker, who set up a roaring rapping that rivaled the distant thunder. Both hawks sprang into flight.

Wind snatched the two and attempted to slam them into the ground. The female Sharp-shinned narrowly missed the trunk of the mesquite from which they darted. The male Cooper's grazed the dirt with his tail and nearly took a tumble, but righted himself masterfully, fighting to ascend. It was clear to all that every effort was being called from both birds to rise toward the cloud that was their goal. Dust obscured the vision of those earthbound in moments. Only Turkey Vulture would observe whether both birds reached their rain cloud. Those below turned their gaze back to the mesquite, where the race was destined to end.

The hawks lost sight of one another in the boiling dust. They felt as if their wings were being torn from their bodies and both were unable to glide. They fluttered to stay aloft and searched for updrafts to carry them higher, thrown viciously in every direction and gasping to breathe in the high winds. Only when they rose above the scouring airborne sand could they sight their cloud and one another. They redoubled their efforts with the return of their vision.

Turkey Vulture fought hard to control his glide and banked to watch the hawks attain their cloud. Male Cooper's hawk dashed ahead, but watched the Female Sharpie's progress as much as where he was going, and carelessly struck his head against Cloud. He bounced off and turned, scraping his back against Cloud's edge, to plummet back to the starting tree. Female Sharp-shinned watched Cloud as she flew and turned against him in one smooth motion, scraping head, neck and back against the Rain he held, then darting back to Earth. She made up time on her turn and was neck and neck with Cooper's hawk as they descended back into the dust. Turkey Vulture dropped down too, so that he could verify that both hawks had reached their designated goal fairly and properly.

Now Cloud released Rain, and everyone was stung with the water's force, but the dust was also knocked down from the air and everyone could see a little better, though not much. The hawks could see enough to spot their tree and crashed toward it with no regard for a safe landing. When both were several hundred yards from their race's end, everyone felt the energy of the lightning Cloud released as blinding light and deafening sound. It destroyed the mesquite tree and both hawks collided in their shock, rolling head over tail to a stop, one against a creosote bush and the other against cowering Coyote, but both miraculously alive.

When everyone's senses had cleared, the hawks rushed to their contestants to ascertain their health. Turkey Vulture spoke of their both having reached the cloud Owl had chosen. All could see the evidence of that. Rain's dark gray stuck to Cooper's hawk's head and back, but the color was broken at the neck, showing how he'd bounced off Cloud. Sharp-shinned was evenly draped with Rain's black-gray, from her head all the way down her back, showing her smooth turn against Cloud's surface.

Everyone wondered who could be said to have won the race when the finish line had been blasted into splinters before their eyes.

Owl said, "Enough. It is enough. These hawks have proven their worth under the most terrible of circumstances. It doesn't matter who might have won. They are both still alive. That is winning enough. Who is fastest will have to remain a mystery forever. Let the issue never again be tested against fate."

Some still wonder who might have won the contest, but neither hawk species cares. They are quite content to test their skills against prey rather than Rain, Wind and each other.

Mesquite Gets a Pruning

It is said there was once a time when Mesquite grew unruly with abundant rain. He grew so well that his branches flowed all the way to the ground in long, thin streamers. Each bough departed the trunk and headed out without branching until it got so long it couldn't hold itself up and leaned into the ground for support. This left Mesquite looking for all the world like a Weeping Willow, which he was not.

Mesquite was rather glad to grow unruly, for it was little bother to him, but the animals that had once sheltered in his shade were no longer able to find their way there, and the plants that grew around Mesquite were raked by his thorns when a breeze blew his limbs. They complained fiercely.

It was only a matter of time before Day and Night were petitioned with the grievances of the desert animals and plants. They notified Mesquite and called for a conference.

"While I can easily reach his seed pods now," Cottontail Rabbit was saying, "I can't crawl under his branches to his trunk. I always had a little wallow dug there where I could dust myself and cool my belly in the dirt."

"That's true," sighed Mesquite, a little embarrassed by all the attention. "I rather miss our afternoon chats."

"And I can't build my nest at a safe height any longer," asserted Verdin, her yellow face highlighted when Sun broke through the cloud-filled sky for a moment to shine upon her. "You know how I love Mesquite for nesting and gleaning tiny insects from his leaves, but it's too dangerous now."

"True again," admitted Mesquite. "I am a little itchy now that no one can reach the underside of my arms to rid me of pests," he told Verdin.

"I used to grow in his shade, where I was protected from burning Sun. Animals would nibble me, spreading my seed to new localities," Grass announced. "Now it's dark as Night under his branches, too dark for me to grow there. No offense...." he nodded to Night.

"None taken," she assured.

"I actually saw Globe Mallow uprooted when she got caught up in his thorns in a windstorm last week," Grass continued. "But not before being sliced to ribbons on those same thorns. It was awful to behold." He trembled just remembering.

"I was so sorry..." began Mesquite.

"It's not really his fault," defended Night. "It's just that he's growing so fast with all the rain we've been having."

"We know," replied Jack Rabbit. "We aren't here to blame. We just miss how things used to be and hope to find a solution. Actually, we do have a suggestion to make."

"What's that?" asked Day.

"Trim him," answered Jack Rabbit. "We'd volunteer our services, as we do for smaller bushes, but Mesquite needs trimming long before we could reach his branches. A pruning would cause his long limbs to branch while still high in the air and keep them branching with additional trimmings. With enough pruning, they'd never grow so long as to reach the ground and Mesquite would fill out and fill in, becoming stronger and more fit in the process, no matter how much it rained."

"What say you?" Day asked Mesquite.

"Sounds a little uncomfortable," Mesquite winced, "but if I could be healthier and a better neighbor too, I guess I'll give it a shot. Depends on who does the trimming, though," he added as an afterthought. "I don't want anyone indiscriminately hacking off as much as they please."

"No, of course not," Night declared.

"We'd allow no such thing," assured Day.

So Day and Night began deliberating, with much consultation with Mesquite, until they designed.... Well, you'll just have to wait for the unveiling.

Since this act of creation came about in response to a particular complaint, and since Mesquite was going to be directly affected by this new creation and had so much input in its development, and since it was only by his good graces that this creation was going to thrive and at the same time be ultimately controlled, Day and Night felt Mesquite should be the one to introduce the new entity to his neighbors.

Another conference was called.

"Yeah, well," began Mesquite, a little embarrassed by all the attention. "It's a beetle."

"A what?" laughed Jack Rabbit.

"What kind of a pruner is that?" scoffed Antelope Squirrel.

"This could work," insisted Grass. "Look what Grasshopper does to me!"

"You were expecting Giraffe maybe?" asked Night.

"Well, sort of..." Jack Rabbit admitted, chewing his hind leg nervously. "Something a lot bigger at any rate."

"Wrong desert for Giraffe," Night said, glaring at Jack Rabbit. "We put a lot of work into this, you know. You might show a little more respect for our efforts."

"Sorry," Jack Rabbit said humbly. "Carry on with the demonstration."

"It's called Twig Girdler," Mesquite continued. "And that's exactly what it does. She cuts a circle around the circumference of one of my twigs in order to lay her eggs."

"In the circle?" asked Verdin, hopping on Mesquite's shoulder for a closer look at the brown, inch-long beetle he held. Its wing-casings were speckled with light orange dots and it had long antennae. She decided it was way too big to eat.

"No," answered Mesquite. "Cutting the circle will cause the end of my branch to die. That's how I'll get trimmed. The beetle then bites holes in the dying wood of my twig to lay her eggs, one to a hole. When they hatch, the larvae will burrow into the dead wood, eating that as food until autumn. Then they'll become adult beetles and climb from their holes to mate and lay more eggs."

"What's to keep you from getting girdled to death?" asked Verdin, concerned Mesquite had not taken his own safety into enough consideration.

"Only my smallest branches can be girdled," Mesquite responded. "And, as my wood dies, it gives off an odor that is attractive to other insects too. They'll also come and lay their eggs in my dying wood."

"How is that any help to you?" asked Jack Rabbit, his eyes growing large with visions of huge insect colonies munching away in the dead tips of Mesquite's branches.

"Some of those insects will be wasps that lay eggs which hatch into larvae that will eat Twig Girdler's larvae-- enough so that they can't overrun all my twigs."

"Ohhhh," said Cottontail Rabbit.

"But," said Verdin, "how about the adult Twig Girdlers? Won't they just keep girdling and girdling?"

"Only the females will girdle," Mesquite answered. "Each will girdle only one small branch. All the adult beetles die in the first frost and none will live longer than a month, even without a frost."

"Twig Girdler, huh?" marveled Cottontail Rabbit. "What will they think up next?"

"Giraffe would have been better," muttered Jack Rabbit under his breath.

Puncture Vine:
The Unwelcome Mat

It is said that there was once a time when Coyote spotted Antelope Squirrel on a rock, singing away to no one in particular, his back turned to Coyote. Instantly, Coyote dropped to the ground, planning to creep up on the preoccupied yodeler. Fate seemed on his side, for Antelope Squirrel sat in the open. A hole Coyote figured to be the squirrel's burrow was at least twenty feet away.

"You are being careless, Friend," whispered Coyote. "And I'm just the one to take advantage of it."

He belly-crawled slowly toward Antelope Squirrel. He could already see himself darting in and snatching up the rodent in the midst of his trilling rhapsody. What a nice snack he would make.

He made his move just as the squirrel took a deep breath and launched into another song. Coyote darted at top speed across a low, sandy area carpeted with green to approach the squirrel's perch. Suddenly he stopped mid-stride, yelping with pain, stepping gingerly through the green mat, no longer intent on his prey. Antelope Squirrel, with the briefest of glances over his shoulder, made off for his home, and escaped easily, for Coyote had lost all interest in him.

"Ouch, ooch, aowww," Coyote howled.

Every step was agony; each of his toes seemed on fire. He yipped and moaned his way off the ground-covering plant he tread upon. It was six feet in width and every inch stabbed him mercilessly. When he was free of the plant he again dropped to the ground, this time to

333

relieve himself of the tack-like stickers he'd picked up from the harmless looking plant.

"Who'd have guessed it would be so nasty?" whimpered Coyote.

He examined his enemy's pleasant, five-petaled, yellow flowers. Each flower nestled at the base of a leaf. The leaves grew opposite one another and were made up of paired leaflets that also grew opposite one another. Each leaf had between four to eight pairs of hairy leaflets.

"You look like you'd be soft to step on," Coyote growled. "Where are you hiding the thorns?"

He plucked stickers from his paws. Many sported two thorns, making them look like goat heads. They were brown, the body about a quarter-inch in length, hard, woody, and irregular in shape. The horns were also a quarter-inch in length. It was a very nasty job to remove them from his pads, of this I can assure you. They caught between his toes and stabbed his lips and gums as he pulled them out with his teeth. Coyote oozed blood from every stab wound, and he had plenty.

He took a closer look at the plant that had nailed him and lost him his lunch. Now he saw that the fruit of each blossom was a green cluster of five goat heads that dried with age and broke apart into the spiked seeds that had impaled him. These hid below the carpet of leaves and blossoms when they fell from the plant, waiting for the next hapless creature they might attach themselves to, the better to spread abroad.

"I see you've met Puncture Vine," squeaked Antelope Squirrel from his burrow's entrance, barely containing his laughter at his foiled would-be predator's distress. "So what do you think of my welcome mat?"

Coyote snarled. "I think you had better learn to watch your back. I think you and I shall meet again."

"Not today, at least," said Antelope Squirrel bravely. He shivered a little at Coyote's threat and slunk back deeper into his hole.

"You won't be giggling when I dig you from your hole some night. You won't find that funny," growled Coyote as he limped away.

"He's really hurting," Antelope Squirrel said to himself as he watched Coyote retreat. "Oh well, couldn't have happened to a nicer guy."

He left his burrow to watch the canine leave the area. He couldn't help saluting his vanquished foe with a final yodel. Coyote looked back with a menacing glare.

"Maybe it's time to relocate," Antelope Squirrel said thoughtfully. "Yeah, a change of scenery would do me good. Perhaps a little bungalow in a new community. I'll want a new neighborhood with an old neighbor, though," he chuckled. "I'll still want a Puncture Vine close by," he called to the plant. "I'll always need my unwelcome mat."

How Turkey Found His Warrior

It is said that there was once a time when Turkey took stock of his clan and bewailed its reduced numbers. Human hunters had killed so many and moved into his forest haunts until he and his family had little space left to call their own. Wild animals like Skunk and Raven raided his nests and ate the eggs before they could hatch. Coyote, Wolf, and Wild Cat hunted adult birds.

"We need a warrior," Turkey said. "Someone to protect us. Someone to stand up for us before the other animals. Someone stealthy enough to hide our young when they are helpless."

It was not breeding season, so Turkey roamed with his fellow toms, searching for acorns, insects and herbs. They discussed the problem and decided to send a representative to discuss it with the creators.

The females were too busy living in the company of other hens, raising their teen-aged young. These were covered with down when newly hatched, but grew quickly and could fly within several weeks, at least enough to take to the trees and a safe roost when endangered. It was the hens who taught each year's hatchlings how to forage and survive in the world. But their best efforts could not replenish the numbers lost to woodland hunters like Coyote, Wild Cat and Man.

Turkey could run thirty miles per hour. He could fly as much as a mile on short, quick wingbeats, not terribly far when compared with other birds, but impressive for his size. He stood about three feet tall and weighed in at twenty three pounds, after all. He decided he would take his request for a warrior to Day and Night, the two primary creators of all and everything, personally, before his kind disappeared from Earth.

Day and Night listened to his case. They were certainly uncomfortable when they examined the numbers. They looked over Turkey history and were amazed at the bird's ability to prevail under difficult circumstances.

"So you were the first animal Man domesticated in this part of Earth," restated Day.

"Correct," answered Turkey. "When European Man first came to our homeland, they found the people already living here worshipped us two times a year, with celebrations in which they thanked us for providing them with food so abundantly. Our numbers were strong then. The newcomers took some of us home with them, where they bred us as barnyard fowl, meatier and heavier than we are. Then some Europeans brought this new turkey back to us. They are dependent on Man, though, no longer able to live in the wild as we do. Man is their guardian and protects their numbers. We need a guardian too."

"A warrior guardian," repeated Day.

"Correct," said Turkey.

"Finding a warrior," said Night, "is primarily a matter of finding a strong heart. It could be you are missing what is right before your eyes."

"How so?" asked Turkey, confused by Night's implication.

"It takes courage and endurance to journey to our home and petition us for audience," she answered Turkey. "This is no small task. It takes great heart."

"Oh, I don't know," Turkey's blue head blushed red at her praise. "Our numbers are small. We are desperate for help."

"Modest too," noted Day. "Always desirable in a warrior."

At Day's compliment, Turkey stood tall, his face turning bright blue, his tail fanned to its full glory.

"You are a warrior for your clan," continued Night dramatically. "You shall now carry that proof." And she fashioned for him a beard. It grew from his heart, a foot-long tuft of strange feathers, black and almost hair-like.

"Let all the toms be similarly marked," declared Day.

"Agreed," said Night.

"How about the hens?" asked Night. "They have all the difficulties of childrearing. They keep the nest hidden and protect the poults when they hatch. That takes great heart too."

"True," said Day. "But I'm concerned a beard might get in their way as they walk or run. Still, the warrior in them should be honored also. How about some of the biggest and oldest hens? It'll show the merit of their hearts too."

"Agreed," said Night.

"And you have Tree," Night reminded. "Tree protects you as you sleep and when hunters stalk. It gives food and shelter from Rain and Sun."

"True," Turkey acknowledged. "We do sometimes take Tree for granted. We stand reminded to give him thanks and praise, but we need more," he insisted. "We are grateful for Tree and stand ready to help ourselves with our wits, flight and speed on foot, but the numbers show this is not enough. We need another warrior, another strong heart."

"I will seek another," promised Day.

"I trust in your word," bowed Turkey, finally content to depart.

Day and Night watched him leave, strutting until he was out of their sight.

"You've shored up his courage," said Day. "The beard's a nice touch, but he's right. Another warrior is needed."

"Who have you got in mind?" asked Night.

"Man," said Day. "He's the only one who hunts Turkey who can also protect him."

"Didn't Man already 'protect' Turkey right out of the wild and into the kitchen?" asked Night doubtfully.

"He can also protect Wild Turkey by controlling his hunts and guarding the forests Turkey needs to survive. And he can bring Turkey back to wild places he used to call home. Man's the only hunter who can, if he will."

"Will he?" asked Night.

"I'll work on it," said Day.

Before long, Man began to work on it too.

Turkey had found his new warrior.

How Little Skink Found His Place

It is said that once there was a time when Little Skink did not know his place.

A strange humming, felt more than heard, urged him to struggle from his egg. Hatching onto a sun-warmed, rocky hillside, he blinked his eyes and watched his nest-mates hatch. Their striped bodies sported pink tails. A glance down his own length showed him he did too. As his six siblings hatched, they slunk away from the nest, their thick bodies slung between four short legs barely long enough, it seemed, to reach the ground. Their smooth, scaled skin glistened in the sun.

"Where are you going?" he squeaked to one hatchling, surprised by the sound of his own voice.

"To hide," it answered, in a voice as squeaky as his own.

"Why?" he asked.

"Because," it answered, but he could tell as he asked each in turn, that they didn't really know why. They crept away, forked tongues flicking from their mouths, tasting the air for something they couldn't yet define. Before long, he alone basked in the sun at the nest site.

"Why am I here?" wondered Little Skink. "Where do I go next?" There was no one to answer.

Again, the strange humming quickened him, filling him with a longing, but for what? He left his rocky hillside, pulling his robust yet slick form over the soil, around rocks, keeping to the shade that helped conceal his passage.

He nosed beneath dry leaves and small twigs, startling small beetles and spiders which he quickly snatched up and swallowed. Bugs, he discovered, were definitely tasty, and he wandered along alert for more. There was a plentiful supply, so in short order he was no longer hungry. Still, he remained dissatisfied somewhere beyond his stomach.

"Where am I supposed to go?" he continued to wonder.

He paused to examine his surroundings. Dry grass loosely thatched his sky, but not enough to shut out the light or heat of the sun. He crept along through crisp grass seed that crunched under his weight. Again he paused. It was utterly silent. All creation held its breath.

The humming touched him again, a warm vibration that stirred something within. He turned downhill.

The shadows deepened; the ground beneath his feet cooled. Trees canopied overhead. Little Skink felt expectant. Something was nearby. He heard someone moving through the cottonwood detritus littering the forest floor. Whatever it was, it was big.

Little Skink stopped to reconnoiter from beneath a branch. Dappled with intermittent sun, he watched an nine inch long lizard move stealthily across the ground. It had legs almost too small for its stocky, heavy, gray body. It's smooth scaled skin seemed stretched taut and glistened like quicksilver. It's tail was a rust red, and its face tinged with the same hue. It moved slowly, but steadily, checking beneath small stones and leaf litter, ever alert for anything that moved. It gobbled up any insects it came across.

Little Skink crouched lower to the ground, though with his short legs that was hardly possible, attempting to be inconspicuous. His movement attracted the attention of the large lizard.

It blinked. It blinked again. Then ambled closer.

"I remember looking like you," it rumbled as it passed.

"Like me?" asked Little Skink, almost too surprised to respond.

"Just like you," the giant answered. "You'll grow up to look like me." He continued thunderstepping through the forest, huge tail glistenslithering behind.

"Wait, then do you know where I should go?" asked Little Skink, hoping this great-sized relation could offer some guidance.

The adult skink cast a glance behind. A slow smile curved reptilian lips. It lumbered on its way. "I'm on patrol," was all it said.

Skink was disappointed and embarrassed not to have been deemed worthy of an answer.

Once more he felt the humming. It was more intense, more encompassing, somehow--and more compelling. He turned to go deeper into the shade, determined to find its source.

He stalked the hum.

He was dragging his body over moist earth now, and for some reason, that filled him with joy. The leaf litter was no longer crisp and easily tossed aside. Now it was soggy and clingy, rotting and fetid. Then he felt it again. The hum.

It was a pulse, a pulse from the center of the earth. A pulse of water which burbled to the surface to form a spring. The vibrations of that pulse coursed in his own blood and his whole being answered it. He crept to the water's edge.

"Ahhh, another," murmured a silky voice.

"Another what?" asked Little Skink humbly, hesitant before the power he felt in the spring.

"Another attendant. Destined to glean insects from my grounds. Destined to resemble granite river rock, smoothed and glistening in my flow. Destined to bond with my spirit and indicate my life-giving presence when

342

drought-stricken creatures seek me out. Destined to be my guardian lizard, patrolling my precincts, maintaining and indicating the health of the world my waters support. Destined to be my faithful companion. "

Little Skink rested in the humming pulse of Spring's words. He knew they were true. Finally, he knew. This was home. This was what he was born to do. Devotion overwhelmed him. While he might forage in the drier uplands from time to time, he would not be found far from the water he served. He would spend his life in close proximity to Spring.

As he grew, he lost his stripes and became a uniform, silvery ghost of the forest floor. He grew to be just like the foot-long lizard he'd seen lumbering on patrol around the water hole, sustained by the hum that had awakened him in his egg.

Black Witch Discovers Hitchhiking

It is said that there was once a time when Black Witch perched on a branch of an acacia and listened to Black-headed Grosbeak tell of lands far away. He was hidden, of course, lest Grosbeak eat him, but he listened carefully.

Black-headed Grosbeak talked to anyone who would listen. He was frustrated--no, more like "frantic," really. He was injured in his wintering homeland of Mexico, unable to journey in the spring to breed in the northern woodlands of the United States, the place where he summered and raised his young. He'd watched his male competition head north first, then later, the females and youngsters from last year. Now he was alone and would remain alone until his people returned in the fall migration. In his agony over missing out on the breeding up north, he talked incessantly of his memories of summers past. Especially the summer of his first year.

In that summer, he'd explored. Too young to have his full adult plumage, he was unattractive to mature females. Since he wasn't tied down, he spent his time cruising about: hunting for butterflies to eat, learning the real estate of the region, and planning where his territory and future nesting site would be located. In his travels, he'd ventured into Alaska. Oh, the nearly constant sunshine. The berry-filled woods. The salmon-filled streams. The beautiful glaciers. What a remarkable land! But he'd never gone back because he'd never been able to talk any season's mate into moving there. No female wanted to risk the adventure and the lives of their offspring. So they stayed in the forests of Idaho, close to others of their species. It was an acceptable trade-off--passing his genes to a new generation rather than adventuring alone. But now, in his isolation, he remembered Alaska. He spoke of the land of his past.

Hummingbird half-listened as he hovered nearby, sipping nectar from the faces of local flowers. His occasional chirp of, "No kidding," or "You don't say," was encouragement enough for Grosbeak.

Another listened silently to the bird's tales of his journey with rapt attention, though. Black Witch Moth. He planned to migrate north this summer. So, why not visit Alaska? He heeded Grosbeak's every word describing the lay of the land and how to use the wind currents to carry a traveler north. Not for a moment was he inattentive.

When Black-headed Grosbeak flew away clumsily to his evening roost, Hummingbird was still canvassing flowers. Black Witch Moth, nocturnal, as most moths are, began to stir. He fluttered his dark, mostly black, wings. With a wingspan of eight inches, many thought he was a bat when in flight. At rest during the day, however, his markings were apparent. When perched under the eaves of a house, or on a protected branch of a tree, he could be closely approached and the single comma-shaped spots of greenish-blue and orange on each of his front wings identified him as a Black Witch. Female Black Witches sported jagged white slashes that ran diagonally down their wings, but males were primarily shades of black and gray.

"How far away is Alaska?" Black Witch Moth asked Hummingbird.

"Far," answered Hummingbird.

"How far?" repeated Black Witch Moth.

"Way far," answered Hummingbird. "I've never been there, but a competitor of mine has. Rufous Hummingbird flies here in the winter and bullies me as I sup at flowers.

(He does not believe in sharing. Fortunately, there are plenty of flowers.) I've heard him boast that he's the best traveled of all hummingbirds because he flies to Alaska each spring. He claims to fly fifteen hundred miles in his migration. That's all I know."

"W-wow! That really is "way far," stammered Black Witch Moth.

"Don't I know it!" agreed Hummingbird.

"How does he do it?" asked Black Witch Moth. "He's no bigger than you, is he?"

"A little smaller, actually," answered Hummingbird. "And as he's quite an unpleasant neighbor, I spend little time with him, so I don't know how he does it," he confessed. "But as Black-headed Grosbeak was saying, I believe it's all up to Wind. There are great storms called hurricanes. They do us horrible damage when they come here, but I don't know of a time when Wind is more powerful. Perhaps a hurricane takes him to Alaska."

"Sounds like a huge gamble," mused Black Witch Moth. "Dare I risk it?"

"I'm told Wind moves in a circle in hurricanes," said Hummingbird. "The center of the circle is calm. It's called an 'eye.' If you rode in that, you might travel far. It would be dangerous, but worth it if you get to see Alaska. How badly do you want to get there?"

"Badly enough to ask how to catch a hurricane," Black Witch Moth said decisively.

"Listen to the seabirds," answered Hummingbird. "They always warn us of storms brewing over the ocean. I'll tell you if I hear anything," he added.

It was not a week later when Hummingbird perched on the bush where Black Witch Moth had hidden beneath broad leaves.

"It's coming," he announced.

The moth gasped and stirred nervously in his hiding place. He could leave so soon?

"Wait out the first of the storm in a protected place. Rain will be terrible. Wind will be awful, but don't come out until the sky clears. That will be the 'eye.' Then fly in the updrafts and move with the hurricane. My informants say it travels north toward the United States, right where you want to go. I can't promise you it will take you all the way to Alaska, but it's a strong start. Good luck. We won't be seeing each other again."

Black Witch Moth gulped and said good-bye with a heart filled with gratitude.

But Hummingbird was wrong. They did see one another again. When the storm's 'eye' passed over and Black Witch Moth took wing from under the eaves of the house where he sheltered, he saw Hummingbird out and about, examining the damage caused to his field of flowers.

"Stay strong," Hummingbird called. "Safe trip."

"Stay well," Black Witch Moth answered. "Take care."

He was off to Alaska.

The hurricane carried its hitchhiker to skies over Arizona before it died away. There he spent one day roosting on the screen door of a house, amazing its residents with his size and beauty. With nightfall, he was on his way once again, guided by Grosbeak's stories and Wind's currents.

Many Black Witch Moths are sighted making their journeys north. They have been seen in every state except New Hampshire. The greatest numbers are spotted after hurricanes pass. The big moths hitchhike storms admirably well.

Not many travel to Alaska, though.

Now you know of one who did.

When Silverfish First Danced

It is said that there was once a time before silverfish danced, when a colony of silverfish was attacked by their arch-enemies, the earwigs. Although Day and Night, the two primary Creators, had made silverfish in ancient times, even before the cockroaches, they were overcome by the predatory earwigs and completely destroyed.

All save one. He returned from his nocturnal wanderings late, hurrying through the damp leaf litter to get back after a night of stuffing himself on a soggy three-day-old newspaper he'd discovered in a human's yard. The vile scent of earwig greeted him just before he dashed into the damp earth below the garden pot he called home. He halted in time to see his refuge was completely overrun. Earwigs loved an environment similar to that of silverfish and set up headquarters under the pot, planning to stay forever.

Silverfish was an inch in length, covered with silvery scales, and festooned with two antennae and three hair-like appendages on his rear end: one pointing off to the left, one to the right, and one directly behind. These were wondrous sensory tools and he immediately raced away before the earwigs became aware of his presence.

But he was alone for the first time in his three years of life and was not happy to find himself on his own. His colony had been thriving, with many adults and youngsters. The young molted six times to gain their silver scales and thrice that to attain adult size and sexual maturity.

Silverfish remained hidden by day, but by night he prowled around looking for more than food. He needed companionship.

Every morning, his first need was to find a safe place to rest. He scurried from rock to rotting cactus, to dried leaves beneath a palo verde, searching for a spot to rest his head that was dark, moist, and where others of his kind resided. By nightfall he was weary, but after a bite to eat, he continued his search. Without daylight to plague him, he could dash about in the open and thus covered more territory, but without success in his quest for a new home.

One morning found him cowering under a creosote, hiding in the dust kicked up by the curved-billed thrasher, a bird up and hunting even before dawn, who was intent on finding and eating him. He played dead and this strategy concealed him from the thrasher's sharp eye, so that the bird gave up and flew off for more productive hunting grounds. He burrowed into the creosote's shadow for cool shade and slept, exhausted and discouraged, but alive.

That evening, under cover of darkness, he emerged and once again began his weary wondering. He couldn't believe his good fortune when he found a bread crumb in his path and ate quickly. This sign of human presence cheered him. People were unwitting benefactors of his kind and, indeed, Silverfish began to sense water nearby. He hurried around the underside of a rock and found newly dampened soil in a garden. He frolicked under stalks of corn and soothed aching feet under fallen bean pods. He soaked up the moisture gratefully. This oasis saved his life, he had no doubt.

As he passed around the third great rock that lined the human's pathway through the garden, he heard a familiar clicking. Silverfish heard his own language and rushed headlong into a settlement where everyone was readying to depart for a night of hunting food. At his entrance, every single silverfish stopped in its tracks to stare. As a stranger, could he expect to be welcomed? No one moved.

After a moment or two of deafening silence, a female approached.

"I have no home," he said. "I am looking for a new one."

The whole community began clicking in rhythm. They swayed and swirled in movements he'd never seen. Fascinated, he watched. The clicking was hypnotic and soon he too began swaying.

The nearby female stood facing him. Her antennae stroked his. He responded in kind. They backed away from each other, then returned to touch antennae, and backed away again. This was repeated many times. No words were exchanged. They both just knew what to do.

After a time, Silverfish ran away, but the female ran after him. They dashed in and around the rest of the silverfish, who continued clicking and swaying.

Then Silverfish stopped suddenly and the female stopped too. They stood side by side and head to tail. Silverfish vibrated his three-part tail against the female. After an hour of such dancing, Silverfish laid a sperm capsule on a thread of gossamer. The female responded by picking it up and placing it on her ovipositor to fertilize her eggs. She would lay them later, a few here, a few there.

The clicking and dancing stopped. Individuals again prepared to head into the night to find food. Silverfish turned to go out with them, feeling deeply pleased and accepted. First, though, he bowed to his mate.

"You have found your new home," was all she said before hurrying away into the darkness they loved.

Mating silverfish dance the same dance to this very day, a story in movement--as much about community as parenthood.

How Wren Learned Mobbing

It is said that there was once a time when mobbing was unknown. Birds did not announce the presence of dangerous characters within their midst. They learned to band together in this activity. But for a time, snakes climbed trees to invade nests, cowbirds laid their eggs in nests of other birds for them to hatch and raise, and predator birds hunted prey without hindrance. These were understood to be simply the bad luck of the individuals suffering loss.

"But with knowledge of sorrow came a sense of responsibility to one another against a common foe," Mother Cactus Wren told her daughter. She indicated the scene taking place below. Fledgling Cactus Wren watched Curved-billed Thrasher--not someone she'd ever much noticed before.

Curved-billed Thrasher trotted along the length of a wall, chortling constantly. He dogged a huge Diamondback Rattlesnake, never taking his eyes from the snake, never getting closer to the slithering snake than was safe, never ceasing his comments. "Keep moving," he scolded the reptile. "You're not welcome here. Get out."

Diamondback had recently eaten. A bulge in his bulk about halfway down his body proved that. He had no gustatory designs on Thrasher, but the bird's heckling kept him slithering along the base of the wall to find digestive peace someplace else.

"Who knows?" Cactus Wren continued. "That snake's last meal might have been that bird's friend. Or it might have been you."

Young Cactus Wren shuddered. "Or you," she realized. "Then who would take care of me?"

"Exactly," her mother said. "So I must now decide what I will do. I can sit here and be safe. Then I will be more likely to be here for you tomorrow. Or, it could be that a Western Screech Owl will kill me tonight in my sleep and I will still not be here to care for you in the morning. These things I have no way of knowing."

The two wrens watched the snake and pacing bird a moment longer.

"Stay here. You do not fly well enough yet," the mother commanded.

She plummeted to the ground, behind snake and thrasher, and began pecking the rattler's tail. The snake flung his huge head around to look behind him and the thrasher dodged away. The wren pecked again and screamed her insults, hopping just beyond the snake's reach. Thrasher squawked louder, distracting the snake from the wren. Five sparrows flying by stopped in a nearby bush to add their voices to the chorus. Young wren began screeching too, but she stayed obediently perched. Diamondback returned to his path along the wall, hastening away, hounded by birds. When he had fled the immediate area, Cactus Wren returned to her child.

"We save ourselves when we help others," she panted, glad to rest at her daughter's side.

"I see," the youngster said soberly. "But what's a Western Screech Owl? How will I know when I see one?"

"The owl is about the size of Mourning Dove, but doesn't act like Mourning Dove. I will show you one soon. In the meantime, watch others. Are they mobbing a dangerous creature? It may be a threat to you too. Then call everyone to help drive off the intruder."

"What if it's really just Mourning Dove?" asked young Cactus Wren.

The adult wren laughed.

"Watch how it acts from a safe distance," she instructed. "Think for yourself, because not every newcomer is dangerous. But let them prove themselves without putting yourself or others in harm's way. Be aware that Thrasher's enemy is usually your own. When he's shouting warnings, you do well to pay attention."

"I will," she promised.

In this way, all new generations of wrens learn about mobbing and an adult's responsibility to others.

When Piracy Entered Creation

It is said that there was once a time when Piracy stirred and sought form. It started as an idea afoot in the halls of creation, but soon became prevalent in a wide variety of shapes and sizes. Amongst insects, one form it took was that of a Robber Fly. Also known as an Assassin Fly, it especially loved preying on all sorts of bees.

Bees ferried supplies of gold pollen between plants and their homestead. They were air transport for the stuff of life and agents of commerce amongst flowering plants. And, they were plentiful in number.

Robber Flies developed spiny legs for grasping their victims. With their three simple eyes and two compound eyes, they had excellent vision. They grew dense bristles on their faces as a defense against struggling captives. With a powerful proboscis, they pierced their prey to inject a substance to paralyze and digest it. The bee's liquid innards could then be sucked up as food for the Robber Fly. Effective predators, Robber Flies were often grey or black in color and not pretty to look at.

These natural thugs sat perched in a sunny spot until a flying bug caught their eyes. Up they would dash for inspection, some insects being more appealing than others. If the potential sacrifice met with approval, it was quickly dispatched and Robber Fly perched again, clutching the carcass, to finish his meal.

Amongst men, Piracy also took the form of robbers who preyed on commerce moving along trade routes on air, land and sea. It is perhaps amongst this species that

Piracy is most diverse and creative. But the similarities are always there between all the forms Piracy takes. Those who know Robber Fly well can see the same principles at work in others of Piracy's forms, and are forewarned. Or enticed for everyone must choose how to relate to Piracy for themselves.

Lesser Goldfinch Gets His Green Back Up

It is said that there was once a time when Lesser Goldfinch rested in the shade after having stuffed himself all morning on the seed from sunflowers lining a sandbar in the riverbed. Others of his race were still at it: bobbing on flower heads, forcing one another off a flower when it got overcrowded, endlessly busy and forever shouting and squabbling for the best position and better seed. He watched them, silent for a moment.

Then he began talking to nearby Verdin, a bird about his same tiny size, though unrelated, for Verdin ate small insects, and Lesser Goldfinch focused on seeds. It was probably the fact that they didn't usually interact that encouraged Lesser Goldfinch to vent his frustrations to his yellow-faced neighbor. Verdin did not stop his constant search amongst mesquite tree leaves for gnats and tiny caterpillars to eat, but he did give Lesser Goldfinch about one third of his attention.

"Then he showed up," Lesser Goldfinch was saying, "with his black back and golden front. He stands out like a sore thumb in our numbers. No one can stand him. He's so pushy and thinks he's so smart."

Verdin looked where Lesser Goldfinch indicated. Lesser Goldfinches by the hundreds swarmed over the riverside flowers, trees and grasses, noisily shoving each other, jockeying for their own best advantage. If there was anyone that didn't belong, he didn't notice.

Then he saw the one his chatty comrade found so distressing. While all the males had green backs and black caps on their heads, there was one in the crowd with a black head and back. And he did stand out from the rest in all his dark splendor. Without having him pointed out, though, Verdin would not have noticed.

"He says all the males where he's from are like him. There, he says, I'd be the oddball. He comes from the southeast, he claims. I wish he'd go back there," Lesser Goldfinch spat angrily.

"Look how the others shove him around. See how he dashes in to steal seed when the others are busy elsewhere? This is our food. He has some nerve taking any for himself. He'd better not plan on staying. He'd better not plan on breeding with one of our kind. Nobody can stand him. See how they all act toward him?

"Look how aggressive he is. Watch how he pushes others away. See how he wants the best for himself and doesn't share?"

Verdin glanced again at the focus of his companion's ire. "Really? He's treating you differently than you treat yourselves?" he asked.

"I hadn't noticed," Verdin said with a shrug.

How Desert Broom Got Herself Noticed

It is said that there was once a time when Desert Broom complained of her anonymity.

"I never get to stand out," she whined. "I'm never noticed among the other desert plants."

Day sighed. As one of the two primary creators, he was listening to complaints while his companion, Night, took a nap in a remote cave, enjoying some much needed peace and quiet. Night would take her tour of duty in a few hours, leaving Day to a bit of respite to spend as he wished. Although alone for no more than twenty minutes, Day already wistfully imagined his role reversed with his co-creator.

Night simply had more patience with this task, he mused. See? He'd already stopped listening because his mind wandered.

"I want something unique and showy," Desert Broom continued. "I want bright, colorful flowers too."

"You are unique," Day reminded her. "You are a large, evergreen shrub. Hardly any animals eat you. You blossom in fall rather than spring, which is unusual, if not unique. And you have your own flowers, quite unlike your mate's. There aren't many other plants that come in sexed pairs like your species. You do stand out. Your creamy, white flowers are all the more noticeable in October and November because there is so little competition for the attention of bees and butterflies. And, you're a pioneer plant, one of the first to move into areas where the soil has been disturbed, which gives your offspring a head start on other plants."

"But my flowers are small, and my mate's are smaller yet. Yes, the bees see, butterflies too, but no one else notices. I've never been told I look lovely."

"That's true," agreed an ornate Queen butterfly. "While I sip from her flowers with delight, I've never thought of her as lovely." She hastened away to spread pollen at another Desert Broom.

"Well, we can't all be so pretentious," muttered Desert Broom under her breath, but Day saw the look of envy she shot at the departing Queen. "I rest my case," she said to Day, sadly.

Day examined his complainant thoughtfully. She was a little drab, he decided.

"Where's your mate?" he asked, realizing, suddenly, that the female Desert Broom had come alone.

"He's over the hill," Desert Broom answered, "and he doesn't care what he looks like. He says his pollen does the job and that's all that matters."

Day hid a smile. He stood and stretched, giving himself time to think.

"Since both your flowers are necessary to produce seed, I can't change yours without changing his as well, and he's happy with his as they are."

Now Desert Broom sighed, in deep disappointment. Her branches drooped.

"But," continued Day, "I believe we can do something more with your seed."

The modifications made that day created one of the desert's greatest displays of autumn. Desert Broom's seed, born only by the female plant, were henceforth fastened to pappus, a puffy, fluffy, blow-in-the-wind-ish white stuff that carried the seed everywhere Wind thought to take it. It collected under Creosote, billowed against Bursage, banked against Brittlebush, and gathered beneath Globemallow.

"It's like snow," exclaimed White-crowned Sparrow, newly arrived for the winter from Alaskan breeding grounds. "I thought I'd left that behind." He romped in the fluff until he sneezed. "Only it's not cold!"

Desert Broom was pleased with Day. "Everyone sees me now," she giggled. "I'm center-stage. Thank you, thank you, thank you."

Day was pretty pleased with himself, too. Night could not have done better, he thought. I handled this affair extremely well.

"What do you think of all this?" Day asked of male Desert Broom.

"Think of what?" he responded, looking around.

"Never mind," Day smirked, shaking his head and winking at Desert Broom in her cloud-like attire. "Most of us see you now," he told her.

Lavender Blue

It is said that there was once a time when Ironwood tree so longed for mobility that he despaired of his roots. Wind tried to convince him of his agility by tossing his branches in a stiff breeze, but that just irritated Ironwood. The tree slipped into such a blue funk he began to lose his leaves. All the verdure at the terminal ends of his branches yellowed and fell to earth.

He watched packrat scamper around his trunk. He gazed at Harris hawk sailing past, carrying branches for a nest. He sighed to see Bee fly hovering nearby. All these could go where they willed, but not he. He would never budge, never dance. He wept.

Desert Spiny lizard heard Ironwood when he returned at nightfall to the mound of sticks, rocks and cactus he shared with Packrat. He was surprised, having never given much thought to his own animation, to find Ironwood so despondent over his stationary status. A tree was a tree, after all. Who'd have guessed Ironwood could want more?

Since he had an appointment the very next morning with Day and Night, the two primary creators, he decided to mention Ironwood's angst to them. Mostly because Ironwood's bark creaked with each shuddering sob, making it difficult for Desert Spiny to get a wink of sleep.

After conducting his own business with Day and Night, which consisted of requesting and receiving permission to enlarge the blue spot on his throat, the better to attract females, he hastened to add, "And, speaking of blue, have you seen Ironwood lately?"

"No," said Day, trying to remember how hot he had ordered Sun to make the afternoon. He'd gotten complaints yesterday from Canyon Wrens, who couldn't find any water at their usual tinaja, it having dried up already in the pre-summer heat. Complaints from the wildlife were nothing surprising, but they were starting a little early this year.

"Why do you ask?" said Night, trying to remember the last time she'd spoken with the grey-green foliaged tree. "Shouldn't he be about ready to blossom?" she speculated.

"I haven't a clue about that," said Spiny, "but his crying kept me up all evening. And, he's so depressed he's losing his leaves. They cover the apartment I share with Packrat. The roof is collapsing under the additional weight and the building inspector is giving us grief."

"Building inspector?" asked Day. He hadn't heard there was one.

"Kangaroo rat," explained the lizard. "No one knows how he got appointed, but he's also making Cactus wren's life miserable because he says they roofed their nest before he could inspect the flooring. He says they have to tear it all down and start over."

"I had no idea Kangaroo rat was such a tyrant!" exclaimed Night.

"He backed off as soon as Cactus wren reminded him he knew where he lived--and he knew where Rattlesnake lived--and he could see to it that Rattlesnake would learn where Kangaroo rat lived too.

"But he's still giving us a hard time, and Packrat and I don't want any dealings with Rattlesnake since he'd eat us just as soon as Kangaroo rat."

"Understandable," said Day.

"But what does that have to do with with Ironwood's being blue?" asked Night.

362

"He's sad 'cause he can't walk around," said Spiny. "He wants to wander."

"But he's a tree," Day said, stating the obvious.

"Well, it seems he thinks being a tree stinks," Spiny replied.

So Day and Night went to visit Ironwood, to see if something couldn't be worked out between the three of them. Ironwood continued to weep throughout the consultation, until Day got frustrated with trying to convince him of the advantages of treeishness and promised to put the abundance of tears to good use, if they could all just think of one. And Night did.

As his tears dripped from Ironwood's budding lavender blossoms, they became Marine Blue Butterflies which sipped from his flowers' nectar and laid their eggs on his blossoms, dancing in sporadic flight. The caterpillars ate from the tree's fruit, and as adults, they carried his substance when they migrated, sometimes even fluttering as far north as Canada.

Ironwood was appeased. He made peace with his roots. He would never see Canada, but a part of him would. He was content to let his passionate longing to waltz take flight as Marine Blue.

Imitation

It is said there was once a time when Rain splattered on the fungus growing from the side of a tree in the forest-covered "sky island" situated in the wintery desert plains of southcentral Arizona. It was night. It was freezing.

The sky island is an Earth-raised jagged summit providing high altitude environs perfect for forest plants and animals. It traps Rain's clouds as they lumber and rumble across arid floors, creating islands of greenery in Sonoran Desert seas.

Winter snows blanket these mountain places with regularity, but on this night, winter was just beginning to grip the highlands. The moisture landing on the tree's fungus was Water. Water that dripped, dripped, dripped off of the slanted edge of the tree's parasite, freezing as it gathered itself to fall to the ground, gradually lengthening into a small icicle.

Fungus watched in admiration.

And the following spring, so they say, a strange creature hatched out on Fungus. It fed from Fungus, as Fungus fed from the tree, and grew through larval stages hanging upside down. Each time it pupated it hung from the last skin shed, so that the living animal inhabited the lowest skin in the chain of exoskeletons. It resembled, as best Fungus remembered and could recreate, the formation of an icicle from drops of Water.

The adult insect, it turned out, was a lovely, three-quarter-inch long beetle with black head and legs, and a Water-colored silvery-blue elytron shell covering its flight wings. The elytron was spotted with tiny indentations, in each of which resided a black dot. The beetle continued eating Fungus and strolled on summer days through stream-lined canyons, making up for the lack of mobility that had confined it to Fungus during all its earlier development.

It was named Pleasing Fungus Beetle, because it did indeed please Fungus. It imitated, in its life cycle, Water forming an icicle in winter, an event Fungus found more beautiful than words could tell. This beetle was his sincerest form of flattery.

Water smiled.

Owl Trumps Hawk

It is said that there was once a time when two Red-tailed Hawks flew together in their courtship dance, locking talons and plummeting together, soaring and circling together. That accomplished, commitments renewed, they began revamping the remains of last year's nest, definitely the worse for wear after the youngsters' antics and the weathering it had endured since. They both carried sticks to the site and worked them into the stack already perched in the many-armed saguaro they'd used for two years already, and very successfully too. They'd raised two generations of two from ugly, featherless, bug-eyed, pimply-pink, squirmy, gaping-mouthed blobs to regal, wide-winged, thermal-hugging, sharp-eyed hunters from on high. No easy task. Now, they began again.

Still in the thralls of courtship and mating, they stick-hunted, added to the nest's bulk, soared overhead, perched in an ironwood tree to mate, then stick-hunted again, blissfully unaware they were watched from a huge mesquite tree crouched in the fork of an arroyo a mile away.

Two tiny Verdins watched the watcher. They had been interrupted in their own nest-building in the mesquite and were calling a warning to all who would listen.

The Great Horned Owl ignored them. She didn't care they didn't want her there. She would stay as long as she chose. She would leave when she chose. For now, she watched. Her mate watched from another tree a quarter-mile downstream.

The Red-tailed Hawks added to their bulky nest, burying evidence of last year's refuse under a tidy layer of fresh sticks. When they had it to the point the female found pleasing, they rested and mated again in another saguaro. Now, to line the nest with finer, softer stuff prior to laying her first egg.

They turned back to the nest to find it occupied. Female Great Horned Owl stared back at them. No amount of soaring and screaming could dislodge her. She didn't care they didn't want her there. She would stay as long as she chose. She would leave when she chose. And she didn't choose to. Her mate snoozed through the day a mile away, knowing the outcome.

The Red-tailed Hawks perched to consult. They knew the outcome too. Time to find a new nesting site. They didn't want owls as neighbors anyway. Too dangerous for their own offspring. Reluctantly, they left.

The Verdins returned to their nest-building in the mesquite where Great Horned Owl had first perched and watched.

"Owl trumps Hawk every time," Verdin said to his mate.

Is It Winter Yet?

It is said that there was once a time when a Sprague's Pipit just stayed put. It's not clear why. He started north in migration with other Sprague's Pipits, leaving behind the grassy plains of southeastern Arizona for the northern prairies of Canada and middle-north United States. But having gotten only a couple hundred miles from the wintering grounds, this one, sparrow-like bird, plummeted into a field not plowed in fifty years which hosted a smattering of mesquite trees, and there he stayed.

Perhaps he had not stored calories enough to fuel the trip. Perhaps he was injured, not so much as to obstruct his typical strolling through the short grasses he found pleasing, but enough to prevent sustained flight. Powerful flight muscles were a must for him, not only for the trip, but for the flight displays that made him attractive to females. His species was known for the capacity for three hour, high altitude courting displays, after all. (Quite surprising in a species so enamored of walking.) Perhaps parasites weakened him. Perhaps he found food plentiful in the old alfalfa field. Perhaps the grasshoppers were emerging from their underground nests. Perhaps his people's solitary lifestyle was especially strong in him. Perhaps he decided to take a year off from procreation. Who knows?

But there he was, where he wasn't supposed to be, facing into a long, hot summer in a desert where he must adapt to survive. Shade of mesquite, water from tree wells in nearby humans' yards, desert insects as diet, and all alone. Well, not really, but none of his own kind. Cactus Wrens, Sidewinders, Curved-billed Thrashers, plenty of

Round-tailed Ground Squirrels, but not another pipit in sight.

Perhaps, though, he sensed there was a problem up north. Maybe he couldn't smell the aroma of soft grasses for tenting over the nests tucked into a dent in the earth. Did he know the wildflowers were drowned? That flooding rivers swept over the habitat he loved? Did he know his people's diminishing numbers would be further diminished by the weather this spring? Who knows?

They'll be back. Those who found a dry spot to nest in what little prairie remains, they'll be back. Fall migration will return them to the warmer grasslands of Arizona. He'll watch for them.

Is it winter yet?

Just For the View

It is said that there was once a time when three coyotes circled a tall, handsome Mesquite tree, calling derisively into it's tallest limbs.

"Why did you say you climbed?" called the biggest. "You are a dog, you know. Proper dogs don't climb trees."

"You don't climb trees," came the answer from above. "But no one mistakes you for proper."

The coyotes snarled and dashed at the tree trunk, jumping as high as they could.

"Come down here and say that!" they dared their treed prey.

"I thought you said you weren't afraid of us," cooed the smallest coyote, in his most cajoling fashion.

"I'm not," declared the voice from on high.

"So where's the bird nest you climbed to raid? Where's the lizard you chased?"

"Wrong season for that," answered the last coyote. "Winter's no time for lizards to be prowling or birds to be nesting."

"But you're not afraid of us. Are you?" the biggest coyote challenged.

"You thugs? Not I," answered Gray Fox, adjusting his weight on his limb, grasping the bark with his thick-nailed claws. His grizzled gray coat hid him when he pressed against the tree's limb, but as he sat up, his reddish flanks and white underparts showed. His fully fluffed gray tail, topped with a black stripe and ending at the black tip, lay along the length of his perch, balancing and anchoring him. He was the only desert canine with the ability to climb trees. Not kit fox, and, thankfully, not coyote.

370

"I didn't climb because of you," he said, licking a paw, watching below, and glancing at the horizon.

Just then the coyotes heard the noisy approach of riders on horseback. They'd been taunting too loudly to notice, and now risked being caught. They fled silently and swiftly.

"I climbed for the view," Gray Fox finished, hopping from his tree just as the horses arrived and before the humans had seen him.

He melted away into the mesquite forest, in the opposite direction taken by the coyotes.

Stirring Up Wind

It is said that there was once a time when two vultures sat together in the top of a mesquite tree, talking quietly and waiting for Sun to warm Air into thermals which they might ride into the blue beyond. They held their wings outstretched, to collect Sun's energy. Nights were cooling now. Vultures were gathering to migrate south.

One was a hatchling of the late spring. He could fly. He had all the grandeur and skill possessed by his family for flight. But his immaturity showed. His bald head was a sickly gray in color. Not the black of youth. Not the red of adulthood. His parents and siblings were already gone. But, as the last hatched and fledged, he still hesitated. He had chosen as his mentor an older bird, one not so eager to travel yet, and this old one had agreed to his company. Vultures are social birds and ready to teach life skills and manners to the offspring of others for the sake of the community as a whole. In his aged companionship, the youth was not abandoned to his own devises.

But the old bird was restless. As they sat preening and conversing, he knew he could not wait much longer. He was being called south.

"I must leave soon," he told his trainee. "You'll come when ready. In the meantime, study the ravens. They take on our task when we depart for the winter. They will lead you to carrion you cannot sniff out for yourself. The cooler temperatures mean the dead do not decay as rapidly, so their stench is less noticeable to our kind, who hunt by scent first, sight second. Ravens, unruly competitors that they are, will show you to your next meal. Let them eat first. You would be injured in a fight with those thugs.

Then feed your fill. You'll get stronger, feel the need more urgently, and you will head south when it's time. Don't be afraid."

The student paused his preening, stunned. "Don't go," he pleaded. "I don't want to be alone."

"You won't be, not for long," comforted the mentor. "Keep flying, keep feeding, keep listening within. You will hear your calling and follow it. We all do."

"But I'm afraid. How will I know what to do without your example?"

"You have had my example enough. You know what to do," assured the advisor.

"How do you know?" asked the apprentice.

"Because I do," stated the teacher, his smile getting lost in the folds of his face and neck. "Look at them," he ordered.

Young Turkey Vulture looked down at the Abert's Towhees trotting from the cover of the mesquite bosque to the water's edge, intent on drinking. At the edge of the forest the towhees paused, leaned forward, then dashed in a footrace to the stream. They drank, then turned, once again raised their tails, leaned forward, and dashed back to the dense brush they loved.

"So?" asked the adolescent Vulture. "You want me to run?"

"No," laughed his elder. "That would be a sight. Leave the trotting to towhees. But look how they lean into the wind when they dash back and forth in their teapot. A bunch of towhees is a teapot," he explained.

"But there is no wind," said Gray Head.

"Towhees create their own.

"Enough. Time to fly," and he flapped his enormous wings, once, twice, awkwardly stepping across his mesquite perch, and was airborne.

The young vulture stared. He had no idea what his patron was talking about. Then he sighed and took flight.

That afternoon the younger vulture settled in a mesquite at streamside and waited to greet his elder, but he never came. One roosted alone.

For a week the vulture sailed in solitude during the day, following ravens as he'd been told. He ate when he could and shivered at night until Sun warmed his black feathers after dawn. During those dark hours he listened for those who hunted by starlight and pressed against his tree's trunk to hide.

That listening brought his own restless yearnings to mind. He shifted his weight from one foot to the other, back and forth, waiting for Sun's rising. One morning, after a night of pacing, he took flight and banked south. With only his inner guide to lead, he was on his way.

The breeze was slight, but the vulture spiraled ever upward toward the high-altitude air current heading south.

Now, he thought. Time to stir up my own wind.

Lullaby

It is said that there was once a time when wintery lands of darkness and tundra exhaled southward, sending Wind and Cloud to pummel all warmth from normally sunny Sonoran desert country. Cloud bumbled along, barely clearing the ground, gravid with moisture shed as Snow over mountains and Rain in lowlands. Every creature turned its back to Wind and scurried to shelter, certain the night would be freezing and black. By late afternoon, Sun hung low on the horizon, peeping underneath Cloud for one last look before departing, a glance too brief to color-tint Cloud. Already Rain splattered the dusty Earth, and the last wayfarers crept into burrows and cover.

The thicket along the canal was riotous with acacia and mesquite trees. The dense forest was edged in rabbit brush and apache plume, rich with seed. It was natural that small birds sought sanctuary here and hunkered beneath low, leafy ceilings to await a dawn when they might breakfast so conveniently. It was also natural that Sharp-shinned hawk should perch above them for the very same reasons. These were very poor bedfellows.

The most impenetrable undergrowth was always home to shy and retiring Crissal thrasher, Rain or not. Knowing the forest paths like none other, trails through the tree branches and trails on the ground, he and his mate felt compelled to hospitality. They shared their refuge with less concern for the hawk, for they were more confident of escape come morning. But the tension through the glen from the others was thick.

Crissal thrasher was like and unlike his Curved-billed cousin who loudly called riddit rit in every dawn's chorus.

Both sported sickle-shaped bills with which they threshed the soil for larvae and grubs for their dining delight, but where Curved-billed bullied and blustered his way into the limelight, Crissal shied from the light, often going unnoticed by all until the need to penetrate his hideouts outweighed the difficulty of doing so. He and his mate nested in the deepest undergrowth, not far above the ground and that was where they nestled now.

Both types of thrashers were also noted for their repertoire of song, but whereas Curved-billed sang from a high perch where all could take note, Crissal sang from the forest depths, anonymous to most admirers, but renown for the sweetness of his serenade. He would have blushed at the praise and his red rump seemed evidence of his bashful temperament.

Now, in shadowless night, harboring distressed and shivering guests in their thorn-forest home, the Crissal thrashers pillow-talked a soothing lullaby. They sang subtle ballads of spring, of green-blue eggs in secure nests, of sunlight filtered through frothy mesquite leaflets, of lifelong friendships between mates. Their songs burbled and gurgled through the forest like a warm breeze, easing shivers of hearts and minds, if not bodies. Listeners took comfort, reminded the storm and winter would pass, that dangers of hunter-hawks would wait til dawn. For now there was refuge in peace.

Sparrows snoozed. Even Sharp-shinned slept.

Owl's Watch

It is said that there was once a time when cold and rain drenched the desert in a winter storm. Cloud settled in low to drape mountains in fog and sleet. There he snagged, and without Wind to encourage his leaving, he wept tears of hail and snowflakes onto peaks and into canyons.

No creature ventured forth.

Little light met the sight of any who peeked from burrow or bush. Feathers or fur fluffed, backs turned to Rain, and stomachs rumbled for food.

Gray was the day.

Black was the night.

Short the day.

Long the night.

Great Horned Owl sat on a naked branch in a dead Palo Verde tree. He shivered. All his feathers were drenched, and he lifted them away from his body, using them as scales to drain Rain away from his skin. He hunched his back. Occasionally he shifted his feet.

He sat all day.

He sat into nightfall.

Little Elf Owl watched from his hole in the trunk of the tree just below Great Horned's perch. Why not seek cover? he thought from his wooden cave. What's he waiting for?

Finally, in the second hour of pitch blackness, he asked.

Great Horned turned his head toward Elf Owl's voice. Then turned back, facing east.

"I'm keeping watch," replied Great Horned Owl.

"For what?" asked Elf. "Me? Because I'm staying in tonight. You won't have me for dinner."

"Not you," said Great Horned, mirthlessly. You're hardly enough to make one swallow, he thought.

"Then what?"

"I had a dream. It gave a prediction."

"Of what?" Elf Owl whispered. He shivered, but not with cold.

"Of Sun's turning," said Great Horned.

"Sun's returning?" asked Elf. "Everyone knows that," he squeaked. "Nights will shorten and days lengthen. The solstice. Who doesn't know that?" he continued.

"Tonight," said Great Horned. "I dreamed this night, this solstice, something new is coming."

"What?" gasped Elf, a little fearful.

"I dreamed I'd see what made Day and Night. If I waited. If I watched."

"Day and Night? Our creators?" Elf gulped. He'd heard rumors. Rumors of something before. Before Day and Night. Unseen. Unknowable. Abiding.

Wind stirred. Cloud parted briefly. Moon looked to Earth and saw Great Horned, alone, unprotected, waiting.

"What are you looking for?" Moon asked.

"I dreamed I'd see what made Day and Night," Great Horned answered. "If I watched faithfully. If I waited patiently."

Moon considered his words, silently.

"Look below you," she whispered.

At the base of the dead tree in which both owls huddled, a puddle had formed. Moon was reflected there.

"You?" asked Great Horned.

"Look closer," smiled Moon.

Both owls leaned out to stare into the puddle. This time they saw their own reflections, next to Moon's. They gasped in unison.

He is waiting for me, Elf Owl thought.

Great Horned bowed to Moon and hooted joyful thanks.

Epilogue

I first read some of Joseph Campbell's works over twenty years ago. It was his belief that we humans needed a new myth. I disagreed at the time. I felt we just needed to remember the old myths. I've come to understand what he meant, though, and that's why I write desert fables. Let me try to tell you why.

We are strange animals who mostly have no clue as to what we fully are, where we come from, or what our purpose is. We constantly forget how little we know, however.

We focus on our rational mind. We believe deeply in logic. Our culture is science biased. We think. We think that's who we are. But we are so much more. That larger identity is what has always been the realm of myth, fable and fairy tale.

Myths connect us to our larger identity. Hearing them reminds us who we are. Myths and fables are roadmaps of the human psyche. They reveal our weaknesses, our strengths, and our connections.

What connections? These connections: to each other, to the environment, to Earth, to the universe at large, to divinity in all the ways we struggle to understand that. We have a sense of that connection, some of us more than others, but knowing this aspect of ourselves involves more than the rational mind. And it will take more than the rational mind to inform us and change us in the ways we must to ensure we have a place in the future of Earth and life upon it, for creation isn't something that just happened way back when. It continues today. It continues eternally. In every aspect, in every creature.

The power of myth, and the storytellers that remind us who we are, reveal to us our larger identity. They reshape "other" as "self."

And they do it so discreetly, slipping in under the radar of the conscious mind.

I hope you enjoy my fables. Please consider giving over more space in your life to myths, fables, fairy tales and other such "fantasies."

They'll provide balance.

www.ingramcontent.com/pod-product-compliance
Lightning Source LLC
Chambersburg PA
CBHW060148260626
47160CB00001B/174